INEVITABLE

5

C.J. PETIT

Printed in the United States of America

First Printing, 2019

ISBN: 9781091033610

TABLE OF CONTENTS

PROLOGUE

**May 12, 1877
Black Hills
Wyoming Territory**

Fuzzy Villers stood holding his gelding's reins as he talked to Charlie Pruitt as four other miners stood nearby listening intently.

"I ain't gonna do this if you boys think you can pull the wool over my eyes," Fuzzy said as he stared down at Charlie.

"Aw, c'mon, Fuzzy. We know better'n tryin' to hornswoggle ya. We got some lonely boys out here and we'll give you top dollar for 'em, but we sure would appreciate some young ones."

"I bet you do, Charlie. Tell 'em it'll take me a couple of weeks, but I'd better not find any sand in with that dust or me and my boys will be back here makin' you wish you never been born."

Charlie grinned and replied, "Don't worry, Fuzzy. You get us some nice ones and you'll be more'n happy with the sale."

Fuzzy glanced back at Ike McCall and said, "Okay, Ike. Let's get back to Laramie and get the boys together. We have ourselves a payin' proposition."

Ike nodded, then both mounted their horses and headed south from the mining camp.

Fuzzy was sure that the miners would pay because he knew how desperate they were getting.

He could understand it easily and he had only been eleven days without spending a night with a woman and some of those randy miners have been up here for months. It was going to be a very profitable sale.

CHAPTER 1

May 22, 1876
Black Hills
Eastern Wyoming Territory

Lin Chase had been on the trail of Hungry Jim Whitacre and his brother for eleven days now and knew he was close, probably just a few hours behind but the mountainous terrain was difficult to navigate and the same treacherous trails made him wary of the ever-present danger of an ambush.

He was just making a nerve-wracking blind turn around a wall of granite when he was startled by the sound of gunfire, but it wasn't directed at him. It was distant, maybe a mile away by the sound, so he had his mottled gray gelding, Homer, pick up the pace as the packhorse trailing behind matched the new speed.

After rounding the turn, the view suddenly expanded with a wide valley stretching for miles surrounded by the Black Hills. As impressive as the sight may have been, it was what was happening down in the valley that attracted his attention.

He kept his eyes focused on the sight as he nudged Homer to a medium trot, and they began their descent into the valley.

The gunfire was coming primarily from the west side of the valley where it rose into the Black Hills, but on the valley floor, there was a group of Indians who he assumed were Cheyenne, returning fire, and they were losing the fight.

The fire coming from the rocky crags at the edge of the valley was from what sounded like Spencer carbines while the Cheyenne were using newer repeaters that fired the less powerful pistol cartridges. Whether they were Henrys or Winchester, it didn't matter. They were outgunned at that range.

As Homer kept the rapid descent, Lin quickly judged the firefight and made out six downed Cheyenne. Only two of the warriors remained in the fight, and Lin didn't think they'd be there much longer. He had no idea why they still continued to fire when they were within range of the two outlaws that he'd been trailing yet not close enough for their shots to be effective.

The same two warriors were still engaged with Hungry Jim and Willie Whitacre when Lin reached the valley then pulled Homer to a stop, dismounted, hurried back to the packhorse and pulled his favored Sharps from its scabbard. He then pulled out a heavy box of .50-110 cartridges from the packhorse's ammunition bag and began sliding the large rounds into the special loops that had been sewn into the inner liners of his heavy, dark gray thigh-length coat.

After filling the twelve slots, he slipped one into the Sharps' breech then returned to Homer mounted and nudged him forward with his knees while holding the long rifle in his right hand.

Tall Bear, the leader of the Cheyenne scouting party that had been sent to investigate the two white men had been shocked by their firepower, spotted Lin as he was riding toward them and naturally assumed that he was there to help the other white men. He knew then that his cause was now even more hopeless, and just stood to face the new threat, ignoring the shots from the rocks. He had fired his last round, so he pulled his war tomahawk to face the rider.

Lin was about eight hundred yards out when he saw Tall Bear stand to face him and began waving at him to get down, which the Cheyenne interpreted as a demand for his surrender which he would never do, so he screamed his war cry and charged at the rider with his tomahawk held high.

The only other Cheyenne still in the fight, Quiet Owl, saw Tall Bear begin his sprint toward Lin but then had to turn back to the first threat when a bullet exploded into the earth just four feet behind him and off to his left by eight inches. He was down to his last three cartridges, so he held his fire.

Lin saw Tall Bear charging at him and essentially ignored him by shifting Homer to his right and rode past the oncoming warrior.

Tall Bear was angered that the rider had refused to fight even though the white man could have killed him with his rifle but realized that he was going to get behind Quiet Owl to shoot him in the back, so he turned to race after the speeding horses, knowing he could never get there in time.

Once Lin knew he had some time to act before the warrior returned, he then turned Homer back toward the west until he got a better read on the position of the two outlaws that were almost invisible behind the rocks and the large cloud of gunsmoke that hung overhead. He waited for a few seconds then one of them fired and he marked the muzzle flare at about twelve hundred yards. He needed to get closer and to their left as the slight breeze would be moving the cloud of gunsmoke to their right, so he nudged Homer more toward the north until he had a decent view of the two men.

He finally pulled Homer to a stop and dismounted with his sole attention directed toward the Whitacre brothers as they continued to sporadically fire at the two Cheyenne and ignored him. He was at the outside of the range of their Spencers, so maybe that was why they didn't target him or perhaps they foolishly believed he was there to help them which would be difficult to comprehend.

Lin had painstakingly developed his reputation as a bounty hunter over the years and wore a very specific outfit when he was trailing wanted men. He was attired in dark gray trousers, a lighter gray shirt, a dark gray leather vest and the heavy almost black coat with the signature ensemble topped by his large, flat black hat, so that those he tracked understood who they were facing. Today it was the Whitacre brothers and they should have recognized who he was and understand that he was the far greater threat.

———

Hungry Jim and Willie had not only recognized him but knew they had a new problem just as they thought they were free of the Cheyenne.

"You think he can reach us from there?" asked Willie loudly as he peered over his Spencer's sights.

"I don't know, but if you see muzzle flash, just duck 'cause it'll take a good second and a half for that bullet to go this far."

"Okay," Willie replied not bothering to tell his older brother that he already understood the ballistic lag.

———

Lin knew that they'd probably drop after his first shot, but he needed to get it downrange quickly so the Cheyenne would understand that they shared a common enemy and not try to kill him while he set up. So, he quickly prepared to take the first shot at eight hundred yards by setting the ladder sight taking into account the altitude and the temperature automatically. This one didn't need to be very precise as he didn't expect them to still be watching once he fired. It was the second or third bullet that would be important.

Once his Sharps' was prepped, he dropped to a kneeling position, quickly set his sights on the head poking out of a rock to the left, released the first trigger then held his breath and gently pulled back the second trigger.

The big rifle roared, and the massive fifty caliber piece of lead was rammed down the rifled barrel by the energy released by a hundred and ten grains of gunpowder. As the smoke boiled out of the muzzle following the bullet's release, he quickly opened the breech and even before it reached its target, was sliding a second round in place of the empty brass.

Tall Bear was still a hundred and fifty yards away when Lin fired and was startled to a full stop when he realized that the tall white man in the black hat was firing at the other two white men.

Hungry Jim and Willie both dropped when they saw the flash and smoke and had their heads below the rocks when almost a full second later, the top of Willie's rock just inches above his head exploded in shards of granite and dust.

"Jesus!" he screamed as his hands wrapped around his head.

"Damn!" shouted Hungry Jim at the same time as he instinctively shielded his eyes long after the exploding rocks from ten feet away had bounced off of him.

Lin had to guess which one would be the first to peek over the rock and experience told him it would be the one on the right as he hadn't been targeted yet. He'd seen where his first shot had hit and adjusted his aim slightly to get his next round exactly where he wanted it before he began to count down from five.

Hungry Jim looked over at Willie and said loudly, "He's probably reloading. I'm gonna check," while Willie simply hunkered down behind his rocky security blanket.

Lin counted, "Three…two…one…" then squeezed his second trigger before Hungry Jim's face appeared.

When Hungry Jim stuck his head above the rock to see if that bounty hunter had moved closer for a better shot, he had but a fraction of a second for his brain to register a new gunsmoke cloud hanging over Lin before the bullet and then the loud report reached him at the same time.

Willie was watching his brother when the massive round took off the top of his head and knocked him back against the rocks, making him shriek in terror drop his Spencer and curl up into a quivering ball.

Lin had seen the hit and waited for ten seconds for any return fire from the second shooter as he finished his second reload, then began to run straight toward the two men in a mild zig-zag keeping his eyes focused as best as he could on the spot as his head bounced with each step.

Willie still had his eyes tightly closed to keep the horrible image of his brother's explosive demise from his mind and failing as Lin reached the rocks quickly set his Sharps against a boulder, pulled his Colt and approached Willie, realizing that he was no longer a threat.

He picked up Willie's Spencer, set it aside then pulled Willie's Colt from his holster and slid it into his left coat pocket before stepping over to Hungry Jim's half-decapitated body pulling his gunbelt then rolling the belt around the holster and dropping it into his expansive right pocket. After leaning Hungry Jim's Spencer against the boulder he'd been hiding behind, he looked at their horses tied behind a wall of rock and finally returned his gaze to Willie.

"Okay, Willie, let's get out of here before those Cheyenne arrive. They're probably not too happy with you."

Willie was suddenly not only aware of Lin's presence but the very real danger that the Cheyenne posed, so he uncurled then scrambled to his feet, trying not to look at his brother's messy corpse.

Lin then took both Spencers and carried them to the horses that still had Winchesters in one of their two scabbards.

He pulled one of the two Winchesters, slipped it into the other horse's empty scabbard then slid both of the still warm Spencers into one of the packhorse's half-empty panniers before untying the horses and handing the reins of the unarmed horse to Willie.

"Get on board this one and if you value your life, you'll stay close to me. If you make a break, I'll just shoot you anyway long before those Cheyenne get you."

Willie just nodded before mounting what was his own horse and once aboard, he was high enough to see the two Cheyenne walking toward them about a hundred yards away.

"*Them Injuns are comin'! Ain't you gonna shoot 'em?*" Willie exclaimed, his recent panic beginning to resurface.

"Shut up, Willie," Lin growled as he led the other two horses out of their hiding place back toward the valley.

Less than a minute later, Lin stopped and waited for the two Cheyenne to approach then when they were within speaking range, he said, "I am Lin Chase. I have been following these men for eleven days."

"I am Tall Bear. Why did you kill them and not us?" Tall Bear asked.

"These two are not men, they are criminals and wanted by our laws. They have killed and done other evil things. I will take this one back to be hanged. It is the death of a coward."

Tall Bear nodded slowly and said, "I must take the bodies of my fellow warriors to our village and admit my shame, but I thank you for what you did. My people now are in your debt and if you place this sign over your lodge or those of your family, we will honor that debt."

Tall Bear used his war tomahawk's handle and drew what looked like an arrowhead with a short shaft then a half circle followed by another short shaft with six short angled lines representing feathers.

Lin then asked, "Tall Bear, why did you stay within range of their rifles?"

"I had to try and get to my wounded brothers and foolishly thought they would run out of ammunition. It is another reason for my shame."

Lin just nodded, hating to agree with him about his poor decision when Tall Bear turned to Quiet Owl and said something that Lin didn't understand before the two Cheyenne walked away to gather their dead and wounded.

Lin led the Whitacre's packhorse and Hungry Jim's animal toward Homer with Willie leading his beside them, still watching the receding Cheyenne. It wasn't as bad as it could have been as only three of the warriors were dead, but the wounded Cheyenne would suffer mightily from the damage caused by those .56 caliber Spencer rounds.

———

An hour later, Lin was back on his gelding leading two packhorses, an empty saddle horse and Willie through the Black Hills heading for Laramie which was the closest town where he could drop off his prisoner. He hadn't tied Willie down knowing he had no place to go but still kept a close eye on the man. Willie knew his fate and Lin didn't doubt that he'd try something if he had the chance. He left Hungry Jim's body where it was without any attempt to bury it because he simply didn't have the time. If he'd had to kill them both, he probably would have brought back their bodies but with Willie coming along, it wasn't necessary.

The two men had a total of over twelve hundred dollars in rewards on their heads and would be the single biggest payout of his career as a bounty hunter. A career that he hadn't chosen but had drifted into after he had finished working for the railroad.

He'd started helping out as an assistant to a guide, using his long-developed tracking and other outdoor skills that he'd honed as a boy. For as long as he could recall, he'd always been an incredibly accurate marksman with whichever weapon he was using, from the old post-war muzzle loaders that could be had for a song, to the latest cartridge weapons from Winchester, Sharps or Colt.

It was on one of those trips into northern Colorado with a group of gentlemen from Philadelphia when they'd encountered an Arapahoe hunting party. Before the guide, Hap Kemper, even had a chance to tell them to hold their fire while he went and talked to the Arapahoe, one of the members of the hunting party had gotten an itchy trigger finger and fired.

All hell had broken loose and after ten minutes of extended gunfire, only he and one of the other members of the hunting party were still left unwounded. Lin had used a combination of his Winchester and the instigator's Sharps and picked off the remaining Arapahoe until the last three disappeared.

Lin expected that they were going to get reinforcements, so he and the other man gathered the six dead bodies, laid them across their horses' saddles then assisted the four wounded men onto their horses and quickly made their way back to Laramie. That was how he acquired his first Sharps as well as four Winchesters and enough horses which allowed him to choose this way of life where he was no longer dependent on what others did, like that ignorant hunter.

At the time he started, it wasn't a well-paying proposition as there weren't a lot of outlaws with prices on their heads in that part of the world, but that changed rapidly as the populations grew in Laramie, Cheyenne and especially Denver. What accelerated his business even more was the discovery of gold and silver all across the Rockies.

By 1872, Lin was covering the wide expanse of territory along the eastern edge of the Continental Divide from Denver to the Black Hills in Dakota and Wyoming and had developed his own unique methods for catching outlaws, beginning with his dress and the use of the Sharps as his weapon of choice. He'd killed or captured twenty-three outlaws since he started and now lived four miles northwest of Cheyenne on two quarter sections of land in a small house that he had built to suit his needs and no one else's.

———

As the sun began to set, he led the horses and Willie out of the southern edge of the Black Hills and pulled to a stop to set up camp. Shortly after dismounting, he pulled his Colt and had Willie step down then after letting him relieve himself, bound his wrists and ankles and set him on his behind while he went about setting up the campsite.

As he was digging a fire pit, Willie said, "You bringin' me in for the reward, ain't ya?"

"That's the idea," Lin replied as he was dropping rocks into a circle around the hole.

"How much are you gettin'?"

"You're worth four hundred and your brother is worth eight-fifty."

Willie replied, "I'll tell you what, Chase. I'll tell you where our stash is if you'll cut me loose. Just give me a Winchester and my Colt back and I'll be out of here. It's over two thousand dollars."

Lin was starting the fire and without looking at Willie, said, "A bird in the hand, Willie. A bird in the hand."

Lin was sure that the two outlaws didn't have anything more than the seventy-three dollars and fifteen cents that he'd found on Willie and in their saddlebags. Of course, he'd neglected to check Hungry Jim's pockets, but doubted if he had another twenty dollars with him. In his years of tracking and catching outlaws, he'd never found one with more than a hundred dollars in his possession.

Once he'd made his almost humorous bribe offer, Willie remained silent for the duration of the night, probably because he was busy trying to figure out a way to escape. Lin spent most of the time cleaning all of the guns, including their Winchesters and pistols.

After Willie had fallen asleep, Lin lay awake in his bedroll, staring up at the stars running through the day's action, looking for mistakes he'd made and things that had worked out correctly. There were always mistakes, but he'd come out of the gunfight unscathed yet again.

The first half dozen times he'd gotten into shootouts with outlaws, he'd primarily used his Winchester, which put him on an equal footing with the men he was after. But when he developed the techniques for the tactical use of the Sharps, he found he had an almost unfair advantage. His only genuine concern was the possibility of an ambush and even that had diminished as he'd become more mature in his profession.

Now his uncanny ability to hit targets at long range made him feel no better than the murderers he chased. He justified the killings as justice served, but it still gnawed at him and knew that the memories that he kept hidden in the recesses of his mind would return, just not today.

He finally closed his eyes and let the sounds of the night sing him to sleep.

———

Lin led the horses into Laramie in mid-afternoon the next morning and headed straight for the Albany County Sheriff's office then stepped down and tied off Homer who had the other animals on a trail rope behind him, including Willie's horse with a bound Willie Whitacre in the saddle. Willie had made a poor attempt at escape during breakfast by throwing some dirt at Lin expecting him to be surprised. He hadn't been and Willie spent the rest of the ride unpleasantly tied to his horse without a break. It had caused some damage to the saddle and Willie's britches, but Lin considered it part of his punishment for the feeble attempt.

Lin walked back to Willie unlashed him from his horse then pulled him down before manhandling him across the boardwalk and into the jail as he whined about his treatment.

"Afternoon, Deputy Wilson," he said as he entered, "I have Willie Whitacre with me, and he seeks accommodation in one of your fine jail cells. I apologize in advance for his malodorous condition, but he proved himself untrustworthy."

"Howdy, Lin," a grinning Deputy Wilson said as he stood, walked around the desk, grabbed the large key ring then turned to the cells.

"Where's Hungry Jim?" he asked as Sheriff Ward appeared from the hallway.

"I left him with half of his head missing. I had to get Willie out of there because these two had engaged and killed some Cheyenne before I got there."

"Great," said Deputy Wilson, "that's all we need."

After shoving Willie into the cell, the deputy slammed the door closed hung the key ring over its peg then returned to his seat as Sheriff Jimmy Ward stood by the desk waiting for Lin to tell the story.

When Lin had completed the relatively short narrative, the sheriff said, "I'll send out the wires to those offering the rewards and have them sent to you in Cheyenne, Lin. You think the Cheyenne are going to be riled up about this?"

Lin had his black hat in his hands as he replied, "I don't think this will change anything because a white man was the one who stopped them. The warrior who had engaged them really screwed up thinking that they could keep moving around until the Whitacre brothers ran out of ammunition. I checked and they still had three more boxes of cartridges for their Spencers and hadn't even touched their Winchesters yet."

Sheriff Ward and his three deputies weren't among the general population that looked down on men like Lin Chase with disdain. He may have gone after the outlaws for the price on their heads, but he was good at what he did, and they appreciated his taking the notorious out of the picture, especially out of their county. If he wanted to get into gunfights with the outlaws, more power to him.

After Lin's initial arrival into the deadly game of bounty hunting, his rate of capture had been continually climbing as his reputation grew. Some of the outlaws had even been getting hold of their own long-range rifles to try to counter his tactics but none had his almost uncanny ability with the Sharps, so many simply surrendered after a few well-placed reminders of his skill.

After writing an official statement, Lin left the office untied Homer and walked the small herd down to Lillie's Café to get some late lunch. On the short ride down the streets of Laramie, he debated about getting a room for the night or starting his ride back to Cheyenne. It was only fifty miles, but it was a long fifty miles. Luckily, he could follow the road that paralleled the railroad which made it easier. He remembered almost every foot of that road having built part of it.

So, after having a mammoth lunch, Lin Chase set out eastward in the late afternoon. At this time of year, he should be able to get a good thirty miles under his belt before he set up camp for the night. If Homer wasn't so tired, he'd just push through to his house, but he knew his equine friend needed a rest. The unnamed packhorse would receive the same consideration, but not the affection.

———

He was about four hours out of Laramie, when he spotted something that surprised him because of its location. Just about a half mile to the north, he saw what looked like a farmhouse and barn. There were several reasons for his surprise. Once west of Cheyenne, most of the settled land was used for ranching, not farming, but he couldn't see any cattle on the place. But what bothered him more was that he hadn't noticed it before. The house looked as if it had been there at least two or three years, too. *How had he missed it?* He must have come this way a half a dozen times in the past couple of years.

He was going to camp soon anyway, so he turned Homer to the north to find answers to his questions and maybe make use of their barn rather than camping out in the open again.

———

Julia Lampley was leaving the barn with a rake over her shoulder when she spotted a rider coming from the north leading a large group of horses and spent another ten seconds examining the stranger, trying to discern his intent before walking quickly to the house with her eyes still trained on the rider.

She stepped onto the low porch, stuck her head in the door and shouted, "Mama! We have a rider coming in! Get the shotgun!"

Her mother was in the kitchen preparing dinner when Julia shouted, so she quickly dropped the heavy wooden spoon she was using to stir her stew then dried her hands on her apron. She turned, snatched the twelve-gauge from its pegs on the wall then hustled down the hallway to the main room where she spotted Julia still standing near the door with the rake still in her hand.

They rarely had visitors on the farm and not one had been friendly, so Mary Lampley cocked both hammers of the scattergun before she and Julia walked out to the porch and waited.

———

Lin had seen the woman run into the house and wasn't shocked when another woman appeared next to her with a shotgun. It was a wise thing to do. He finally made out other family members working on what looked like another house about half a mile to the northwest.

When he was closer, he took his hands from Homer's reins and put his palms facing the house to show that he was no threat, but the woman with the shotgun didn't lower it which he appreciated as a wise precaution.

When he was within fifty yards, he pulled to a stop and said loudly, "Howdy. My name's Lin Chase. Do you mind if I dismount?"

"Go ahead," Mary replied but kept the shotgun trained on the stranger.

Lin stepped down then led Homer toward the front of the house, tied him off at one of the porch supports but stayed twenty feet away to appear less threatening.

"What made you stop by?" Mary asked as she stared at him.

"I left Laramie a little while ago and was headed for my house in Cheyenne when I spotted your farm and my curiosity was aroused. I've made this ride a few times and didn't recall seeing your farm here before, but it looks as if it's been here for at least two years now. I was going to ask if I could spend the night in your barn, too."

"You have a lot of guns with you, Mister Chase. Why is that?" Mary asked sharply.

Lin turned, glanced at the two packhorses and three saddled horses, all with various-sized rifle stocks jutting into the air before returning his eyes to Mrs. Lampley.

"Well, ma'am, two of them were mine when I started this trip almost two weeks ago, but I added the others when I caught up with Hungry Jim and Willie Whitacre a couple of days ago. We had a gunfight and I wound up with their property."

Julia finally spoke when she asked, "You killed the outlaws?"

"Just one, ma'am. The other one is in Laramie and will probably be hanged shortly."

"Are you a lawman, Mister Chase?" Mary asked.

"No, ma'am. I'm what they refer to as a bounty hunter," he replied.

Mary was about to tell him to ride on when Julia suddenly asked, "Won't you come in and have some coffee, Mister Chase?"

Mary shot her an angry glance before Lin smiled then replied, "I believe the lady with the shotgun would prefer that I move along. I do thank you for your offer but before I go may I ask a few questions, so I can sleep tonight without having those small mysteries keeping me awake?"

Mary just wanted him gone, so she said, "Go ahead."

"Why did you select this location for your farm? There aren't many that homestead this far west."

"My husband chose this spot because he liked all the trees nearby that he could use to build our homes rather than build those sod houses like they have to use on the prairie. The soil here was good, and the trees block the wind, too. The Barber family has a farm just a few miles northwest of here, too."

Lin nodded then asked, "Are you well-armed, ma'am? I can see you have the shotgun, but do you have anything that had better range than that?"

Mary was suspicious of his motives and asked, "Why do you want to know?"

"Yesterday, the Whitacre brothers were engaged with some Cheyenne and had killed a few of them and wounded others before I stopped them. I'm not convinced that they'll seek revenge for what they did because I was the one who stopped them from killing all of the warriors, but you really should have better protection than just a shotgun."

Mary wavered then replied, "We have a Springfield rifle and a Henry repeater, too."

"How many folks do you have on the farm that can fire a gun?"

"Six."

"Now I don't have any use for the weapons that I picked up yesterday and I don't have any place for the extra horses, either. There are two Spencer carbines, two Winchester '73s, and two Colt pistols. I'll leave them all with you and you can have those two saddle horses and the extra packhorse, too. There's a lot of ammunition for the guns as well. That should give you a better chance at defending yourselves."

"Why would you give us all that? What do you want?" Mary asked with her cocked shotgun still pointed at Lin.

Lin sighed and said, "To be honest, ma'am, right now, I'd just as soon keep riding, so I'll just leave the three horses and be on my way."

He turned, walked to his packhorse untied the trail rope to the other three animals then let it drop before he stepped back to Homer, mounted and tipped his hat.

"Have a nice day, ma'am," he said then smiled at Julia and turned his horse to leave.

Julia glanced at her mother then put down her rake and shouted, "Wait!"

Lin almost didn't but pulled Homer back around and looked at Julia.

"We don't know how to use them," she said quickly.

If they had a Henry using the Winchesters wouldn't be a problem but the Spencers were altogether different, so he said, "I can stay here and wait for you to get your menfolk, so I can give them a brief explanation how to load and use them."

Julia then surprised both Lin and her mother when she bounced off of the porch then approached one of the saddled horses untied it from the other two that Lin was going to leave behind and mounted. She was wearing bib overalls so it wasn't difficult.

"I'll take you to see my brothers," Julia said as she set the gelding off at a walk.

Lin glanced at her still astounded mother then set Homer to a slow trot to catch up still trailing his packhorse.

When he did, Julia looked over at him and said, "I have to apologize for my mother. She really is a very nice person. It's just that she's worried about strangers."

"I thought she was being very reasonable, actually. I haven't shaved in a while and I had all of those guns, so I would probably scare Satan himself."

Julia laughed and replied, "I doubt it. How long have you been a bounty hunter?"

"About six years."

"Really? You don't look that old. How old are you?"

"Twenty-six. I started early."

Lin guessed she was in her early twenties and assumed that he would soon meet her brothers and her husband, although she hadn't said 'husband' only brothers. Maybe she was a widow which was hardly unusual.

———

Julia's brothers, Jim and Bill and his wife, Marge, and her youngest brother, Pete, had been busy working on Jim's house and soon spotted Julia riding a strange horse accompanying an unknown rider leading a packhorse. They all stopped working and stepped down to the ground as they approached the half-built structure.

When they were within thirty yards, Julia quickly dismounted, but Lin stayed in the saddle.

Julia then turned to him and said, "Mister Chase, step down and I'll introduce you to the rest of my family."

Lin dismounted as Julia said, "Everyone, this is Mister Lin Chase. He just stopped by," then she turned and said to Lin, "This is my brother Jim, then there's Bill and his wife, Marge, and finally my brother, Pete. Jim's wife, Anna, is in the house with their little boy, Teddy."

Lin offered his hand to Jim, who shook his hand as he said, "Pleased to meet you Mister Chase. What brings you to our farm?"

Julia quickly answered, "Mister Chase has offered to give us three horses, saddles and some guns and ammunition, but I don't believe you know how to fire some of the rifles, so he is going to show us how to use them."

Lin glanced at the almost effervescent Julia and had no idea why she was so downright happy about his being there but figured he may as well get it over with, so he quickly looked at her puzzled brother.

"I'm a bounty hunter," he said, "I acquired the horses, weapons and supplies from two outlaws that I tracked down. I have no use for them, but I believe they could help your family."

Lin was surprised that he didn't get the expected look of distaste when Jim smiled and replied, "Well, Mister Chase, we most assuredly could use the extra firepower and your expertise. We're just sodbusters out here and there have been a few occasions where I wish we could protect ourselves better, but we haven't made a lot of money since we got here, so we put off acquiring more and better weapons."

"Well, then I'm glad I can help. I was told there were six who could use the weapons, does that include that young man standing beside you?"

Jim turned to his wide-eyed, expectant brother and smiled as he said, "Pete just turned ten, so I guess he's getting old enough."

Pete turned his dancing blue eyes to Lin and asked, "Do I get my own?"

"Well, son, whichever gun you use will be up to the men of the house," Lin replied before turning to Jim and adding, "I've got two Spencers, two Winchesters and two Colt pistols you can have."

"That's a lot of firepower," Jim replied.

"As I told your sister, they were using the Spencers to shoot Cheyenne about forty miles northwest of here. I don't think that the incident will spur the Cheyenne to do anything, but there are a lot more dangers than just Indians and having the guns will help to keep your family safe."

"I know. We had an incident with some men last year that could have been a lot worse, so the guns will be appreciated."

His wife then said, "Why don't we all head back to the house, it's almost dinner time anyway."

Lin nodded then Julia turned and stepped beside Lin as they began to walk to the farmhouse. It was only then that Lin noticed how tall she was. She had to be within an inch or two of his six feet and wondered why he hadn't noticed it before.

Pete trotted to Lin's other side and asked, "Mister Chase, may I ride your horse back?"

Lin smiled and handed Homer's reins to the boy who thanked him, managed to get into the saddle despite his short legs then set Homer off at a trot the house.

Jim watched his brother ride away and said, "He's all boy, that one."

"I think we all are inside, but we don't let too many people know it."

Everyone laughed as they continued the long walk then Julia asked, "Can you tell us about how you caught the two outlaws?"

Lin gave a very quick summary of the gunfight and was still answering questions as they reached the back of the farmhouse and Julia tied off the gelding to a small hitchrail. When she turned and smiled at him, Lin figured out why he hadn't noticed her height before. It was those intense dark blue eyes that had distracted him. Having them almost at his eye level made them more noticeable, too.

The back door then opened, and Pete popped outside before his mother walked out behind him without her shotgun and an apologetic countenance.

"Mister Chase," she said, "Pete tells me that you let him ride your horse and thought you were a good man, so I would like to apologize for my brusque manner."

"That's alright, ma'am. I don't blame you a bit. Most folks think of bounty hunters as just a whisper above the outlaws that we track, and I've learned to live with it."

"No, it's not that. It's just, well, never mind. I do sincerely hope you'll accept my apology and join us for dinner. It's the least we can do in light of all that you've already done for our family."

29

"I appreciate that, ma'am," he replied as Pete hopped off the short back porch and grabbed him by his hand to lead him inside.

Mary Lampley turned and was the first into the kitchen followed by Pete towing Lin inside then Julia and the rest of the family entered behind him.

When Lin entered, he spotted a young woman holding a baby in her arms sitting at the large table, smiled at her, nodded then removed his hat. He assumed she was Jim's wife, Anna and their son, Teddy.

Julia quickly walked to the cookstove, stirred her mother's stew then continued to the table and pulled out a chair for Lin before she took a seat.

Pete usurped the chair, so Lin waited for everyone else to take their seats before taking the next empty chair at the end of the table next to the Anna and her son. There were still two open chairs around the expansive table which reminded him of the enormous kitchen table he used to share with his family so long ago.

"So, Mister Chase," asked Mary, "what made you decide to go into that line of work?"

It was one of the more common questions that he was asked, which irritated him a bit because he knew that no one would ask that question of a farmer, rancher or any other profession, but he had his stock answer.

"I just fell into it, mostly. I wanted to be able to do whatever I needed to do without answering to anyone," then he paused and said, "I've been introduced to each of you, but I don't know your family name."

Mary then replied, "Oh, I'm sorry. I thought someone had mentioned it. It's Lampley."

Lin nodded and said, "I believe I scared everyone when I arrived which was completely understandable. I really need a bath and a shave when I get back to Cheyenne, and all those guns didn't make me any less frightening either."

There was a light chorus of laughter when Julia asked, "Are you going to stay the night, Mister Chase?"

Although that was the original plan Lin was already feeling uncomfortable around Julia who seemed to have already set her cap for him which was disconcerting, so he replied, "No, ma'am. I don't believe so. I'll show everyone how to use the guns and then ride back to Cheyenne."

"Please call me Julia, or Julie if you wish. I answer to both. But why would you leave so late? You can always just sleep in the barn loft."

Those intense blue eyes made Lin waffle, so he replied, "I'll think about it, Julia."

She still had her eyes boring into him when she asked, "May I call you Lin?"

"Lin is fine," he replied, then looked at rest of the family and said, "everyone else can use my Christian name as well."

Mary could see how Julia was unsettling their guest, so she said, "Pay no attention to Julia, Lin. She's the oldest, so she thinks she's in charge. Everyone here knows I'm the one who runs this place with an iron hand."

Everyone laughed as the others filled their chairs while Mary began to hand out bowls of stew and Julia and Marge helped by putting out large plates of biscuits along with cups of coffee or milk depending on preference. Julia assumed he was a coffee drinker and set a large mug of coffee before him and smiled before returning to her seat.

"Where do you live?" Julia asked before taking a bite of her stew.

"I have a small house on two quarter sections about four miles northwest of Cheyenne."

"Do you live alone?" she asked as soon as she swallowed.

"Yes, ma'am," he replied before taking a big spoonful of stew to preclude any speech for a minute.

Lin wasn't sure, but it seemed as if Julia Lampley had done more than just set her cap for him and was acting as if she was already planning on returning with him to Cheyenne. He'd never met such a brazen woman before in his life and it made him much more than just nervous. It disturbed his concentration which was always a bad thing in his business.

Pete then asked, "Have you killed a lot of outlaws?"

Lin had to recover his wits enough before he swallowed then replied, "Twelve, but I've captured eleven and now, I'm capturing more than I'm having to shoot. It's why I dress the way I do and use the Sharps rifle. Once they know I've got them in my sights, some would rather just give up and take their chances with the courts or try to kill me when I'm taking them in."

As he answered Pete's expected boy question, he noticed that Julia was still staring at him and tried not to notice so much, but it was very difficult. He'd attracted the attention of a few young women over the years, but none had the directness or intensity of Julia Lampley. As curious as he may be about her status as a widow or single woman, he decided that leaving that question unanswered might be a safer way to go.

As the dinner progressed, he answered and asked questions, so by the time it was done, they knew he'd grown up on a farm in Iowa and he knew that they had left their farm in Ohio after the local bank failed taking all of their savings with them, but the creditors still wanted to collect on the mortgage on the farm.

It was almost sundown when Lin, Jim, Bill and Pete moved the horses to the barn, unsaddled them and let them drink and feed while they brought the two Spencers, Winchesters and Colts to the house.

As everyone sat in the main room, Lin demonstrated how to use the Spencer first because it was so different with its tube of seven cartridges in the stock and the extra actions of using the lever to bring in a new round and cock the hammer manually after it was in the chamber. Then there was the weak ejector that required the shooter to just about turn the carbine on its side to have the empty brass pop free.

The Winchester was much easier to demonstrate because they had a Henry and the biggest difference between the newer gun and its forebear was the ability to load individual cartridges though the loading gate rather than having to carefully slide them into the tube under the barrel. The Colt was surprisingly new to all of them, so it took a bit longer to explain how to load and fire the pistol. Lin hadn't met a lot of men who didn't know how to use Sam Colt's handgun.

Throughout the lessons, Lin kept letting his eyes drift back to Julia who he swore never blinked once as she kept her eyes focused on his face. His decision about staying in the barn had already been made for him when they unsaddled Homer and his packhorse, and he began to believe that he would have to deal with her later.

Why she was behaving this way had him baffled. He wasn't so falsely immodest not to admit that many women found him attractive, but Julia was far from being a plain young woman and should have already married, yet apparently wasn't and no one had mentioned that she was a widow, either. With the paucity of women in Wyoming Territory even given their remote location it was a true mystery. His earlier decision to keep his curiosity about her status unanswered was tested, but he was able to refrain from asking, lest she get the impression that he'd somehow proposed.

"Well, folks, that's about all you need to know," Lin said as he handed the Colt to Jim Lampley.

"We really appreciate this, Lin," Jim replied as he examined the revolver.

Lin stood and said, "I'll be leaving early in the morning, so I'll say my farewells now. I'm glad to have met everyone and hope you get that house finished before the snows arrive."

Jim laughed and said, "We're trying. I know how early that can happen, though."

Lin nodded then gave the family a short wave, picked up his hat then turned and left the house, intentionally avoiding Julia's gaze.

Once on the front porch with the door closed behind him, he exhaled sharply, pulled on his hat and quickly trotted to the barn in the dark to get his bedroll set up in the loft. After almost two weeks on the trail, sleeping under any roof was a blessing.

He entered the barn, closed the door behind him then lit the one lamp and hung it from its hanger under the center beam. He picked up his bedroll and headed for the ladder at the back of the barn more than ready to get a quiet night's sleep.

He had just set his hand on one of the rungs when he heard the ominous creak from the barn door hinges then sighed and slowly turned around and was unsurprised and even more worried when he saw Julia closing the door behind her. He wished that he'd just saddled Homer and headed back and cursed his curiosity for even turning down the access road.

"Julia, you shouldn't be in here. Are you trying to get me shot with one of the guns I just gave your brothers?"

"They'd do no such thing," she said then walked closer before plopping down on a stack of hay.

Lin set his bedroll down, sighed then walked back to the center of the barn, turned to face her and folded his arms across his chest.

"What do you want, Julia?" he asked without a hint of friendliness to almost spook her into leaving.

"I want you to take me with you," she said bluntly.

Even though he'd already mentally suggested that possibility to himself hours ago, when she said it, it stunned him. *How could anyone be so bold?*

He stood in silent for almost thirty seconds and his shock must have shown on his face because he swore it was as if Julia was almost dissecting his thoughts.

He finally said, "Julia, at the risk of sounding rude, are you insane? I've known you for less than six hours and you want to run away with me?"

"Maybe I should have phrased it differently. I want you to teach me what you do. If you want to stay here while you do it, then that's even better."

Lin stared at her then slowly turned and sat down on the hay beside her, utterly flummoxed. He was so off balance, he had to search for any kind of answer to her request. Maybe he'd been reading too much into her intentions and there was no romantic interest at all which was better, but not by much. *How would he teach a woman how to do his perilous work? Why would she even want to do it?*

It took him another minute before he said, "Miss Lampley, I'm not sure if that isn't even more outside the realm of sanity than what I initially thought you'd asked. I'm a bounty hunter, not a baker or a tailor. I go after murderers and engage them in gunfights. I'm out on the trail for weeks at a time in harsh conditions."

"I know all that, but I have a problem."

"Obviously."

"No, I'm not close to being crazy, Lin. My problem is that I'm a woman."

"Strangely enough, I noticed that. How is that a problem beyond the obvious issues?"

"I want to kill two men."

Lin blinked twice and almost asked her to repeat what she'd just said. He could understand why some women would want to kill a man, but he'd never heard one so calmly state that she wanted to do it and to kill two of them. There must be a reason, and it had better be a good one for him to even consider it.

For almost thirty seconds, neither spoke until Lin finally asked, "Why?"

Julia didn't look down or wring her hands but let her dark blue eyes bore into him as she replied, "Last year in April, my parents were in the house while the rest of us were out in the fields. My father was in bed with some sort of stomach ailment. Two men rode to the house and just walked in the door with pistols drawn. They didn't see my father and while one watched, the other raped my mother and then the second one raped her while the first one watched.

"By then, my father, who was already weak, stumbled out of the bedroom saw what they were doing and turned to get the shotgun out of the kitchen. One of the men shot him then they both left the house and rode away. We heard the gunshot and raced to the house, but we were too late. My mother was curled up and sobbing and my father died three weeks later from an infection. We notified the sheriff's office the next day, but my mother was too shaken to describe them, and they had nothing to go on, so there was nothing they could do. Nothing.

"It took her a while to get over that attack, which was why she was so hostile to you when you first arrived. It took me a long time to get her to give me the description of the two men, Mister Chase. I can't be a sheriff or deputy because I'm a woman, so I want to be a bounty hunter like you.

"When I saw those guns, I knew almost instantly that you were a bounty hunter, which is why I've been so aggressive. I couldn't let you leave. When you said you were a bounty hunter, it was as if God had sent you as an answer to my need to punish those men. I wanted you to show me how to do what you do so I could give my mother the justice that the law couldn't."

Lin could understand her rage but knew she had no idea what to expect. At the same time, it let him be more comfortable with her now that he understood her intent wasn't what he'd initially thought.

"Julia," he said softly, "I understand your need to deliver justice to those men, but you are seeking revenge, and that's a dangerous thing. One of the reasons I'm so successful at what I do is that I have to do it with an almost complete lack of emotion. Emotions will cause mistakes, and mistakes can get you killed. Even if you had as much skill as I do, if you approach these men with hatred and an urgent desire to kill them both, it's much more likely that they'd kill you."

"So, you won't help me either?"

Lin didn't reply but asked, "Can you give me the descriptions?"

Julia knew she might be losing the argument but answered, "One was tall, about your height, but thinner. He had dark hair and brown eyes. The second one was a few inches shorter with dark hair and brown eyes, too."

"That's a pretty vague description, Julia. Do you have anything else that might help? Were either of them left-handed or have any scars?"

"The first one had a missing left earlobe."

Lin's eyebrows peaked before he said, "That sounds like the Hilliard brothers. Ron is the one with the missing earlobe and Dick is the shorter one. I didn't know they were operating this far north. They're both wanted for assault, robbery and rape and

Dick is wanted for murder while Ron is only an accessory to murder."

Julia asked, "Why do you know so much about them?"

"They're wanted criminals. It's my job, remember? I study those wanted posters in case I ever run across one of them accidentally," he replied then added, "I'll tell you what I'll do. After I return to Cheyenne to get settled and resupplied, I'll run them down for you."

"I still want to come with you. I need to be there when you find them."

"No, you don't. I'll take care of it myself and come back and tell you when I get them."

"I need to do this! I need to be there when they die. If you won't take me with you then I'll just take one of those rifles you left and go after them myself."

"You're not that stupid, Julia. A young woman alone in this country wouldn't last two days. Now I've got to go back to Cheyenne in the morning and I'll start after them in a few days."

"Then I'll come with you. Please let me do this."

For thirty seconds, Lin looked at her determined face as he ruminated. He doubted if she'd really go off on her own, but there was one reason for letting her come along, and it was a surprise. He was already fascinated with her direct demeanor and admitted she was pleasant to the eye. He didn't want to lose the chance to know her better. Granted, there was the chance that once he understood Julia, he'd change his mind, but he'd never met a woman like her before.

Lin finally said, "Okay, you can join me on the search, but on my terms. I need to return to Cheyenne for a few days to resupply and handle some other routine jobs then I'll return and spend some time showing you the basics, so you don't get yourself killed. You will always do exactly what I tell you to do without hesitation. Okay?"

Julia smiled, nodded and replied, "Thank you, Lin. I promise I won't be a problem."

"I find that hard to believe but now, Miss Lampley, may I get some sleep. Please?"

Julia began to stand then stopped, looked at Lin with those unsettling eyes and asked, "Do you promise to come back in two days?"

"Give me some leeway, Julia. Make it four and I promise I'll be back by then."

"Good. I'll hold you to that promise. I'll see you when you return."

As she stood, Lin asked, "Does your family know why you came here?"

She smiled and replied, "No. They're under the impression that I came to join you for some hanky-panky."

His face registered his shock as she laughed and then just walked past opened the door and left, closing the squealing barn door behind her.

Lin sat unmoving for almost five minutes, unable to match the solemn Julia who had told him that she wanted to kill two men to the mischievous Julia who may or not have told her family that she was joining him in the barn for some 'hanky-panky'.

Finally, he stood picked up his bedroll then climbed the ladder to the loft. After spreading it on the floor, he simply removed his hat, gunbelt and boots before sliding into the bedroll.

By the time he drifted off to sleep, he was still perplexed by the woman and doubted if it would get any better. But it would be the most interesting manhunt he'd ever undertaken. He was almost regretting that she hadn't set her cap for him. Maybe that would have been easier for both of them.

———

Lin was up with the predawn and was saddling Homer twenty minutes later. The whole idea was to leave the farm before anyone was up, but he should have known better. This was a working farm and despite having grown up on one, he still thought he could steal away without notice.

He was just beginning to saddle his packhorse when the creaking hinges announced the arrival of a guest, so he slowly turned then smiled when he saw Pete enter the barn and not Julia.

"Good morning, sir," Lin said as he threw the saddle blanket over the packhorse's back.

"Julia said not to let you leave until you had breakfast."

Lin leaned against the gelding and thought this was an unexpected opportunity to have his questions about Julia's status resolved without having to have her provide the answers.

So, he asked, "Pete, what do you think of your sister?"

"What do you mean? Ain't you gonna get hitched?"

"*What?*" Lin asked with wide eyes and yet another stunned expression forgetting about his questions.

Pete shrugged and said, "Everybody was saying that you and Julia were gonna get married."

Lin was about to set the record straight but knew he was talking to the wrong person to get this issue clarified.

"I'll come with you, Pete," Lin finally said as he pulled the blanket from the packhorse and draped it over the pack saddle.

As he walked with Pete to the house, Lin answered his rapid-fire questions related to guns which had a surprisingly calming effect on his turbulent mind. *Marriage? What was that woman doing?* And just when he almost thought they had made an unusual, but non-romantic arrangement.

When they entered the back door into the packed kitchen, it was Bill's wife, Marge, who was the first to break the news of his un-proposed upcoming nuptials when she said, "Well, congratulations, Lin!"

Lin smiled at Marge, mumbled "Thank you," then sought out those blue eyes of his unintended intended.

As he shook Julia's brothers' hands and accepted similar well-wishes from them and Jim's wife, Anna, he was finally able to make eye contact with Julia, who had been talking to her mother as they stood in the corner. When their eyes finally met, he expected her to be sheepish and embarrassed, but she was nothing of the sort which utterly destroyed the soothing impact of the gun talk with Pete.

Julia read the total confusion and probable growing anger in his eyes then said, "Mama, I'd like to take a short walk with Lin. We'll be back in a few minutes."

Mary smiled and said, "We understand, dear. We'll feed everyone else and you and Lin can eat privately when you get back."

Julia smiled at her mother crossed the large kitchen put her arm through Lin's and dragged him out of the house. Neither spoke as they crossed the short porch and stepped out onto the dirt heading north to the furrowed fields.

Once they were a hundred feet or so away, Julia asked, "I imagine this is all a big surprise for you, isn't it?"

Lin had managed to bite his tongue waiting for her to explain, so he quickly said, "You might say that. When Pete casually mentioned that we were going to be hitched, it almost knocked me over. Why did you say such a thing, and why was everyone so happy about it? Nobody here really knows me that well. I could have lied completely about who I was. I could be some murdering outlaw who made it all up."

"I knew better from the moment I saw you on your horse with all those guns. Why do you think I stopped you from leaving?"

"You wanted me to show you how to become a bounty hunter."

"I do, but before you even said what you did for a living, I could see in your eyes that you were a good man and an honest one. That was no façade of being polite and almost innocent. For a man whose killed as many bad men as you have, your eyes are incredibly innocent. You're probably more innocent than I am."

"I doubt that, Julia, but that still doesn't explain this whole marriage fib that you've obviously told to your family."

"Yes, there is that; isn't there? That is totally my fault, and I'm afraid I've dug the hole even deeper."

Lin dug in his heels, turned and looked at Julia before he asked, "You didn't tell them that we were intimate last night, did you? I mean, you only were only in the barn for twenty minutes."

"No, I didn't even suggest that. Remember that I told you I'd mentioned to my family that I was going to see you for some hanky-panky? Well, I wasn't the one who said it. When I said I was going to go to the barn to talk to you, Bill said, 'Enjoy your hanky-panky time, sister', and I just laughed which to the whole family, seemed to confirm what Bill had said."

"Oh," Lin said as they resumed walking.

"Anyway, when I returned, Anna asked me in front of everyone if I was going to run away with you, which surprised me, and I answered that you had to go to Cheyenne for a few days before you came back. It was the truth, but they interpreted it to mean that you were smitten and would be coming back to call on me and it took a life of its own after that."

"Didn't you at least try to derail the whole idea?"

"No."

"*No? Why not?*" Lin asked sharply.

"Because I think it's a good idea," she casually replied.

Lin threw on the brakes again, turned to look at her, feeling almost as if he was caught in an imaginary wonderland where nothing made any sense.

"Why would you even suggest that? I've talked to you for just a few hours and less than one of those was alone. How do you know if I even like you?"

"Do you?"

"Do I what?"

"Do you like me?"

"Does it matter? You seem to already have us married and with eleven children for some reason."

"It matters, but it's not like that at all."

"Alright, I'll admit that I like you. But if it's not like that at all, what is it like?"

Julia started them walking again and said, "You agreed that you'd show me the basics of how to do what you do and that I'd come with you to find those two men. Right?"

"Yes. So far, we're in agreement."

"Now, if we're out in the great empty world out there together for days, what do you think will happen?"

"Meaning?"

"Meaning that you're a young man and I'm a young woman. What will happen is inevitable, don't you think?"

Lin was totally flustered with Julia. His only close encounter with a member of the opposite sex was with his school sweetheart Edith, and that was nine years and over five hundred miles ago. *Have women changed this much or was it just Julia?* He placed his bet on it being just the tall young woman walking beside him.

They walked a good hundred feet before Lin answered, "I suppose that could happen, but I'd never force myself on you."

"I know that. I told you that I saw the innocence in your eyes, but can I tell you something else?"

"You will anyway, so go ahead."

"You have probably been wanting to ask me why I had never married since you first arrived. Is that right?"

"Yes, I'll admit it had crossed my mind. There aren't many women in the territory, and especially young, handsome women like you. I would have thought that even when you were in Ohio that you would have had many suitors."

"I did have a few young men try to visit me, but I had a few reasons for spurning them all. The first was that I was the oldest and even though I was a girl, I worked hard around the farm."

Then she held out her hand and said, "Shake my hand."

They were still walking as Lin shook the calloused and rough hand of a working farm woman.

After releasing her hand, Julia continued, saying, "Then there was the issue of my height. I was always taller than the boys in my school, and when I was young, I was ridiculed by both the girls and boys for being a beanpole. I remembered that and wasn't about to forgive those young men when I filled out. But I could have looked past those early years if I judged any of them to be the man with whom I wanted to spend the rest of my life. I needed a man who could challenge me and still treat me as an equal and a woman. Do you understand that?"

If another woman had asked the question, he wouldn't have, but with Julia, he understood completely.

"Yes, I can."

"The moment I saw you on that horse, I could see something in your eyes that told me that you could be the one who would do both. I couldn't let you leave, even before you said what you did for a living. When you said you were a bounty hunter, everything just slammed together in my mind."

"So, you're actually serious about getting married?"

"Yes."

"Don't you even care what I think about all this? I said I like you, Julia, and that's true, but like isn't love and there's a big difference between the two. You realize that you've thrown a giant obstacle into the whole idea of you coming with me to find those two men, don't you?"

Julia didn't miss a step as she replied, "I don't believe that it has, but would it make a difference if I told you that I loved you?"

Lin had finally stopped trying to anticipate what Julia would say next and replied, "No, because I wouldn't believe you anyway."

Julia glanced over at him but didn't say anything as they walked around the field of young corn plants.

Lin decided to push the whole marriage episode aside for the sake of his own sanity and return to the original proposal, although the word now had a whole new context.

"Julia, I promised you that I'd return and show you the rudiments of what I do, and I always keep my promises. So, here's what I suggest we do. I'll go along with the whole courting story to mollify your family before I return to Cheyenne for a day or two and then come back. Okay?"

"I'm grateful for that, Lin, and I do apologize for putting you into this situation."

"I accept your apology, Julia, and there's one other thing. If it's okay with you, I'd like to spend one more day here with you to get to know you a little better before I head back to Cheyenne. I've already been gone two weeks, so one more day won't hurt."

Julia broke into a big smile and said, "I'd enjoy that, Lin. Will you shoot your Sharps? I'm sure that everyone, especially Pete, would love to see it."

Despite his earlier turmoil, Lin couldn't help but to respond to Julia's infectious smile, so he smiled back and replied, "I think that can be arranged."

They turned to go back to the house, now almost half a mile away, and Lin surprised himself and took Julia's rough hand in his when they headed back, convincing himself it was to add support to her whole courting story.

Julia was neither surprised nor displeased when she felt his hand take hers. She hadn't told him one thing that she didn't believe. She knew it was fate that made him turn down the farm's access road yesterday evening. As soon as she'd heard his voice, she knew. All those years of pushing away those boys and unworthy men had prepared her for his arrival. It was almost as if the finger of God had nudged him to the front of the farmhouse.

"So," Julia returned to her other purpose for joining him when she asked, "how long do you think it will take to find the Hilliard brothers?"

Lin was relieved to be back on his home turf when he replied, "First, we'll have to go to Laramie and see Sheriff Ward and ask if he's heard any rumors. Then we start asking around. Usually the best places are livery stables, saloons and cafés. After that, we start going to other towns until we get a lead. On a case like this, it could take weeks unless they commit some crime and are identified."

"When we're in towns, do we stay in a hotel?"

Lin glanced over at Julia, saw her slight smile and replied, "You don't think I'd make my wife stay in the livery, do you?"

Julia laughed then said, "Only if I'm naughty."

"Then I guess you'll always be sleeping with the horses, because you haven't been anything but naughty since I've met you."

Julia continued to laugh as they walked, and she tightened her grip on his hand.

Lin was astounded by how comfortable he suddenly was being with Julia. Maybe she was right and that it was inevitable that they should find each other. Either that or she somehow planned everything including some sort of distant mind control which he was beginning to think wasn't as strange as it sounded.

The rest of the family, except for Mary, Anna and her baby, were all leaving the house as Lin and Julia approached.

Jim smiled and asked, "Did you enjoy your walk?"

Julia replied, "Yes, oh nosy brother. Lin even said he'll be staying for another day and will give us a demonstration of his marksmanship with his Sharps rifle later."

Pete exclaimed, "Wow! I can't wait!"

"So, you won't be working in the fields with us, Julia?" he asked.

"No. I think I've earned a day off. We're going to go have breakfast now."

They all waved and headed for the barn to collect hoes and rakes while Julia and Lin entered the house.

Lin had expected to find Julia's mother, sister-in-law and her baby in the kitchen, but he found it empty. He could hear their voices down the hallway but didn't know from which room.

Julia walked to the cookstove, slid the still greasy frypan to the hotplate and began cracking eggs while Lin set their two place settings.

Lin took a hand towel to pick up the hot coffee pot as Julia began scooping the scrambled eggs from the frypan then poured the coffee into the two cups on the table as she set the plates of eggs and already fried bacon nearby.

After they sat at the table, Julia then asked, "How long does it take to become a sharpshooter?"

"Most people can't come close to becoming a marksman no matter how much they practice and most of the marksmen don't have what it takes to be a sharpshooter. I was lucky to be born with an almost innate sense of understanding where a bullet will go. It just all seemed so logical to me and I can't recall a time I wasn't very accurate with any firearm that I used.

"It wasn't until I had been a bounty hunter for three years and built my house near Cheyenne that I learned about ballistics. I bought every book I could find on the subject and nothing I read seemed baffling at all. It all confirmed what I already understood. I'll be honest with you, Julia, and this isn't meant to impress you or just braggadocio. I'm the best that I've ever seen with firearms."

"Then I can't do what you do with your rifles?"

"I don't know, Julia. Have you ever fired one before?"

"No. I've shot my father's shotgun, but that's not the same; is it?"

"No, ma'am," he replied before snapping off a big chunk of thick bacon with his teeth.

"When you were talking about facing those two brothers in the Black Hills, you said that you were eight hundred yards away. That's almost half of a mile. Is that normal?"

"For me, it is. I usually take my first shots between six hundred and a thousand yards to let them know that I'm serious."

"How long does the bullet take to get that far?"

"Now, that, Miss Lampley, is a very insightful question as most people seem to think the bullet arrives almost instantly, probably because so few have witnessed a long-range shot. The answer is that it depends on a few variables. If I'm shooting my Sharps with the .50-110 cartridge, the muzzle velocity is almost fifteen hundred feet per second, or five hundred yards per second when it leaves the gun. But it starts slowing down as soon as it leaves the barrel, so at a thousand yards, it takes around two and a half seconds to reach the target."

"That long? I always thought bullets traveled a lot faster than that."

Lin smiled as he was in his element now.

"My Sharps' muzzle velocity is higher than most of them, but the air has to be pushed out of the way and gravity, altitude, wind, temperature and even the humidity all act on the bullet as it heads downrange. Even the size of the bullet makes a difference. If the Sharps fired a smaller round, then it would drop less and have even greater range, but to be honest, at a thousand yards, it's almost impossible to pick up a target without a telescopic sight. All of those factors have to be calculated when you set your sights."

"And you do all that in your head?" she asked in astonishment.

"Yes, ma'am. It's second nature, really. Even with my inherited ability to shoot, I still practice a lot and make sure that they're in different conditions so when I take the shot, my brain does the calculations almost automatically."

"If it takes that long for the bullet to get there, can't the bad guys get out of the way?"

"Yet another excellent question, ma'am. When you're in a long-range shootout, as I was three days ago, and the bad guys are looking at you, it's impossible to hit them because as soon as they see my muzzle flash, they'll drop behind whatever rock they're hiding behind or just move left or right. Now if they're trying to hide behind a wooden wall then it doesn't matter because the bullet will blast right through even two inches of wood."

"So, how did you hit him?"

"When I fired my first shot, I saw them drop behind the boulders then quickly reloaded and set up to fire again while they were hiding. They know that because they can see my muzzle flash, they can always drop back down again before the bullet arrives, and I'd just be wasting ammunition. But they're also usually worried that I'll rush them while they're hidden, so one of them will poke his head over his rock to see where I am.

"After I reloaded, I aimed at the other man's spot then counted down from five. That gives them about ten seconds altogether. When I hit zero, I fire the rifle and the bullet is on its way without a target. Sometimes the timing is right, as it was this time and the outlaw is sticking his head up as the bullet arrives. If I'm wrong then it'll keep their heads down again, and I close in."

"You do all this at half a mile?"

"I have excellent eyesight, but I'm really aiming at a spot."

"How accurate are you with your Sharps?"

"At eight hundred yards, I'll put a round through a six-inch target nine out of ten times."

"And you'll show us this afternoon?"

"Yes, ma'am."

Julia looked at Lin with a newfound awe as she finished her eggs as much by his lack of braggadocio for his skills as for the skills themselves.

"Why do you have to return to Cheyenne? Can't you get your supplies in Buford?"

"Not the ammunition for my rifles and I have a special order that I placed a few months ago and it should be in now, too."

"Can I guess it's another gun?"

53

"Two, in fact. Winchester came out with a new model late last year, the Winchester 1876. They call it the Centennial model. It's a lot beefier than the '73 and uses a bigger, .45 caliber cartridge. When I was talking to the gunsmith in Cheyenne, he told me that they were chambering some for an even larger caliber cartridge to use for big game hunting. So, I had him special order two of fifty caliber model with the musket length barrels and eight boxes of the cartridges. They'll give me more range and power that will fill the gap between the Sharps and the '73s."

"And that's the only reason you have to go back?"

"That and I check my mail and my house and barn. I need a shave and a haircut, too," he said as he rubbed his heavily-stubbled chin.

"Are you going to bring a shaving kit with you this time?"

"I think so. Normally, I spend so much time in the saddle, I don't want to waste the time to shave, but this won't be one of my normal chases."

"I don't believe it will be," she said with a smile before taking a sip of her coffee.

Lin took his cup in his large hands and looked into those dark blue eyes as he sipped his coffee and was sure that she was absolutely right. This would be far from one of his normal chases on so many levels.

––––––––

Ten minutes later, they were in the barn while Lin unsaddled Homer and Julia sat on the same stack of hay that she'd used last night but this time, she held one of his Sharps in her hands.

"It's awfully heavy, Lin," she said as she slid her fingers along the octagonal barrel.

He was uncinching the saddle as he replied, "Mine are heavier than most because I had Paul Bergerson, the gunsmith in Cheyenne, balance them by putting lead weights into the stocks and then putting brass plates on the butt."

"Is balance important?"

"Very. Without it, a long-range shot is much more difficult unless you're using some form of support. If you notice, each of them also has a special fitting that allows me to sit them on a tripod that I keep with me in one of my panniers on the packhorse. I use it for really long shots of up to a mile."

"Can you even see that far?"

"At that range, you fire at shapes, but I can hit them."

He finished unsaddling Homer, walked to his ammunition pannier, pulled out one of the mammoth .50-110 cartridges from its box and handed it to Julia.

"My God, Lin! This is scary," she said as she held the large cartridge between her thumb and index finger.

"Only if you're on the receiving end, Julia," he said before taking a seat beside her.

She handed the two-and-a-half-inch long cartridge back to Lin and said, "You said you had to check mail when you get back to Cheyenne. Do you write to your family?"

"Yes, ma'am. I write to my parents back in Iowa at least once a month. I usually go and visit them in the middle of winter when business is slow."

Julia smiled and her eyes sparkled as she said, "Maybe I'll get to meet them the next time you go."

Lin laughed then said, "Maybe. But we need to find the Hilliard brothers first, and that might take a while."

They kept their eyes locked for another thirty seconds, already amazingly comfortable with each other. The bigger change, of course, was Lin's. After all of the time being kept unbalanced by Julia, he'd come to appreciate just how unique she was, and began to believe that what would happen between them was indeed inevitable and now quite desirable. He couldn't imagine being able to spend very much time with her alone on the trail and not have it lead to intimacy.

―――

In Harney, just east of Laramie, Fuzzy had his boys sitting around a table at Robinson's Saloon as they finalized their plans. Sitting opposite from Fuzzy was Ike McCall, his long-time partner. Arnie Jacobsen and Hound Jones sat on his right and on his left were the two Hilliard brothers who Lin thought would be difficult to find. The brothers, Hound and Arnie Jacobsen had been recruited for the job once Fuzzy had come up with the scheme.

Fuzzy Villers was using beer mugs for his outline.

"This is the first farm northeast of Buford, the Lampley place. We get four from there. I'll go with Dick and Ron to do that place 'cause they're already familiar with it. Arnie, you, Hound and Ike take care of the Barber farm right here. That'll give us three more. Then we all ride northwest and make our final stop where those squatters are livin' and get the last two."

"How do you know about the squatters, Fuzzy?" asked Ron Hilliard.

"I passed by their poor excuse for a cabin about a year ago when I took a different route to Laramie for supplies. They'll be the easiest 'cause there's only two men and I didn't see a gun at anywhere."

Hound Jones asked, "What about the law?"

"By the time they get wind of it, we'll be long gone. They'll be dealin' with the miners, if they even have the balls to go into the camp."

"Are they really gonna pay that much?" Ike McCall asked.

Fuzzy grinned before answering, "You saw the faces on those miners, Ike. They were practically droolin' when I told 'em we'd be bringin' them women. Those boys have been in that camp for a long time now and they know if they leave their claims for even a little while, they'd lose 'em. They'll probably pay more than we expect, too."

"How much do you figure?" asked Dick Hilliard, the greed apparent on his face.

"It depends on what they look like. I caught a glimpse of some of the Barber women and those squatters, but you and your brother said the Lampley women were all good lookers, so we could get quite a haul, especially if they ain't been deflowered. But what makes it likely we'll get more is the way we're gonna sell 'em. We're gonna make 'em bid against each other. There are fourteen of 'em in the camp, and with only nine women, there'll be a regular biddin' war."

"Won't some of 'em just team up and buy one to share?" asked Ron Hilliard.

"Most likely. But the young, good lookin' ones will get us a big payday. We should leave the camp with more than fifteen pounds of gold. That's almost a thousand dollars apiece, boys. And the beauty of it is that the law will blame the miners and not us even if they bother chasin' us down at all."

Arnie Jacobsen asked, "What about supplies and horses? We ain't got the money for 'em."

"That's the beauty of all this. We pick up a wagon at the first farm, load it with supplies and the women from both farms and the squatter cabin then head to the camp where we sell what we don't need to the miners. Hell, we can afford to give 'em away once we sell the women."

Dick Hilliard then asked, "Say, Fuzzy, about the women. We can use 'em, can't we? I mean, it's a bonus."

"We ain't got the time for it. We need to grab 'em, get 'em to the camp and sell 'em real fast. If the law finds out about it sooner than we expect, we'd run into 'em before we got there. Once you get your gold, you'll be able to buy any woman you want."

"Okay."

"And we don't kill anybody either unless we have to. We tie up the menfolk in a locked room and leave 'em. By the time they get loose, we'll be in Colorado. If they die, then it won't be by a bullet."

Ike nodded and said, "Okay. It looks like were ready to go tomorrow night, so let's get another beer. I'm kinda thirsty."

Fuzzy laughed and said, "You're always thirsty, Ike."

The basic outline was set. In a few days they'd all be rich men.

———

After a very sociable lunch with the entire family, Lin, Julia and Pete went out to the fields to set up a target for the Sharps demonstration.

They walked all the way to the half-finished house where Lin selected a split board with a seriously large knot that was pretty useless for construction before they headed for the nearby forest.

"This will work," Lin said as he leaned the board against the trunk of an eighty-foot tall Ponderosa pine.

"How do you measure the distance?" Pete asked.

"I estimate it in my head but in this case, Pete, you will pick the distance. First, I want you to measure one of your strides."

"How do I do that?"

"Go ahead and take two long steps then stop."

Pete nodded, took the two long steps then turned and looked behind him.

Lin looked at the distance between his heel marks left by his right foot and said, "Each of your strides is about thirty inches, Pete. So, do your cyphering and tell me how many steps it will take to get eight hundred yards."

Pete squinted his eyes and furrowed his brows before saying, "Nine hundred and sixty."

Lin grinned at him then said, "Very good. Now, I'll walk with Julia and talk with her, so I can't count. What I want you to do is start counting numbers to yourself and stop somewhere around a thousand. Okay?"

"Not nine hundred and sixty?"

"No, sir. Anywhere between eight and twelve hundred. Let's add some mystery to this."

Pete grinned and said, "Okay. I'm ready."

Lin took Julia's hand and they stepped away from the target.

"Why did you do it this way, Lin?" she asked.

"Estimating distance is critical to putting a shot on target. If Pete stopped at exactly nine hundred and sixty paces, then I'd almost be cheating by knowing it was exactly eight hundred yards. Now it'll be between less than seven hundred and more than a thousand yards. It's just another variable."

"You know he's probably going to go for the longer distance, don't you?"

Lin smiled at her and replied, "I'd be surprised if he didn't count to two thousand."

"I think he'll get bored by then."

"I hope so, because that would be out of range for anything less than a howitzer."

When Pete finally said, "Here!" they stopped, and Lin marked the spot with a long heel drag in the dirt.

"Okay, folks, let's go and get one of my Sharps and we'll see if we can make that board nothing but splinters."

The two tall young people and Pete all walked quickly toward the barn, but Pete had to change his direction after a few hundred yards to go and tell his brothers and sister-in-law that the show was ready to begin.

As Julia and Lin entered the barn, Pete had already danced into the house to let his mother and Anna know that Lin was ready to fire his Sharps, so two minutes later Mary, Pete and even Anna, with ten-month old Teddy in her arms left the house and joined the parade heading to the northwest behind Lin, who was wearing his heavy coat with six extra rounds of cartridges in their inner lining loops.

Once they arrived, Lin had them stand back about twenty feet and warned them of the loudness of the report. They formed a semi-circle at that distance, but Julia was just six feet to his left and Lin understood her need to be close. She had to become acclimated to the Sharps' impressive bark.

As he opened the breech, Lin glanced downrange, estimated the distance at almost eleven hundred yards then glanced at Pete before smiling and shaking his head. He watched the pine needles for estimating the wind direction and speed downrange before he closed the breech, adjusted the ladder sight to near the end of its travel and cocked the hammer.

He knew he should have used the tripod for the shot or at the very least, chosen a prone or kneeling position, but he didn't see this as just a show. He wanted to challenge himself with what was an incredibly difficult shot. Even before they began walking, he knew at this range he wouldn't be able to make out the knot at all and would barely be able to sight on the board itself. But the lighter board stood out in dark contrast to the darker bark of the tree and he knew the knot was about eight inches from the top. It would be more of a guess, but that's what made it a real challenge.

Everyone was silent as he took a deep breath, let it out slowly then released the first trigger. He held his breath as the sights settled where he wanted them to be then slowly pulled back on the second trigger. The Sharps surprised him as it should, when it rammed back against his shoulder and the fifty-caliber aerodynamic slug of lead raced downrange.

The Lampleys all thought he'd missed after the first two seconds, but Julia knew better because Lin had explained the basics of ballistics to her just a few hours ago. It wasn't until more than three seconds had elapsed before they all saw the board fly away from its supporting pine trunk, eliciting cries of surprise.

Julia just turned, grinned and said, "That was an impressive piece of shooting, Mister Chase."

Lin smiled back and said, "Luck, Miss Lampley. Just luck."

She took his arm and as they all began to walk to the target, she replied, "In a pig's eye, Mister Chase."

"I could barely see it, Julia. There really was a lot of luck involved."

She knew that he was telling the truth but also suspected that luck played a much smaller role than he believed.

It wasn't until he was within a hundred feet that Lin realized how close he'd been to actually hitting the knot. At eleven hundred yards, he'd been high by six inches almost missing the board entirely, but it was in perfect alignment with the center of the board.

He was incredibly pleased with the shot, but said, "I missed the knot."

Julia laughed and said, "None of that false modesty, Lin. Admit it. You're tickled pink with the results."

Lin laughed as well before saying, "Okay. I'll admit that it was an extraordinary shot."

"Now set it up again and try once more now that you know the conditions."

Lin didn't want to risk a miss but decided to make a second attempt because Julia had asked and because he wanted to see if he could do it.

Ten minutes later, he not only repeated the shot but hit the knot this time splitting the now useless piece of lumber right along the grain which cemented his own confidence if he had to make a similar shot in the future. He'd never come close to this level of accuracy before but wasn't sure if it was simply because he had never tried. He rarely engaged any serious target at much over eight hundred yards, which was still an incredible range.

As the family returned to where they had been before the shooting, Lin and Julia went to the barn, so Lin could clean his rifle.

While he slid the long cleaning rod down the barrel with the cleaning fluid-soaked cloth, Julia asked, "Lin, why can't I come with you when you leave tomorrow to go to Cheyenne?"

"Because, Miss Lampley, we aren't married, and I'll be back in three days anyway."

"Not four?"

"No, ma'am. Not four. I said that when you were irritating me."

She laughed before she asked, "And I'm not irritating you anymore?"

Lin slid the rod out of the rifle, looked at her, smiled and answered, "Not as much."

"I can live with that. So, after you come back, how long before we leave?"

"Probably a day or two if it's okay with your family."

"Why should I need their permission? I'm an adult woman and I thought you understood that. Are you worried about what they might think about you?"

"Not at all. I'm just concerned about what they might think about you."

She laughed and said, "When they first thought I was going to run off with you, they were ecstatic. They thought I'd be an old maid and never leave."

Lin just shook his head at the thought of Julia ever being considered an old maid or even a middle-aged maid. He was surprised that she was still a maiden now.

After he had his Sharps cleaned and stored and the remaining cartridges put back into their box, he and Julia remained in the barn, as everyone must have expected, and just talked mostly about his job, including the tracking and dealing with the men when he caught up with them. He also went into more detail about his house, including his bath contraption and his odd method of entry.

By the time they returned to the house, the sun was low in the sky and Julia helped make dinner with her mother and Marge while Lin talked with the male side of the family in the main room. The subject matter in the main room was about guns and how Lin used them.

———

Most of the evening was spent in the main room as the family gathered to chat about the new house, the crops, and Julia's approaching departure to leave with her new husband. There were some expected jabs from Jim, Bill and even Pete as they chided Lin about his choice in brides. Lin just accepted the jibes and grinned as expected, still somewhat spinning when he realized that he went from passerby to dangerous stranger to interesting guest to imagined fiancé in less than a day.

When he and Julia finally left the house to go to the barn, he wasn't sure how she would react to all of the talk about her impending marriage because it had sounded as if the family expected to come to Cheyenne for the wedding.

Once behind closed doors and the lamp lit, Lin asked, "So, Julia, how long do we let this go on?"

"Let what go on?"

"This whole marriage story. They're going to find out sooner or later that we're not getting married."

"My mother knows. I told her what I was going to do because I wanted her to have justice."

"Then why did your brothers all act like they were planning on coming to our wedding in Cheyenne?"

"Because they don't know yet. Either my mother or I will tell them when we think it's the right time."

"Why wouldn't you tell them right now?"

She tilted her head slightly, then replied, "Because, Mister Chase, I'm not convinced that we aren't going to be married."

Lin felt as if he was almost back to square one with Julia, but as he looked into those confident blue eyes, he suddenly realized that he wasn't. He knew her much better after another full day and was beginning to think that she might be right after all.

Julia could see the revelation blossom behind his eyes then smiled.

"Give it time, Lin. You'll see."

Lin just quietly replied, "Okay."

There was a very pregnant pause of about twenty seconds before Julia asked, "What am I going to wear when I'm with you? I don't think bib overalls would be appropriate."

Lin had to clear his mind for a second before he answered, "Oh. I'll pick up some clothes for you in Cheyenne. They'll be men's clothes, so you might have to tailor them to fit you."

Julia stood then pulled her overalls tightly around her waist before turning away from Lin and asking, "You mean to fit my female form?"

Lin slid back into a state of disfunction as he stared then finally squeaked, "Uh-uh."

Julia laughed as she released her overalls and said, "I was right, wasn't I? You really are incredibly innocent, at least when it comes to women."

"How did you get this way, Julia? I mean, from what you told me, you never spent a lot of time with boys or men."

"No, but I have three brothers and the two older ones talked constantly about girls and what they appreciated when they looked at them. I knew that I had what boys and men appreciated, but I didn't care, at least not until now."

"Okay, but why are you so, I don't know, open about it?"

"Why not? Are you embarrassed?"

"Not embarrassed, but I am a bit uncomfortable."

"I'll have to work on that while we're alone. Have you ever been with a woman before?"

"A few times, but not with a woman I cared about."

"What about that girlfriend you had in Iowa?"

"No, not with Edith, either. We kissed, but that was all."

"If it makes you feel any better, I haven't been with a man yet, either. You're going to be my first."

Lin just stared at Julia and expected her to laugh, but she didn't. Instead, she just leaned over, put her hands behind his neck and kissed him softly before sitting back.

He thought that he was now supposed to kiss her back, but he just looked into those blue eyes and tried to fathom where this all was headed. Nothing about this seemed remotely normal.

Julia smiled, said, "It's inevitable," then stood and left the barn closing the squeaky door behind her.

Lin just sat on the hay for another ten minutes, the foundation of his world shaken by that one, short but incredibly powerful kiss. He'd kissed other women, beginning with Edith, but she was just a girl and six inches shorter to boot, and the others were just part of his released lust. But Julia disrupted his whole thought process. She simple threw him off balance almost constantly, and he'd never had such sensations. He was sure now that despite his protests just minutes earlier, that marriage was definitely in the picture, but they had a lot to do before they reached that stage.

Julia, once she closed the door, stopped and closed her eyes. She had never been kissed at all before and had felt an almost explosive need to kiss him to discover what it was like. Yet even in her wildest imaginings she hadn't expected this. Now all of her almost frivolous talk about marriage and what was inevitable had much more meaning when she had first spoken the words. Now they became real and she wanted them both desperately.

After returning to the house, she was able to corral her sisters-in-law into a private conversation and after extracting promises of silence on the matter, she told Anna and Marge about her plan to go with Lin to find the two men who had assaulted her mother and killed her father which had shocked them both. That was compounded when she had told them what she had done in essentially offering herself to Lin Chase.

Both of her sisters-in-law, while younger than her but much more knowledgeable in the ways of men, had told her that men were very sensitive about their perceived roles as the one in control and that her forward behavior might have the opposite effect and drive him away.

When she finally slipped beneath the blankets that night, she believed that regardless of his reaction to her conduct, she really had no choice if she really wanted to make those two men pay for what they had done. If she hadn't been forthright and direct in her request, she wouldn't have had a chance. Besides, being subservient wasn't in her personality.

She fell asleep with a confidence in her decision and believed that Lin Chase would be returning in three days to take her with him.

CHAPTER 2

Lin wasn't up nearly as early as he had been yesterday yet was already saddling Homer shortly after sunrise. When he finished, but before he started saddling the packhorse, he took a quick look out the house saw the smoke from the cookstove pipe then returned to loading the packhorse.

After slipping in his spare Sharps and Winchester into the packhorse's scabbards, he began lashing down the panniers for the day's short ride. Cheyenne was just three hours away, and he'd be going into town before heading out to his house. He'd already decided to make it just two days before he returned, giving in to Julia's magnetism.

"Inevitable," he thought then just shook his head and smiled.

He led Homer and the packhorse out of the barn, closed the noisy door then walked to the front of the farmhouse and tied his gelding to the porch support before striding around the side of the house to the back porch.

He'd barely stepped onto the small porch when the door popped open and Pete said, "I was just gonna come and get you, Mister Chase."

Lin smiled as he took off his hat entered the doorway and said, "Well, I'm glad to have saved you the trip."

"Sit down and have some breakfast, Lin," Mary said as she waved her spatula at him.

"Mary, I'll just grab some coffee and be on my way if that's alright."

"You're a grown man and can decide for himself, Mister Chase," she replied as Lin picked up a checkered kitchen towel to grab the hot coffeepot.

Lin grinned and replied, "That's debatable, ma'am"

Lin poured himself a mug of coffee then after setting the coffeepot back to the cookstove and returning the towel to the countertop, he walked to the table and took a seat next to Julia.

Everyone was dressed for another day's work either tending the fields or continuing to build the second house while he appeared to be more of a preacher enroute to his church to conduct Sunday services.

"What's your house like?" Marge asked, "Is it as big as the one we're building?"

"No, ma'am. It only has four rooms. The main room and the kitchen take up about two-thirds of the house, and the bedroom and my equipment room take up the rest of it. It only has one door and no fireplace. I have a small barn that's a lot closer than most barns. It's about a hundred feet to the east of the house, and it's only big enough for two or three horses and their feed and tack, but it still has a loft."

Julia was sipping her coffee as she watched him describe his house, hoping she'd get a chance to see it.

Even though she had confirmed her actions to herself last night, what Marge and Anna had told her had simmered in her mind, so she had anxiously awaited for him to show up for breakfast to discover if their evaluation of the situation was right or hers was. When he had just said he'd be having coffee so he could leave sooner, she thought that maybe she'd been wrong after all.

Lin had been avoiding making eye contact with Julia for a very simple reason, He needed to leave for Cheyenne and knew it wouldn't take much for her to convince him to stay for another day or two.

He finished his coffee quickly set the cup into the sink then said, "I'll be heading back to Cheyenne now. I'm grateful for your hospitality and happy to have met such a fine family."

Then before Julia could say anything, her mother asked, "Will you be coming back, Lin?"

Lin smiled then took the risk and looked at Julia as he replied, "Yes, ma'am. I'll be back in three days. I promised Julia and I always keep my promises, especially to my intended."

Julia looked up at him, felt an enormous sense of relief then stood, walked close to Lin took hold of his arm and walked him out the back door, crossed the small porch then continued around the south side of the house.

"I was worried that you might leave and not come back," she said as they strolled beside the house.

"Why would you think that? I promised you, didn't I?"

"Marge and Anna think I might have pushed you away because of my aggressive behavior."

Lin looked at her and said, "I'll admit it startled me, Julia. I've never met a woman who talked or behaved as you do. But once I understood your motives and knew you better, I found that your manners were refreshing and admirable and the more I understand you, the more I like you. You're an honest woman, Julia, and that is something I appreciate even more than I did when you pulled those overalls tight."

Julia laughed before saying, "I'm glad to see that you're honest and forthcoming as well now that you know me better. I appreciate you calling me your intended, too."

"Maybe it was more than just to bolster your story, Julia. It might take some time to find the Hilliard brothers and maybe we should count it as visiting or courting time."

"I'd like that, Lin," she said softly.

Julia was gratified that her sisters-in-law were wrong. If Lin had felt as if he had to be in charge or was deterred by a strong woman, then he wasn't the man she thought he was. He was not only not intimidated, he liked her that way which cemented her decision to stay with him well beyond the chase for the Hilliard brothers.

They soon reached the horses, and Lin untied Homer then let the reins drop as he turned to face Julia.

"I'll be back."

"You'd better be," she said with a smile on her face.

Now that he was sure that she wasn't going to try to keep him at the farm for another day, he decided he may as well give himself a little more incentive to return as quickly as he could.

Lin then cupped her chin in his hands took a long gaze into those dark blue eyes then kissed her softly. Julia felt her knees weaken and her toes curl before she was able to regain her balance.

He stepped back slightly, smiled then turned and mounted Homer.

She was still smiling as he turned the gray gelding around, gave her a short wave and rode down their access road trailing his packhorse. She continued to watch him as he rode southeast on the road to Cheyenne and her eyes hadn't left him until he almost disappeared then waved his hat over his head. She returned his wave, then finally headed back into the house.

It was going to be a long three days, she thought. Even her initial plans for just joining him to hunt down those two outlaws were now thrown into disarray. She was on unfamiliar ground now, but knew it was territory she wanted to explore.

———

For the entire ride back to Cheyenne, Lin had to struggle to maintain anything close to his normal level of alertness, but thoughts of Julia kept haunting him. He had simply never met anyone, man or woman, who was like her. She was a formidable person who had allowed him to touch her soul just as she had touched his. It was almost a religious experience that had become a dangerous distraction. Any distraction in this business could cost him his life and his biggest worry now was how much more of a distraction she would be when they rode off to hunt down those two.

He was startled when he heard the screech of a train whistle from behind him and then just moments later, the rumble of a Union Pacific locomotive hauling a train of coal cars. As he waved at the engineer, he was embarrassed that he hadn't noticed it until it was so close. He'd knew that he'd been drifting but this was beyond a momentary loss of focus. To let an entire train sneak up on him was unnerving. It served as a hammer blow to force him to revisit the whole idea.

Giving in to Julia seemed perfectly logical while she was smiling at him and he had to try to detach Julia from the mission itself. It would be hard, but he had to at least give it a try. The biggest problem was that he had already promised to take her along.

He finally decided that he'd make that decision when he returned to the farm and was able to talk to Julia again. Regardless of what his decision about taking her would be, he knew he'd have to return, and not just because of the promise. That last short kiss had sealed his decision that Julia would be returning with him to Cheyenne after the Hilliard brothers had met their end, one way or the other.

————

He was less than an hour out of Cheyenne when he turned northeast off of the road to go to his house. There was a set of wagon tracks that went to his land directly from Cheyenne, but when coming from the west, he always cut the angle and saved himself a mile or so.

He had to pass through what was now the Double L ranch to get to his house but there weren't any fences yet, so it wasn't a problem. He knew the Lewis family reasonably well, and they didn't mind it when he crossed their property. They were comfortable having him as a neighbor too, as it gave them a sense of security.

He had passed their ranch house ten minutes earlier when he spotted his house and barn in the distance. His property wasn't anything spectacular other than it had a nice stream that cut across the northern part of the land. It was what him decide to take this quarter section when he had been searching for a place. It was close enough to Cheyenne that he could get anything he needed quickly or have shipped in yet far enough away for privacy. He had quickly bought the second quarter section to the north just to increase the length of his target range.

Homer seemed to be getting excited about being home and picked up the pace on his own which made Lin laugh, but the packhorse wasn't overly pleased.

Lin patted Homer's neck and said, "Your job won't be done when we get home, Homer. We'll be heading down to Cheyenne after a short break."

Homer obviously didn't care as he continued his fast trot to his home and after twenty more minutes, Lin pulled him to a stop before the small house.

He was honest when he told the Lampleys about his house. It was small, just forty feet by thirty feet. But it was very well built and because it only had four rooms, it seemed much larger inside. The main room ran the length of the house along the front then there was a short, wide hallway with his one large bedroom on the left, a smaller room that he used as his equipment room across the hall then the large kitchen in the back. The kitchen was smaller than the main room as the large bedroom took the west side, but even with the missing twelve feet, was still enormous and very well equipped.

Getting into the house was intentionally difficult because of his extended absences. He had them hang what appeared to be a typical dinner bell triangle from the porch roof that was really the only way to open the front door. One good tug opened the latch inside and had to be held until the door was pushed open. He almost didn't even notice the unusual entry method any longer.

Aside from the absence of an entry latch and the lack of a back door there was one other oddity in the kitchen. When he had first worked with the engineer at East Construction and Building, they'd come up with an unusual contraption for heating bathwater that had worked out much better than either had expected.

First, they had arranged for the bathtub to be placed in the large kitchen near where the back door would have been if it had been there. Then they had installed a large cistern near the sink and mounted it with the base eight feet off the floor. They had a standard hand pump installed in the kitchen, but then added a second, rotating hand pump to move water from the sink to the cistern.

When Lin wanted to take a bath, he'd fill the sink then use the hand pump to fill the cistern which had a small outlet pipe on the top which indicated when it was full. Then he'd fire up his cookstove, walk to the bottom of the cistern and open a valve.

The water then exited the cistern into a long copper pipe that ran along the back wall then wrapped around the cookstove pipe before reaching the cookstove where it went through a grid of pipes that were attached to the back of the cast iron cookstove like lines on a paper.

Lin usually made himself some dinner while he waited for the heat from the cookstove to heat the water and by the time he was finished eating, he'd simply disrobe, open the valve above the tub and let the heated water fill it in less than a minute. He'd test the water's temperature, which could be close to boiling, then have to refill the cistern with cold water and let it immediately empty into the tub to bring the water temperature to a reasonable level.

As he began unloading the packhorse and bringing his weapons and unused supplies into the house, he was anxious to put the contraption to use but knew he had to go to Cheyenne first. He'd been gone for almost three weeks and his new Winchesters should be in by now.

So, he led both horses into the barn, left Homer saddled and stripped the packhorse while Homer munched on some oats. After both animals were feeding, he returned to the house and made himself a quick lunch using some of his returned supplies knowing he'd have to make a grocery run. He'd only get enough perishables to last a couple of days as he'd be leaving again, but he'd have to get enough trail food for two now. Then he'd have to shop for Julia's clothes and other thing she'd need for the trail. That would have been difficult if he'd had to buy women's clothes, but he'd be buying slightly smaller versions of what he wore but would have to add other things he normally didn't carry and double his supply of food.

Just ninety minutes after returning to his home, Lin Chase was back on Homer's saddle and riding to Cheyenne. When he made the short ride, he only had one of his Winchester '73s, knowing there was no reason for additional firepower over the four-mile trip but did have two extra scabbards for the two new Winchesters.

The thought of having the rapid-fire capability of the Winchester coupled with the power of the .50-95 Express cartridge made him almost giddy. When he'd read about the new repeater and that Winchester was offering it in the larger caliber round with almost as much power as his Sharps, he had immediately put in his order. He knew that the Winchester, even in the musket version with its longer barrel that he'd ordered, didn't have the range of the Sharps and probably not the accuracy, but they were still a big step up from the .44 caliber pistol rounds that his Winchester '73s fired.

The drawbacks were that it was more unwieldly, it had a diminished capacity even with the long barrel and the cartridges were a lot more expensive. They still didn't reach the cost of the Sharps cartridges, and even though Winchester had begun manufacturing cartridges for the Sharps that undercut what Sharps charged, Lin preferred to use the manufacturer's cartridges. Cost was irrelevant to him, but now that the Sharps company had closed its doors, he'd have to switch to the Winchester rounds when he was low on stock.

He reached Cheyenne in the early afternoon and thought about stopping at Kreiser's Barber Shop for a haircut and shave but was too anxious to feel the new Winchesters in his hands, so he headed for P. Bergerson, Gunsmith and Dealer in Firearms.

Lin dismounted, tossed Homer's reins across the hitchrail and bounced onto the boardwalk and through the doorway to the gun shop spotting Paul Bergerson behind the counter explaining the workings of a new pistol to a customer.

He didn't say anything but just walked to the counter and let his eyes search behind it for his new Winchesters but knowing that they were probably in back. After new guns arrived, Paul would spend a few hours on each one, cleaning up the factory's tiny mistakes. As each gun left the factory, except one of the rare 'One of a Thousand' Winchesters, it would have small imperfections that a highly qualified gunsmith could correct, and Paul Bergerson was one of the best. When he was finished doing his magic, the finished Winchester would have qualified for the 'One of a Thousand' title.

Paul glanced his way, smiled, but then continued to explain to his customer the differences between the Colt 1873 model he was buying and the Colt New Army in his holster.

Lin patiently scanned the inventory, looking for anything new, but not finding anything different. It hadn't even been two months since his last visit, so he wasn't surprised.

Paul reached behind him, took two boxes of .44 cartridges and set them next to the pistol then the customer asked for a gunbelt with loops for the cartridges, so Paul left the counter with the man and walked down the hallway toward the leather section, where they found a holster that he liked. When they returned, Paul finally was able to complete the sale, at least Lin hope that was true, but it wasn't as the man asked how much Paul would give him in trade for his old pistol, which started a round of negotiations.

If Lin didn't have the patience required of a sniper, he probably would have just left the shop and returned later, but he waited and thought about Julia and her need for weapons. He had two Winchester '73s that would be redundant now, but he did like having a spare Colt, so he decided he'd buy her a pistol and gunbelt.

The deal was finally consummated, and Lin let the grinning man pass him without comment before he turned and headed for the counter.

"That took a while," Lin said.

"He wasn't too bad. It seems to me that you've spent a lot longer buying some of yours."

"That's just because we talk about them and other things. So, did my Winchesters arrive?"

"Yes, sir. I've got them in back along with the six boxes of .50-95 Express cartridges and your order of four of the .50-110 cartridges for your Sharps. I'll be right back," he replied before he turned and walked through a curtained doorway to his workshop.

Like a six-year-old on Christmas, Lin eagerly watched the curtain until it parted, and the gunsmith walked out with two long-barreled Winchesters. He handed one to Lin, who snatched it with a greedy hand, and set the other on the counter before returning to his workshop area for the cartridges.

Lin was examining the new musket with practiced hands and an eye for details while Paul was setting the ten heavy boxes of cartridges on the counter next to the Winchester.

"How much work did you have to do on it, Paul?" Lin asked with his eyes still glued to the repeater.

"Not too much, but I put a few rounds through each of them when I finished, and I think you'll be happy."

"I know I will. You do good work."

Paul was smiling as he said, "I have something else you may be interested in."

Lin glanced up and replied, "Probably. What do you have?"

"This," Paul answered as he slid a single cartridge across the counter.

Lin set the Winchester on the counter near its sibling, then picked up the cartridge and whistled.

"Where'd you get this thing? Is it for the Sharps?"

"Yes, sir. It's a .50-140 cartridge. As you know, Sharps is out of business, so this was made by another company."

"I've heard of them but hadn't bothered ordering any because I didn't see the need. I can reach out as far as I can with the .50-110s. This thing is almost an inch longer than my .50-110s. Why did you order them?"

"I didn't order them. Give me a minute," he said then re-entered his workshop.

Lin was still examining the three and a quarter inch cartridge and rethinking his policy about not buying another manufacturer's ammunition when Paul exited almost making him drop it when he saw what was in the gunsmith's hands.

Paul was grinning as he handed the large, very different Sharps to Lin.

"I got this three weeks ago from some feller who had brought it with him to do some big game hunting. He shot a bear with it, then after he dropped the carcass off at Hosick's to get stuffed and shipped home, he came here, and I bought it from him. I figured it might sit in my shop for a while unless one particular customer of mine might want it which was the only reason that I bought it from him. Was I right?"

"Of course, you're right, Paul. That Malcolm scope can make good use of those monster cartridges because I'll be able to see what I'm shooting. I don't care how much you want for it either."

"That's good, because it'll cost you ninety dollars, but that includes two and a half boxes of those .50-140 cartridges that you can still use in either of your other Big Fifties."

Lin finally pried his eyes from the Sharps-Borshadt and asked, "Did you take a look at the workings?"

"Yup. I didn't have to do much, either. He was from Boston, or as he said, Bah-stahn, and had a local gunsmith make a lot of modifications. That man sure did talk funny."

"I'll bet he thought we all talked funny, too. I reckon that he didn't say reckon very often."

"I reckon not," Paul said then chuckled and added, "See the wood in the stock? Well, the gunsmith was really good at his job, maybe as good as I am. Anyway, he used what the man said was called ebony to replace the original stock. It's really a heavy wood, so the balance was better. Then he finished balancing the rifle by adding a center support for a tripod, just like yours. I had to modify the size of the hole a bit to fit your tripod, but that lost weight wasn't enough to throw off the balance."

Lin was lovingly running his fingers over the weapon as he asked, "How big was the bear? I imagine this beast with those cartridges would have made a mess of the animal."

"Would you believe he shot a black bear from less than a hundred yards and almost missed? He hit the bear on the right shoulder and almost took the whole joint out. That bear probably didn't even weigh two hundred pounds."

"Why would anyone humiliate a weapon like this by taking that shot?"

"He seemed happy and said he'd never have to use it again anyway. I actually put more rounds through the barrel than he did. It took three to adjust the Malcolm scope, and you won't believe what a difference it makes. I was hitting a four-inch target at eight hundred yards when I was finished, and I imagine you could do almost double that."

"I couldn't even see that far without a scope, but that extra piece of hardware makes it possible. Okay, Pete, I'll write you out a draft for the total, and you can help me get them situated on Homer."

"Who'd you run down this time," Pete asked as he began gathering boxes of cartridges.

"Two brothers name Whitacre. They had Spencers and were picking off Cheyenne when I arrived."

"Tell me about it while we load you up."

Lin narrated the story while they made three trips to Homer and managed to get the three long guns into scabbards as the Winchester '73 was relegated to the bedroll behind the saddle.

After writing his draft, Lin rode Homer to Kreiser's and finally had his beard shaved off and his hair cut. He was going to ride straight back to try the new Winchesters and the Sharps-Borshadt but remembered to stop at the post office to see if he had any mail.

He had to wait in line behind a woman who was being instructed on the proper way to tie strings around the package she wanted to mail, but eventually walked to the window and was gratified to find a letter from his mother.

After slipping it into his left coat pocket, he left the post office, rode to the Western Union office, picked up his two vouchers, then stopped at the bank and made his deposit, keeping a hundred dollars in cash before mounting Homer again and beginning his short ride to his house. It was only then that he realized that in his excitement over the Sharps-Borshadt, that he'd forgotten to buy a pistol for Julia, but he could take care of that tomorrow when he returned to town to start getting his supplies.

It was early evening when he finally was able to move the three new acquisitions into his equipment room to join his already extensive armory. It was too late to try the weapons today, but he planned on engaging in some serious target practice in the morning before he returned to Cheyenne to do his shopping.

He fired up his cook stove, filled his cistern then stripped off his clothes and dropped them all in a laundry basket near the hallway. He'd drop them off at the Chinese laundry in town before he left. He didn't mind cooking, but laundry was one job he wouldn't wish on any human being.

He cooked and ate sans clothing then after washing his dishes, he walked to the bathtub, opened the valve and the steaming hot water rushed out into the tub. It was too hot to use but once the water stopped flowing, he closed the valve, walked to the other side of the kitchen, pumped cold water into the sink and then began spinning the wheel to the rotating pump to move the cold water to the cistern but not filling it.

He then walked to the tub, opened the valve again then after a few seconds, he stuck his fingers into the water and waited until the cold water had reduced the temperature enough before closing the valve, sliding into the tub and emitting a loud sigh. Other men may think him odd for enjoying a warm bath as much as he did, but none had ever been there to watch, so it didn't matter. No women had seen him either, but maybe that would change.

After scrubbing off all of the accumulated trail dust, he stepped out of the tub, pulled the drain plug from the bottom and dried himself as the water level began dropping. When it was almost gone, he opened the valve again to let the clear, cold water rinse out the tub. He cleaned the tub once a month or so, but this kept it from getting too grimy between serious cleanings.

———

As Lin was cleaning his tub, less than twenty miles west, the six men who would throw everything into turmoil were meeting in Fuzzy and Ike's hotel room in Buford. Fuzzy was the only one seated on a chair while Ike and Hound sat on the bed and the Hilliard brothers and Arnie Jacobsen were on the floor leaning against the hallway wall.

"You boys all got this down?" Fuzzy asked.

Arnie Jacobsen sighed then replied, "We're not idiots, Fuzzy. We head north to the Barber place while you and the brothers

85

go to the Lampley farm. We wait for you to show up and then we all go and pick up the two squatters."

"Alright. After we eat, let's get the horses saddled and ready to go. We leave around midnight and then make our move with the predawn. Okay?"

There were nods of almost bored agreement before everyone stood and left the small room to head for Smith's Café for supper.

————

Lin spent another hour reading, mostly about guns and ballistics as if he didn't know enough. But he really wasn't paying that much attention to what he was reading either. He was thinking about Julia and the changes that would be coming in his life, one way or the other. For such a short initial meeting, she was becoming an obsession which did nothing to reduce his concern about how he could track killers with her along.

It was only when he closed his book that he remembered the letter from his mother that was still in his coat pocket and was seriously annoyed with himself for getting so forgetful. First the Colt for Julia and now the letter. He was beginning to believe that he was getting senile already as he stood, set the book down and left his equipment room to head for the kitchen and his letter-bearing coat.

Lin pulled out the letter then had to light the lamp near the table before sitting down.

It was a pretty standard letter, letting him know about the crops and his sister and brothers. He was going to be an uncle again which would make a total of eight nephews and nieces. There was no earth-shattering news, so it wasn't going to change his plans at all.

After turning out all of the lamps, he finally slid beneath the quilts in his own bed for the first time in weeks and thought he'd be able to fall asleep quickly but couldn't because there were too many things on his mind, mostly Julia.

———

Eight miles away, the Lampleys were all getting ready for sleep. Little Teddy was already in his handmade cradle while his parents changed nearby. Mary was already under her covers and Bill and Marge were already under the covers, and Marge had just whispered to Bill that he was going to be a father which he had already suspected but was ecstatic to hear.

Julia had to make her bed in the main room as the bedrooms were all taken. Pete had a mattress that he dragged out into the kitchen for his bed. They really needed that second house if not a third.

All of the new weapons that Lin had given to them were out in the barn. They hadn't had time to move them inside the house yet believing there was plenty of time. It wouldn't have mattered if they had moved them into the house anyway even if they did manage to find the space.

———

It was a new moon which didn't make travel any easier as the two groups of three men left Buford then split up with one trio headed due north and the other continued eastward on the road.

The two Hilliard brothers and Fuzzy Villers were leading the almost empty packhorse as they walked their horses along the roadway. They weren't in any rush as they had another four hours before the predawn arrived and only another hour's ride before they reached the Lampley farm.

Fuzzy's only real concern was how Arnie, Hound and Ike would do in trying to find the Barber farm. They shouldn't have any problems following the wagon trails, but Fuzzy wasn't overly confident in any of their abilities. He was most concerned about Hound Jones simply because of his reputation. The whole idea was to get the women to the mining camp quickly and in good condition, so they'd bring the most money, but Hound was a loose cannon. He wasn't too sure about the Hilliard brothers either but thought he could control them.

When he'd first talked to them, they had gleefully told him of their aborted attack on the Lampley farm, and Fuzzy had stressed to them that they had to keep their pants buttoned this time. It wasn't about the women. It was about the gold.

Fuzzy and the Hilliards made the same turn that Lin had made two days ago somewhere around two o'clock in the morning then dismounted and walked their horses closer to the house but not close enough to attract attention. They hitched their horses to some nearby trees then sat down and waited.

———

Arnie Jacobsen hadn't had any problems in following the wagon trail in the light of the Milky Way but had to walk their horses more slowly than Fuzzy's group, so they didn't get to the farm until almost an hour later. What made it easier to find was the smoke from the chimney made by the dying fire.

Like the other three, Arnie, Hound and Ike all dismounted about two hundred yards from the house and hitched their horses. Everything was ready.

———

When the stars began to fade in the predawn, Arnie was the first to move as he stood and told the others it was time. Hound

Jones and Ike McCall grinned as they rose brushed themselves off then all three began walking toward the house. They left their heavy coats, their hats, and their Winchesters on their horses wearing only their Colts. Their pockets were filled with pigging strings.

Henry and Wilma Barber were still asleep in their bedroom as was their daughter, Mary and her husband, Joe, were in theirs. Their two-year-old daughter, Sissy, was sleeping beside them. In the next room their son, Mike was snuggled in next to his wife, Bess. The house was chilly and silent as the three men approached the front porch.

Arnie and Hound stayed out front while Ike trotted around to the back of the house.

Arnie then counted to thirty then he and Hound pulled their pistols, cocked the hammers and walked confidently onto the porch and ripped open the front door slamming it against the outer wall.

Sleep in the three bedrooms was suddenly interrupted by the loud noise which caused confusion among the family for a few seconds.

That confusion evaporated when Arnie shouted, "Everybody out of those bedrooms! Now!"

Ike entered the back door and had to wait for his eyes to adjust to the gloom in the kitchen before he could see the family members beginning to cautiously exit their bedrooms.

"Who are you?" Henry Barber shouted as he stared at the leveled muzzles of the two men.

"Who we are don't matter," Arnie snapped then said, "We don't want to kill anybody, but we will if you don't do what we tell you."

Henry glanced at his son and then noticed a third gunman in the kitchen which squashed any idea of retaliation.

"What do you want?" he asked quietly.

Arnie didn't answer but told him to turn around. Once he did, Arnie quickly bound his wrists with a pigging string then just minutes later, they had all three of the men tied and sitting in the first bedroom before they tied up the women and put them into the second bedroom with little Sissy who had only awakened momentarily before returning to sleep.

The family was now totally subdued and even Arnie was surprised how simple it had been. The farmers just hadn't been prepared for it. *Why should they?* They didn't have anything valuable or so they believed. It was only after all of the adults had been bound and gagged when Arnie told the men that they would now be bachelors again.

Arnie, Hound and Ike then went to the kitchen to make some coffee and breakfast while they waited for Fuzzy to arrive with the four Lampley women.

————

Fuzzy had waited a little longer because he wanted more light when they moved, so just about the time that Arnie's group was making coffee, he and the Hilliard brothers stood and began walking to the Lampley farmhouse with their Colts and their pigging strings.

Inside the Lampley home, most were still sleeping, the exception being Pete who was already stirring in the kitchen, but

Fuzzy and the Hilliards hadn't expected anyone to be sleeping in the main room or the kitchen as they reached the house.

It was Dick Hilliard who was assigned to go to the back door, so Fuzzy began counting as Dick disappeared around the side of the house.

When he reached thirty, both he and Ron Hilliard made their loud entrance into the house with their pistols drawn.

Pete was the first up as he scrambled out of his mattress bed and quickly turned to try to get to the barn and the guns when he ran into Dick Hilliard who had just entered the door.

Fuzzy shouted, "Everybody out!" as a still-confused Julia popped up from her own portable bed in the main room.

Just seconds after she stood, Ron Hilliard saw her in her nightdress and said, "Well, well. Ain't you pretty."

Even in the low light of the predawn, Julia spotted the missing earlobe and snapped, "You bastard!"

Fuzzy pointed his pistol at her and snarled, "Shut up! All of you, just shut up!"

Julia just glared at Ron but folded her arms over her chest for some semblance of modesty.

Even as Fuzzy had shouted, there was a commotion in the kitchen when Pete had tried to scramble past Dick Hilliard and Dick had slammed the boy back toward the table and after he lost his balance, he'd smashed into one of the chairs and toppled two others.

"You try anything again, boy, and I'll drill you with a .44," Dick said as he glared at Pete.

Pete slowly stood and felt a trickle of blood slide down the corner of his mouth. He knew there was nothing he could do now and doubted if anyone else could do anything either.

Fuzzy's group then began tying up and gagging the men and shoving them into one bedroom. But unlike Arnie's group, they had the women all change into normal clothes and pack the rest of their things into used burlap bags. Once the women were changed, they were all bound and left in the main room while Dick went back outside and harnessed the Lampley's wagon.

As Dick was getting their transportation ready, Ron and Fuzzy began loading food and supplies onto the porch then Ron trotted back to the trees to get their four horses. Once the horses were behind the house, they loaded the packhorse with the supplies. None of them noticed the guns stored beneath a tarp in the barn.

The women weren't gagged, so they were talking about what was happening because nothing made any sense to any of them.

"What do you think they're doing, Julia?" asked her mother who had surprisingly not recognized the Hilliard brothers in the dim light; the same men who had raped her last year.

Julia wasn't about to bring that subject up if she didn't have to, nor did she mention what she expected them to do to the women before they left.

"I don't understand this. We don't have much money and they're just taking our food. Why would they take such a risk for just food?"

Anna said, "What about Teddy? How can I take care of him if we're all tied up?"

"I'm sure he'll be fine, Anna," Julia said, "Nobody hurts babies, not even this sort."

"But how will we get loose?" asked Marge.

None had an answer as they all just waited while Fuzzy and the Hilliard brothers prepared to make their departure for the Barber farm.

Pete was bound and gagged in the kitchen and wondered why he wasn't with his brothers.

The answer was that Fuzzy had decided to use Pete as a hostage to ensure the good behavior of the women. He couldn't threaten any of them once they realized their fate, so he thought if he brought the boy along and threatened to shoot him, they'd behave themselves. What happened to the kid after the sale wasn't important.

It was just thirty minutes after the dawn arrived that the women finally were told the motive for the invasion.

"Alright, ladies," Fuzzy said as he entered the bedroom, "We're gonna to move you all to the wagon outside then we'll ride out of here and head north to a mining camp where you're all going to be the new wives of some lonely miners. We're also takin' the boy out in the kitchen with us, and if you so much as shout, I'll personally shoot the little bastard. We'll cut your wrists free when you're in the wagon."

The women all exchanged glances knowing that there was nothing they could do, so they all watched as Fuzzy began cutting their ankle bindings and standing them on their feet.

In the bedroom where the men all remained bound and gagged, all they could do was listen to what was going on and feel totally useless.

Pete had heard Fuzzy's threat and now understood his purpose as insurance for good behavior. Like everyone else, he felt helpless and hated it.

Fuzzy and the Hilliards each grabbed some food before they walked the women out to the wagon and put them onto the bed, not caring about their obvious discomfort. Once Pete was put in back, Fuzzy cut the wrist binding of the women but not Pete's. He had Julia get in the driver's seat to handle the reins and let her sisters-in-law ride next to her as the wagon began rolling west toward the Barber farm, nine miles away.

———

At the Barber farm, things had gotten a bit out of hand when Hound raped Bess while she was still bound, so Ike then took Mary and after arguing with them both, Arnie finally decided he'd join in and assaulted Bess after Hound was finished while Wilma watched her daughter and daughter-in-law being violated and simply wept.

After they were finished, Arnie had the women change to prepare for the arrival of Fuzzy and the wagon. He told them if they said a word about what had happened, he'd kill little Sissy before they left.

———

It was two hours later when the wagon appeared out of the east and after moving the three Barber women to the bed of the wagon, the six men rode beside the wagon heading for the squatters who had built a crude cabin northwest of the Barber farm.

Despite the Barber women not saying anything, Fuzzy strongly suspected that they had been assaulted by Arnie and the others but didn't chastise them at all because he didn't think it would affect their sale price and the last thing he needed now was a schism in the group. He didn't care what happened after they got their gold.

———

Lin was out on his target range with his three new weapons arrayed on the large flat rock that he thought was a gift from the heavens. He already had targets set at a hundred, three hundred, six hundred and a thousand yards. He knew he should practice more with his pistols but so far, he'd only had to use them twice in gunfights with outlaws. He'd had to use his Winchesters a dozen times and had almost taken a hit when he'd gotten that close. At least the new Winchesters would give him another advantage.

He really wanted to try the Sharps-Borshadt but convinced himself to try the Winchesters first. Both had the ladder sights that his '73 had, but the markings were differently scaled, and he could see that the top marking was for five hundred yards. He smiled when he compared it to Winchester's claimed effective range for the new '76 to be the same hundred yards as the '73, even with the standard .45-75 cartridge.

Lin loaded the first Winchester with just five cartridges and sighted on the hundred-yard target to check on the sight's accuracy. He didn't doubt Paul Bergerson's skill, but it was his life that might depend on the gun, so he had to be absolutely sure.

He levered in the first round, adjusted the sights then quickly snapped the Winchester to his eyes, picked up the target and fired. He kept his eyes downrange and was rewarded with a solid hit almost dead center. The power of the repeater had surprised him even though he had expected it. It was almost the same as his Sharps. He then moved to the longer ranges and was able to put a round on target at five hundred yards, but not centered. He tried at the thousand-yard target just out of curiosity and saw the dirt kick up about thirty feet short of the target.

After trying the second Winchester with similar results, he finally was able to try out his scoped Sharps-Borshadt. It had to be one of the last weapons produced by the Sharps company before they closed their doors and vowed one day to do some research to find out the last few serial numbers of the guns they produced.

The Sharps-Borshadt was almost like a big Henry with smooth brass sides after the external hammer had been moved inside of the rifle. He opened the breech, slid in one of the enormous .50-140 cartridges then closed it. He didn't want to waste the cartridge on one of the closer targets, so he adjusted the scope for the thousand-yard target. It was a reasonably temperate day with a west wind at about seven miles per hour. He wasn't sure what the wind was downrange, but there weren't many obstructions, so he used that number.

He brought the long gun level then sighted the target, released the first trigger, held his breath and had to adjust his eyes to the moving glass. He'd never used a telescopic sight before, and while he appreciated the expanded image and the reticles, the decreased angle of view meant that any motion at all was magnified.

Lin held his breath steadied the sight then squeezed the second trigger. The hundred and forty grains of gunpowder's released energy slammed the butt of the rifle against his shoulder and the equal and opposite reaction hurled the fifty-caliber bullet out of the muzzle at almost seventeen hundred feet per second. Even at that enormous speed, it still took almost two seconds for the slug to strike the target, disappointing Lin when it did. He was aware that most shooters would have been tickled pink to be within nine inches of center at a thousand yards, but he'd expected better out of the new gun. He routinely was within six inches with his other Sharps.

He then tried his next shot with one of the .50-110 cartridges, realizing that he probably had over-compensated for the more powerful round.

After firing, he discovered that was indeed the problem when the second shot was just two inches low of dead center.

He fired two more of the larger cartridges, storing the difference in his mind for future reference.

Satisfied with his day's shooting, he returned to his house to clean the new guns before he went to Cheyenne to get his supplies for the Hilliard Hunt.

———

Julia was still driving the wagon and her stomach protesting the lack of food, as were all of the women. She still had Anna on her left and Marge on her right and felt guilty as her mother was still sitting uncomfortably on the wagon bed with the three Barber women and Pete, who was still bound. All of the Lampley women knew what had happened to the Barber ladies and wondered why they hadn't been violated, especially knowing that it had been the same two that had invaded their house last year.

She didn't know their names yet, but was determined to find out, so she could tell Lin when he found her and the others. Julia had already concluded that he was their only chance for deliverance. She just hoped that none of her family mentioned that he was expected to return to their farm in the next few days.

As they approached the squatters' small cabin, Arnie, Hound and the Hillard brothers rode away at high speed with their

Winchesters at the ready. Because the squatters were there illegally, they felt their tactics didn't have to be as refined as it had been at the two farms. But things were different than they had been when Fuzzy had last seen the squatter's cabin, yet the change wasn't noticeable yet as the two young men who were out working their fields spotted the riders and the wagon and began to run back to the cabin.

Fuzzy and Ike remained to guard the women as it continued to roll toward the cabin.

The women watched the two young men as they shouted warnings to the cabin but began to slow. One of them almost reached the house when Arnie fired his Winchester from less than forty yards. The man spun to the ground and began writhing and screaming in pain while the second man turned and ran away only to be run down by Hound who shot him from point blank range dropping him face first into the ground.

Arnie then fired a second shot into the screaming man then the four men all turned to the cabin just as two women stepped out of the front of the cabin saw the armed outlaws nearby then ducked quickly back inside. It was only then that Fuzzy and the others realized that their plan had been altered as both women were in an advanced state of pregnancy.

Julia pulled the wagon to a halt and felt as if she were in a dream as she watched the four men run into the cabin after the very pregnant women wondering if they were still intent on taking the women to the mining camp in their condition.

Inside the cabin, the decision about whether to take them to the mining camp was rendered moot when one of the women had grabbed a shotgun and the Hilliard brothers barged into the one-room cabin saw her trying to cock the hammers and shot both women without hesitation.

The women both dropped to the floor at the same time as their blood began pooling across the floor while the men began to search the cabin for anything worth taking but finding nothing.

A frustrated Dick Hilliard then tossed the lone kerosene lamp onto the floor and threw a lit match onto the spreading liquid as his brother Ron laughed. They trotted out of the cabin giggling as they mounted their horses joined Hound and Arnie and fast trotted them to join the departing wagon as smoke began to boil from the cabin.

"What are you two so all-fired happy about? Did you find something?" asked Fuzzy already knowing that they wouldn't be taking either of the squatter women with them.

"Nope, but take a look back there," shouted Ron.

Fuzzy turned in his saddle and blanched when he spotted flames licking along the outer wall of the cabin. He wanted to scream at them for letting everyone for miles around know that they'd been there but there was no point now. All he could hope for was that no one would notice. At least the bodies of the two pregnant women wouldn't be found.

———

But someone did notice. John Longtree, whose claim had tapped out almost a year earlier but was still holding out hope of rediscovering his lost vein had offered to go to Laramie for supplies and was riding six miles southwest of the northbound wagon and soon spotted the smoke from the fire. He wasn't in a rush to go to Laramie anyway, so he turned his horse and three pack mules to the source of the fire to see how extensive it was and was curious about its origin. Most forest fires were caused by lightning strikes but there hadn't been any thunderstorms in over two weeks now. That meant the other cause for the blaze had to be a neglected campsite.

The wagon full of women was already eight miles north of the still blazing cabin when John arrived and was surprised to find that it was a cabin that was burning and not the forest. He was about to turn back when he spotted what looked like a body on the ground and headed his horse and pack mules in that direction and soon found the body of Al Spangler with two bullet holes in his back. He then spied the second body trotted his horse to that spot and looked down.

"Lordy!" John exclaimed as he quickly wheeled his horse back toward Laramie before setting him and the mules off at a fast trot.

———

As the wagon rolled, the women were all talking about the shootings especially of the two pregnant women. *How can any man be so cruel?* They were chatting as much to keep their thoughts away from what awaited them when they arrived at the mining camp in the morning. But by discussing the horrific events they had just witnessed had the side effect of raising their fear even higher as they understood the soulless nature of the men who had taken them.

Julia may have considered herself stronger than the other women but was affected just as deeply. Those men were laughing after killing the women. Laughing! She had told Lin that she would be willing to kill the two men who had raped her mother even before watching them murder two pregnant women. Seeing them behaving as if it was entertainment horrified her far more than the killing itself.

Yet now she began to doubt that she could do what she so easily had told Lin that she wanted to do and began to wonder how she would react if she had to kill those two knowing that it was highly unlikely now. She doubted if she would even be able to sleep at night, much less think it was funny to watch people die. *Are all men who killed often that way? Was Lin?*

She found it hard to imagine that he enjoyed doing it, *but how did he live with killing so many men?* She spent some time trying to imagine how it had affected a good man like Lin Chase. All she could imagine was that he understood he was killing evil men like the six who had taken them and murdered the two pregnant women, but it still must be taking its toll.

———

Lin had dropped off a reply to his mother at the post office then had walked across the street to Harrington's to begin his shopping. He bought two outfits similar to his for Julia but instead of the flat hat, he bought her a dark gray Stetson. He then added a pair of boots, two Union suits and a heavy black jacket.

With that order complete and loaded onto the packhorse, he stopped at Bergerson's and picked up the extra Colt and gunbelt before heading over to the Bon Ton Livery. He had already given three horses to the Lampleys but didn't think either of them was good enough for Julia, so he picked out a brown Morgan gelding with a black mane and tail and no markings and then stopped at Meanea's Saddles and Harnesses for a new saddle for the small gelding. The Morgan had a nice gait, was only five years old, and he knew that the breed was sure-footed for the mountains they might have to climb.

While he was at Meanea's he bought two more scabbards, including one that was large enough for the Sharps-Borshadt and the scope. He had been worried about throwing the scope out of alignment when he'd put it into the tighter scabbard earlier.

After he'd had lunch, he went to Underwood's and bought more food and other supplies than he'd ever bought before including food items that he thought Julia might appreciate. With all of his shopping complete, he led the Morgan and the loaded packhorse out of Cheyenne to return to his house.

As he reached the intersection for the north trail off of the westbound road, he was tempted to continue riding west but just smiled to himself and made the turn. If he'd known what was happening just thirty miles away, he'd have raced westward like a man afire, but he rode Homer back to his house still wearing the smile knowing that Julia would be riding beside him in a few days.

He'd already made the decision to let her come with him and it hadn't been nearly as difficult as he'd expected.

———

The group had stopped for a break to let the horses drink and the women were allowed to get off the wagon to take care of their personal needs as the men watched.

Julia said to Fuzzy, "Cut my brother's ties. He's not going anywhere, and he needs some water."

Fuzzy was ready to argue with her but didn't see the point, so he just walked to the wagon cut Pete's bonds and stepped away. Julia trotted to the back of the wagon climbed onto the bed and helped her young brother to sit on the tailgate while he rubbed his wrists.

"Thank you, Julia," he said before he gingerly stepped down to find someplace to relieve himself.

He managed to unbutton his britches and finally empty his bladder before returning and getting some water from the stream and splashing some onto his face. He thought about running away but felt he needed to stay and protect his mother, sister and sisters-in-law. He was the only Lampley man with them now.

The men had the women make a quick lunch out of the food they had stolen from the two farms and after they ate, they let the women and Pete finish off the rest.

After the forty-minute break, they all boarded the wagon again, and Julia was surprised when they had Pete drive the wagon rather than her. She was put in the back with the other women while two of the Barber women were allowed to sit in the driver's seat with Pete.

Once they were underway, Dick Hilliard asked Fuzzy, "How much longer to the gold camp?"

"We should be there by noon tomorrow."

"Then how long before we get our money and get outta there?"

"Not long."

Dick turned to Ron and grinned. They'd soon be richer than they ever thought possible.

———

John Longtree arrived in Laramie about the same time the wagon began to roll again and rode directly to the sheriff's office, pulled up outside and quickly hitched his horse before entering the office.

Deputy Orville Smith was behind the desk and was arguing the advantages of the Remington over the Colt with Deputy George Cobb when he looked at Longtree.

"What can we do for you?" Orville asked.

"I found a burnin' cabin about three hours northeast of here with two dead bodies outside. They both had bullet holes in their backs."

"Hold on," Orville said as he stood to go find Sheriff Ward.

As he stood waiting for the sheriff, John Longtree decided he'd buy some supplies with the other miners' money, sell two of the pack mules and go find another claim in Colorado. The killings had left him shaken and he didn't want to run into the killers.

Sheriff Jimmy Ward entered the main office and asked John what he'd found with as much detail as he could remember. There wasn't much more information than he'd given to the deputies because he hadn't stayed around very long as he was worried about getting shot himself.

After the sheriff listened to John Longtree's short description of what he'd found, he questioned him about anything else he'd seen that could help but got nothing more.

He then said to Deputy Smith, "Orv, you and George get some supplies and ride out there to find out what happened. If you can track the killers, go ahead and do that."

"Okay, boss," Orville replied, "Did you want me to send Andy back right now?"

"No, he's still not right after that flu. I'll hold down the fort until you get back."

"We're out of here," Deputy Smith said before walking to the gun rack and taking a Winchester from the wall, tossing it to Deputy Cobb then taking a second one for himself.

Forty minutes later, the two deputies were riding northwest, and just an hour later, they were able to pick up the smoke from the remains of the cabin which saved them time by providing a direct line to the bodies.

It was late afternoon when they arrived at the sight of the murders and soon found the tracks of the wagon and horses which presented a dilemma to the two young lawmen. They didn't find the charred remains of the two women under the debris but spotted some of their footprints.

"There are seven horses and that wagon, Orv," Deputy Cobb said as he looked down at the tracks.

"Why would they have a wagon with them?" Orville asked.

"Did you see those footprints out front? There were women in there, and there aren't any now. I'll bet some of those miners came down from up in the Black Hills to get some women and are heading back."

"So, what do you think, George? Do we go back and tell the boss, or do we chase after them right now?"

"I'm not sure. What do you think?"

"Well, I don't figure having the sheriff with us will make much difference. They won't be looking for us, so we can surprise them. Besides, they're miners and not outlaws, and we've only got a few more hours of daylight."

"Okay, then let's go," George replied.

The two deputies then set out at a medium trot following the wagon trail knowing that the wagon couldn't move all that quickly over the rough ground.

———

They may have expected that the wagon could only make slow progress, but they were wrong as the wagon couldn't move at all after the right rear wheel had broken just ten minutes after they had resumed their northward journey. There was a spare wheel under the wagon, so the task of replacing the wheel fell to Hound and Ike.

Fuzzy had explained to them that the women had to be in good condition when they arrived at the mining camp which had mollified the grumbling duo somewhat as they moved all of the women and Pete from the wagon to a clearing where they were kept under the muzzles of two Colts while the wheel was changed.

Neither man was familiar with the task, nor were any of the other men, so the job took a lot longer than it should have. If they had asked any of the women,or even Pete, they could have finished sooner, but they weren't about to ask for help from a bunch of sodbusters.

———

The two deputies were still five miles behind the stalled wagon when they were spotted by Ron Hilliard who had climbed a tall rock to see if the burning cabin was still visible. He stood there watching for another fifteen seconds before racing back to the wagon and calling Fuzzy over.

"What?" Fuzzy asked.

"We're bein' followed. There are two riders down south following our trail."

"How far?"

"A few miles, and they're still comin'. I figure they'll be here in another hour or so."

Fuzzy then took off his hat and quickly walked to the same boulder Ron Hilliard had used, climbed on top and looked south into the lower elevations where he spotted the two riders then slid down and trotted back to the others.

"Which of you boys is best with a Winchester? And don't go braggin' if you ain't."

They all looked at each other for a few seconds until Hound said, "I'm pretty good."

Ike then said, "You know I'm damned good, Fuzzy."

"Alright. You two are gonna walk back down our trail leavin' your horses here. They're only here because of that damned fire anyway. Find a good ambush site and take out those two comin' behind us. Okay?"

Hound nodded then jogged to his horse slid his Winchester from the scabbard and waited for Ike to do the same.

Fuzzy then said, "We're gonna get the wagon and everyone out of sight into those trees over there. When you're sure they're dead, come back and we'll head north some more. We already wasted too much time on that damned broken wheel."

"Okay, Fuzzy," Hound replied before he and Ike began walking quickly south.

Fuzzy had to wait until the wagon was repaired before moving them all into the trees about eighty yards to the east. Once hidden the women were all warned to keep quiet or Pete would be the first to die.

Hound and Ike found a good ambush location about a half a mile south and split up so they could engage the two riders in a crossfire.

––––––

Fifty minutes later, the deputies were talking as they had their horses at a slow trot making the climb into the Black Hills following the easy trail of the seven horses and the heavily loaded wagon.

"How far ahead are they?" asked George.

"Not far, less than three hours, I think," Orville replied as he looked at the hoofprints.

Deputy Cobb then looked ahead and said, "I don't see them yet. Shouldn't we see them soon?"

"Not if they're three hours ahead of us. That's a good six or seven miles even with the wagon going into the Black Hills. I don't know how much longer they can use the wagon either. I've never been up this far north. Have you?"

"Nope. I know the sheriff has and maybe even Andy made it up here."

Orville laughed and replied, "A lot of good that does us now."

George looked at his partner and laughed as well just as a Winchester rang out and he felt a .44 slam into the right side of his chest knocking him from his horse.

Orville didn't panic but quickly pulled his Winchester turned to the shooter's gunsmoke and put his sights on the man when a second shot sounded from his left causing his horse to scream then buck and twist when the bullet drilled into his neck. Orville and his horse then dropped to the ground in a large cloud of dust while the horse continued to writhe in pain.

Hound, who had fired the first shot into George Cobb fired his second at the downed deputy his shot passing through Orville's left arm and into the horse silencing the animal as Orville lay still beneath him groaning in pain.

Ike assumed he'd killed the deputy then bounded from behind his rocks and trotted over to Hound.

"We sure got 'em, didn't we?" he exclaimed happily.

"Let's get that first one's horse," Hound said as he began to jog to retrieve George's horse that had begun to trot away.

Orville could hear them talking and knew that his almost miniscule chance for survival was if he played possum, so he kept his breathing shallow and his eyes opened wide trying not to blink.

Hound and Ike both ignored him in their chase after George's horse and after catching the gelding finally approached Orville. Hound picked up his Winchester then Ike grabbed his Colt, but neither noticed that the deputy was still breathing even though blood was still flowing from his bullet wound.

With their new weapons in their possession, the two led George's horse back up the long rise to the wagon.

Fuzzy had watched the ambush from the distant trees and was pleased with their performance, so by the time the two men returned, the women had all been put back in the wagon and all that Ike and Hound had to do was to slip the deputies' Winchesters into their bedrolls and drop their pistols into their saddlebags, mount then set a trail rope to the new horse before continuing north.

————

After they were out of sight, Orville knew he had several problems. He was still bleeding and had to staunch the flow of blood first. Then he had to extricate himself from his dead horse before he did anything else. He couldn't feel his left leg anymore, so he wasn't sure if it was broken or not.

Behind all of his problems, he felt immensely troubled by the death of his friend and the failure of their mission. He almost wanted to die, but knew he had to tell Sheriff Ward what had happened first. Then he could die of shame.

He just hoped that the sheriff or Andy made it to them before he died.

————

Lin had unsaddled Homer and the Morgan before unloading the packhorse. He left the full panniers in the barn as he brushed the animals down and let them have their oats and water. It was a tight squeeze having three animals in the barn, so after they'd eaten, he led them into the small corral behind the barn before heading to the house with his Winchester.

Once inside, he unlocked his equipment room went inside and placed the Winchester '76 in the large rack then pulled a sheet of paper from his desk and took a seat. He wrote out a short checklist to make sure he hadn't missed anything because of his growing obsession with Julia then when he finished writing, he leaned back and examined the list.

Satisfied that he hadn't missed anything, he stood then walked to the kitchen to make himself some dinner.

————

Julia and the other women were huddled around the campfire under the watchful eyes of three of the men. None had been bothered after the three Barber women had been violated at their farmhouse, yet they seemed to be less affected than Julia's mother, Mary. She had finally recognized the Hilliard brothers and had shrunk into a shell, not speaking to anyone as she awaited her fate. Even Pete hadn't been able to get his mother to talk to him.

Pete was the only one bound now as the six captors thought he was the only one who might try to escape because he'd heard them tell the women that he'd be shot if they didn't cooperate. They didn't realize that Pete now saw his role as a protector before they had trussed him like a calf about to be branded.

They had all eaten and Julia, Anna and Marge were washing the dishes in the nearby stream when Anna asked, "We're never going to get out of his alive, are we? They just killed those two deputies back there and I don't think there are any more lawmen coming."

Julia glanced at the two men who were watching them and replied, "You have to have faith, Anna. I think that you'll be back home in a few days with Teddy and Jim."

Marge whispered, "Do you really think so, Julia?"

Julia nodded and whispered back, "Lin promised to come back and I hope he's as anxious to return as I was for him to come back. When he does, he'll track them down and make them all sorry that they ever set eyes on us."

Anna was about to argue the point when Ike shouted, "You shut up over there!" ending the hushed conversation.

––––––

Orville had finally stopped the blood from leaking from his left arm by pulling off his belt and wrapping it tightly around his bicep. He was sure that he'd lose his arm if he ever got back to Laramie, but it was a small price to pay if he could get justice for George.

He was so weak and tired from the loss of blood that after drinking the last of his canteen's water, he just let his head lean to the ground and fell asleep.

––––––

Lin had gone to bed early because he planned on leaving with the dawn, if not earlier. He'd set his pocket watch's alarm for four o'clock and expected to be at the Lampley farm before eight. He had tried to think logically about the upcoming mission to find the Hilliard brothers but there was no use. He drifted off to sleep thinking about Julia.

CHAPTER 3

The wagon was moving north at dawn. Everyone, even the six kidnappers were hungry having eaten all of their food the night before. None of them had realized how much food fourteen people consumed in a day even on the severely reduced rations that they had with them.

They were just six hours from the gold camp when they set out.

———

The men at the Lampley farmhouse were in bad condition, having gone more than a day without water adding to their misery of being bound and gagged. They were all worried about their wives, but Jim was worried just as much for his baby boy in the next room who had been wailing almost constantly.

They all shared added concerns for Pete after having heard the men threaten to kill him if the women didn't behave and expected they'd kill him anyway when they left the gold camp. All of them knew that they wouldn't last long unless someone came to the house and that wasn't very likely. The only hope they had was if Lin Chase not only kept his promise to return but decided to return earlier than he had told Julia. None believed they'd be alive in another two days.

The Barber men who were in equally bad shape had no such hope at all. Little Sissy was crying as much as Teddy Lampley, but was wandering the house looking for anyone but not finding a soul. She was simply terrified and lost when she couldn't find her mama.

The obnoxious smells that permeated both houses only exacerbated the worries of the bound men.

———

Lin's alarm had done its job and peeled away his slumber then he'd hopped out of bed quickly and began to rush in an organized pattern to prepare for his departure.

He washed and shaved in cold water then dressed and quickly fashioned a rudimentary cold breakfast before leaving the house retrieved the three horses from the corral then saddled Homer and the Morgan before beginning to load the packhorse. When he finished, he had the Sharps-Borshadt and one of the new '76s in his scabbards on Homer one of his other Sharps and the second '76 on the packhorse and a single Winchester '73 with the Morgan. The saddlebags on Homer and the Morgan each had ammunition in addition to their typical contents. Most of the ammunition was stored in the packhorse's panniers.

He rode out of the small barn before sunrise trailing the Morgan and packhorse and cut across the Double L ranch reaching the main road as the sun peaked over the horizon. He set Homer to a medium trot as he was anxious to see Julia.

———

Lin was just an hour out of the Langley farm when Orville awakened to a mushy, dry mouth a throbbing left arm and a numb right leg. His horse was still stretched out across him, so he tried for almost twenty minutes to pull his leg free from under the horse then finally collapsed and began to sob in frustration. He didn't even have his pistol to shoot himself.

———

In Laramie, Sheriff Ward was alone in his office and wasn't overly concerned with his missing deputies. He had confidence in them both and knew that he'd sent them on a job that could take a couple of days. That didn't mean he wasn't a bit worried, though. He just wished that his third deputy, Andy Wilson had been feeling better then one of them could ride north and make sure things were still okay.

His concerns were put aside when he had to leave the office to investigate a complaint of a stolen mule from the Faraway Livery.

———

Lin felt his pulse quicken as the Lampley farm came into view and still wondered how he'd missed seeing it for so long. The only thing that came to mind was if he'd always passed the spot at night which wouldn't be unusual. Whenever he reached Laramie, he'd normally press straight on through to Cheyenne but wondered if he had stopped before the Hilliard brothers had paid their horrific visit whether Julia would still have talked to him the way she had.

None of that mattered as he turned Homer down their access road and immediately noticed the absence of smoke from the cookstove pipe and the chimney. Then there was the lack of hammering and sawing from the new house construction, too. Most of the time, such anomalies wouldn't have bothered him, but this was Julia's home and his worries escalated quickly.

He then nudged Homer to a medium trot but kept his weapons where they were as he studied the house still not seeing anything out of the ordinary other than what he'd already noticed.

That changed before his foot touched the ground and the sound of little Teddy's crying reached his ears and the foul odors of human waste reached his nose. He didn't bother pulling his Colt as he just dropped Homer's reins and hurried up the three steps onto the porch and yanked open the door when he was hit by a wave of nauseating smells.

The only sounds were still coming from Teddy's wails in the second bedroom, but Lin shouted, "Is anyone here?"

In their bedroom, the two Lampley men began to unashamedly weep in their sudden relief yet were unable to so much as mumble.

Lin trotted down the hallway looked into the bedroom where Teddy's legs were kicking in the air above his cradle then despite his instinct to help knew that the smells weren't from the baby alone and quickly turned and went to the only other closed room and threw the door open only to be assailed by an even more powerful stench.

But even more horrifying than the smell was the sight of the Lampley men all bound and gagged. He quickly ran to the brothers then pulled off the gags of Jim and Bill Lampley.

"What happened?" he asked hurriedly as he pulled his knife and began to cut away Jim's bonds.

Jim tried to talk but his tongue was like a rock and all he could croak was, "Water…"

Lin nodded, realizing that neither of them could move either, so after cutting Bill's ties, he sheathed his knife then quickly ran to the kitchen and pumped the coffeepot full of water, He returned to the bedroom and poured some down each man's throat as they began to try to restore circulation into their wrists.

"I'll get some water to Teddy and be right back," Lin said as he stood, left the coffeepot with them then raced back to the kitchen, filled a glass with water and hurried to the baby's room, picked him up and slowly poured some water into his gasping mouth making sure that he didn't pour too much.

Once Teddy had enough liquid, he finally stopped crying as he was exhausted.

Lin then carried the little boy into the first bedroom where the two brothers had worked themselves into a sitting position and set the baby on the bed.

Jim finally said in a rasping voice, "Three men, Lin. Three men came here yesterday morning and took our mother, wives, Julia and Pete. They said something about selling them to miners."

Lin was stunned but not shocked enough to lose focus.

"Did they take anything else?"

"I don't know. Go and check, we'll try to become useful again while you do."

"Alright. I'll be back in a few minutes," Lin replied before checking on Teddy's position and quickly rushing out of the room and through the kitchen, noticing the empty larder and pantry before heading out to the barn to check on the horses and the guns that he hoped they hadn't moved into the house yet.

It wasn't long before he found the missing wagon, but the three horses he had brought with him when he first arrived were still there with their saddles, so he wasn't surprised to find the guns all still accounted for under the tarp. He quickly returned to the house again assaulted by the stink but ignoring it as he entered the first bedroom and found the Lampley men trying to gain their feet.

"They took the wagon and your two plow horses but left the other three, the saddles and the weapons. They emptied out your larder and pantry, but you have the packhorse and saddle in the barn. I'm going after them right now because I don't want to let them get too far ahead. They could be at the mining camp already. I know where it is."

"Lin, Bill and I can come with you," Jim said.

"No, Jim, you'd be more of a hindrance than help. Besides, you need to look after Teddy. I'll get those bastards and bring the women and Pete back safely. Bill, I need you to ride into Burton and send a telegram to Sheriff Ward in Laramie. Tell him what happened and that I'm trailing them."

Bill then said, "Lin, please help my Marge. She just told me that she's having our baby."

Lin was taken aback by the news but nodded and replied, "I'll have her back in a few days, Bill."

Bill nodded but didn't say anything else, fearing he'd never see his wife again and never know their child.

Lin then reached into his pocket, counted out fifty dollars and set it on the bed near Teddy.

"This is for the food and whatever else you might need," he said then without waiting for a reply, he hurried out the door, quickly mounted Homer and headed to the back of the house where he found the wagon tracks leading off to the northwest.

He was surprised by the direction even after following it for just a few minutes. The mining camp was almost due north from the farm, yet they were heading northwest. To Lin, that meant only one thing: they wanted to collect more women.

He set off following the trail with the Morgan and packhorse trotting behind them.

————

As Lin was setting out from the Lampley farm, Fuzzy spotted the mining camp in the distance and shouted back, "Just another hour or so, boys!"

The other five all cheered while most of the women all slipped into an even deeper despondency. The lone exception was Julia, who knew all she had to do was hold out for three days at the most and then Lin would arrive and make things right. She needed to tell him that the two men she had wanted to kill were among the six men too, but it would have to be Lin that delivered the justice. After watching them kill the squatters and their pregnant wives then the deputies, she had been shaken deeply and knew that she couldn't pull the trigger.

She could tell how upset the others were with the news of their pending arrival at the mining camp, so she said as loudly as she dared, "Listen. You all need to stay strong for just a few days and then we'll be out of this place."

Marge said, "I hope you're right, Julia."

Anna then added, "So, do I."

Marge didn't mention the baby that was growing inside her for fear that one of the men would overhear her and shoot her as they had done to the two pregnant women back at the cabin. None of them knew that the woman had a shotgun, but it wouldn't have mattered anyway not to murdering men like these six evil bastards.

Julia was deeply concerned about her mother who had remained distant and silent for the entire ride. She was sure that her mother knew what awaited her and that horror had already been visited upon her once.

The wagon trundled up the last long rise before settling onto a narrow plateau and Fuzzy told the others to stay put while he went and talked to the miners about the upcoming auction.

———

Lin saw the tracks heading for a second farmhouse that must have been the Barbers that Julia had mentioned, and he nudged Homer to a fast trot.

When he pulled the gray gelding to a stop, he was still in the saddle when the eerie similarities between the Lampley farmhouse and this one struck him. He could already hear the wail of a baby accompanied with the same smells that had drifted out of the Lampley home.

He dropped down quickly grabbed his canteen then hurried into the house and headed straight for the bedroom with the closed door.

He swung it open and found three men all trussed up as the Langley men had been and in equally bad condition. He quickly undid the gag of the oldest man then moved to the other two removed their gags before he cut the bonds of the father before tilting the canteen to his lips and letting him take two long swallows before repeating it actions with the other two.

Before anyone could say a word, he said, "I just left the Lampley farm and their women were all kidnapped as well. I told Bill Lampley to go to Burton and send a telegram to Sheriff Ward. All of their food was taken, but their horses were still there. I'm going to go after them as soon as I can."

Henry rasped, "Who are you?"

"My name's Lin Chase," he replied before taking his canteen back and asking, "Do you think you can handle this for now? I need to be going."

"We'll be okay," replied Joe Barber as he struggled to find his feet.

Lin nodded and trotted out the front door across the porch then mounted Homer and quickly picked up the trail again.

In the house, the three men began to move a little better, and Joe was finally able to get to the next room and help little Sissy.

———

Deputy Orville Smith was drifting in and out of consciousness as he lay under the hot sun with his eyes closed. Every part of his body was in pain and he wasn't sure he'd last until sundown. He had long since stopped worrying about dying because he knew he would be gone soon. It only bothered him that he'd never get a chance to tell the boss what had happened to George.

———

Fuzzy was leading the fourteen miners out of the camp toward the wagon. Each man had his pouches of diggings hung over his shoulder, but no one except the man himself knew how many smaller bags of gold he had inside the heavy pouches. Each of them was anxious to buy himself a wife today but didn't want to spend too much unless she was worth it.

The women saw the crowd of men coming and all of them were revolted by the sight. None of the miners looked as if they'd even seen a bar of soap in a year and the very thought of even being touched by any of them was enough to make even the strongest stomach rebel.

The miners gathered around the wagon and began to examine the merchandise, each of them picking out his favorite quickly and more than half had settled on the tall woman with the blue eyes even before Fuzzy started his sales pitch.

Fuzzy stood on the wagon bed and pulled Julia to her feet to stand beside him as he said loudly, "Okay, boys, we did all the hard work, now you get to choose a woman to have for yourself. I'm gonna start with the tall one here because I've been told that she's unspoiled. What one of you lucky boys is gonna be the one to deflower her?"

Julia thought she was about to vomit at the thought and almost shouted that she'd rather die but glanced at her bound, ten-year-old brother and remained silent as the bidding began.

Saul Baker was the first and said, "I'll give you a pound of dust for her."

Fuzzy was going to laugh at the bid but before he could comment, Charlie Pruitt outbid him at two pounds. The bidding quickly passed Fuzzy's desired price of three pounds and finally ended when MoMo Nesbitt placed a bid of six pounds of gold dust for Julia. The fact that someone had paid over two thousand dollars for her didn't matter at all to the women as the dust was given to Fuzzy and he practically shoved Julia off the back of the wagon into MoMo's waiting arms.

None of the other women went for that much but even the two mothers went for three pounds apiece as the losing bidders began to get desperate. When the bidding ended, the seven disappointed miners began to bargain with the buyers for part-time use of their new wives and Fuzzy had collected twenty-seven pounds of gold dust. Even if it was salted with sand, which he didn't think was likely because they hadn't had any time to taint their pouches, it was quite a haul and after they cashed in the gold, they'd each be over fifteen hundred dollars richer.

Fuzzy was standing holding onto the reins of his red gelding as he shouted, "It's been a pleasure doin' business with you boys, but we're gonna leave now. Enjoy your new lady friends. I'm sure that they'll all be real happy to keep you satisfied."

None of the winning miners paid him any attention as they towed their wives away but one of the ones who didn't get a woman asked, "How much do you want for the wagon and mules?"

"You just keep 'em, Will. You came up on the short end this time," Fuzzy said as he mounted his horse.

"You gonna bring some more?" Will asked.

"Sure. Give me some time. You can keep the kid, too."

Willie grinned and said, "Thanks, Fuzzy. Bring me a good one, will ya?"

"You bet," Fuzzy shouted back as he and the others began to ride southwest to avoid any contact with the law that might be on their trail after shooting the two deputies.

Once they began their downward trek, Ike McCall asked, "Are we really gonna do this again?"

Fuzzy laughed and replied, "Hell, no! I just wanted to give them hope."

The others all laughed but noticed that Fuzzy had kept all of the bags of gold in his own saddlebags rather than divvying them up already.

———

Lin spotted the vultures to the northwest with the wagon tracks pointing directly toward their pivot point. Someone had died up there and he hoped that one of the sick bastards who had done this thing had met his maker but knew it was unlikely. He had picked up the trail of six horses after stopping at the Barber farm, so he knew it was a large group now. He just hoped they hadn't killed one of the women or more likely, Pete.

The remains of the cabin were still smoldering, and he could see the two bodies being set upon by the vultures. It didn't take him long to realize that they were just unknown victims of the six men and just turned Homer north knowing where he was headed.

It was already close to sundown when he spotted the dead horse and what he assumed was a body underneath then saw the second body a few feet away identified them both by the badges first and then by their faces soon afterward.

He sighed before he dismounted to check on George Cobb who was out in the open found him dead then walked slowly to Orville's body.

Lin was about to leave to resume his pursuit when Orville moaned slightly which startled him into turning around and grabbing his recently refilled canteen and rushing to the fallen lawman.

He knelt near Orville's face and gently poured some cold water across his forehead. Orville's eyes slowly opened to slits before Lin lifted his head slightly and poured some water into his mouth.

Orville swallowed the water and tears began to fill his eyes.

Lin said, "You got yourself into a fix here, Orv."

Orville squeaked, "I know."

"Okay. I'm going to give you a little more water and then I'll see if I can get you out of there. Okay?"

Orville nodded slightly as Lin gave him some more water. After a few more swallows, Lin gently lowered his head then stood and walked a few feet away turned and looked at the situation. It wasn't going to be easy to remove Orville's leg from under the carcass without doing a lot more damage, but he knew it couldn't be helped. All he could do was to get him moved quickly to reduce the pain.

He walked back to Orville sat on his heels and asked, "Orv, how bad does your leg hurt?"

"It's been numb from almost the start, Lin. Can you just pull me out?"

"It's going to be awfully painful, Orv."

"Maybe I'll pass out."

"Let's hope so," Lin said then worked his way behind Orville's head, sat down and slid under him so his head was on his lap. He then braced both of his feet on the carcass, put his hands under Orville's armpits and took a deep breath.

"Okay, Orv. Hang on," he said before using his powerful legs to push against the carcass and began to pull Orville free.

Orville began screaming as he moved then suddenly quieted as he passed out, but Lin kept pulling until his legs suddenly straightened and the deputy slid free of the horse.

Lin was sweating from the exertion as he slid out from under Orville and then quickly walked down to examine the leg. He ran his fingers down the long bones of the leg and found them intact which was surprising to say the least. Then he felt the ankle and found the fracture he'd expected to find. His ankle was ninety degrees from the rest of the lower leg, so while Orville was still unconscious, Lin quickly snapped it straight which still elicited a loud grunt from the unconscious deputy.

"Sorry, Orv," Lin said as he stood then looked down at the deputy trying to come up with a way to get him back to Laramie. It was about a three-hour ride to Laramie at a slow trot, but this would be longer, and he'd have to somehow get Orville into the saddle.

First, he took Orville's bedroll carried it to George Cobb's body and covered it then began gathering rocks to keep it in place long enough for someone to come and pick it up.

He then emptied his canteen to quench his thirst hung it back on Homer then returned to the still passed-out Orville and tried to think of some way of getting him into the Morgan's saddle.

Finally, he just threw up his hands slid them under Orville, then stood while lifted the deputy and walked back to Homer as Orville's head just hung over his right elbow.

"Sorry, Homer, but this is going to be hard on both of us."

He then turned, put Orville over his shoulder like a heavy sack of flour then carefully mounted Homer. Once in the saddle, he slid Orville back to a sitting position in front of him then held onto him with his right arm and started Homer back toward Laramie.

As he rode south at a better pace than he would have been able to achieve if he'd managed to put Orville in the saddle, he thought about the delay this was costing him in his pursuit of the six men who had taken the women and hoped that it wasn't going to make the women especially Julia, suffer irreparable damage. He was so upset about the lost time that he almost wished that Orville hadn't lived through the gunfight but amended it to wish that neither of the deputies had left Laramie in the first place.

———

Four of the seven women had already been taken by their miner husbands by the time Lin had set out for Laramie, so he wouldn't have been able to prevent that horror. Anna, Marge and Mary Barber had screamed and fought the men as they forced themselves on them while Julia's mother, Mary, just wept.

The remaining three women including Julia all waited for their turn to be violated as they heard the other women's screams. Julia had been surprised that she hadn't been taken yet until she realized that her 'husband' was out negotiating for more miners to use her after he'd ruined her.

When he finally walked into the small shack with eyes full of lust, Julia thought that she would be able to remain strong but only felt overwhelming terror fill her soul. Just two days ago, she had been lightheartedly telling Lin how sex between them was inevitable, but now that filthy, ugly little man staring at her was what was truly inevitable, and she wondered if it was some form of punishment for her desires.

Julia didn't scream when he finally took her, but simply closed her eyes and shuddered in revulsion while he huffed and pawed her with his disgusting smells nauseating her as he rutted with her as if she were nothing but a warm mattress.

When he finished, he rolled onto his side and fell asleep as Julia closed her eyes then curled into a ball and began to cry. It wasn't supposed to be this way.

Over the course of that first night, Julia had to undergo another even more nauseating experience when MoMo sold her for a single use by another, even filthier miner. She didn't think it was even possible as the larger and sweatier man slid all over her and even tried to kiss her, but she had turned her head which hadn't seemed to bother him at all.

There were screams from other tents and Julia had no idea who was making the horrendous sounds but was sure that one was her mother and she wanted all of the miners to die horrible deaths. She didn't blame Lin for not arriving soon enough to stop this, but prayed he'd show up as soon as he could and make them all suffer as badly as they were making the women suffer.

It wasn't an hour later when a different miner arrived to use her as MoMo was trying to make his money back.

————

Pete had been left bound in the bed of the wagon almost forgotten by everyone as each of the women dealt with her own private hell. But as he lay there, he finally was able to slide to the back end of the wagon and reach the rusty hinge of the wagon's tailgate.

He began to rub the leather pigging strings that bound his wrists while the dried wood that surrounded the hinge jabbed splinters into his hands and wrists, but he had to fight through the pain as he continued to work the leather against the old iron.

After almost ten minutes of agonizing work, the leather string suddenly snapped, and Pete felt like crying as he pulled his wrists free from the leather and then quickly untied his ankles. He had to stay put for a few minutes until his blood flow returned to his suffering wrists and ankles, and as he sat on the wagon bed, he had to decide what to do now that he was free.

It was dark, but he didn't know where they kept their guns and even if he found one, *what would he do with it?* He knew he couldn't help his mother, sister or sisters-in-law himself but thought that more deputies might be coming, so he decided that his best chance was to walk back the way they had come and hope to run into another lawman.

He was hungry, thirsty and still only ten years old, but Pete Lampley was going to do what he could to stop the screaming that had been torturing him all night.

So, just around the same time that Lin had almost reached Laramie, Pete slipped out of the miner's camp and made his way down to the small plateau then picked up the wagon tracks and began to quickly walk south clutching himself against the chilly night air.

———

Lin arrived with his still somnolent cargo sometime before midnight. Orville had awakened twice but hadn't made any sense when he'd spoken. Lin didn't know if his arms would ever work again as he walked his horse down the unlit streets of Laramie. The only lights belonged to the two saloons that stayed open until the wee hours, so he headed that way hoping he didn't have to dismount because he didn't think he could.

He finally stopped in front of Burleigh's Saloon, and shouted, "I need help!"

Nothing happened for almost a minute but just as he was preparing to shout again the bartender, who was probably the only sober person in the establishment appeared at the doorway.

"What's your problem?" he asked loudly.

"Deputies Cobb and Smith were ambushed a few miles north of here. Deputy Cobb was killed, and I have Deputy Smith with me. He's been shot and his ankle is severely broken. I can't get down with him."

The bartender threw his bar towel over his shoulder then turned to the barroom and shouted, "Billy, you and Mel get out here and help. I'm gonna go and wake up the sheriff. Don't any of you boys dare to take anything either."

The bartender then ran from the saloon and crossed the street disappearing into the darkness before two somewhat inebriated men walked out through the doors and approached Lin.

"I need you to help me get Deputy Smith down and my arms aren't working very well."

"Okay, I'll take his legs," one of them said then walked next to Lin's left leg and put his arms under Orville's legs.

Lin then managed to get Orville moving from the saddle and grunted as he tried to hold him up while the second man slid his arms under Orville's back. Between the three of them, they were able to get Orville onto the boardwalk.

Once he was on his back Lin dismounted and knelt beside his head as Orville opened his eyes again.

"Where am I?" he asked softly.

"You're back in Laramie, Orv," Lin replied then asked one of the two men, "Could you get some more water? My canteens are dry."

"Just water?" the man asked before the other man replied, "Just get the water, Billy."

The first man re-entered the saloon just before the bartender returned and said, "Sheriff Ward will be here in a minute."

"Thanks. I really appreciate the help," Lin said before the bartender went through the batwing doors to take control of the barroom again.

Billy returned with a glass of water just as Sheriff Ward appeared out of the blackness, stopped and knelt beside Lin.

"What happened, Lin?" he asked anxiously as Lin took the water and began to give some to Orville.

"It looks like Orville and George got bushwhacked about six hours northeast of here. I was tracking six men who kidnapped seven women to sell to the miners in that gold camp. Orville got shot in the arm, but his horse must have been shot at the same time and I found him trapped underneath the carcass. His ankle is in bad shape and he's lost some blood, but I think he'll make it. I covered George's body with Orville's bedroll and some rocks, but it won't last long. There were two squatters' bodies just south of where George's body is, too."

"I heard about the squatters. That's why I sent George and Orv. I stopped by and told Doc Phillips that Orville was wounded, so he'll be here shortly. Did you catch up with any of those bastards?"

"No. I had to bring Orville back or he'd die. I'm going to turn around right now and start back."

"You oughta rest, Lin. You're not going to be in any condition to take on six killers and a bunch of miners."

"Jimmy, those six low-life bastards invaded the homes of two good families, tied up all of the men and didn't care if they or the two babies that were in the houses died or not. They sold those women to a bunch of men so they could be raped.

"Now I aim to get those women free and if they want to shoot those miners, I'll give them the guns, and I don't care if you or any other lawman knows about it. Then I'm going to track those six men to the ends of the earth if I have to and every single one of them will know that he's going to die. I'm not going to play nice with any of them, either. Just don't try and talk me out of this, Jimmy."

Sheriff Ward had no intention of talking him out of anything as he replied, "Just make sure you kill them all, Lin. Every last one of them."

Lin stood finished off the glass of water then handed the empty glass to the sheriff and growled, "You can count on it, Jimmy."

"Okay, Lin. I'll take care of things here."

He turned, mounted Homer and walked his horses to the trough, let them drink for a minute then turned them back to the north.

Doctor James Phillips arrived just as Lin was walking his horses away and asked, "Who's that?"

Sheriff Ward simply replied, "That's Lin Chase and to the men who did this, he'll be Satan himself but to the rest of us he's an avenging angel."

———

Lin knew for all his brave talk, the sheriff was right that if he didn't get some sleep, he'd be useless in the morning. He also knew that he had to restrain the incredible rage that had been bottled inside him since he'd arrived at the Lampley house. As he had explained to Julia what now seemed a lifetime ago, emotions can get you killed in this job.

He kept Homer moving north in the moonless night. He was so familiar with the landscape that he didn't care about his exact location but simply followed the North Star. He figured he'd ride for another two or three hours before he let the horses rest then he'd get some sleep, but he needed to plan his approach to the miners.

He had a good idea how many were working that mine camp and put the number between a dozen and twenty but probably at the lower end of his estimate. He doubted if any of them were very good with whatever weapons they had in the camp which were probably Winchester '73s and a few pistols.

His only real disadvantage were the women and Pete. He couldn't just ride into the camp and start blasting away. He needed to get the women out of the camp first before he did as he said he would and kill them all. He knew it had to be done because none of them would leave the camp and the women would most likely choose not to tell any prosecutor what had happened to them. Justice had to be delivered there and it had to be delivered by him.

Regardless of the righteousness of it, shooting men who really were no contest still didn't sit right with him. For six years now, he'd been hunting and killing men. He still remembered each of the men and despite his best efforts at pushing those memories behind a wall of happier memories almost like a vault, he knew that sooner or later, they'd all rush free and haunt him.

It was just a question of how many more he would kill before they sprang free but there was no question that he had to do what was necessary when he reached the mining camp. His only concern was the six men who had stolen the women. If they were still in the camp maybe sharing the women then he'd finish them off, too.

He knew that it was unlikely that they were miners themselves because they wouldn't leave their claims, no matter how horny they got, but they sure would pay a lot for someone else to bring them women.

By the time he finally pulled up to stop for the night, he estimated that he was more than halfway to the camp. He unsaddled the two horses unloaded the packhorse and let them drink and graze while he ate some dried sausages that he liked and filled up on a can of cold beans rather than make a campfire.

Lin slid into his bedroll having no idea of the time but doubted he'd get more than two hours of sleep and hoped it would be enough. He set his pocket watch alarm to get an early start as tomorrow would be a killing day.

———

Six hours earlier, the men who had instigated this tragedy had already reached the town of Howell just one railroad stop northwest of Laramie where they settled in for the night at the small hotel. Once they were in their three rooms, Fuzzy finally divided up the take after some bickering about the weights of the different bags of gold dust.

Once the issue was settled, they headed for the local saloon to have a beer. Tomorrow they'd all leave and avoid big towns. The original plan had at least a few days of safety built into it, but once the two deputies had been killed, they had to modify their escape plans by riding east then avoid Laramie and turn south to leave the territory altogether. Once in Colorado they could split up and go their separate ways to convert their gold into cash.

CHAPTER 4

Lin was awake with the predawn then hurriedly prepared for what lay ahead as he rounded up the horses brought them back to the camp and began saddling the two riding horses and loading the packhorse. Once the horses were ready, he made himself a reasonable filling breakfast of more sausages and a can of cooked potatoes that he salted before devouring cold.

The sun was up now and once he mounted and began heading north, he wasn't surprised when he found he was just fifty feet off of the wagon tracks even after riding blind through the night.

———

Julia awakened and almost vomited when she felt the miner's hand on her naked stomach. She quickly slid out from under him as he stirred and asked, "Where do you think you're goin'?"

"I need to pee, unless you want me to do it here."

He dropped his head back down and said, "Go ahead, but you'd better come back soon. You're my wife now."

Julia didn't reply as she quickly threw on her dress to cover her nakedness but didn't find the rest of her clothes before she quickly left the small shack that the miner called home and was blinded by the morning sun as she exited.

She threw her hand up to shade her eyes and found several miners already outside and eyeing her up as they had a fire going for a communal breakfast. She forgot about nature's urges as she scanned for her mother but only finding Marge, Wilma and Bess Barber.

She strode across the rocky ground in her bare feet noticed that all of the women were barefoot then understood that it must be a way of keeping them from running.

Not finding her mother, she headed for the unharnessed wagon to see how Pete was doing knowing he had been left bound and without water. When she reached the wagon, she was startled to see it empty and thought that one of the miners who had been denied a wife had used her little brother instead. She felt her knees weaken as she grabbed the side of the wagon and looked down as her stomach heaved at the thought. Then she saw the cut pigging string on the ground and another a few feet away and suddenly realized that somehow, Pete had escaped and felt as if a great victory had been achieved.

She then remembered her own bodily needs and walked behind the wagon and squatted there, feeling the humiliation rise within her again.

Julia then turned to walk back to the camp but lingered for a few seconds to look south for signs of Pete or maybe even Lin, but knew it was too soon to expect him to arrive. She would have to survive at least another full day of this treatment before there was any chance that Lin would appear.

But as much as she hoped to see Lin, she already began to feel ashamed knowing he would know what had happened to her. She knew it wasn't her fault, but it wasn't a matter of rational thought.

By the time she returned to the big cookfire, she saw more women who were being told to do the cooking now and finally found her mother who was being held closely by her two sisters-in-law. Julia hurried as quickly as her injured bare feet would allow and when she drew near, she looked into her mother's almost catatonic face and almost began to cry.

Instead, she whispered, "Mama, Pete has escaped. I saw his cut bonds and he's gone."

Mary Lampley slowly looked at Julia then said in a distant voice, "It doesn't matter anymore. We're going to die here."

Julie put her hands on her mother's shoulders and said, "No, Mama. We're going to be home by tomorrow night. You'll see."

Mary slowly shook her head but said nothing.

––––––––

Lin knew he was about an hour away from the camp, so he was more vigilant than usual although he really didn't expect the miners to be waiting to drygulch him. What he suspected was that the six others might have spent the night in the camp and would be leaving soon and maybe returning the way they had entered. Their only other real option was to go to the southwest and exit the Black Hills to the west of Laramie.

If they were planning on going to Cheyenne to cash in their gold, they'd be coming back this way, but if they went the other direction, they'd most likely be heading for Colorado. He doubted that they'd take the train after shooting the two deputies. They were a hot item now and needed to get out of the territory altogether. He placed his entire bet on them going to Colorado.

He still had the wagon wheel tracks stretching out before him when he spotted a body a mile north. With his dress and size, it didn't take long for his extraordinary eyesight to reveal that it was Pete on the ground.

He picked up the pace but already knew that Pete hadn't been shot just by the fetal position of his body. He must have escaped or been abandoned without anything warm to wear. Lin's only worry now was Pete's condition after spending hours out in the cold. Luckily, it hadn't been that cold last night but even though it stayed above freezing, the boy didn't have a lot of fat on that small body to protect him.

When he was within a hundred feet of Pete, Lin slowed Homer, pulled him to a stop then quickly dismounted and hurried to the boy, kneeling beside him seconds after stepping down. He laid his hand on Pete's chest and could feel his heart beating, so he opened his heavy coat, picked him up then held him against his chest and closed the coat around him. His own torso felt the sudden chill of Pete's body as he embraced him.

Pete felt the sudden rush of warmth and murmured, "Mama?"

Lin replied, "No, Pete. It's Lin Chase. Can you hear me?"

Pete's eyes remained closed as he replied, "Mister Chase?"

"Yes, sir. I'm just trying to get you warm before we go up to that mining camp and get your mama and all of the other ladies out of there."

"How are my brothers?"

"All of the men and babies are fine now. We need to go soon. How are you doing?"

"Cold."

"I kind of noticed that. Do you think you can stand?"

"I think so."

Lin walked to the Morgan with Pete still hanging on then gently set him down removed his heavy coat and wrapped it around the boy.

"Okay, Pete?"

"I'm really thirsty and hungry."

"I'll get you something to hold you over," Lin said as he took one step toward Homer pulled a sausage out of his left saddlebag then grabbed his canteen before turning back to Pete.

Pete took the canteen first and guzzled half of the water before exchanging the canteen for the sausage and wolfing it down.

"Pete, do you know how many miners there were?"

"I'm not sure, but I think fourteen or fifteen."

"Did the men who took the ladies leave already?"

"Yes, sir. They left right after selling the ladies for gold and rode west."

Lin felt his stomach flip hearing out loud what he knew had happened to the women but just replied, "Okay."

Pete finished the sausage and said, "It was horrible what they did to my mother and the other ladies, Mister Chase. They were screaming all night."

"I can't imagine how bad it was for them, Pete. All I can do is get them out of there and make those miners pay for what they did."

"I'm better now. Can I ride the small horse?"

"That's what he's here for. Let me help you up because the stirrups are too long. I adjusted them for your sister."

As he was being hoisted onto the saddle, Pete asked, "How did you get here so fast?"

"I wanted to see Julia."

"Oh. Are you gonna marry her?"

"That's the plan, or as Julia would say, it's inevitable," he replied as he handed the Morgan's reins to Pete.

"What's 'inevitable' mean?"

Lin untied the trail rope from Homer and attached it to the Morgan as he answered, "It means that it's bound to happen."

Pete nodded and said, "Like what is going to happen to those miners soon."

Lin mounted Homer and said, "Exactly. Now let's go and free the ladies, Pete."

The horses resumed their path northward as Pete felt the growing heat from the sun coupled with the warmth of knowing that Mister Chase was going to save his mother and the other ladies.

———

Just ten minutes later, the gold camp came into sight and Lin still hadn't come up with a firm plan of action which he knew would be a waste of time anyway until he had a better grasp of the current situation. He remembered the basic layout of the large camp. It was in a narrow valley with their claims on both sides of what was essentially a shallow box canyon. There were a series of small shacks on both sides that each miner had built on his own claim but none were more than three hundred feet apart.

When they were within a mile of the camp, Lin turned and said, "Pete, I want you to stay back about a hundred yards if it comes to gunfire. I won't have time to help you and I need you to keep the packhorse from bolting. Can you do that?"

"Yes, sir."

"Good. Let's go and talk to these bastards."

Pete wished he could stay closer to Lin but knew that he was right, so he began drifting back slowly as he walked the Morgan with its attached packhorse behind the gray gelding.

Lin slipped his Winchester '76 out of the scabbard on the right side and just held it in his right hand as he let Homer maintain a slow trot toward the camp. He knew there was a round already in the chamber, so all he'd need to do was cock the hammer. He had fired from Homer's back many times and knew the horse hadn't been skittish even when he'd fired a Sharps from the saddle. If he ever needed Homer to be steady, it was today.

———

The miners were bringing their dirty clothes to dump near the fire so the women could do their laundry when one of them shouted, "Riders comin' in!" and everyone turned their faces to the south.

Julia instinctively shouted, "Lin!" then quickly realized that she'd made a mistake.

MoMo, her self-proclaimed miner husband grabbed her by the arm and asked, "You know him?"

Julia thought about lying but knew that it didn't matter, so she answered, "Yes, I know him, and if you had half a brain, you'd just let us all go before he kills all of you."

MoMo pulled his Remington pistol shoved the muzzle against her ribs and said, "You're not goin' anywhere."

He then walked Julia out of the camp with his pistol never further than two inches from the left side of her chest as the remaining miners and women all stared at the approaching rider.

———

Lin had heard Julia's shout and was fighting to squeeze his anger and concerns into a box in the back of his mind. He needed to remain calm as he watched a very short miner marching Julia away from the large group of miners and women another fifty yards behind. He had to be at least six inches shorter than Julia.

He cocked the Winchester's hammer as he slowed Homer to a walk not taking his eyes off of the miner. He could see the pistol pressed against Julia's left side but noticed that the hammer wasn't cocked which gave him a short window. He'd have to wait for them to stop to even have a possible shot.

MoMo was about eighty yards away from the others when he pulled Julia to a stop then just to play it safe, he swung behind Julia keeping his pistol against her back and just peering around her left elbow at the rider.

Lin halted Homer when he was about sixty yards away from Julia and was annoyed with the small miner's decision to use

Julia as a shield. It was a cowardly but smart thing to do even if he didn't know Lin's reputation as a sharpshooter.

Lin held the Winchester at the ready position as he shouted, "My name is Lin Chase. I want you to harness the wagon and release all of the women within ten minutes. If you don't comply, I'll kill each and every one of you."

His threat didn't seem to impress any of them least of all the miner who held Julia, yet his arrival and warning had an immense impact on the women except for Julia's mother who was still in her own world.

MoMo yelled back, "I don't think so, mister! We've already had our fun, so if you come close, we'll just shoot the women and then you."

"What's your name?" Lin hollered.

"I'm MoMo Nesbitt. What do you care?"

"I don't. But just so you understand, MoMo, I'm a bounty hunter. I've killed over a dozen men and captured more than that. Those men weren't miners like you but killers, gunfighters and outlaws who knew a lot more about guns than you do. So, I'm giving you ten minutes to harness their wagon and let the women go. That's my final warning."

For added protection, MoMo slipped his head back behind Julia and bent his knees to hide completely behind her as he licked his upper lip. He had some doubts now but still thought he was safe. The other miners were all exchanging glances. While none had recognized the name many had heard the stories and those that had them began to rest their hands on their pistols.

MoMo finally shouted from behind Julia, "You got one minute to ride away, or I put a .44 through her."

Julia then shouted, "Shoot him, Lin! I don't care if you have to put a bullet through me! Kill him!"

Lin almost didn't hear her desperate, fateful shout as he had been working out a possible shot, but it would take Julia's cooperation and an enormous amount of sand. He had to be as cold as ice and be more accurate than he'd ever been before.

He looked into Julia's blue eyes from across the distance and shouted, "Julia, did you spread your legs for that man?"

Despite her precarious position and her last shout that he put a bullet through her, Julia was horrified that he would ask such a thing. *Didn't he understand that she'd been raped? Not once but four times?*

Her anger flared as she shouted back, "What do you think I am?"

Lin then kept eye contact with her and repeated more slowly, "I said 'spread your legs', Julia. You know what I mean. You might want to close your eyes, too."

While MoMo was trying to understand why Chase was so concerned if she had spread her legs, Julia finally understood what he was planning to do and even though she'd just told him to shoot her, she felt a cold fear slide over her. She had to override her fear and trust that he was that good, remembering those long-range shots with his Sharps.

Julia closed her eyes and even if he hadn't told her to do so, the thought of what he was going to do made her knees weak, as she spread her legs as far as she could and still remain standing. She began to silently pray, "Please, dear God. Please."

Lin saw Julia's eyes close, her knees push away as she dropped two inches then concentrated on the patch of thin yellow cloth that was about four inches above her knees, grateful she wasn't wearing a dark dress as the sunlight cast shadows leaving a brighter space where her legs weren't.

MoMo then shouted from behind her, "I don't hear your horse movin'!"

Lin instantly brought his Winchester in line knowing he had a second or two before one of the other miners shouted a warning to MoMo aimed at his predetermined target and just as soon as the sights settled, he squeezed the trigger.

The half-inch diameter slug of lead shot down the barrel, where its grooves imparted the much-needed spin for accuracy before the expanding gases from the burning gunpowder shoved it out of the muzzle at fifteen hundred feet per second. As the bullet left the business end of the Winchester, it passed through the sound barrier while the sound wave that the shot created traveled around five hundred feet per second slower. It didn't matter much as the tip of the bullet penetrated the thin yellow cloth of Julia's dress less than a quarter of a second after leaving the Winchester, passed between her thighs then left the dress and struck MoMo's privates an instant later.

MoMo heard the sound at the same moment that his brain registered the excruciating pain caused by the .50 caliber slug passing though his crotch. He screamed dropped his pistol and crashed to the ground in agony as his hand grabbed to protect what wasn't there any longer.

Julia despite her eyes being closed felt the heat of the bullet as it passed less than an inch from her inner thighs making her

146

eyes pop open in shock before they rolled back into her head and she collapsed to the ground.

Lin knew he'd made the shot and Julia had probably passed out from shock, but he had other issues now.

He nudged Homer forward, levered in a fresh cartridge and maintained his sights on the startled group as MoMo continued to scream.

When he was close to Julia, he stepped down keeping his Winchester aimed at the group some of whom slid behind the women then walked to Julia and said loudly, "Julia, can you hear me?"

Julia's eyes fluttered as she heard his voice then quickly put her hands where the bullet had passed through her dress but didn't feel any blood, just a big hole. She sat up, glanced at the screeching MoMo then rose onto her bare feet and would have kicked him if she was wearing boots but stepped over to Lin and stood beside him without saying anything.

Lin then yelled to be heard over MoMo's cries as he still squirmed and bled, "I'm giving you the same choice I gave MoMo. Ten minutes from now, I want to see that wagon harnessed and all the women on board with their things or each of you will get the same treatment. If any of you even think of taking a shot, I want you to understand that I never miss, boys."

Charlie Nesbitt had made his decision even before Lin restated his ultimatum but wanted assurance as he shouted back, "How do we know you ain't gonna kill us all after we let 'em go?"

"I promise that I won't shoot any of you, and you can ask anyone who knows me. I always keep my word."

Julia glanced at Lin but still remained silent.

Charlie scanned the faces of the other miners then yelled back, "You can't let the other women kill us either and you can't go get the law to come back."

"I won't let the women shoot you and I won't tell or send anyone here after I'm gone and neither will the women or the boy. You have my word."

Before Charlie could reply, Julia looked at him and exclaimed, "Lin, you can't do this! You can't let them get away with what they did to us!"

Lin didn't reply, but waited until Charlie shouted, "Give me a minute."

Lin watched as the miners had a quick conference as the women listened in the sudden silence when MoMo's screaming had ceased.

Julia was beside herself thinking that Lin was going to let them all live free from any punishment for what they had done to her and all of the women but remained silent as she stewed in her anger. *Why was he letting them all live? He should be shooting them all right now!*

Charlie yelled back, "Alright. We'll get the wagon harnessed and let the women get their things, but you gotta back off five hundred yards and we'll send the women."

"I'll do that," Lin shouted then turned to Julia and said, "Go and get your things, Julia, and trust me."

Julia looked into his eyes then nodded and began walking to MoMo's shack to get her clothes. She assumed one of the miners would get their shoes from wherever they had put them.

Lin back stepped toward Homer then mounted and wheeled him back to Pete who was almost as disappointed as Julia about Lin's decision to let the miners get away with what they'd done.

Lin understood how Julia felt and was sure the other women felt the same way, so he wasn't surprised when Pete asked, "Why'd you let them get away with it, Mister Chase?"

Lin just looked at the youngster and replied, "I didn't, Pete. I'll keep my promises, but they won't get away with it. Now let's move away a few hundred yards like the man said."

Pete nodded turned the Morgan and packhorse away from the mining camp and rode beside a silent Lin Chase who was scanning the terrain as they walked the horses.

They were well past the five-hundred-yard mark when Lin pulled them to a stop then wheeled Homer around to face the camp.

"Okay, Pete. This is where we'll stay. Now we wait for the ladies to drive the wagon over here."

Pete didn't know how Lin could keep his promises and still make those miners pay for what they did, so he didn't reply.

———

In the camp the miners were grumbling about paying so much for one night's pleasure but had quickly harnessed the wagon and moved it to the center of the camp while two men kept watch on Lin now almost eight hundred yards away.

The shoes were all piled in the bed as the women began to board, their fear of not quite being free keeping them quiet until they were at least outside of the camp.

Like Julia, each of them was angry that justice wasn't going to be delivered to the men who had not only raped them but had inspired the whole thing. What made them even angrier was that the bounty hunter had promised the miners that none of them would either shoot them or notify the law about what had happened. To a woman, they were determined to tell their husbands about this and expected those miners to pay for what they did.

Anna and Marge Lampley were almost as much disappointed in Lin as they were angry.

Not surprisingly, it was a barefooted Julia who took the reins of the wagon while the other women began sorting out their shoes in the bed. She snapped the reins the horses lurched forward and soon had the wagon rolling past MoMo's body as they left the camp.

All of the women except for Julia and her mother were glaring at the miners with looks of absolute hate as the wagon pulled away. Mary Lampley still sat in a daze.

The miners were a noisy, angry bunch of men for the lost gold and now the lost women.

"I say we get our Winchesters and go after that bastard!" shouted Saul Baker.

Charlie Nesbitt replied, "Didn't you see that shot he made to kill MoMo? I ain't goin' out there."

There was a murmuring of agreement with Charlie as they all continued to watch the wagon recede and approach the distant bounty hunter as he waited about a half mile away.

———

"Here they come, Mister Chase," Pete exclaimed as the wagon drew closer.

"Strangely enough, I can see that, Pete," Lin replied as he watched the wagonload of women being driven by Julia, but also glancing back at the mining camp beyond to see what the miners were doing. He wanted them all to stay put for another few minutes. He was counting on their burned-in need to stay with their claims and remain within the mining camp.

When the wagon was within fifty yards Lin dismounted then slid the Sharps-Borshadt from its scabbard and leaned it over his shoulder before he and Pete walked away from the horses.

Julia had planned on pleading with Lin to break his promise, just this once when she saw him take his big gun from his horse and decided not to ask. He had said that she should trust him, and now she would. She didn't know if he was going to ignore the promise or not, but she had to believe he wasn't about to let those bastards live much longer.

She pulled the wagon to a stop and before she could clamber down, Lin and Pete stepped to the wagon and Lin said, "Ladies, I know you've all had a horrible time, but I'm going to set things right. You probably heard me promise that I wasn't going to shoot them, allow you to shoot them or go to the law. I always keep my promises, and I'll keep this one. The difference is that I usually keep to the spirit of my promises but in this case, I'll only stay true to the words that I spoke."

Except for Mary Lampley, there was a hubbub of questions and chatter from all of the women who seemed just as determined that the miners should all be sent to Hell, but Lin held up his hand.

"Ladies, please trust me. Now you'll all be able to watch as justice is served. Just get ready to cover your ears. It's going to get noisy."

Lin then turned, walked to Pete, opened his heavy coat took the two .50-140 cartridges from the loops slipped them into his vest pocket then left the wagon and walked to the packhorse. When he reached the animals, he removed his tripod then stepped behind a three-foot tall rock outcrop before he leaned the rifle against the rock then set the tripod on top and made sure it was stable. He then removed the two lens covers from the Malcolm scope opened the rifle's breech and slid the long cartridge inside before closing it again and setting the mounting hole into the tripod's mounting point.

The women all watched now curious as much as angry with what he was planning on doing. Surely, he couldn't expect to shoot them all at this distance as most of the women had a hard time even seeing the miners.

Lin hadn't a single thought of shooting a miner as he adjusted the telescopic sight for the range, then modified it for the altitude. The temperature and the wind didn't play much of a role and he'd make those adjustments off of the reticle. Besides, he didn't need to be that accurate now anyway. He probably could use one the smaller .50-110 cartridges, if one dared ever to apply the word 'small' to a Sharps cartridge, but he wanted to be sure.

He looked through the scope and slowly angled the sight down the row of shacks until he found the one that he wanted. The others, while all small, were bigger than this one. It wasn't far removed from the wall of rock, either. It was even built into a recess in the mountainside which suited his purpose.

It was too small for a man to lie down in but it was more than large enough for their supply of dynamite. His only question was how much they had remaining, and he'd only know that when it went off.

Lin was ready so he released the first trigger and shouted, "Cover your ears!"

Then he held his breath let the sight steady on the base of the small hut and squeezed the second trigger.

The big rifle roared as a giant plume of gunsmoke filled the air above him and all of the women and Pete thought that was the sound that Lin had warned them against, but it hadn't seemed that bad.

It was only when they all watched to see if they could spot what he had tried to hit did their eyes tell them what was coming before the sound arrived.

The large mass of lead traveled the eight-hundred and forty-six yards in a little over a second and a half. The miners had all been returning to their shacks to begin the day's work after having dismissed the thought of any retaliation.

The sound wave from the shot hadn't arrived yet, but one of the miners, Larry Pinchot, had seen the large muzzle flare in the distance and shouted, "What's that?"

No one had a chance to reply when as soon as the question had been asked, the bullet drilled through the wood of the dynamite hut then penetrated one of the three cases of dynamite that were stored inside along with a box of blasting caps. Not that the blasting caps really mattered once the bullet crushed into the first stick of dynamite which had the same effect as a blasting cap and set off the massive explosion.

Even Lin was stunned with the size of the blast as the hut evaporated and the shock waves then penetrated the rock face of the mountain behind it and ripped through the air in front of it. The miners were blown from their feet in the blast of debris and most were already dead when the mountainside succumbed to the massive fractures in the stone that held it in place creating a massive avalanche.

All of the witnesses around the wagon were staring with their hands over their ears as the sound reached them and rolled past them into the surrounding Black Hills. The dust cloud from the explosion rose like an enormous mushroom over what used to be a valley but was now just a canyon filled with crushed rock.

For almost a minute the sound continued to echo as the observers continued to watch in stunned disbelief.

Yet, when Lin finally lifted his rifle tripod and walked back to the wagon, he looked at the women's faces and saw a mixture of satisfaction and relief on each of them, even Julia's. On the other hand, he felt a deepening sense of emptiness. He'd just killed fourteen men but only MoMo had posed a genuine threat. He had never even shot at an unarmed man yet now, he had killed more than a dozen. He knew he could justify what he did because what they had done but still, it made him almost disgusted with himself. He had to push it aside for now because he still had things that needed to be done.

He lifted the rifle from the tripod opened the breech pulled out the empty brass case then closed the breech and replaced the lens caps. He leaned the Sharps-Borshadt against the rock before he took down the tripod and collapsed its legs. He then took them both back to the packhorse slid the tripod into its small case returned to Homer and slid the Sharps-Borshadt back into its big scabbard before he walked back to the wagon and all of the women turned at his approach except for Mary Lampley.

He held out the empty cartridge case to Julia and asked, "Did you want to keep this, Julia?"

She took the still-warm brass in her hand then turned to the wagon and held it out to her mother.

"Mama, I think you should have this."

Mary blinked then accepted the metal cylinder and stared at it for a few seconds before looking at Julia and asking quietly, "What about the others?"

Julia didn't look at Li, but answered, "Lin will get them all, Mama."

Lin then said, "Julia, I'm sorry for having to take that shot, but it was the only one I had."

"I know," she replied, "it was just the shock of having that bullet pass so close that I could feel the heat."

Lin nodded then said, "Ladies, we have enough time to get you home. All of your men are safe and so are the two babies. Would you rather go there or to Laramie? We can get to Laramie a couple of hours earlier."

The women all voted to go directly home, which didn't surprise him.

The destination settled, Julia snapped the reins and the wagon began to roll forward again as Lin returned to Homer, mounted and trotted beside the wagon while Pete rode the Morgan on the other side trailing the packhorse.

———

In Howell, the six men needed to buy some more supplies for the packhorse then ride as group to Colorado before going their separate ways.

They didn't pay much attention to the earthquake and thunder that had passed through the town a little while earlier.

———

Lin glanced over at Julia as she drove the wagon and wondered how badly she had been affected. She was a strong-willed woman and appeared to be functioning normally, but he suspected that she was wrestling with the recent nightmares just as the others were, each in her own way. It was probably worse for her because she had never been with a man before, and he really wanted to talk to her but knew that it was impossible now.

He hoped that her mother and sisters-in-law would be able to help when those nightmares returned but could already tell that her mother wasn't doing well either. He knew he'd be chasing those six down and now, he was almost certain that he'd be doing it alone. It was also possible that Julia would no longer see him as anything other than a killer and forget about their other arrangements as well. He wouldn't blame her at all.

Julia may have been wearing a façade of normalcy, but she was far from feeling like herself as she almost robotically drove the wagon. She thought that she would be able to almost ignore what was happening as the miners had raped her a total of four times. She'd closed her eyes and imagined better things, especially her short time alone with Lin, but it hadn't worked to deflect the smells, sounds and sensations as they climbed on top of her and slammed themselves into her.

Yet, as horrible as that memory was, it was the very real thought of carrying a child as a result of the revolting night that really terrified her. She had been so strong for the other women since she'd been taken from her home, yet she knew that she couldn't maintain this façade if she discovered she was pregnant. *What would become of her if that happened?*

If Anna or Marge became pregnant, at least they had husbands to care for them and help them to cope with it just as they'd be there for them when their wives were returned safely to them later today. She knew that she'd have to stay now, for many reasons. Her mother seemed to be off in another world, and Julia knew she'd have to try and help her. *But who did she have to help her?*

Lin would be leaving to go after the six men, and she already felt the impending night of terror that awaited her as she slept alone in the main room.

While taking a short break to water and rest the horses, Lin had to spend some time with the women and Pete answering questions, mostly about how he would find the six men who had done this horrible thing. Julia had remained standing silently by his side as he answered still acting as if she were totally unaffected by the ordeal.

But before they all returned to the wagon, Lin took Julia's elbow and guided her away from the others a few feet.

"Julia, are you, all right? I'm really sorry I had to take that shot, but it was the only one I could take."

Julia nodded as she replied, "No, I knew what you were going to do, but the shock of the bullet passing by so closely shocked me. I'll be fine."

He looked into her dark blue eyes and asked, "Are you sure? You've been through a lot. Things that no man can really understand."

Julia averted her eyes and replied, "No. I'm fine. Really."

Lin wanted to tell her that she was lying to him and maybe to herself but said, "If you need me to stay tonight, let me know. Will you?"

"Okay," she answered tersely then stepped quickly to the wagon climbed into the driver's seat and waited until everyone was settled and snapped the reins.

Lin watched the wagon rolling away then sighed mounted Homer and set him at a slow trot to keep up with the wagon.

He pulled up beside Pete and had him back off until they were fifty yards behind the wagon.

"How are you doing, Pete?"

"I'm better."

"Good. Pete, I'm going to ask you for a favor. Okay?"

"Sure."

"When you get back home, I'm going to have to go after those six men, but I'm very worried about Julia. I think she's going to feel very alone tonight, so can you move your mattress into the main room after she's under the blankets? Talk to her and tell her silly stories."

"Why?"

"What happened to her and the other ladies was a horrible thing and I think Julia's bottling it all up inside. She needs someone to help her, especially tonight."

"Telling her silly stories will help?"

"I think so, but I'm not an expert on women at all and especially not women who have been hurt like this. I just go by how I feel after I kill a man."

"Like what?"

"It's a hard thing to kill a man, Pete. You're taking away something that God had given him and now after blowing up that mountainside, I've killed more than two dozen men. I know that what I did had to be done but that doesn't make it any easier. I feel empty and dirty for having done it. It's a haunting feeling that stays with you for a long time."

"Okay. I'll help my sister all that I can."

Lin smiled at the boy and said, "You're a good man, Pete Lampley."

Pete smiled back then had to catch up when Lin nudged Homer forward to catch up to the wagon.

―――――

Lin was about fifty yards ahead of the wagon and it was late afternoon when the Barber farmhouse and barn appeared in the distance. Lin pulled out his Winchester that needed cleaning anyway and fired a round into the air to let the men know they were coming.

It must have worked because by the time the wagon was within a mile, Lin could already see three men standing on the small back porch waving. He didn't bother looking behind him as he expected that their wives were all returning the waves. He was sure that they were all happy to be safely returned and hoped they could return to a semblance of a normal life now.

Julia guided the wagon to the back of the house and Henry, Joe and Mike Barber each raced to the back of the wagon to help their wives down. Joe had little Sissy in his arms.

As Wilma reached the ground, she began to cry as her husband embraced her. Mike almost pulled Bess from the wagon bed, and he was in tears as much as she was as they held each other, but Joe had to let Mary Barber step down by herself before he could give Sissy to her then hugged her as Mary kissed her daughter then her husband.

Henry finally turned to Lin, who had remained on horseback, said, "Mister Chase, I can never thank you enough for what you did. Did the men who did this pay the ultimate price?"

"The miners who created this mess by offering to buy women are all dead, but I'm going to chase down the six who made it happen."

Wilma Barber snapped, "Kill them all! Every last one of those bastards!"

Her two sons glanced at their mother having never heard her talk like that before as Lin replied, "Yes, ma'am. I intend to do just that."

Joe and Mike began to ask questions, but Lin stopped them by saying, "I'm sure Jim and Bill Lampley are just as anxious to get their wives back as you were, so we've got to be rolling."

Henry then said, "Of course. I apologize, but be sure to stop by sometime, Mister Chase."

Lin just smiled nodded and tipped his hat before setting Homer off at a walk while the Barbers started talking to each other as they returned to the house.

After dropping off the three women and accepting their well-meant thanks, the wagon was moving just ten minutes after stopping. Lin didn't pull ahead so much this time but still rode a few yards before the team that was probably pleased with the reduced weight.

He was already modifying his plans about returning to Cheyenne tonight primarily because of the tired horses. He'd need Homer to be well-rested tomorrow when he chased after the six men who had caused all this misery. Besides, he'd have to start his search to the west now as that's where their trail would begin.

The sun was almost gone when the first structure on the Lampley farm, the unfinished house that would soon belong to Jim and Anna, appeared on the horizon. Five minutes later, Lin fired another shot to alert Jim and Bill Lampley that they were close and soon saw the two men trot onto the back porch and begin waving wildly just as the Barbers had. It was the same eerie similarity as it had been on his journey to find the women when he had noticed the same smells and baby cries in both houses. This time it wasn't tragic at all.

Lin finally brought his gelding to a halt when he was fifty yards from the house and waited while the family had their reunion. It was another mirror image of what had just happened a few hours ago when Bill helped Marge down and hugged her as Jim handed Teddy to Anna before kissing her. Julia then helped her mother down while Pete dismounted and walked to his family.

He then nudged Homer forward until he was just fifty feet away then stepped down and hopped onto the porch where Jim and Bill pumped his hand and slammed his back as they expressed their sincere appreciation for saving the women.

"Jim, if it's alright with you, I'll stay in the barn tonight. I'll be leaving early in the morning to go after the six men who kidnapped the seven women."

"There were seven?" he asked incredulously.

"Yes, sir. They stole the three Barber women as well, but they're all safe now. The miners who started this whole scheme and bought the women are all dead. I'm sure your wives can tell you the story. So, is it all right if I use your barn tonight?"

Bill said, "Of course, it's alright. You should be embarrassed for even asking."

Jim then turned to Anna and said, "I have some food cooking, but I'm not sure that it's very good."

"Anything would be wonderful right now," she replied before she entered the house with Teddy on her hip.

Julia had already guided her mother through the open doorway without even looking at him.

As the others turned to follow them into the house, Lin said, "I'll take care of the wagons and the horses. I'll be in when I'm done."

"I'll help," said Bill, which was soon echoed by Jim.

"No, you all need to spend some time with your wives. This won't take me long."

The three men understood nodded and gave him a small wave before going into the kitchen and closing the door.

Lin trotted back to Homer temporarily hitched him to the back of the wagon with the Morgan then clambered into the driver's seat flicked the reins and headed for the barn. Once inside, he lit the one hanging lamp as the light was almost gone.

It took him almost an hour to unharness the team, move the wagon back into position, unsaddle Homer and the Morgan then unload the packhorse before he brushed them all down. He'd already made his decisions about how to find the six men, but it was a gamble at best. It depended on what they had decided to do now that they had all the gold dust, and the fact that they'd been paid in gold dust rather than currency made all the difference.

There weren't a lot of banks that were set up to assay the gold and then convert it to cash and they were usually in larger cities. He knew that Laramie and Cheyenne both could handle it but was sure they weren't going to head into Laramie, not after having killed two deputies. He didn't believe they'd go to Cheyenne, even if they knew that one of the deputies had lived.

They'd want to get out of the territory altogether and that meant they'd probably ride to Colorado which meant they could go to a number of places like Fort Collins, Boulder or Denver. With a full day's lead, he knew he probably couldn't run them down and he'd lose them once they arrived in the city.

It was his years of chasing outlaws that gave him the confidence to take the gamble that Denver was their destination. He would take the train to the capital of Colorado then ride north to meet them head on if they rode that far or press on to the other places if they didn't. If they decided to take the difficult cross-country route, he'd miss them, but their most likely path would be on the road that paralleled the Denver Pacific Railroad.

He estimated his chances of finding them at less than fifty percent, but it was better than trying to hunt for them in a town, and that was assuming they chose to go to Denver in the first place.

Once the horses were all settled, he pulled out his Winchester and the Sharps-Borshadt for cleaning. He decided that it was too late to eat and doubted if Jim had made enough food for that many mouths, so he pulled the last of his sausages from his saddlebags stuck it between his teeth and began to clean the Winchester.

He was humming 'I Ride an Old Paint' as he slid the cleaning rod down the barrel of the Sharps-Borshadt when the squealing door announced a visitor. He kept humming but stopped sliding the rod as he turned to the door and saw Jim Lampley enter.

"Everybody wondered why you didn't come back to the house."

"After I finished with the horses, I had to clean my guns. Then I needed to get ready to leave early tomorrow morning, too. How are the women, Jim?"

He thought about it for a few seconds before replying, "My mother isn't doing well, but Anna, Marge and Julia seem as good as could be expected. Did they tell you that the two who had killed my father and raped my mother were among the six men that did this?"

Lin stared at Jim pulled the cleaning rod free and answered, "No, they didn't. Of course, I didn't spend much time talking to them, but I'm surprised that Julia didn't say anything. I'm really worried about her. She's like an overwound clock spring that's ready to break."

"I know. I think both Anna and Marge are dealing with it better than she is. Maybe because they know we love them, but I'm not sure."

"I told Pete to sleep in the main room tonight just to help her through the night. She shouldn't be alone."

"That's a good idea. So, are you going to come into the house?"

"No, I don't think so. I already had a sausage, so I'm okay. I don't believe that you had made enough for as many mouths that had to fed anyway."

Jim smiled and said, "I didn't, but the ladies all pitched in and whipped up a good dinner."

"Good. I'll be leaving before sunrise tomorrow then head to Cheyenne. I'm going to take a risky approach and ride to Cheyenne rather than try and pick up their trail over near Laramie. I'll board the train to Denver and after I arrive, I'll ride north and hopefully catch up with them on the ride north or keep riding until I get to Colorado Springs."

"You're not going to face off against six of them, are you?" he asked.

"Even if I do, It's not bad, Jim. I have all of the advantages, believe it or not."

"I hope you know what you're doing."

"I do."

"Well, I'll be going then, and I still owe you fifty dollars, too."

"No, you don't owe me anything. I'll take it from those six bastards after I kill them all."

Jim nodded then acted as if to he was going to say something but just smiled at him and left the barn, nudging the door closed with his foot.

As Lin did the last bit of cleaning on the Sharps-Borshadt, he wondered why Julia hadn't told him that the Hilliard brothers were among the six that had taken them to the mining camp. He was sure that she knew who they were yet hadn't expressed any desire to go after them as she had the first time they'd met. She had specifically said to her mother 'Lin will get them all', not 'we will get them all'.

He was growing more convinced that she now saw him as little more than those murderers who had killed Deputy Cobb and those two squatters, and he could understand that. But when he had thought of the squatters, he suddenly realized that there weren't any more women. *Why would they go to the squatters' cabin if there weren't any women?*

He'd like to ask Julia, but he thought it might not be a good idea. If those men had murdered women then Julia would probably be even more afraid of him.

He stood set the two rifles where they belonged then walked to Homer and began to absent-mindedly rub his neck as he thought about confronting those six men.

They were murderers, kidnappers and to him, much worse. They had sold those women into nothing less than slavery. He'd have no problem shooting every one of them, but it was a question of how. He knew the landscape well north of Denver, mainly because there wasn't much to remember. The mountains were a few miles west of the city, so the terrain was flat with some large hills off to the west before the mountains began. The railroad and the roadway beside it were a good half a mile from the start of the hills which was why the tracks were there in the first place. There were gullies and streams that cut into the earth that would make a good place for them to use for a defensive position as well as the occasional forest.

He was still rubbing Homer when the door creaked again and this time, he found himself looking at Julia who had a mug of what he assumed was coffee in her hand.

"I brought you some coffee. My brother said you had already eaten something."

He stepped over accepted the mug and took a sip before replying, "This is very thoughtful, Julia."

"Why didn't you come to the house as you said you would?"

"After I took care of the horses, resorted the supplies for tomorrow and cleaned my guns, it was a bit too late. Besides, I didn't think there was going to be enough food for everyone."

"Is that the real reason?"

"Mostly. But I thought that the family needed to spend some time together to say things that only family can say to each other."

Julia slid what used to be a milking stool to the center of the barn floor sat down and said, "Don't you think that you've earned the right to be there now?"

He resumed his seat on the nearby hay and replied, "No, Julia, I really don't. I've only known your family for a few days. It doesn't matter what I've done, I'm still a stranger."

"Not to me, you're not."

"Are you sure? Why didn't you tell me that two of those men were the Hillard brothers? What made you change your mind about joining me in seeking revenge, Julia? Are you afraid to be with me now? You watched me blow up an entire mountain after I put a bullet between your legs. You have no idea what kind of monster I could be inside, and if that thought scares you, I'd understand."

Julia shook her head and said, "No, no, you've got it all wrong. I'm not afraid of you in the least. I'm just worried that I could become like one of those men. I watched them shoot the deputies, and two pregnant women and then laugh about it. I don't ever want to be like that. I don't want to take the chance."

Lin was startled and asked, "Pregnant women?"

Then even before she replied, he realized why they had stopped at the squatters' cabin yet hadn't added any more women to the wagon.

"They were at the squatters' cabin. The Hilliard brothers chased them inside shot them and then burned the place down."

"I was wondering why they had gone there. But about the other part of what you said. Julia, you could never be like that, you know. The fact that you're worried about it makes it impossible that you could kill and not feel the pain of remorse."

Lin could see the pain already behind her eyes as she asked hurriedly, "Then, how do you do it? I saw your eyes after the mountain exploded and you were far from happy about it, but you still did it. Doesn't it bother you?"

Lin folded his fingers and answered, "It bothers me immensely. I feel incredibly empty each time I have to take another man's life even if he's trying to kill me. What I do is something I learned after I killed the first one. I found that if I

168

created an imaginary vault in my mind made up of happier memories, I could store those bad ones away and keep them at bay. Sometimes, it takes me longer to get the memories into that vault because of their size, like today. Then when the vault door is opened, I can see the other memories waiting to leap out at me, so I slam it closed quickly. My biggest worry is that one of these days, I won't be able to close it fast enough and I'll go mad."

"Then what will happen?" she asked quietly.

Lin shuddered but said, "Never mind. It doesn't matter."

He took a long sip of the lukewarm liquid then set the cup back down.

Julia then asked quietly, "Do you think I could do the same thing? Make a vault in my head to hide the bad memories?"

Lin looked at her closely but shrugged and replied, "I don't know, Julia. Knowing it's there is kind of scary to me at times. I think it might have been smarter for me to deal with the problems one at a time rather than storing them away."

Julia then lowered her eyes to the barn floor in the flickering lamplight as she thought about what he had told her, and let those horrific memories slide back into the forefront of her mind.

Lin then quietly asked, "Will you be all right tonight, Julia?"

She just shook her head slightly and began to quiver ever so slightly.

"Stay with me tonight, Julia," Lin said softly.

She nodded then Lin stood, took her hands pulled her to her feet and softly wrapped his arms around her. She lowered her head to his shoulder, closed her eyes and began to quietly weep.

Lin felt the tears soaking through his shirt as she began to tremble, but he was doing all he could knowing that words wouldn't help her now as she wrestled with those horrible memories that assaulted her mind.

Julia tried to do as Lin had done and create a vault to hide them away but failed. The more she tried to forget them, the more vivid and real they became: those horrible faces, the disgusting smells, the filthy groping and the obnoxious grunting. It happened again, again and again. She could see their eyes as they violated her and cared only about themselves. She was nothing.

Lin thought she'd stop quivering after a minute or two, but Julia was getting worse as she passed trembling and went to full shaking when she suddenly began to fight his embrace and tried to wrestle away from him as if he were about to rape her as the others had done.

Her eyes were screwed tightly shut as she suddenly screamed, "Don't touch me!"

Then she began she began to pound him with her fists, "Get away from me! Get away!"

As Lin tried to calm her as she fought her demons, she suddenly reached up with her fingers and clawed at his face, leaving long bloody scratches along both of his cheeks while she continued to struggle.

Lin ignored the blood and held on even more tightly before he exclaimed, "Julia, Julia, it's me! I'm with you now, and I'll never hurt you."

Julia's continued to cry but stopped struggling as she felt Lin's tears fall on her forehead, or that's what she thought they were until she opened her eyes to the horror of what she had done when she saw Lin's bleeding face just an inch from hers. She then she exploded into a new round of crying as she clutched onto him with an amazing amount of strength.

She then began saying, "I'm sorry…I'm sorry…I'm sorry," continuously as she wept and still shook.

Lin let her work her way through her horrors as he continued to ignore the blood sliding down his cheeks.

When she stopped apologizing, Lin said softly, "It's all right now, Julia. You'll be better now."

She relaxed her grip and finally began to breathe normally, then stepped back slightly, looked at his face then touched his blood-stained cheek with her fingertips and said softly, "I need to clean your face. I did such a terrible thing."

"No, that's alright, Julia. I'll take care of it," he said as he turned to his saddlebags took out a small towel, dumped some water from his canteen onto the cloth, wrung it damp then as he began to press it to his face, Julia intercepted his hand, took the towel and began to gently wipe the blood from his face as he looked into her sorrowful blue eyes.

"I'm a real mess, aren't I?" she asked as she wiped his face.

"You'd be a heartless woman if you weren't," he replied.

"I tried to make a vault like you did, but it didn't work. All that happened was everything came back to me as if it was happening all over again. They raped me four times, Lin. Four times! The first one, the one you shot through my dress, rented me to each of the others to make back some of the money he had paid to buy me."

"Julia, I know this doesn't make any sense, but I think it was better for you to let it your pain out the way you did rather than keep it hidden inside you."

She softly touched his face again and said, "But it wasn't better for you, was it?"

"I've had worse, ma'am."

Julia asked, "Have you ever been shot, Lin?"

"No, ma'am. Not even once."

"That's amazing," she said as she wiped the last of the blood from his chin then carried the towel to the trough and rinsed it somewhat clean then wiped her own face of Lin's blood, rinsed it again then tossed it on top of a stall fence.

When she returned, Lin asked, "Are you better now? Do you still want to stay here, or do you think you can return to the house?"

She quickly replied, "I'd rather stay, unless you're worried that I might do something worse than scratch your face."

"No, I'm not worried and Julia, there's something else that you shouldn't worry about."

"What's that?"

"Just because we'll be together alone tonight, nothing is inevitable."

Julia surprised him when she smiled then replied, "That was a pretty stupid thing to say."

"No, it wasn't, but I didn't want you to be afraid."

"I'm only here because this is where I want to be and where I know I won't be afraid, Lin."

Lin nodded then turned and took the second bedroll that had been on the Morgan and laid it out next to his.

Julia removed her shoes then had to wrap her yellow dress around her legs to slide inside the bedroll before Lin blew out the lamp, pulled off his boots and gunbelt then slid under the second bedroll just inches away from Julia.

Even in the almost completely dark barn, there was just enough ambient light that they began to make out each other's features as they talked just eighteen inches apart.

Julia said, "I'm sorry I scratched your face, Lin. I really am."

"I know you are, but you had to let those demons escape, so it doesn't bother me. Can you tell me about the six men now? I need to know who I'll be chasing."

"Oh. I'm sorry. I forgot. You know about the Hilliard brothers. They called the leader Fuzzy. He was average height with dark hair and a full beard."

Lin said, "That's Fuzzy Villers. I know about him."

"Another man he kept calling Ike and the others were Hound and Arnie. I didn't get any last names."

"You don't have to, Julia. I know all of them and that makes it easier and harder, too. None of them are amateurs, so I need to be careful, but it also means I know what to expect and can find them."

"I'm sorry for sending you out alone, Lin, but my mother needs me."

"I know she does, Julia. Did you want to return to the house for her now?"

Julia thought about it and conceded it was probably a good idea for her to return, so she replied, "I think I'd better. I wish I could stay with you, though."

"You're a good woman, Julia. I'll see you in the morning."

Julia slid out of the bedroll, slipped on her shoes then stood and said, "Goodnight, Lin."

"Goodnight, Julia," he replied then rolled onto his back felt his scratches and closed his eyes.

Julia then left the barn and as she walked back to the house, she wondered if what Lin had said was true about her letting the demons take control of her rather than trying to hide them away.

She entered the house and went to the bedroom where she found her mother staring into the darkness.

"Mama, did you want me to sleep with you tonight?"

Her mother didn't answer, so Julia pulled off her shoes then slid under the blankets next to her mother and wrapped her in her arms, noticing that her mother hadn't put on her nightdress and was still wearing her shoes.

CHAPTER 5

Lin slid out of the bedroll while the barn was still dark knowing that the predawn was probably just brightening the sky outside. The southbound Pacific-Denver train left Cheyenne just after noon, so he'd have to ride at a good pace, but he'd leave the Morgan here along with the panniers that contained all of the clothes he'd bought for Julia when he thought she'd be joining him.

He had Homer already saddled and was loading the packhorse when the squealing barn door announced Julia's arrival and let in some of the early morning light.

Lin turned then Julia saw his face and grimaced.

"I really did scratch you badly, didn't I?" she said as she approached.

"It's all right, but I'm just worried that everyone who sees me will believe that I tried to assault you last night."

She shook her head and replied, "No. I already told them what had happened last night."

Lin stopped loading the packhorse and asked, "How did you do last night, Julia?"

"I had bad dreams, but I'm still better than my mother, I'm afraid. She's lost somewhere in her mind. I had to get her changed this morning as if she were a toddler. I'm very worried about her, Lin."

Lin had nothing he could say that could help, so he just nodded his agreement.

"Will you come back?" she asked quietly.

"Yes, I'll come back. I'll tell you what happens and maybe if I get those men, telling your mother will help her to get better."

Julia nodded as she looked at him.

He stared into her dark blue eyes and saw so much pain and fear that he didn't know if Julia would ever get better. He hated those men for what they had done to the women but knew that no matter what he did to them, the damage could never be undone. He wished he could stay here and help her to recover but knew the best thing he could do was to find those bastards and make them pay for what they did. When he'd finished with that task, maybe there would be a future for him and Julia, but he wouldn't know until he was done.

He reached to her face and let his fingertips barely touch her left cheek.

"Are you going to leave right away?" she asked.

"As soon as I finish loading the packhorse. I need to catch the southbound train from Cheyenne, so I'll leave the Morgan and the pannier with all of the clothes I'd bought for you when you were going to accompany me."

"Okay," she replied then said, "Please be careful, Lin."

"I will."

Julia took his hand from her face kissed his fingers then turned and left the barn.

Lin watched her leave then took in a deep breath before he finished loading the packhorse and led the two horses out of the still-open barn door. He mounted then looked at the quiet house turned Homer toward the road and set him off at a walk.

Julia watched Lin ride away from the main room. She hadn't been completely honest with him about the tormenting nightmares that had dominated her night which had become so intense that they made her leave the bedroom and sit in the kitchen in the dark. The horrible treatment by itself had been horror enough, but the underlying fear of pregnancy had intensified the nightmares. She felt lost and alone and had almost asked Lin to forget about the six men and help her but knew it would have been a selfish thing to ask. Her mother needed something, and maybe the desperately desired deaths of those men would be the nudge that returned her to this life.

————

Fuzzy Villers, the Hilliard bothers, Arnie Jacobsen, Hound Jones and Ike McCall had departed Howell the afternoon before and had to follow the road to Laramie but were able to turn south before entering the town. They were trailing the packhorse which was loaded down with supplies.

Despite all of the gold that each man carried amounting to over fifteen hundred dollars, purchasing the supplies had left the six men with a total of fifteen dollars and forty-six cents among them. It didn't matter to them because they knew that they'd soon cash in their gold and be awash in cash.

————

Lin had accelerated Homer to a fast trot to give him as much time to get to the Cheyenne before the train left. He pulled his pocket watch as he rode into the morning sun and was pleased to see it was only 7:10, so he'd have plenty of time.

177

He slowed Homer to a medium trot knowing he didn't have any reason to go to the house as he already had his supplies and his weapons.

Lin shifted his thoughts to the six men he hoped to be confronting later that day. It was only a three-hour train ride to Denver and the road ran right past the train station because it paralleled the tracks all the way to Cheyenne. So, if things worked out, he could be in a gunfight by four or five o'clock this afternoon.

―――――

But the six men didn't travel all the way to Denver. They stopped at Fort Collins and had their gold assayed and converted to cash. They then took rooms at the Harris House and went to Fuzzy's room to split the cash into six equal amounts. When they finished dividing the money, they were tickled when each man soon had spendable cash of over fifteen hundred dollars.

Once they had the money, there was no reason for them to stay together except for the Hilliard brothers, so they adjourned to their own rooms before heading over to Markel's Saloon and Billiard Hall across from their hotel. It also housed the town's best brothel on the second floor.

―――――

Lin arrived in Cheyenne around ten-thirty, so he first headed for the bank where he withdrew a hundred dollars, noted his balance of $9438.65 then left and trotted over to the sheriff's office. No one had commented about his scratches, but they sure did stare.

He had barely crossed the threshold when Deputy John Draper exclaimed, "Jesus, Lin! What the hell have you been up to? We're getting all sorts of stories out of Laramie, and what happened to your face?"

By the time he reached the desk, Deputy Ralph Scranton and Sheriff Luke Templeton had both reached the desk.

"I'll give you the quick version, but I've got to get onto the train for Denver."

"Okay, let's hear that version, but you'll have to give us the full story when you get back," Sheriff Templeton said.

"Okay. But I need you to send a telegram to Sheriff Ward, too. I don't have the time. I assume he sent you a telegram about the six men who kidnapped the women after shooting his deputies. Tell him I'm still chasing after them and will be going to Denver where I think they're headed. Let him know that the women are all safely back home and all of the miners are dead when I blew up their mountain, and before I start, I'll give you the names of the six men and I'll need their latest wanted posters, too."

As he began to tell the story, he wrote the names of the six men who had murdered George Cobb, shot Orville, the squatters and their pregnant wives. The sheriff then gave him the updated wanted posters on the six men.

It took fifteen of his precious minutes to tell even the abbreviated version, but when he finished including how he had gotten the gouges on his face, there were no questions just a stunned silence.

"Can you send that telegram for me?" Lin asked.

Sheriff Templeton shook his hand and said, "We'll send the telegram and good luck finding those bastards. I wish we had the jurisdiction to come with you."

"I'll take care of it, Luke," Lin said as he gave them a short salute then turned and headed back out the door.

After the short ride to the train station, he left Homer and the packhorse with the stock manager then bought a ticket to Denver. He only had to wait another thirty minutes before he heard the whistle of the southbound train and soon saw the locomotive pulling into the large station.

He waited while six passengers departed from the cars then hopped onto the steel car platform and swung through the door found an empty seat and plopped down before setting his saddlebags on the seat beside him.

When he turned to the window to look outside, he caught his reflection and was startled by the damage that Julia had done. The scars looked much worse than they had felt, and his biggest concern now was that they would remain with him for the rest of his life. He didn't consider himself a vain man, but to most people the scratch marks would mean that he'd tried to force himself on a woman who'd had to scratch his face to defend her honor. How ironic that would be, he thought.

Twenty minutes later, the train lurched forward and within ten minutes it had reached its maximum allowed speed as it rumbled south toward Denver.

———

Only Ike McCall and Fuzzy Villers had decided to ride south to Denver that morning and had cut cross-country rather than follow the road that led to Boulder. It would cut some distance from the ride and be on more level ground. It would also take them directly into Lin's path.

The Hilliard brothers had stayed in Fort Collins while Hound and Arnie had decided to go to Boulder.

———

It was early afternoon when Lin mounted Homer and left Denver following the road north. He felt a little odd because he wasn't tracking his targets but hoping to run into them. His biggest advantage was that he was expecting to find them, but they probably wouldn't be suspicious of a lone rider coming from Denver. His other almost as important advantages were his skill with his weapons and their added range. His disadvantage was one that he'd groomed to be noticed: his dark, almost black outfit and broad flat hat. It was too late to change now.

Still, he wasn't sure that he'd be running into them today, thinking they might have stayed in Greeley or some small town rather than pressing on to Denver, assuming that it was their destination in the first place. He could see a good three or more miles ahead and with the road clear ahead, he was trying to keep his mind from drifting into his concern about Julia, but the warm temperatures and the lack of company soon had him woolgathering.

———

Fuzzy and Ike reached the southbound roadway that paralleled the Pacific Denver Railway when Lin was fifteen miles south of them. They'd picked up the pace as they wanted to reach Denver today. Fuzzy had the packhorse tied to his horse.

Almost an hour later, it was Ike who first spotted the rider in the distance and shouted, "Fuzzy, we got somebody comin'."

Fuzzy was daydreaming about what he would do when they got to Denver and was startled by Ike's warning, but soon spotted the speck about three miles south.

"What do you figure, Ike? It ain't likely he's the law."

"I don't think so, but he's in an odd place for a lone rider. Let's just keep an eye on him."

———

Lin had committed the cardinal sin of letting his mind drift, so it wasn't until another five minutes had passed when he caught sight of the two men and a packhorse and cursed his lack of attention. They were already less than two miles away and they'd be within rifle range in another five minutes.

There were only two men, so it wasn't likely that it was any of the six, but it was possible. He didn't do anything hostile yet, but reminded himself of his identifying clothing which was almost as bad as pulling his rifle and waving it over his head.

———

Fuzzy glanced to his left and said, "You know what, Ike? I think he's that bounty hunter that uses a Sharps."

"Chase? You figure that's Chase?"

"It doesn't hurt to be safe. If it's him, then we got a problem."

"Not if he doesn't know who we are, Fuzzy. Let's keep goin' and see how close we can get. Once we get within Winchester range, it doesn't matter how good he is with that cannon of his."

"You're right, Ike. Keep an eye on him until we get close. He might just be some gambler, or maybe he's a preacher comin' to convert us into good Christians."

Ike snickered as both men kept their horses at a slow trot, closing the gap.

———

Lin identified Fuzzy and Ike at six hundred yards because one was riding a deep red horse and the other a buckskin. Neither was that rare in itself, but both together would be too much of a stretch to be a coincidence.

His adrenalin level kicked up a notch, so he had to pull it back down when he was becoming too fidgety. They may be within range, but there was that tiny chance that they weren't who he suspected them to be and they hadn't shown any hostile intentions yet.

So, Lin and the two outlaws continued to trot their horses closer as if neither was aware of the other, and soon they would just tip their hats as they passed enroute to their destinations.

The gap was shrinking as each man watched without appearing to watch, and each right hand ready to pull a Winchester free of its scabbard.

They passed three hundred yards, and no one made a move as tension heightened.

Lin had been monitoring his ever-decreasing range advantage with his '76 when his eyes caught a flash of light off of a brass plate on the butt of Ike's Winchester and everything changed. He was carrying a '76 as well and even though it was probably chambered for the .45-75 cartridge, he'd just lost his edge. He couldn't delay much longer, so at two-hundred and fifty yards, Lin quickly pulled Homer to a stop then snatched his Winchester from its scabbard which had the expected result when both Fuzzy and Ike pulled their repeaters free.

But that extra second that Lin had gained by being the first to arm himself was now critical as he pointed his muzzle at Ike McCall and his Winchester '76 then used that extra second to let his sights settle on his target.

Ike's built-up anxiety made him rush his shot, so he was able to fire before Lin pulled the trigger. His .45 sped across the seven-hundred and thirty-nine feet in about a half a second and ripped through Lin's left coat pocket just as he squeezed his trigger. His sights had pulled to the left just a fraction of an inch sending his shot four feet to Ike's left, missing Fuzzy by just inches.

Fuzzy had been ready to fire himself when the .50 caliber bullet whizzed past his left ear making him yank his shot, sending the .44 wildly off-target.

The two outlaws had kept their horses moving to cut down the range but had angled away from each other as Lin took his second shot at Ike who had already fired his second round and missed Lin entirely.

Lin's shot slammed into Ike's gut just to the right of center as he was turning his horse, so the large slug of lead ripped into his liver before it severed his spinal cord as it pulverized the twelfth thoracic vertebral body then exited his body.

Ike screamed as his arms flew into the air and he was thrown to the left side of his horse, slamming into the dirt.

Lin then shifted his aim to Fuzzy who was now rapidly firing at under two hundred yards. Then even as he had Fuzzy in his sights, he hesitated. Despite the sound of .44s now buzzing within inches of him, Lin felt as if he was cheating.

Fuzzy's sights were bouncing as his red gelding maintained his speed, still trailing the packhorse, but he wanted the gap closed. He'd seen Ike go down and had an almost fatalistic outlook as he continued to fire as his Winchester's barrel became too hot to touch.

The gap was just over a hundred yards when Lin's trademark flat black hat flew from his head making him understand that the odds were now even. He had to reacquire Fuzzy in his sights after the near miss then squeezed the trigger.

Fuzzy was levering in a new round when Lin's last shot reached him and punched into his left upper chest, vaporizing sections of two ribs before mauling the top of his heart and leaving his body. He then rolled over backwards over his horse's rump and was trampled by the packhorse.

Both animals then began to slow and by the time Lin started Homer forward again, they had stopped in a cloud of dust just off the roadway.

Lin glanced at Fuzzy's body and knew he was dead, so he turned Homer to where Ike McCall lay on the roadway fifty yards away. He thought it was highly unlikely that he'd survived the gunshot and the fall to the ground but when he drew close, he spotted movement when Ike's head turned.

Lin dismounted and walked to Ike McCall, whose eyes were following him but wasn't moving beyond that.

"You're dying, McCall," Lin said as he looked down at the fallen outlaw.

"I don't feel nothin' below the waist and my right arm's broke," Ike replied in a surprisingly strong voice despite blood still leaving his body, then he asked, "Are you that bounty hunter, Lin Chase?"

"I am, but I'm after you boys for taking those women to the miners."

"Are you gonna go and kill them too?"

"I already did. I took the whole mountain down on them when I put a round into their dynamite shack."

Ike closed his eyes and chuckled at the thought as Lin said, "I'm going after the other four. Where'd you leave them?"

"Why should I tell you? I'm dyin' anyway."

"If you want me to leave your carcass out here for the critters to chew on then you keep quiet. If you want to be buried properly in Denver, just tell me. There isn't any use lying either. I'll find them soon enough."

Ike really didn't care in the first place. He'd never liked the Hilliard brothers and Hound was downright spooky. Arnie Jacobsen was just there.

"Two of 'em were goin' to Boulder and them brothers were stayin' in Fort Collins for a while."

"Okay. I'll get Fuzzy on his horse and then come back."

"Can I get some water before you go? I'm mighty thirsty."

Lin turned removed his canteen from Homer, pulled the stopper free and handed it to Ike's only working appendage, his left hand. He began guzzling the water as Lin mounted Homer and walked him and his packhorse over to Fuzzy's gelding and packhorse then took his reins and led them to Fuzzy's body.

He unbuckled Fuzzy's gunbelt, rolled it and slipped it into the gelding's saddlebags then recovered his Winchester '73, slipped it into his scabbard before picking up the body and tossing it over the saddle.

After tying down the body, he mounted Homer again and led the three horses back to Ike who was still alive, but much less

186

animated with Lin's empty canteen on the ground by his side letting a small river of water flow across the dirt.

Lin stepped down and Ike's eyes followed his approach, but he remained silent after Lin arrived. Lin picked up Ike's '76, did a quick examination of the rifle then slipped it into his buckskin mare's scabbard before returning to Ike.

Ike was staring at him as Lin dropped to his heels to ask him a question, but he soon realized that Ike's stare was permanent, so he reached over and closed his eyelids. He remained sitting on his heels just looking at Ike McCall's body for almost a minute before he sighed unbuckled his gunbelt then slid it out from under his body, rolled it, stood and dropped it into the saddlebag.

Ike was heavier than Fuzzy, and Lin was getting tired, so Lin decided to wait for a little while and pulled off Ike's saddlebags. He wasn't sure if he'd find gold or cash but was relieved to find almost fifteen hundred dollars in bundled twenty dollar notes inside. It would save him from having to get the gold assayed. He put the money into his right-hand coat pocket as the one on his left was now useless after Ike's first shot.

He then walked to Fuzzy's horse, opened his saddlebags and found a similar amount, shoved it into his pocket before taking Fuzzy's canteen and emptying it before taking a deep breath and returning to put Ike's body on his horse.

It was sundown when he finally began his ride back to Denver, four hours away.

As he rode, he reviewed the gunfight as he always did to find where he'd made mistakes, and the most glaring one he'd made was when he'd hesitated before shooting Fuzzy Villers. *Why hadn't he taken the shot right away?* He knew that he'd felt a sense that he was cheating because of his superior range, but he'd always had that advantage. *Why did he wait until Fuzzy had a better chance of killing him?*

He knew it had nothing to do with Julia because if it had, he would have shot them both when he had a real advantage. It had to be something else, and he thought it had to be because of the miners. He'd killed fourteen men, and maybe even one or two of them hadn't abused the women. He'd never know the answer to that question either. As much as the terrifying memories of killing all of the outlaws had bubbled away in the back of his mind, dropping that mountain on the miners was much worse.

Now he had to go to Boulder and Fort Collins and kill four more men. He hoped that he could do it without trying to give them a fair chance to kill him.

It was about an hour before midnight when Lin stepped down in front of the sheriff's office, tied off Homer and crossed the boardwalk.

He must have looked a sight when the deputy on duty looked up and saw the freshly scratched face with its five-day growth of beard covered in dust and the blood left on his clothes from the bodies he had loaded onto their saddles.

But he was impressed when the nonplused deputy simply asked, "Can I help you, mister?"

"My name is Lin Chase. I'm a bounty hunter and have the bodies of Fuzzy Villers and Ike McCoy outside."

The deputy rose and asked, "You sure it's them?"

"Yes, sir. I talked to Ike McCall before he died. He told me where I could find the other four men who kidnapped seven women up in Albany County in Wyoming Territory and sold them to miners. I got the women back home safely, but I'm hunting those bastards down."

"Let's go look at them and I'll see what we can do."

"I appreciate it, Deputy."

Lin followed the deputy out to the horses and watched as he began to examine the bodies. He was shocked by the damage caused by the .50 caliber rounds, but all of the holes were in the front, more or less, so there was no question of drygulching.

He turned to Lin and asked, "What did you use to take them down?"

"I have a pair of Winchester '76 muskets that are chambered for the Winchester .50-95 Express cartridge."

"Maybe we should get one of those, Mister Chase. Can you help me lead the horses a few blocks down the street to Lysander's Mortuary?"

"Absolutely."

As they led the two body-laden horses, Homer and the two packhorses down the gaslit street drawing the stares of the few inhabitants still awake, Lin began telling the deputy the story from the day he found the Lampley farmhouse devoid of the women. When they reached the mortuary, Deputy Harry Torrance had to wake Herbert Lysander, the son of the owner who was living in an apartment above the morgue before they could start unloading the bodies.

It was well after midnight when they left the mortuary to take the horses to Hembree's Livery, again waking the owner.

Lin was still telling the story when they returned to the sheriff's office and walked inside.

They sat down and Deputy Torrance said, "I need you to come by later this morning and write a statement, but I don't see a problem. We'll wire Sheriff Ward to let him know what happened, too."

"I appreciate it, Deputy. I'll head over to the Metropolitan so I can get some sleep and get cleaned up."

"I'll see you in the morning."

"Yes, sir," Lin said as he stood.

Deputy Torrance gave him a short wave then began writing his report as Lin left the sheriff's office, turned left and headed for the Metropolitan Hotel.

He entered the Metropolitan Hotel, saw the clerk behind the desk gape at his appearance but didn't say anything, so he just asked for a room, paid the four dollars for the suite because of the bath then climbed the stairs to room 211 with his saddlebags over his shoulder.

After he was in the room, he lit one of the four lamps then removed his bloody coat, looked at the damage from the .45 and knew it was beyond salvage. After removing the cartridges from the loops and the cash from the pocket, he tossed it and his hat into the trash can then stripped and set his clothes aside before walking into the bathroom carrying the kerosene lamp.

He set it down and saw his face in the mirror then understood why he had spooked the desk clerk. The scratches were swollen and still red giving him a monstrous appearance. There were two on the right and three on the left side of his face. As he examined the scars, all he could think of was how tortured Julia must have been when she made them.

He walked back to his saddlebags took out his toothbrush and powder as well as his shaving kit that hadn't had much use lately. He set the shaving kit near the sink but brushed his teeth and washed his face in plain white soap before leaving the bathroom with the lamp then blowing it out and crawling under the covers.

As he lay there, he spent some time trying to push the fresh memories of the gunfight behind a heavy iron door of good memories that all included Julia but was failing as he drifted off to sleep.

———

Lin was dreaming and he knew it was a dream even as he sat in the saddle. His first clue was that he wasn't riding Homer, but a sad excuse for a horse with a swayed back and a thick rust-colored coat that bordered on fur. He scanned the horizons and found them empty. They were more than just unpopulated, there were no mountains or streams or even trees. It was just a brown emptiness that surrounded him as the ancient horse plodded along.

He suddenly heard hoofbeats behind him and twisted in the saddle wondering how anyone could have snuck up on him so quickly. He saw Fuzzy and Ike both just fifty yards away with their Winchesters leveled at him, but they weren't normal Winchesters. They were enormous even bigger than his Sharps.

Lin panicked dropped to the old horse's neck and rammed his heels into the animal's flanks demanding that he run, but the nag just kept walking.

His heart was exploding in his chest as he began to shout for the horse to gallop as he turned to see Ike and Fuzzy then screamed when he saw that they were just a few feet behind him and had the muzzles of their oversized Winchesters just inches from his face with the bores looking like cannons.

It was Fuzzy who said in a normal voice that echoed from the mouth of his gun, "It's inevitable, Chase."

As Lin continued to scream giant clouds of gunsmoke and flame erupted from both muzzles and he tried to close his eyes as he could see the two cannonball-sized bullets screwing their way towards him.

He bolted into a sitting position with his heart still pounding wondering if he had screamed in the room or just in the nightmare. He wiped the sweat from his forehead as he sat up, still shaking from the incredible fear that had just left him.

He crawled out of bed pulled his pocket watch from his pants pocket and checked the time. It was close enough to morning that there was no reason to return to bed and risk another nightmare. He'd had them before but none this intense, and he believed it would only get worse. His mental trick of keeping the bad memories at bay was failing.

So, in the wee hours of the morning, Lincoln James Chase walked to the bathroom and drew a bath to cleanse the outside, wishing he could do the same for his soul.

CHAPTER 6

A clean shaven, freshly bathed Lin Chase left his room at the Metropolitan Hotel early the next morning having left his gunbelt in the room. He had the money-filled saddlebags over his shoulder and was coatless as he stopped at the desk paid for another night's stay then walked to the hotel restaurant for breakfast.

Shaving had been a challenge with the scratches, but the swelling had diminished, and the angry red had already faded to just plain scarlet, so they weren't so bad. He still was concerned that others would misinterpret the scratches and brand him a womanizer who had gotten his due, but no one knew him in Denver, so he supposed it didn't matter.

When the waitress took his order, she did look at him askance, but he still smiled, placed his order and began to sip his coffee, thinking about how the best way to get to Boulder to find Hound Jones and Arnie Jacobsen. He'd probably take the train rather than ride. Once he arrived in Boulder, he'd ask around about the two men and maybe he'd use the local law in this case.

The waitress brought his order almost startling him having not realized that he had been deep in thought for almost five minutes.

As he ate, he began setting the day's schedule. He'd go to the sheriff's office first to write his statement then go to the large clothing store for a new not-so-recognizable wardrobe before taking the noon train for Boulder.

He pulled out his pocket watch after the waitress had cleared the table then stood, left fifty cents next to the empty coffee cup, hung his saddlebags over his shoulder and left the restaurant.

Once outside in the brisk Colorado air, he shivered slightly then turned right and began to step along the already crowded boardwalk studying the townsfolk as they went about their daily lives and wondered what he would be doing with the rest of his life.

Lin reached the sheriff's office, opened the door and stepped inside finding two different deputies drinking coffee and talking, one behind the desk and the other sitting on the desk. Both turned to look at him as he closed the door behind him.

"Can we help you?" the one sitting on the desk asked as he stood.

"I came in late last night with some bodies and talked to Deputy Torrance. He said I needed to stop by this morning and write a statement."

"We read his report. You're Lin Chase?"

"Yes, sir. Where can I write my statement?"

"Come with me if you don't mind. I think we need to see Sheriff Anson first."

Lin nodded, not surprised by the need to see the top man, then followed the deputy down a long hallway before reaching an open office door.

The deputy rapped on the door jamb then said, "Boss, Mister Chase is here."

"Send him in, Lee, and you stick around."

Deputy Lee waved him into the office and a few seconds later, Lin was sitting before the sheriff of Arapahoe County, Colorado with Deputy Lee Gunderson standing behind him.

"I read Deputy Torrance's report but if you could, I need to hear it myself."

"Yes, sir," Lin replied then began his narration.

When he finished, the sheriff said, "We already sent a telegram to Sheriff Ward. I'm sure he'll be grateful for killing two of the bastards that had bushwhacked his deputies. Deputy Gunderson will show you where you can write out your statement. I'll notify the ones who offered the rewards on Fuzzy Villers and Ike McCall."

"Thanks, Sheriff," Lin replied then rose and followed Deputy Gunderson to a surprisingly large office space where he sat down and began to write his statement.

It took longer to write the statement than the actual gunfight had lasted by quite a large margin. He spent over thirty minutes writing while it had only taken three minutes to kill the two men.

When he dropped off his report at the front desk, Sheriff Anson said, "You can take those horses and gear when you leave. They're yours to dispose of as you see fit."

"Thanks, Sheriff. I'll be leaving on the noon train to track down the other four. The two who shot the deputies are still out there."

The sheriff shook his hand and said, "Good luck then, Mister Chase."

Lin nodded, hung his saddlebags over his shoulder then gave the three lawmen a short wave turned and left the office.

The temperature outside was already moderating into the mid-fifties as he headed for the clothing store.

They had a wide selection of clothes, and he started by buying a new heavy coat with large pockets. This one was a light brown but the three pairs of britches he bought were all either tan or light gray. The four shirts were all lighter shades of brown or gray as were the two vests. He finally added a light gray Stetson to replace his destroyed flat black hat.

After paying for the large order, he donned the coat and hat, left the store and headed for the livery where he had left the horses. He was undecided what he'd do with them but held off the decision until he examined them more closely.

He found all of the animals in the corral beside the livery mixed with other horses before he entered the big barn doors of the livery and he found two liverymen inside. One was mucking out stalls and the other was shoeing a short mare.

"Mornin'," shouted the one mucking out the stalls.

"Howdy. I dropped off my gray gelding and four other horses last night and need to take a look at them."

"Sure thing. Let's go and check on 'em," he said as they turned to the right toward the corral.

He opened the corral gate and Lin walked in behind him.

Lin had originally thought about selling all three of the horses, but after more closely examining the buckskin mare and the red gelding, decided he'd keep the two animals and sell their packhorse.

They led Homer, his packhorse and the two new horses out to the barn where they began to saddle the three riding horses as they negotiated a price on the outlaws' packhorse, saddle and gear. Lin only wanted the Winchester '76, the two boxes of ammunition, and their pistols, which were already in their saddlebags anyway.

By the time that the animals were all ready to go, Lin had settled for just sixty dollars for the packhorse and the rest of the gear and supplies.

He pocketed the money and with the packhorse loaded again, he mounted Homer and headed for the train station with his bag of new clothes hanging from the buckskin's saddle horn.

Lin reached the train station with not much time to spare as the northbound train was pulling into the station. He quickly bought a ticket and tags for the four horses then after taking his bag of new clothes from the mare and putting it in one of the packhorse panniers, he led them to the stock corral and with his saddlebags over his shoulder hopped back onto the platform.

———

Hound Jones and Arnie Jacobsen had been in Boulder when Ike had told Lin of their location but that was before they had a minor altercation at Bisbee's Bar that night. For most men, it would have had no consequence at all, but Hound and Arnie knew that they had prices on their heads and a recent murder of two lawmen that might have made them not only more wanted but under greater scrutiny.

It had been a simple poker game and despite all of the cash that each man now had in his pocket, Arnie had dealt from the bottom of the deck to win a three-dollar pot. One of the other players had called him on it and tempers flared, and as all four men stood, the bartender put a quick end to it by pulling his shotgun and ordering all of them out of his establishment.

Hound and Arnie had quickly returned to their rooms at the Charlton House hotel, but were concerned that the incident would draw the interest of the local law.

So, the next morning, they rode out of Boulder heading south to Denver. Hound thought they might hook up with Fuzzy and Ike again.

By the time Lin's train was pulling out of Denver, they were already twelve miles south of Boulder.

———

Lin was staring at the mountains to the west of the tracks as the train hurtled north. He wasn't woolgathering but reviewing the descriptions of the next two outlaws he was hunting, Hound Jones and Arnie Jacobsen.

Neither was particularly notable as far as physical descriptions went, but Hound Jones had a nasty pedigree that eclipsed that of the other five in the group. He seemed to be nothing less than an evil, soulless man who enjoyed inflicting pain. His was the highest reward of the six men, and it was so with good reason. He'd murdered four men that they knew of, had raped six times that had been reported, and had assaulted and maimed over a dozen. Lin wondered how the seven women, or even the male members of the family had avoided even worse treatment with Hound in the mix.

His nickname wasn't because he had a dog-like appearance, but because early on in his criminal career, he'd bitten off the ear of one of his victims then howled. He was the one who gave himself the moniker after that because he thought that Wolf was overdone.

Arnie Jacobsen was almost gentlemanly by comparison, having committed just a single murder before the recent killing of George Cobb. But these two men were the ones who, according to Julia, had been the ones that had ambushed the two deputies.

He may be risking even more intense nightmares, but Lin really needed to find these two and put them under the ground.

The train was already slowing down to take on water at Coal Creek when Lin spotted the two riders heading south on the nearby roadway. If there had been more traffic on the road, he might not have paid them so much attention, but they were the only ones there to attract his eyes.

They were just thirty feet away as the rider closer to the train looked straight at Lin but was probably just looking at the passenger car. It was those cold, lifeless eyes that told him he was looking at Hound Jones. Normal men looked at trains with a hint of curiosity, but the man looking at him had a malevolent stare.

Lin didn't waste time as the train continued to slow. He stood, tossed his saddlebags over his shoulder and walked down the aisle to the front of the passenger car.

As the train crawled into the small station, Lin stepped down onto the platform and walked to the stock corral.

He spotted the stock manager standing near the loading ramp holding the reins of a handsome black gelding, opened the gate and trotted over to the man.

"Excuse me, sir. Could I get my four animals out now? I have a ticket to Boulder, but I need them now."

"Sure, mister. Got your tags?" he asked.

Lin pulled the four tags out of his left pants pocket and handed them to the stock manager. He then led the black gelding up the ramp, opened the doors to the stock car and after taking the departing horse inside, he emerged with all four of Lin's animals three minutes later.

Lin then asked, "Could I leave the packhorse and the other two with you? I should be back in a few hours. If I'm not back by tomorrow, you can keep them."

The man grinned and said, "You got yourself a deal, mister."

Lin nodded, then quickly mounted Homer and left the corral then the station as he headed south on the road at a fast trot.

It wasn't long before he spotted the two men and then slowed Homer to a medium trot knowing he'd still be gaining on them.

———

Hound and Arnie had no reason to suspect that anyone was trailing them now. They'd been checking their backtrail after leaving Boulder, but once the town had disappeared from sight, they relaxed their vigilance.

They'd stopped for a quick lunch at a local eatery in Coal Creek but weren't worried about the law trailing them anymore.

So, they kept their slow, rhythmic pace as they headed for Denver expecting to be there by six o'clock.

———

As Lin closed the gap to less than a mile behind the two outlaws, he was thinking about how to approach them and the feelings of guilt were already beginning to tickle his mind. He kept trying to convince himself that the two men were murderers and worse and even if he shot them both in the back at five hundred yards, he'd be innocent in the eyes of the law. His arguments failed as he knew they would, but he still had to come up with some way of stopping them.

Twenty minutes later, he was less than a half a mile behind the two men and they still hadn't seen him, but he was about to change that.

He pulled his Winchester free cocked the hammer then just pointed it into the air and pulled the trigger.

———

Hound and Arnie weren't even talking when the loud report rippled across the open ground startling them both before they wheeled their horses around and spotted Lin still riding toward them.

"Who the hell is that?" Arnie shouted.

"Must be the law!" Hound yelled back.

Arnie quickly scanned the surrounding landscape for cover and yelled, "To the west, about two hundred yards!"

Hound didn't even look that way before he ripped his horse's reins in that direction and set him off at a gallop and was soon joined by Arnie.

Lin watched them both bolt from the roadway and could see where they were headed. It was a good defensive position almost like the one the Whitacre brothers had used but without the mountain behind it. There were a series of large boulders before a low ridge that was no more than twelve feet high. He slowed Homer to a slow trot and turned off the road to follow, feeling more in control of the situation now.

———

Hound and Arnie reached the boulders and had their Winchesters in their hands as they hurriedly dismounted and let their horses loose before they raced behind the protective rock.

Once they were safe or at least believed that they were, Hound said loudly, "What do you think, Arnie? He can't get too close to us without exposing himself."

"He could shoot our horses."

Hound thought about it before replying, "I don't figure he'll do that."

Arnie then asked, "How'd he get so close? We didn't have any trailers when we left Boulder."

"How the hell do I know? He's here now, and that's the only thing we gotta worry about."

With the hammers to their repeaters cocked, both men just watched as Lin approached wondering what he was planning.

———

Once they had made their run, Lin had simple returned to his routine methods for tracking and capturing criminals. Both of them were facing hanging, and Hound could be hanged in any of four different jurisdictions, so Lin didn't expect them to surrender.

He slipped his Winchester back into its scabbard and pulled the Sharps. His new coat didn't have any loops sewn on the inside yet and probably never would, so when he was about six hundred yards out, he pulled Homer to a stop then dismounted, walked back to his saddlebags and took out a box of .50-110 cartridges. He then took eight of the big rounds and slipped them into his right coat pocket before chambering one, returning the box to his saddlebags then taking off his new hat and hanging it on the saddle horn.

He then pulled the Winchester back out of its scabbard and walked fifty yards away from Homer to keep him safe.

————

Arnie squinted in the high sun and said, "Hound, how come he's got two Winchesters?"

"That other one with the scope ain't no Winchester, Arnie. I think we might have Lin Chance over there."

"He ain't wearin' no black hat or coat. How do you figure that it's him?"

"He rides a dark gray horse, and I don't care about that hat or coat. I'm pretty sure it's him."

"So, what do we do?"

Hound laughed and said, "Nothin'. What the hell can we do? We'll just have to wait him out. He ain't gonna fire that long gun forever, then we can rush him 'cause he's away from his horse."

Arnie smiled and replied, "You're right, Hound. How many shots do you figure he'll take?"

"Beats me, but it'll take him about four or five seconds to reload that beast, so after he fires, there'll be enough time to take a peek."

"What if he's faster than that?" Arnie asked.

"He's about six hundred yards out and if you stick your head out, you'll have about a full second to duck back down before the bullet gets here."

"Oh," Arnie replied having no intention of risking the accuracy of Hound's estimate. If he wanted to peek, let him do it.

———

Lin laid the Winchester on the ground with the barrel resting on a loaf-sized rock as he set up for his first shot with the Sharps.

He'd seen Hound hide behind one of the boulders on the left side and Arnie was on the right. Now it was just a question of what strategy they would use to get closer to him. The smart thing for them to do would be to sneak around the other side of the boulders and wait for him to fire. Then they could rush him with a zigzag, knowing how difficult it would be to hit them with the Sharps at range. With the reload delay, they would only need thirty seconds or so to get within lobbing range of their Winchesters.

Lin always assumed that they'd be smart which is why he had the Winchester with him.

He finally settled the reticles on the Arnie's rock released the first trigger then held his breath and squeezed the second. The Sharps announced its presence as the big gunsmoke cloud billowed from the muzzle and the fifty caliber round pushed the air aside as it crossed the six hundred and four yards arriving at the boulder above Arnie's head before the sound reached their ears.

The granite exploded causing Arnie to screech, "Jesus!" before ducking and covering his head from the shards and dust that surrounded him when the rolling sound wave arrived.

Knowing what might be coming and having it show up were two different things.

Hound didn't make a sound but quickly ducked his head letting his hat deflect the rocks that peppered the brim and crown.

Lin quickly reloaded then shifted the sights to Hounds rock and began his countdown. When he reached zero and pulled the trigger but wasn't surprised when his second shot passed over the top of Hound's boulder and slammed into the dirt of the ridge behind them.

"What's he shootin' at?" asked Arnie loudly.

Hound snickered then answered, "I heard he has this trick where he figures one of us is stupid enough to take a look after he shoots his first round."

Arnie glared at Hound and asked, "Why didn't you warn me?"

Hound shrugged then replied, "I figured if you wanted to look and get your head blown off, it'd be fun to watch."

Arnie stared at Hound but said nothing as he sat behind his boulder and waited for more shots.

Lin reloaded the Sharps but after another fifteen seconds, figured that they weren't about to stick their heads out from behind those rocks for a while, so he decided to waste a round then move in closer.

He took a few seconds to aim at Hound's rock then fired, making a big notch in the top of his boulder and showering the two men with more rocks and dust.

As soon as he'd fired, Lin snatched the Winchester then began to run toward their hiding place. The only thing he was worried about was if they suddenly decided to go around the outside of their boulders to rush him. It would put him in a bad situation.

The echoes of his last shot were still bouncing off of the rocks when Hound decided to move from under his big boulder and duck walk behind some smaller rocks, hoping that Lin didn't see him when he crossed between the gaps.

Once Arnie watched him leave, he felt exposed then turned and followed him rather than going in the opposite direction.

Lin hadn't spotted Hound when he was briefly exposed as he crossed the space between the boulders, but he caught the flash of movement as Arnie passed right behind him which let him know that at least one of them was moving. To Lin, it meant that they were now moving in opposite directions in preparation for a rush.

He was less than two hundred yards out when he dropped to the ground setting the Sharps to his side, before he cocked the hammer to the Winchester and waited for them to appear, aiming at the left side where he'd seen the motion. He was certain that one would come from that side but believed the other would appear from the other side as well. It was just going to be a matter of timing.

Hound knew that Arnie was behind him but didn't really care. He knew that Chase was six hundred yards out and he'd be able to take a good look before he could swing that Sharps in his direction, so when he slowed and took his peek from the side of the boulder, he was surprised not to see him at all. He could see his gray horse standing where he'd left him, so he hadn't ridden anywhere. *Where the hell was he?*

Lin spotted a head pop out from the side boulder and realized that they weren't going to rush him after all. He shifted the Winchester's sights slightly to the left and soon had the head targeted, but he didn't fire. He waited.

Once Hound had concluded that Lin wasn't where he'd expected to find him, he stuck his head out a little further then quickly scanned to his left and spotted him on the ground around two hundred yards away.

He yanked his head back behind the rock and turned to Arnie.

"He's lyin' on the ground a couple of hundred yards out."

"What do we do, Hound?" Arnie asked almost in panic.

Hound had no idea what to do. He had never been trapped like this before, and he regretted leaving their horses out in the open ground.

Then he had a revelation of sorts when he turned to Arnie and said, "I got it, Arnie. I'll stay here and after a few seconds, I'll start throwing shots in his direction while you circle around the other side and sneak up behind him. Don't fire until you're in range though."

Arnie thought about it for a few seconds then said, "Okay," turned and headed back.

Hound watched him leave and was sure that Chase would spot him as he passed the gap. Then he'd change his attention to Arnie's side of the rocks. He knew at this range, the bounty hunter's Winchester was as ineffective as his was, but once Arnie popped out into view, it would give him enough time to get close and start throwing .44s at Chase before he could turn that Sharps in his direction.

Lin did see the sudden shadow pass the gap and if it hadn't been for the head popping out and taking a look, he might have turned to look for the moving man, but he wouldn't have to worry about the one heading to his right for another thirty seconds, so he kept his eyes and sights trained on where he'd seen that head.

Hound slid close to the end of the boulder and cocked his Winchester's hammer. Arnie should be close to the end by now, and he didn't want to waste a lot of ammunition, so he waited a little longer before slowly sliding the barrel of his repeater out from behind the boulder without exposing himself then pulled the trigger.

Lin had seen the first six inches of Hound's Winchester and expected to see the shooter a few seconds later. He took aim, but when the muzzle stopped moving then blossomed with gunsmoke, he was confused as to the shooter's motive for a few seconds. The man who'd fired had no intention of either hitting him or showing himself, which meant he was a distraction for the second man.

He didn't have much time, so rather than shift his attention to his right, he aimed at the man's Winchester barrel and forearm. He could barely make out the edge of his fingers as he held the repeater but took careful aim as accuracy was more important than speed despite the possibility of the second shooter coming around behind him.

Lin squeezed the trigger but didn't wait to see if he'd hit the target as he quickly shifted to the right as his .50 caliber shot slammed into the wooden forearm just two inches in front of Hound's fingers. After splintering the wood support, it struck the magazine tube shattering the steel and causing one of the rimfire cartridges to ignite, firing its bullet into the one before it, creating an almost instantaneous chain reaction. The destruction of Hound's Winchester took a fraction of a second, and Hound never understood what had happened to his trusty firearm as pieces of hot steel, wood and lead ripped through the air with many of them finding a home in Hound's face and chest.

The sounds of his exploding repeater overcame Hound's screams for a second before his howls were all that came from behind the boulder.

Arnie had crossed around behind the last boulder on the other side when Hound was hit and momentarily stopped when his panic returned with the horrendous sound, but his need for self-preservation took control, so he cocked the hammer to his Winchester and raced past the last few feet of protection spotted Lin on the ground and began to fire.

The ground around Lin began erupting in dirt volcanoes as he centered his sights on Ike and squeezed his trigger.

Arnie had just fired his fourth shot when he watched the flame and gunsmoke belch from Lin's Winchester and never had the chance to lever in a second round as the large caliber bullet slammed into his chest obliterating his breastbone then his heart and lungs before it left through his back.

Arnie wobbled on his feet then dropped straight to the ground as his legs gave way.

Hound's wailing was the only sound left as gunsmoke hung over the open ground.

Lin stood, picked up his Sharps and began to walk back to Homer temporarily ignoring Hound's screeching. He still didn't know which one was still alive as he slid both of his rifles back into Homer's scabbards pulled his hat back on then mounted and started walking the gelding to the boulders. He pulled his Colt but didn't cock the hammer yet as he passed their horses and continued toward the center of the boulders rather than give the screamer a chance at shooting him. He didn't think the man was faking the injury, but injured men could still shoot.

He dismounted then walked behind the boulders and headed to the left where the volume of Hound's howls had dropped.

Lin spotted him lying on the ground with his face bleeding profusely as he shook, so he holstered his pistol as he drew closer.

When he was within a few feet, he knew that it was Hound who had been hit by the exploding rifle that laid next to him. His face was a disaster with the right part of his jaw missing and blood still leaking out from all over his chest and neck.

Lin didn't say anything as he walked past Hound and picked up the stricken rifle. He'd never seen anything like it before. He'd seen a Henry that had a barrel explode but this Winchester was little more than a stock, a receiver and trigger assembly attached to a mangled mass of metal.

He knew he couldn't do anything for Hound, so he turned and walked back to where their horses stood with Homer. He led one of them to where Arnie's body lay in an awkward folded position then laid the body out flat went through is pockets and was surprised to find a huge wad of cash in his pants pocket rather than his saddlebags. After sticking it in his new jacket's left pocket, he stripped the gunbelt from the body, wrapped it and dropped it into his saddlebags before lifting Arnie and tossing him onto the saddle.

Lin didn't tie him down yet but led him back to the other horses and tied him to Homer before leading the second horse back to where Hound's silent body lay on the ground.

After stripping his gunbelt, and putting it away, he searched the body found his cash and put it with Arnie's before he took a drink of water from Hound's canteen then took a deep breath and hoisted the body onto the saddle. He led the horse back to Homer fashioned a trail rope for the two horses then lashed down the bodies.

He took one quick look through their saddlebags but found nothing special before he mounted Homer and started back toward Boulder.

For some reason, killing these two hadn't bothered him nearly as much as it had when he'd killed Fuzzy and Ike McCall. He wasn't sure if it was because he'd only shot Hound's rifle or that Arnie had been close to hitting him. Whatever the reason, he was in a decent mood as he headed north to collect his horses.

———

When he arrived in Coal Creek an hour later, he picked up his packhorse and two spare horses without explaining anything to the stock manager then stopped at the same diner that Hound and Arnie had eaten lunch before quickly setting out for Boulder.

He kept moving at a medium trot as he rode allowing himself some much-needed time to think about Julia. He'd only been gone two days, but so much had happened during that brief time that it felt more like two weeks and he wasn't done yet. He still had to go to Fort Collins and find the Hilliard brothers.

———

At the Lampley farm, the entire family was in a state of great concern as Mary hadn't come out of her catatonic state. She hadn't eaten since she'd been back, and Julia had been her nurse as she'd cleaned her and was able to get her to drink some water.

They'd tried everything including bringing Doctor McIntyre from Cheyenne to see her, but Mary Lampley still was non-responsive. The doctor had put in a tube down her nose to give her some nourishment, but they all knew that if she didn't come back to them soon, she'd die from starvation.

No one would say it, but they all thought that it might be the only way she'd ever find peace again. Mary Lampley had simply surrendered.

———

Lin rode into Boulder after the sun had dipped below the horizon, but he still attracted a lot of attention as he rode to the office of the Boulder County sheriff. He'd never met the man or any of his deputies, so he wasn't sure what to expect as he dismounted before the office and tied off Homer.

Boulder had grown considerably since his last visit, so he wasn't surprised to find the office open and manned even at this late hour.

The deputy behind the desk glanced up as he entered and asked the customary, "What can I do for you?"

"My name is Lin Chase, and I have the bodies of Hound Jones and Arnie Jacobsen outside. I need to have you verify their identities before we get them to the morgue."

"You the bounty hunter?" he asked as he stood.

"I am. These two were among the six men who kidnapped seven women and sold them to a bunch of miners. I dropped off the first two last night in Denver and I'll be heading out after the last pair tomorrow. These were the two that ambushed two Albany County deputies a few days ago, killing one of them."

"I heard about that," he said as he grabbed his hat and followed Lin out the door.

As he examined the two men, Lin asked, "How'd you hear about it?"

"It was in this morning's newspaper. I guess they wired the story from Denver."

Lin nodded as the deputy turned to him and said, "I'll go ahead and write this up. Hound was a real mess. What did you shoot him with, a cannon?"

"Nope. I hit his Winchester's barrel and it must have set off some of his cartridges because it went off like a loud firecracker."

They entered the office again as the deputy asked, "How far out was that shot?"

"Around two hundred yards, I think."

The deputy took a seat behind the desk and shook his head as Lin sat down and gave him the information for the rewards then had to give him the details of the story in the paper as he wrote his statement.

It was close to a repeat of what had happened in Denver when they led the horses down to the mortuary dropped off the bodies then left the horses at the closest livery. The deputy was awed when he saw the mangled Winchester that had killed Hound, so Lin told him he could keep it for evidence.

It wasn't until almost midnight before Lin was able to finally get a room and strip out of his old clothes. He slid under the covers thinking that he was safe from nightmares tonight because he hadn't had the same sense of guilt he'd had after killing Fuzzy and Ike.

He was wrong.

Less than an hour later, he bolted upright soaked in sweat as his heart raced. He knew he hadn't screamed this time but that didn't make it any less terrifying.

But he knew he needed sleep, so even though another nightmare might arrive, he laid back down and closed his eyes falling back asleep just minutes later.

––––––

Lin was already having breakfast at seven o'clock, not having experienced another nightmare. He was dressed in his new clothes, giving him a totally different appearance. His scars were still there and didn't look much different than they had the day before, but he didn't pay them much attention anymore.

After breakfast, he left the hotel with his saddlebags over his shoulder and headed for the livery. He didn't care for either of the two horses he'd gotten yesterday, so he briefly negotiated with the liveryman for the sale and let them both go with their saddles for a hundred dollars.

He was planning on riding to Fort Collins but changed his mind when he found that the northbound Colorado Central train left at 11:10, so he led the buckskin mare, the red gelding and his packhorse to the train station again and left all four animals with the stock manager before buying his tickets and tags, bringing the tags back to the station manager then walking to the newsstand near the platform and buying a copy of the *Rocky Mountain News*.

After taking a seat at one of the benches, he opened the newspaper and just as the deputy had mentioned, there was the story of the gunfight between the notorious bounty hunter Lin Chase and the two infamous outlaws, Fuzzy Villers and Ike McCall. He assumed they got the story from his official statement, because it was reasonably accurate, including referring to him as 'the notorious bounty hunter'.

———

In Fort Collins, Dick and Ron Hilliard had also read the story that morning, and it had a dramatic effect on their plans to stay in town for a few more weeks.

"You figure he's comin' our way?" asked Ron as they ate breakfast.

"It sounds like he's comin' north from Denver. He caught Fuzzy and Ike when they were ridin' south. It even said he was heading for Boulder next. I'll bet one of 'em talked."

"So, which way do we go?"

Dick shook his head and replied, "Really, Ron? Which way do we go? We can't go south, and there ain't much east of here. We could go west, but there's nothin' there either. I think we'd best be headed north again before he gets here."

"And go where? They're lookin' for us up there, too."

"We follow our own backtrail and cut behind Laramie and then head west from there. We can ride to Green River and get the train west to California."

"It's a long way to Green River, Dick. What will we do for supplies? We don't even have a packhorse."

"We got a lot of money, Ron. We get out of here fast, we head north, stop at Lone Tree pick up supplies and a horse then cut northwest."

Ron wasn't sure it wouldn't be better to ride straight west, but Dick was right that there was nothing there, so he finally nodded.

After finishing their breakfast, they checked out of their hotel room then headed for the hotel's livery to get their horses saddled and just as Lin's train was pulling into Boulder, the brothers left Fort Collins riding north.

———

By the time Lin stepped down in Fort Collins, the Hilliards were already twenty miles north of town.

After claiming his four animals, Lin began his search for the brothers at the nearest livery but still hadn't had any clues after visiting the last of the four liveries in town. That left the hotel liveries, and there were four of those, too.

He had a quick lunch before going to the first of the hotel liveries, the Manhattan House's, where he finally got an answer to his question, but it wasn't a good one. The hotel's liveryman told him that the men had saddled their horses and left about five hours earlier, saying that they wouldn't return.

Lin gave the man a silver dollar then walked quickly out of the livery mounted Homer and headed to the eastern edge of Fort Collins and stopped at the crossroads. The road ran north and south from here and he had a choice to make. He hadn't seen anyone riding south as the train headed north, but that wasn't a sure thing. There were a few places where the road wasn't visible, and it was unlikely that they would ride north back toward Wyoming.

He sat on Homer for almost five minutes knowing that with each passing minute, they were getting further away. Finally, he turned Homer north. There were two reasons for his choice: he hadn't seen any riders, which decreased the likelihood that they'd headed south, and that newspaper story about Fuzzy and Ike meeting their ends north of Denver. It had even included his next destination, so it was more likely that they'd run away from the threat rather than into it.

Besides, heading north was getting closer to Julia and if he was close enough, he'd take a detour and see how she was doing.

He had the horses moving at a medium trot as Fort Collins receded in the background guessing that the Hilliards were a good thirty miles ahead of him by now. The distance was almost secondary as long as they stayed on the road. There was almost a full moon tonight and as long as the clouds stayed away, he'd be able to see them if they were camped out near the road. He didn't think they'd be camping out, as they didn't have a packhorse with them.

As he rode, he wondered where they were headed. Surely, they wouldn't show their faces in Laramie or Cheyenne, and he was a bit surprised they hadn't just taken the train out of town, but that didn't mean they couldn't board a train at one of the small stops along the way.

———

The Hilliards weren't thirty miles ahead, but only eighteen as they'd stopped at Bristol City rather than Lone Tree to buy a packhorse and some supplies. It was just a matter of good timing when they had arrived in the small town and spotted the livery across from the dry goods store. They didn't negotiate on the price of the packhorse and the sad excuse for a pack saddle, and only spent an hour and a half in the town before leaving again feeling much better about having the flexibility to leave the roadway whenever they chose. It was the main reason they had shied away from using the train. They didn't want to be so easily tracked and locked in a rolling coffin. All it would take would be a conversation with a ticket agent and a telegram to have some lawmen waiting for them. The next time they took a train, it would be to Oregon.

But on the road, they felt safe as they continued north and even stopped in Lone Tree for dinner before continuing north, looking for the northwest trail that passed south of Laramie.

―――

Lin stopped in Bristol City and asked the liveryman if they'd been seen and was pleased to hear that they'd passed through but displeased somewhat to learn they'd bought a packhorse. That meant he had to be more careful after dark to avoid overshooting them.

After letting the horses drink from the trough, he set out again as the sun began to set.

―――

Ron and Dick Hilliard were in Wyoming Territory and followed the trail they had followed leaving the territory as it cut northwest through the mountains. It wasn't an easy trail as it wound through passes and around almost impassable terrain, but it would take them past Fort Saunders before it reached the flatlands south of Laramie.

"When are we gonna stop, Ron?" Dick asked as they climbed a shallow pass.

218

Ron replied, "Just on the other side of the rise. We can even have a fire 'cause the moon is so bright we'd be able to see anybody that's followin'."

"That's good 'cause I'm kinda hungry."

Ron didn't answer as he guided his horse up the narrow pass. Neither man was really worried much about Lin Chase anymore after they'd spent their time in the saddle discussing the possibility. They concluded that even if he was chasing them, he'd have to find Hound and Arnie before he went to Fort Collins. Ron had convinced his brother that Lin was still in Boulder.

––––––

Lin was twelve miles behind the brothers and had been fortunate to have caught their departure from the road. A hay wagon had pulled onto the roadway just south of Lone Tree and churned up the Hilliard brothers' trail, so Lin had actually ridden past where they'd made the turn to the northwest but noticed the decrease in hoofprints a few hundred yards later.

After chastising himself, he'd turned Homer and the three trailers around and searched the west side of the road and found the trail that they'd followed. It wouldn't have been devastating if he'd ridden all the way to Lone Tree, but it would have cost him a few hours.

Once he left the road, he found that their trail was more pronounced, and he noticed that there had been more horse traffic going in the opposite direction a few days before their trail and guessed that they were returning to where the six outlaws had started for Colorado.

Lin decided to stay on their trail after moonrise because he really didn't want to fall asleep and have another nightmare. He knew he was about four hours behind them and if they stopped to camp, he could catch up with them by morning.

————

Twenty minutes later, Ron and Dick Hilliard followed a crossing stream and left the trail then entered the trees before dismounting to set up their camp. Even though neither believed Lin was even in Fort Collins yet, it was always a good idea to make a campsite less visible.

After unsaddling their horses, Ron unloaded the packhorse while Dick built the fire and less than forty minutes after dismounting, they were sitting near the fire that was heating their coffeepot while they fried two small steaks in their new cast iron skillet that they'd bought in Bristol City.

"Say, Dick, we don't have to ride all the way to Green River, do we? I mean, now that we got the money, why don't we pick up the train in Howell? It's a lot closer."

"I don't know, Ron. It's still pretty close to Laramie. I'll tell you what, though. Let's head for Cooper's Lake. That's just another fifteen miles or so past Howell."

Ron grinned as he flipped the steak and said, "That's a good idea. We can reach it by tomorrow late and take the mornin' train to Oregon."

Dick smiled back at his brother. The enticing smell of the frying beef made him feel relaxed and confident that all of their problems were behind them.

————

Their problems were exactly six miles behind them as they began to eat their dinner. Lin had lost his light for almost an hour after sunset because the moon hadn't risen yet, so he'd had to slow down. But the trail itself didn't allow for deviations, and now that the almost full moon flooded the landscape with light, he was able to speed up slightly.

His only concern now was noise. In the night, it seemed as if every strike of those horseshoes on the rocky ground was amplified, and he had sixteen clad hooves making a lot of racket. He'd stopped twice since leaving the roadway to rest the horses and to check the droppings left by the Hilliards' horses, and knew he was getting close.

There was enough moon for him to check his watch and was surprised to find it was almost midnight. He thought briefly about setting up camp, but he wasn't tired as his adrenalin was keeping him awake, and he wanted to end this, so he kept his horses plodding along.

————

The Hilliards had let their cooking fire die as they unraveled their bedrolls and prepared to get some sleep.

Ron had just kicked off his boots when Dick said, "I'm gonna go and check the trail."

"What for? There ain't nobody there."

"I just got this feelin' all of a sudden. I'm probably just wound up too tight."

Ron snickered as he slid into his bedroll without further comment.

Dick walked away from the hidden campsite and headed for the trail about sixty yards away as Lin was reaching the summit of the small pass they had passed earlier.

Dick reached the trail, stopped and turned to the southeast and spotted Lin and his horses outlined on the top of the rise in the bright moonlight. He didn't panic but began backing away as he kept his eyes on the oncoming rider.

Once he was in the trees, he turned and ran the last few yards, grabbed his Winchester and said in an excited voice, "Ron, he's comin'! He's only about a mile back or so!"

Ron had already started extricating himself from his bedroll when Dick announced Lin's presence and was soon yanking on his boots. After strapping on his gunbelt, he snatched his Winchester and both brothers then made their way deliberately toward the trail, using the cover of the trees to hide their movement.

_____

Lin had missed Dick Hilliard and not because he was woolgathering. It was just one of those quirks of nighttime lighting where the shadows of the tall trees had hidden Dick from sight. If he had turned and run, then Lin probably would have spotted him. But now he was riding into an ambush and wasn't ready as he led the horses along the downslope.

_____

The Hilliards were waiting with cocked Winchesters behind trees just forty yards from the trail and could already hear the many hooves as the horses drew closer.

Their only real problem was that neither brother could see the other very well in the shadows of the trees even though they were only fifteen feet apart.

Dick was on the right side had a better view down the trail, so Ron loud whispered, "Can you see him yet?"

"No. Shut up, Ron!" Dick replied in a hushed voice.

———

Lin was four hundred yards away from their ambush site and hadn't heard them over the sound of the horses. He was completely unaware of their presence as he rode closer to their killing zone.

There was almost no wind, but almost meant didn't mean none, and there was an almost undetectable movement of air from the northwest carrying the scent of their horses with it.

When Lin was about eighty yards from where they waited, his horses picked up that scent and the buckskin mare flared her nostrils and nickered. None of his other horses reacted, but the Hilliards' newly acquired packhorse nickered in return.

Dick Hilliard swore under his breath and knew they'd lost their advantage, and as he already had Lin in his sights, he fired. His startled brother followed suit and pulled his trigger.

At eighty yards, they shouldn't have missed even in the moonlight, but both men had jerked their triggers in their haste and their .44s ripped past Lin without causing damage.

Lin had already been reaching for his Winchester when the muzzle flashes announced their locations, but he knew he was outlined by the moonlight, so he dropped across Homer's neck then slid off the side of the saddle to the ground then tossed aside his new hat.

Both brothers had seen him dismount but soon lost him in the same shadows that had kept Lin from spotting Dick. Ron thought he saw him and fired a second shot.

Lin was on the ground just on the other side of the trail. It was a very uncomfortable position with so many rocks pressing against his torso and legs, but he wasn't about to move as he cocked the hammer to his Winchester just before Ron took his second shot.

Lin marked the place of the muzzle flare and after setting his sights on the location, squeezed the trigger and quickly and painfully rolled three times to his right.

Just as Ron's right shoulder was being demolished by Lin's shot, Dick fired at Lin's muzzle flare before turning and rushing to help his brother.

Lin heard Dick's .44 ricochet off the rocks he'd just vacated as he waited in the shadows for another muzzle flare announcing the second shooter's location. He heard the scream from the one he'd hit but didn't know how badly he'd wounded him. With the power of the '76, any hit would probably be fatal, it was just a question of time.

Dick had set his Winchester down as he tried to stop his brother's bleeding.

"I'm dyin'! I'm gonna die, Dick!" Ron sobbed as his older brother looked down at him.

Dick could see the blood squirting out of a severed artery and knew it wouldn't be long and rage burst inside him.

"I'll kill the bastard for you, Ron!" he snarled

Ron was already drifting away as he gasped, "Kill him bad, Dick. Kill…"

Dick angrily picked up his Winchester levered in a fresh cartridge and turned back toward the trail.

He couldn't see the bounty hunter, but he was in a killing fury and nothing else mattered than to shoot the bastard who had killed his brother.

He took a step out of the trees and yelled, "Come and get me, Chase, you damned coward!"

Lin was startled when he saw Dick Hilliard step out and then shout a challenge. He could have put a fifty-caliber slug of lead through him without a problem but instead, he stood, leaving his Winchester by the side of the trail, and released his Colt's hammer loop.

Dick saw the bounty hunter as he stepped out of the shadows onto the trail without a Winchester and was momentarily confused, but it didn't matter. He had a rifle in his hands and his brother's killer didn't.

Lin stepped slowly forward and shouted, "You're the last one, Hilliard. Do you know why I'm hunting you?"

Dick had his Winchester aimed at Lin's chest and should have pulled the trigger but instead, he yelled back, "I've got a price on my head. That's all. I don't believe that newspaper story about chasin' after us 'cause of us takin' those women."

"Last year, you and your brother invaded the Lampley farmhouse and raped Mary Lampley and murdered her husband. You destroyed a family and took away someone they loved. I was going to chase after you and that bastard brother of yours even before you took the women. What you did to the women, especially my Julia, makes killing you even more necessary."

Dick couldn't have cared less about what Lin had said other than he'd called Ron a bastard and that hit him hard.

He muttered, "You're the bastard!" as he squeezed the trigger.

Lin was already moving to the right as soon as he finished his explanation, but he wasn't quite quick enough before Dick's Winchester erupted in flame in the moonlight and the .44 reached Lin in a fraction of a second ripping off a piece of his left bicep. He felt the bullet's heat but had to ignore the pain when he hit the ground on his right side as he cocked the hammer of his Colt and aimed at the moonlit Dick Hilliard a hundred feet away.

Dick thought he'd hit Lin, but was so angry, that he planned on emptying his Winchester into the bounty hunter. So, he was levering in another cartridge when he saw the muzzle flare from the ground and felt Lin's .44 slam into his chest. He staggered as the bullet blasted through ribs, his left lung, then more ribs before it left his body.

Dick went to his knees muttered, "Sorry, Ron," then fell onto his face.

Lin slowly stood, holstered his pistol and flipped the hammer loop in place before examining his wound. It wasn't much, but it was the first time he'd ever been shot, so he didn't know how bad he should feel right now.

He crossed the trail and when he reached Dick Hilliard, gave him a hard kick to make sure he was dead then walked to the trees to find his brother.

After finding Ron's body, he then walked to their horses, opened one of their saddlebags and pulled out a spare shirt and walked to the nearby stream. He cut off the the shirt's sleeves, then gingerly removed his own shirt and splashed icy water on the wound, examining it again in the moonlight before wrapping one of the sleeves around the damaged arm, tied it off then wrapped the second one around it. He then walked back to the trail and headed to his four horses who had wandered off the trail and were drinking from the stream.

He pulled one of his new shirts from the packhorse's pannier and put it on before leading the animals back to the Hilliard brothers' campsite then began to unsaddle all of the horses. With his arm wound, it took him a lot longer, and he wasn't looking forward to saddling so many horses in the morning but that was a problem for the morning.

He already decided that he wasn't going to bring the Hilliard brothers' bodies to Laramie. He'd tell Sheriff Ward what had happened. If they wanted to waste the time to send someone up on the trail to find the bodies, they could do that, but he didn't care if those two were eaten by the critters that were probably already nearby.

It was almost predawn when he had finally settled into his bedroll. He'd found their money but didn't bother counting it before he put the bundles of cash into his saddlebag with the others. Altogether, the six men had over nine thousand dollars on them. They'd been paid that much money by the miners so they could rape innocent women. *Why should he feel the least bit of guilt for killing such men?*

As he closed his eyes to get some sleep, he hoped that being shot would end the nightmares.

———

It was still dark when he opened his eyes and was confused. It had almost been the start of a new day when he had fallen asleep. Then as he stood, he realized he wasn't outside anymore but in the hallway that might have been a hotel, but there was only one door and it beckoned to him.

He walked slowly toward the door and hesitated, fearing what was on the other side. He tried to leave, but his feet were frozen to the floor. He watched as his hand, without his mind telling it to, reached for the brass doorknob and rotated it. Lin felt the coldness of despair flush though him as he heard the muffled click, then he swung the door open on its silent hinges seeing a room he'd never seen before but felt that he belonged there.

Everything in the room was either black or shades of dark gray and even the paper stacked on the desk was dark. Lin wondered how he'd be able to write on the black paper as he suddenly didn't want to be in the room anymore.

Then he knew why he was there. He had six memories that had to be put into the enormous vault on the other side of the room.

He shook his head and said aloud, "I'll do this later," but when he turned to leave, the six memories he was going to sentence to his vault were all standing behind him with grins on their faces, or in the case of Ike McCall, half of his face, the .50 caliber Winchester round having taken the other half away.

"You gotta do it, Chase," whispered Fuzzy Villers, "you can't leave us out here all alone."

Lin shook his head as he replied, "I can't. Not this time. Let me pass!"

Dick Hilliard put his icy cold palm on Lin's chest and laughed before he said, "You ain't goin' anywhere. Are you a sissy or somethin'? You were the big brave man when you shot all of us."

"That was different. Let me leave!"

Then the half-faced Ike McCall stepped so close that Lin could smell the putrid stench of death flowing from the massive cavern on the left side of his face.

"I'm gonna kiss you if you don't open the vault, Chase."

Lin quickly stepped away turned back to the room with his heart pounding wildly and approached the vault door, feeling the chilling presence of the six dead men behind him. The massive steel door seemed much larger and even more forbidding than he could have imagined, but Lin knew that if these six weren't placed inside, he'd never find peace again.

He reached the enormous, foot-wide dial and suddenly realized that he couldn't remember the combination. His mind was racing and approaching panic as he tried to recall the first number, but it just wasn't there anymore.

He turned to Fuzzy Villers and said, "I can't remember the combination. I can't!"

"I know the numbers, Chase. The first one is six."

Lin nodded, then turned back to the giant lock and spun it to six, each passing line sounding like a hammer striking an anvil.

When he reached six, Fuzzy said, "The next number is six."

Lin was about to argue that it had to be a different number, but as he rotated the dial slowly past zero and returning to six again, suddenly knew what the last number would be.

Fuzzy cackled, leaned close to his right ear and whispered, "Six."

Lin then rotated the dial counterclockwise back to six hearing an unearthly wail when it reached the number then placed his hand on the black handle that was the size of a rifle barrel and wasn't surprised to find that it wasn't cold steel that touched the palm of his hand but almost painfully hot metal.

He turned the handle but didn't have to pull the vault door open as it slowly began to move on its hinges. He quickly stepped back knowing that the six men weren't going into the vault, but all those that were inside were coming out. It was time. There was no more space in the vault.

He began slowly backpedaling as the six men behind him stood waiting off to the side as the others began to exit. But the first to leave weren't the miners. Leaving the vault first was a naked Julia followed by the other women, all of them not wearing a stitch and each one smiling contentedly as if they were happy with what had happened to them.

Lin kept backing up wanting to ask why they were there, but his mouth couldn't open as the miners began to exit the vault behind the women, their bodies mangled and misshapen. At their forefront was MoMo with his bloody groin then the women all turned and accepted the hands of their miner husbands as they all continued to step toward him.

Lin's eyes were bulging at the gruesome and horrifying sight when the Whitacre brothers finally emerged, the top of Hungry Jim's head missing and Willie with a rope around his neck. Then it was a crowd of other men that he'd killed that began to file out of the vault's abyss, all of them with black, colorless eyes.

When his back finally pressed against the back wall, his head whipped to the right to find the door, but it wasn't there anymore. There was no escape as he knew there wouldn't be.

He finally looked for Julia, her blue eyes gone having been replaced with the same lifeless black eyes of the others.

She and MoMo left the others and stepped before him.

In a deep, terrifying voice, MoMo said, "You think you stopped me from pleasurin' my wife, Chase? You didn't. I take her all the time now and she loves every second and begs me to do it. She spreads her legs, just like you told her to do."

Lin shook his head violently before searching Julia's eyes for even a speck of color but found nothing but blackness.

Julia then said in a chilling, un-Julia voice, "It's time now, Lin."

She then reached to his waist, pulled out his Colt and held it out to him.

Lin finally found his ability to speak and said, "Kill me then, Julia. Do it now!"

Julia shook her head slowly, smiled and took his hand, placed the Colt's grips in his palm and said, "No, Lin, you must do it. You killed all of them, and you are the only one who can kill yourself. You know that. It's inevitable."

Lin slowly lifted the Colt cocked the hammer, and as he brought it level, he looked at Julia then the other women before quickly scanning the thirty-one grinning faces of the dead men. Julia was right. This is inevitable.

He slowly pointed the muzzle at the bridge of his nose, the .44 caliber bore looking like a cave as he felt the trigger under his finger. He didn't close his eyes as he squeezed the trigger then saw the flash of gunpowder deep inside the chamber and then the point of the bullet as it began its spinning approach to end his life in slow motion.

Then he heard a nightmarish scream as the bullet left the muzzle and the heat and light exploded in front of his eyes.

He bolted upright in his bedroll, bathed in sweat with his heart thumping crazily against his ribs when he realized that he had been the source of the scream of terror.

The sun was already sending beams of light through the pines as Lin sat and recalled each second of the worst nightmare he'd ever experienced. It had been so vivid that he could replay the entire dream from the moment he'd seen that door.

He stayed sitting in the bedroll for another five minutes before he let out a deep breath and slipped free of the bedroll, pulled on his boots and prepared to complete the killing journey.

CHAPTER 7

As he led the six horses behind him, Lin was still shaken by the nightmare. He began to believe that he was close to madness for what he had done and could be a danger to others, especially at night. He was certain about one thing. He couldn't kill another man, no matter what he'd done or was about to do, including shooting him.

By the time the buildings of Laramie appeared on the horizon around mid-day, he had returned to a semblance of normalcy, having been able to concentrate on what he'd need to do now. He'd already taken the cash and created nine bundles of a thousand dollars each and knew what he would do with them. Two were already in his coat pocket.

It was just after two o'clock when Lin entered Laramie, attracting attention solely because of the number of saddled horses behind him.

He pulled up before the sheriff's office, dismounted and tied off Homer before crossing the boardwalk and entering, spotting Deputy Andy Wilson at the desk writing a report.

Andy looked up as Lin closed the door and said, "Lin! Am I glad to see you! We've been wondering what had happened since we received that telegram from Arapahoe County saying you got Fuzzy and Ike McCall."

"I'll let you and the sheriff know in a second. Is he in?"

"Sure. Let's go back to his office."

As Andy stood, Lin asked, "How's Orville?"

"He's doing as best as we could hope for, but we're not sure he'll be able to work as a deputy again. The doc was able to keep his foot, but he'll always walk funny. If he comes back, it'll be a while."

They reached the sheriff's office and Deputy Wilson tapped on the door before opening it and said, "Boss, Lin Chase is here."

"Come on in," Sheriff Ward said as he automatically stood behind his desk.

Lin followed Andy Wilson inside and after shaking the sheriff's hand, they all took their seats.

"So, Lin, what happened north of Denver? I only got the gist of it from Miles Anson down in Arapahoe County in that telegram."

Lin explained about the gunfight north of Denver with Fuzzy and Ike then when he finished, he told them how he'd engaged in a second shootout with Hound and Arnie Jacobsen south of Boulder. Lin went into great detail about how Hound and Arnie died because they were the two that had killed Deputy Cobb and crippled Orville.

"What about the Hilliard brothers," the sheriff asked, "Are they still on the loose?"

"No, Jimmy. I trailed them north out of Fort Collins and they almost ambushed me just a few miles southeast of here last night. We traded gunshots and I got both of them. I didn't bring their bodies with me because I took a hit in my left arm, but that was really just an excuse. I just didn't care enough to bring them back."

"I don't care, Lin. I'll still send out messages that you got the Hilliard brothers."

"I appreciate it, Jimmy, but this really wasn't about the rewards. I wanted those two bastards even more than the other four. Shooting the two that killed George was worthwhile, too."

Then after a pause, Lin said, "After I killed each pair, I went through their saddlebags and found the money that they'd been paid by the miners. I didn't tell any of the other lawmen about the money but this morning, I divided it into nine bundles of a thousand dollars each. I'm going to give one stack to each of the women that they kidnapped, and I want you to give one to George Cobb's widow and the second to Orville, so he and his wife won't have to worry."

As Lin removed the two bundles from his pocket, Sheriff Ward said, "I won't report it either, Lin. That's as good a use for that money as I can think of."

Lin laid the two stacks of twenty-dollar notes on the sheriff's desk and said, "I appreciate that, Jimmy. I was a bit concerned that I could be charged with theft myself for not turning it in."

"Hardly. You were entitled to it when those men were listed as wanted dead or alive. You knew that."

"I know, but it sounded better when it sounded as if I didn't know that."

"So, now can you tell me what the hell happened to your face?"

Lin explained about Julia and her nightmares. Then, he surprised himself when he segued into his own nightmares then when he finished, he said, "I don't think I can do this anymore, Jimmy."

"You're giving up being a bounty hunter?" the sheriff asked.

"I have to, Jimmy. I can't kill a man again. It might push me over the edge."

"You could always come to work for me, Lin. I'm down two deputies now and you know my county better than I do."

Lin knew it was no different than being a bounty hunter with limits but replied, "I'll think about it, Jimmy."

Then as he stood to leave, Sheriff Ward said, "Oh, not that it matters much, but after Willie Whitacre was sentenced to be hanged, he was visited by his father. Orville said that before he left, he said that he was going to kill that bastard. He assumed it meant you. We get those threats all the time, but I figured you'd want to know."

"I appreciate it. Did you see the man?"

"I did. He's about what you'd expect. About five feet and eight inches with not much extra fat on his bones. He wore his gray hair long and had had a full beard."

"How did he even find out about it?"

"Would you believe that he lived just up the road in Howell?

"That is a surprise. Maybe that's where they'd go when they weren't causing mayhem."

"Well, I wouldn't worry about the geezer myself."

Lin nodded then both lawmen shook his hand before he turned and left the sheriff's private office before exiting the jail, mounting Homer and going to see the doctor about his wound.

After having the damage repaired, he headed first for Tanner's Livery where he sold the three horses and gear from the Hilliards, but still kept the buckskin mare and the red gelding. The mare had earned points by warning him of the ambush and the red gelding was too handsome to give away.

So, with another hundred and thirty dollars in his pocket, he then rode to Carter's Restaurant where he had a big lunch, left an even bigger tip then rode out of Laramie heading east.

After two hours on the road, he angled off the road and cut northeast, anxious to see Julia again, wondering how she was coping with life. He may have had his problems with his nightmares, but Julia had to defeat her own demons. One of the advantages or disadvantages of spending so much time on horseback was that it allowed for a lot of time to think.

The more Lin examined his problems and Julia's own nightmares, he began to wonder if there was any chance at all of them being together.

He was still deep in thought when the Barber farm rose from the horizon and he had to shake off his depressing mood. It wasn't long before he caught sight of the family working in the fields.

———

It was Joe Barber who spotted him first, and shouted, "Papa, we have a rider coming in from the east."

His father shielded his eyes against the high sun and said, "I think that's Lin Chase. At least, that's his gray gelding. He's just dressed different."

They all stopped working as Lin waved and they returned the greeting.

He angled Homer to the southwest to avoid trampling their crops, and the family began to walk toward the house to meet him.

Lin reached the house first then stepped down and let Homer's reins drop as he untied his saddlebags and hung them over his shoulder while he waited for the Barbers to arrive.

When they were close, Henry smiled and asked, "What brings you back, Lin?"

"I have some news about those six men, Henry. Could we talk inside?"

"Sure, I'm sure Wilma will want to hear it, too," he replied as the three men and two women all walked with Lin to the back porch.

Henry opened the door and shouted, "Wilma, Lin Chase is here!"

Wilma smiled as she let a pair of her husband's britches drop back into the wash water, dried her hands on the front of her skirt then turned to greet their welcomed visitor.

"Lin has news about those six men, Wilma," Henry said as the family walked toward the kitchen table.

Wilma's smile disappeared as she joined the family at the table while Lin dropped his saddlebags to the floor.

"What happened to your face?" asked Bess.

Lin smiled and said, "I learned never to help a trapped black bear cub. They're never grateful."

Everyone laughed, but Lin wasn't sure they bought the excuse as he continued.

"I won't be staying long. I just left Laramie and I'll be heading to the Lampley farm shortly. But I wanted to let you all know that all six of those evil men are dead."

"Thank God for that!" exclaimed Mike.

Mary asked, "Did you get shot?"

"Just a slight arm wound that the Doc Peters stitched up in Laramie."

Lin then said, "After I shot them, I found that they had converted the gold that the miners had paid them to cash, and it came to just over nine thousand dollars. I broke it down into nine bundles."

He then opened his saddlebags, took out three of the bundles and set them on the table.

"I'm giving one to each of the women that those men had kidnapped. I thought it was right that the money goes to all of you. I also gave a stack to the widow of the deputy who was killed by those bastards and one to the deputy they shot and left for dead."

As he finished, they all stared at the large amount of currency on the table for another fifteen seconds.

Then Wilma looked up at Lin and said quietly, "You didn't have to do this, Lin. You risked your life to come and rescue us, then chase after those sick men. You should have kept the money."

"No, Wilma, I don't need it. Besides, you can do a lot of good things for the family with that much cash. I know the one thing my mother always wanted was a sewing machine, so last Christmas, I had one sent to her. She told me that it was the greatest gift she had ever received."

Wilma smiled then looked at her husband and said, "A sewing machine would be wonderful to have, Henry."

Henry smiled at his wife then at Lin before he said, "I think we should do that. When we go to Cheyenne, we can order one for you."

"You don't have to order one, Henry. F.E. Warren & Company have them in stock. That's how I was able to pick out the one for my mother."

The idea of taking the wagon into Cheyenne and buying a sewing machine and some other luxuries they had never dreamed of brought broad smiles to all of the family, who then began to stand and walk to Lin to thank him for doing what he did and his generosity.

"You'll have to come by and see my new sewing machine, Lin," Wilma said after kissing him on the cheek.

"I will, Wilma, but now I need to go the Lampleys, so I'll be leaving. Besides, you've all got to get back to work!"

Lin then smiled, picked up his saddlebags then turned and headed for the door, leaving a chattering family, not believing that much more work would be done in the fields today.

He mounted Homer and led the three horses east, already feeling a bit of excitement about seeing Julia despite his earlier concerns about their future.

He'd spent a lot of hours thinking about Julia, mostly about the nights before she had been taken, and it was those memories more than anything else that had let him keep his balance.

————

The Lampley family was eating dinner a bit early to discuss what could be done about Mary. She had her eyes closed now as if she was sleeping but never awakened. Now they began to worry that she never would. Julia had been pouring a beef broth and then some milk and water down the tube that the doctor had inserted in her nose but knew it wasn't enough.

As Mary's only daughter, Julia felt it fell on her to care for her mother, and she was exhausted. She'd started wearing the dark men's clothes that Lin had left for her because she found them more comfortable and reminded her of the man who had given them to her and so much more.

Her worries about her mother had pushed her own horrors to the back of her mind but not intentionally as Lin had tried to do with his. But now even Julia was at wit's end about what she or any of them could do to bring her back to this world.

"There's nothing we can do, Julia," Jim said softly, "I wish we could, but we've tried everything."

Julia nodded slowly and whispered, "I know."

Pete looked at his family and felt tears beginning to well in his eyes just as the sound of hooves outside the back door startled everyone.

Jim and Bill bolted for the Winchesters that had finally been moved into the house when they heard Lin's voice shouting, "Where is everybody?"

"Lin!" Julia cried as she shot out of her chair and rushed past her brothers slamming the back door open as she slid onto the small back porch.

Lin was stepping down and smiled as he caught sight of Julia wearing a black outfit that he no longer wore but filled it much better than he ever had.

Julia smiled when she first saw Lin, but her overwhelming concern for her mother quickly pushed it away as he stepped onto the porch and took her hands.

He looked into those pained eyes and asked quietly, "What's wrong, Julia?"

"It's my mother, Lin. Ever since she's been home, she hasn't spoken or eaten. Doctor McIntyre came from Cheyenne and put a feeding tube down her nose, but she just lays there. We're all so horribly worried about her."

Lin nodded then walked with Julia into the house, still holding her hand.

As soon as he saw the deep worry on each of the Lampley faces and Pete just short of tears, the reasons for his visit were shoved aside as he thought about anything he could do. Maybe the news that he had killed the six men who had done this would help.

Before anyone could speak, he turned to Julia and asked, "Could I speak to Mary for a few minutes, Julia?"

"Of course, you can, Lin, but I don't think you can help."

"I got all six of those men, Julia. If she knows that she's safe now, maybe she'll get better."

Julia wasn't surprised that he'd done what he said he'd do, so she just replied, "I hope so," then walked with him to her mother's room.

When they entered the room, Lin was stunned by the deathlike appearance of Mary Lampley. He pulled a chair up close to the head of her bed and took a seat.

He leaned forward slightly then said in a conversational tone, "Mary, this is Lin. I just returned after tracking down those six men and they're all dead now. You're safe, Mary. No one will ever hurt you again."

Mary didn't so much as change her shallow breathing as Lin leaned back then looked at Julia's stressed face.

He was about to give up when a swell of anger bubbled inside of him, so he said, "Julia, could you give us a few minutes of privacy? I'd like to talk to your mother alone."

There was a short pause before Julia replied, "Alright, Lin," then turned and left the room, closing the door behind her.

Lin knew that whatever he said in a normal voice could be heard past the door, so he leaned very close to Mary's left ear.

"Mary, I just trailed and killed six men and was almost killed in the process. It was only dumb luck that one of those bullets didn't punch into my chest. I didn't do it for the money. I did it to find justice for you and the other women and this is how you repay me for risking my life? You don't even care if you live or not. And do you know what? It's also very selfish.

"You are the most selfish woman I've ever met and a terrible mother. Right now, your only daughter, a wonderful, innocent woman who suffered even worse that you did, is having to take care of you while she has no one to take care of her, Mary. No one. What kind of mother thinks of herself more than her own daughter? I'm ashamed of you, Mary Lampley. You should be thinking of Julia, not yourself."

He then stood and just before he turned, Mary's eyelids slowly opened and she whispered, "Julia?"

Lin smiled leaned down and kissed Mary on the forehead then whispered, "I'll send her in, Mary," before he walked to the door, pulled it open and wasn't surprised to find Julia standing before him.

"Your mother just asked for you, Julia," he said quietly then stepped aside to let her rush past.

He watched as Julia sat on the edge of the bed, looked into her mother's open eyes and heard Mary say, "I'm sorry, Julia," before he turned and walked down the hallway to the kitchen.

When he reached the kitchen, he smiled at the family and said, "Your mother asked for Julia," then had to get out of their path as they stood en masse and hurried past him down the hallway.

He was listening to the sounds of crying and chattering as he walked to the cookstove, took a towel in his hand lifted the hot coffeepot and poured a cup of coffee then walked to the table and took a seat.

While he was sitting, he took the last four bundles of money and set them on the table among the dirty dishes then took a sip of coffee.

He had finished the coffee when he heard footsteps coming from the hallway and Pete popped into the kitchen and took a seat beside him.

"What did you tell my mother, Mister Chase?"

"Nothing much. I told her that she needed to help Julia. Now that you're here, can you tell me how your sister is doing, Pete?"

Pete scrunched up his face and replied, "I think she's still scared. She helps my mother all the time, but at night when she's sleeping, she has nightmares. I even told her silly stories, but I don't think they helped much."

"That's okay, Pete. I think she just needs more time now."

Pete then asked, "What's all that money for?"

"For your mother, sister and sisters-in-law. I'll explain when they come back out."

"Okay."

When the others except for Julia returned, Jim and Bill walked to the table while Anna and Marge began to prepare some food for Mary.

Jim and Bill noticed the large pile of money on the table and Jim said, "What's that?"

Even though Julia wasn't there, Lin explained the story behind the money and its purpose. By then, both of their wives had drifted to the table.

"All that money is for us?" asked Anna.

"One bundle is for each of you. I know the money itself doesn't begin to make up for what happened, but I couldn't think of a better purpose for the money. You'll be able to get your house built a lot faster now and buy some nice furniture, too. You can even build a third house and a barn."

Anna looked at Jim and said, "He's right, Jim. We could have a builder finish it."

Lin said, "I used East Construction in Cheyenne. They do good work. You could have the whole family make a trip to Cheyenne for a day and contract for the house, order your furniture and just take a couple of days away from work."

Even Pete seemed to be uplifted by the news, so Lin set the cup down, assumed that Julia wouldn't be returning soon then stood and said, "If no one minds, I'll take my things to the barn and get my horses settled. They've had a long few days."

"How about you, Lin?" asked Anna, "How are you doing?"

"I'm fine," he replied with a smile that he didn't feel then turned, glanced down the empty hallway and walked out the still-open door, closing it behind him.

He hadn't been surprised at all when Julia had remained with her mother. She must have been so relieved that she'd probably be there for hours.

He untied Homer and led him and the other three horses to the barn. It was going to be too crowded for them, so he just began unsaddling the horses and once they were finished and the packhorse unloaded, he led them out to the corral and let them graze on the hay that was piled against the barn.

It wasn't until the sun was setting and he'd already made himself a cold dinner from his supplies that the barn door opened, and Julia entered in her dark outfit.

"Lin," she said as she closed the door behind her, "What did you say to my mother? She spent almost ten minutes telling me how sorry she was."

"I just told her that you needed her help. It's the truth, isn't it?"

Julia didn't answer but walked past Lin and sat on the same stack of hay she'd used the last two times they'd been in the barn together.

Lin sat beside her and asked, "How bad has it been for you, Julia?"

She thought about downplaying the impact of what had happened but knew that he'd see through it, so she whispered, "Bad."

"Pete tells me that you're having nightmares, Julia. Are they getting worse or better?"

"I don't know. Sometimes I think they're getting better, then I have a bad one."

"I wish I could help, Julia, but I'm not sure if there's anything I can do."

Julia then looked at him and said softly, "Marry me, Lin. You could marry me."

"You probably know by now that I love you, Julia, and I've wanted to marry you very much, but I'm worried now."

Julia dropped her eyes and whispered, "It's because of what happened, isn't it?"

He took her hand and replied, "No, Julia, that least of all. It's me that I'm worried about, not you. Remember I told you about how I'd hide my bad memories behind good ones like a bank vault?"

"Yes."

"My biggest concern for some time now was that sooner or later, the number of those killings would reach a point where they would take over my mind and drive me into madness. After I killed the miners that began to grow because I felt as if I'd murdered them. Some of those men may not have brutalized the women and still died."

Julia interrupted him, saying, "All of them used us, Lin. There wasn't an innocent man among them."

That news was somewhat good to hear, but Lin continued.

"Then after I killed Ike McCall and Fuzzy Villers, I began having nightmares. Bad ones. They got worse after I killed Arnie Jacobsen and Hound Jones, who was probably the worst man I've ever killed. Then after I killed the Hilliard brothers last night, I thought that maybe because it was finally over and the two men who had hurt your mother and killed your father were dead, I'd have a good night's sleep. But it was the worst nightmare I'd ever had. I can still recall each moment, too."

"Can you tell me about the dream?" she asked.

He looked into those deep blue eyes and said, "I can't, Julia. I just can't."

"Why not? Was I in it?"

Lin sighed and nodded, but said, "Please don't ask again, Julia. Please."

"Alright, but why does that mean we can't be married. If I'm willing to put aside my own fears of being intimate with you, and I'm still not convinced I have, why are your concerns a barrier?"

"I'm worried about hurting you, Julia. When I awakened from my last nightmare, I felt that in my madness, I may hurt myself or someone close."

"I'm not afraid of that, Lin."

"Maybe not, but the thought that I might hurt you is horrifying to me."

"Then what are you going to do? Are you going to leave me forever?"

"Tomorrow, I'm going to ride into the Black Hills and just try to find peace. If I can go two nights without a nightmare then I'll return and see you."

"Then will you take me to Cheyenne with you? Whatever you told my mother was wonderful. She's talking and eating now. She's still not a happy woman, but she's my mother again. I'll never be able to thank you enough."

"You'll never have to, Julia. If I can get past my nightmares and know that you'll be safe, then I'll spend the rest of my life making you happy."

"I'll be waiting for you, Lin, and I'll try to get past my own troubles. But I believe that the best way for me to do that will be to be with you."

Lin then said, "Julia, if you'd like, you can sleep here with me tonight, but I'd only have one request."

"I'll do anything you ask, Lin," she said softly with no double entendre hidden in her reply.

"I want you to bind my wrists with pigging strings. Not tightly, just enough to keep me from doing something bad when the nightmares arrive."

"Okay, I'll do that. But maybe we'll be able to keep both of our nightmares at bay."

"I hope so," he replied

Lin then laid out the two bedrolls under the light of the single lamp, as Julia removed her new boots as he slid his free and took off his gunbelt.

Then Julia wrapped Lin's wrists in some pigging strings as they stared into each other's eyes and when she finished tying the last knot, she blew out the lamp then slid into her bedroll.

Once in their bedrolls, they faced each other across the twenty-two inches of semi-darkness illuminated by the light of the full moon that filtered through the gaps in the wood.

"Now that you can no longer see my eyes, will you tell me about your nightmare, Lin?"

Lin was about to argue that it wasn't her eyes that had prevented him from telling her about the nightmare, but then realized that's exactly what had kept him from telling her.

"I will, Julia, but please don't be hurt or offended by what I tell you. It was only the terror of my mind creating the most abominable images possible to try and take control."

"I understand, Lin," she said softly.

"I was sleeping outside, but found myself in the hallway of a hotel with only one door…"

Lin kept his eyes on Julia's face as he described the hideous experience barely being able to see her eyes but just enough to catch a glimpse of blue which allowed him to continue.

Julia listened and found herself disgusted and ashamed when he reached the naked Julia with MoMo part but then when he finished, her hand flew to her open mouth.

"Inevitable?" she asked quietly.

"Each of my nightmares now end with that word."

"Oh, my God! I'm so sorry, Lin. This is my fault, isn't it?"

"No, Julia, it's not your fault at all. It's just a nightmare."

"But, the 'inevitable' part of your nightmares is from me, isn't it?"

"I suppose, but it's just a word, Julia. It just had a much better connotation when you used it the first time."

"The first time?" she asked.

"When you came and sat right there and said that when we were alone on the trail after them, what would happen between us was inevitable."

"That was a brazen thing to say, wasn't it?"

"I'll admit that it was startling, but it was much better than when I hear it in my nightmares."

"Do you believe that you'll do it?"

"Kill myself?"

"Yes."

"I don't know, Julia. That's why I need to go away for a while. I need to find peace."

Julia then said, "I'm not sure if that other inevitability will ever happen either, Lin. I'm just as hurt and confused as I was the day after it happened, and now I'm worried about being pregnant, too."

Lin had his arms outside of the bedroll, so he reached across with his bound wrists and gently caressed Julia's cheek with his fingertips.

"Julia, could I ask you not to worry about that? When I return, we'll get married and even if that first inevitability never happens, I'll always love you and make you happy. We'll raise the baby as ours and love him or her with all of our hearts."

Tears began to drip to the top of Julia's bedroll as she took his fingers in her hand and kissed them softly.

"Then you've got to get better and come back to me, Lin."

"I want that more than anything in this world, Julia."

Julia kissed his fingers once more before letting his hand go and saying, "I love you, Lin."

Lin smiled and said, "Good night, Julia."

"Good night, Lin."

After they had closed their eyes, they shared a common wish for a nightmare-free night before they soon fell asleep.

Lin didn't know when he shot upright in his bedroll, but it was still dark and Julia was still asleep, so he hadn't screamed.

He laid back down and could only remember the last part of the nightmare and it was just the Hilliard brothers that he'd seen but knew the others were all just out of sight watching. They'd been out in an open field at night and they had said nothing as they cackled and watched him turn his own Colt into his eyes.

Then, just before he squeezed the trigger, they all began a low chant, "In...ev...it...a...ble," then he'd shattered into wakefulness as the bullet headed toward him.

He spent the next fifteen minutes watching Julia's peaceful face and was happy that at least she may have a peaceful night's sleep.

————

Lin opened his eyes as bright shafts of sunlight poured through the gaps in the eastern wall. Julia was still sleeping just inches from him and he smiled.

Now he knew he had a problem as he slipped his bound wrists out from the bedroll but was surprised to find that his bindings were already close to falling off already. He quickly pulled them off and tossed the leather strings aside before sliding out of the bedroll and slipping on his boots.

As he was pulling on his second boot, he heard Julia say, "No nightmares," then turned to smile at her.

"I'm glad to hear that," he replied.

Then she asked, "You still had one, didn't you?"

"Yes."

"Was I in this one?"

"No. Just the Hilliard brothers."

"It doesn't mean that mine are gone though, does it?"

"I don't know, Julia, but even one night without them was a revelation."

She slid partially out of the bedroll, sat up and asked, "Are you still going away to be alone?"

"I have to go. I don't know how long it will take but I have to do this."

"Don't be gone too long, Lin."

Lin nodded then said, "I need to leave the two new horses here, if that's okay."

"I didn't even see them."

"There's a pretty buckskin mare and a red gelding. You can have either of them if you'd like. Their tack is over there. I bought the Morgan for you, but I believe that Pete has grown attached to him."

Julia smiled and said, "He has. I'll take a look at the other two. Now, if you don't mind, I need to use the privy."

"You go ahead. I'll just run behind the barn."

"Meet me in the kitchen when you're done."

"Yes, ma'am," he replied as she slipped out of the bedroll and hurriedly pulled on her shoes.

He was putting on his new hat as he watched her race from the barn. He had already made his mind up about what he'd be taking with him on his trip into the Black Hills and it would be the lightest he'd ever traveled into the wilderness.

———

After his morning ablutions which included shaving, he joined the Lampleys for breakfast. It was a much more congenial time as everyone talked about their plans for getting the two houses done within a couple of months now that they had the means to do it. Mary remained in her bedroom but was eating normally to gain her strength back.

Before he left, Julia told him that her mother wanted to talk to him privately, so Lin stood and walked down the hall, turned into her bedroom and closed the door before taking the chair that was still near the head of her bed.

Mary smiled at him and said, "I heard what you said, you know."

"I'm sorry, Mary, but I needed to make you angry."

"You meant it though, didn't you?"

"Sort of. I had just looked at Julia and knew she needed someone badly and you were the best one to help her."

"I think you could help her more, Lin."

"I'm not so sure. When you talk to her again, have her tell you what I told her last night. I'll be leaving shortly, and I don't know when I'll be back. If, I mean when I do, I'll marry Julia and do everything I can to help her and make her happy."

Mary looked at him in silence for a few seconds then said, "I'll talk to her about it. Maybe I can help her before you get back…not *if* you get back."

Lin smiled then stood and kissed her on the forehead as he had before and said, "Good-bye, Mary."

"Good-bye, Lin, and come back to make my Julia happy."

"Yes, ma'am," he replied before opening the door and leaving the bedroom.

He walked to the kitchen collected Julia and walked with her to the barn.

Julia helped him saddle Homer and the packhorse but didn't comment on his lack of firepower as he slid the lone Winchester '76 into the scabbard and left his other weapons including the new Sharps-Borshadt under a tarp.

With everything ready, Lin hung his Stetson on his saddle horn then took Julia in his arms and smiled at her.

"I'll be back as soon as I can, Julia."

"I hope so, Lin."

He kissed her softly then whispered, "Not a hope, Julia. I'll be back."

Julia just nodded as she kept the tears at bay as a terrible sense that she'd never see him again washed over her.

Lin led the two horses out of the barn, mounted Homer then quickly rode out of the yard and turned northwest not looking back at Julia. He had to leave and knew that if he saw those dark blue eyes again, he'd have to turn around.

Julia didn't know why Lin hadn't even waved but just sighed and slowly stepped toward the house as he disappeared into the distance.

———

Lin passed the Barber farm far enough to the north that no one took notice then continued due west for a while. The clouds had rolled in and rain threatened, but Lin gambled that he'd have enough time to get his slicker free before he was drenched in a sudden downpour and kept riding.

He stopped for a lunch break sometime after noon and then mounted again and headed west where he soon picked up wagon tracks accompanied by seven horses and guided Homer to the center of the wagon ruts as he followed the same course.

In mid-afternoon, he spotted the charred remains of the squatters' cabin and continued past where the wagon turned north to take a closer look.

The bodies had been removed, but he dismounted and walked to the chimney, burnt wood and ashes which was all that remained to mark the existence of the two couples and their unborn children who had never been given the chance to experience life.

It had been Julia who had told him about the two pregnant women who had been murdered inside the cabin and despite his revulsion, he stepped onto blackened mess.

He kicked away some of the charred rubble and wound his way to the fireplace. There he found the burned remains of one of the women and saw where a large bear had dragged away the second. He should have been nauseous, but he was just sad at the grisly sight.

He didn't inspect it closer but simply stared down removed his hat and said, "I'm sorry, ma'am. I know it doesn't help you any that those bastards that did this to you are suffering in hell, but I hope that you're in a better place now with the rest of your family and your baby. No man has the right to take a woman's baby from her. Give your child a kiss for me."

He kept staring at what had once been a young woman with child when he noticed that one of the stones on the outside of the fireplace had popped loose from the heat, exposing a small hiding place. He pulled the rock free then slipped out a thin tobacco tin.

He popped it open dumped its contents into his palm. It must have been used as their vault as sooty coins dropped out amidst charred one-dollar notes. Maybe it had been all of the money they ever had. If so, it hadn't been much. The silver amounted to thirty-seven cents, but when he shifted the coins, he found something else inside that wasn't money. After digging under the change, he picked out a small chain with a cross. It was probably made of tin but for some reason, the woman hadn't worn it. She'd hidden it away, and he would never know why she had.

He looked back down at what was left of the woman and asked, "Why weren't you wearing this?"

He finally exhaled sharply, slid the thirty-seven cents and the chain into his pocket then turned and stepped out of the burnt cabin.

He walked slowly back to Homer mounted then turned back north to follow the wagon trails, the mystery of the cross and chain still on his mind.

———

Back at the Lampley farm, Mary was making her first foray outside of her bedroom assisted by Julia as they walked to the kitchen.

"I need to take a bath, Julia," her mother said as she sat down at the table.

"I'll draw one for you after I get some more food into you, Mama."

"Alright, Julia. If you insist," she said then asked, "What are you going to do when Lin returns?"

"I'll marry him, Mama. I just don't know if I'll ever be able to consummate the marriage. I love him so much but I'm still such a mess inside."

"It hasn't been that long, Julia. It'll get better."

Julia turned to her mother and asked. "Mama, you were almost lost to us after what happened. I know it was the second time for you, but how can you tell me it will get better?"

Mary looked at her daughter and answered, "It wasn't the second time, Julia. It was the third."

Julia blinked and asked softly, "Third?"

"I never told you or anyone else about the first time because your father and I agreed that no one should ever know, but I believe that it's time that you heard the truth."

Julia left the cookstove and took a seat at the table across from her mother but didn't say anything.

"Haven't you ever wondered why you're so much taller than your brothers and have those dark blue eyes?"

Julia had never really paid any attention to the differences until her mother mentioned it.

"No."

"The first time I was violated was back in Ohio when I was seventeen. I thought I was going to be shunned and thrown out of the house, especially after I discovered I was pregnant. At the time it happened, your father and I had just started seeing each other, but he hadn't officially started calling on me. When he asked if he could, I was honest enough to tell him that I was already with child because of the attack and all he said was, 'Then I guess it will be a short courtship.' We were married two weeks later, and no one ever knew. The man who had raped me was a passing stranger and I never saw him again."

Julia asked softly, "So, papa wasn't really my father?"

"Yes, dear, he most certainly was your father. Did you ever know a day where he didn't love you?"

"No. I loved him just as much."

"That's because you were his daughter as much as mine. It was his love for me that let me get past that first time and survive the second because I had to be there for him. He wasn't here to help me with the third one, and I think that's why I went into that shell.

"If it wasn't for your Lin, I'd still be there. What he said to me sounded so much like my Earl would have said that, for a moment, I thought he'd returned. So, Julia, let him love you and push those demons away. Don't forget, your father and I had three more children after you, and I enjoyed every second that we shared in creating them. It was just because we loved each other, Julia."

Julia stood then hugged her mother as she began to weep.

"Thank you for telling me, Mama."

Mary patted Julia on the shoulder then asked, "Weren't you going to feed me, young lady?"

Julia stood, laughed lightly as she wiped the tears from her face and said, "Yes, ma'am."

––––––

Lin spotted the remains of Orville's horse ahead and noticed that in addition to critters feasting on the flesh, someone had taken the saddle from the carcass. He knew it wasn't the Cheyenne, so he imagined that someone in Laramie had heard about the shooting and ridden to the spot to salvage what he could.

He examined the area as he passed but didn't see any new hoofprints which didn't bother him. The scavenger could have shown up with the men who'd picked up the squatters' and George Cobb's bodies. He continued past the location and soon arrived at the spot where they'd had to repair the broken wheel and pulled off to camp for the night. It wasn't that late, but this wasn't a tracking mission, so there was no hurry.

After unsaddling the horses and setting them to graze, he dug a small pit and soon had a fire going to make supper. He ate his food and drank his coffee as he stared into the still-cloudy sky. The full moon brightened a portion of the clouds to mark its passing but did little to improve his view of the night landscape. But he didn't need the light because he wasn't following anyone as he just sat, leaning against his saddle and staring into the night, having no doubt that the nightmares would return.

As much as he was concerned about his own problems, he was even more worried about Julia's. It wasn't because it would prevent them from being intimate, but that they caused her pain. He wanted Julia to be the same happy, teasing woman he'd met before they'd taken her from her home. Her sisters-in-law and each of the Barber women had someone who loved them and had been with them before the mass violations, but Julia had no one to let her understand the difference between making love and being raped and no one to help her recover afterward. His Julia was suffering alone. He believed that he was the only one who could help her, but he had to fix himself first or he could make things so much worse.

So, when he finally slipped into his bedroll, he tried to reason away his fears and doubt but wasn't close to finding an answer as he drifted off to sleep and was soon engaged in a never-ending gunfight where his bullets were never even close to his targets, driving him into faster, more inaccurate firing as his rifle's barrel began to glow red hot from the constant passage of bullets and hot gases. He never had to reload as he kept firing and the unhurt killers kept laughing at his ineptitude.

When he finally ripped himself free from the dream, he found his heart pounding, but in this nightmare, there hadn't been the suggestion of the inevitability of suicide.

He returned to the bedroll, believing he had somehow made progress and was asleep again ten minutes later.

———

The next morning, Lin started a small fire and cooked himself a reasonable breakfast and made a pot of coffee. There was no rush because he had nowhere to go and no time limit.

So, by the time he started riding again, it was already mid-morning. The day was still cloudy and threatened rain, but he decided to call its bluff and left his slicker in his bedroll as Homer climbed the incline of the Black Hills.

He had to stop and let the horses rest twice on the long climb, but just after before noon, the scene of the massive landslide came into view, and he felt his stomach turn knowing that there were fourteen bodies under those rocks. He could see vultures still circling the valley and some among the rocks searching for nourishment.

He soon looked to his left and saw the spot where he had taken the shot and kept riding as he let the bile rise in his throat almost as a penance for what he had done.

When he reached the edge of the rubble-filled valley, he dismounted and let Homer's reins drop as he stepped forward a few feet, scaring off some of the big, dark birds who spread their giant fingered wings and took to the sky to watch and wait.

As he stepped closer, he saw that MoMo's body hadn't been covered completely by the rocks and had been providing food for the vultures and other carrion-eaters. As he looked down at his feet, he could see tracks of other predators that had probably gorged on the bodies he'd left behind.

It was that thought that sent his breakfast back out onto the ground as he bent over and heaved.

When he finished retching, he turned and walked to Homer, removed his canteen and washed out his mouth. He hadn't been sick when he'd seen either Hungry Jim's half-head or that of whichever of the six men he'd shot through the eye. Nor had he been this affected in any of the others that he had killed. *Why was he so sickened by this sight? That was the bastard who had bought and raped Julia.*

He took in a deep breath and returned to the avalanche debris. He then wound past MoMo's body and began climbing rocks and stepping past others as he made his way deeper into the field of dead miners.

Lin found some remnants of their shacks among the rocks as well as parts of their bodies, but he didn't vomit again.

He finally climbed one tall rock, stood on top and did a slow, rotating scan of the destruction, seeing the freshly exposed rock on the west wall before he finished his examination and looked back at Homer four hundred yards away.

He shook his head, realizing just how exposed he was now. His lone rifle was the Winchester '76 that was in Homer's scabbard a quarter mile away.

Lin took one more scan of the valley then climbed back down the boulder and began to make his way back to Homer.

The sun was past noon as he reached his gray gelding, took his canteen and drank it dry before mounting and heading east just a few hundred yards to a stream that was just outside a small forest.

He dismounted and began unsaddling Homer to prepare for his second night alone. He planned on returning to the rock-filled valley in a little while on foot, only this time, he'd bring his Winchester.

———

The Lampleys had a visitor that morning when Henry Barber arrived to tell them of his family's plan to take a wagon into Cheyenne on Friday then stay overnight and do some serious shopping with some of the money that Lin had left for them. He asked if the Lampleys would be interested in coming along. It didn't take long for them to agree and soon there was a quick outline of a plan. The Barbers would drive their wagon to the Lampley farm then both wagons would head for Cheyenne.

The Lampleys had enough horses now that all of the Lampley men and Julia could ride, leaving enough space on the wagon for anything they might purchase.

By the time Henry Barber departed for home, all of the Lampleys including Mary, were excited about the trip to Cheyenne in a couple of days.

———

Lin left his campsite in mid-afternoon and headed back to the mining camp valley. He didn't understand why he was drawn to the location as it seemed to send him even deeper into a pervasive sense of doom. Maybe that was the whole purpose of his journey, to drive him into madness sooner.

He again passed MoMo's remains but didn't have the same reaction as he walked past and began climbing onto the rocks, only this time, he began heading for where the dynamite shack had been. It was easy enough to find as it had created a deep gouge into the rock.

When he arrived there, he was surprised to find that there were still pieces of wood nearby and some had actually been driven into the rocky wall behind the shack.

He explored the damage for another hour, and as he was leaving, found a Remington pistol on the ground among the sharp rocks. He picked it up and found it was an 1858 Model that used percussion caps, but none of the cylinders were loaded. He tossed the pistol back to the ground and continued to leave the valley.

One of the interesting things he'd seen was a large vein of gold near the site of the blast. He didn't care, but he might mention it to someone in the future.

He returned to his campsite and decided to take a bath in the stream while it was reasonably warm. So, he quickly stripped and soon was freezing in the icy water as he scrubbed away a couple of days' worth of dirt. He took the time to examine his sutured wound and despite the swelling, he thought it looked okay then wondered how his scratches looked.

After he dressed, he restarted his fire then reheated his coffee. He held off making himself something to eat until after sundown as he just sat and enjoyed the serenity of the mountains.

That night, after he'd gone to sleep, any serenity he'd found during the day evaporated along with his hope that last night's nightmare was a portent of less self-destructive dreams. The nightmare that attacked his mind that night included a return to the theme of suicide when he'd been told that he must shoot himself, only this time it was Mary who gave him the order and the Colt.

When Lin woke up shaking and sweating, he was still mystified that Mary would even appear in his nightmare. Because of the intensity of the nightmare, Lin just slid out of his bedroll, pulled on his boots and began to pace beside the stream as he relived the terrible dream, searching for some way to stop them.

He paced until the predawn then built a fire to have his breakfast while the two horses still slept. The sky was clear again and not a drop of rain had fallen.

As he ate, he gazed at the valley which was already busy with vultures and wondered if the proximity to the miners' impromptu burial sites had caused the powerful nightmare. Whatever the reason, he knew he was no closer to finding peace than he had been when he started.

He didn't get underway until mid-morning again and rode northeast further into the Black Hills.

He continued to climb until he reached the spot where he had initially heard the Whitacre brothers' Spencer fire at the Cheyenne just two weeks ago.

As he began walking Homer down toward the wide valley, he began calculating the number of men had killed in those two weeks and came up with the astonishing total of twenty-three, not including Willie, who'd been hanged. No wonder he wasn't able to squeeze those last six into his vault.

The descent into the valley was much slower this time as there was no rush to reach the bottom. Unlike the visit to the smaller, rocky valley, this one had no vultures circling overhead but he did see some white-tailed deer racing across the eastern edge before they disappeared into the trees. This was a much more peaceful atmosphere and Lin decided that it might be better to stay here for a couple of days.

After reaching flat ground, Lin kept Homer at a walk as they headed toward the spot where the Whitacre brothers had stayed and almost wiped out that band of Cheyenne with their Spencers.

He pulled up a hundred feet from the spot, dismounted, then slid his Winchester from its scabbard as he approached the shooting location. He could still see the damage his shot had inflicted on the one boulder that had dropped them both back down.

When he reached the spot, he looked down and all that was left of Hungry Him was a few scraps of clothing that had been ripped away. He imagined that a big carnivore, probably a brown bear, had dragged away most of the carcass, but there were too many animal prints on the ground to identify them without serious examination, and he wasn't about to waste the time.

He then turned and walked back to Homer, mounted, and slid his Winchester home. He then turned and rode toward a creek that ran along the center of the valley and dismounted.

It was well past noon when he set up what would be a more permanent camp.

———

The sun was low in the sky as Lin built a small fire to cook his dinner. All he had to keep him company were the two horses, who were grazing quietly nearby, the constant drone of cicadas, and his thoughts.

He was humming *Uncle Sam's Farm* as he dumped a can of beans into his skillet, then added one of his sausages that he'd already cut into pieces. After adding some salt and pepper, he let it simmer while he leaned back and sipped his coffee.

It was so tranquil, he believed if he couldn't find peace here, he never would.

While he waited for his supper to cook, he scanned the area and visualized the scene that he'd first encountered when he'd cleared that block of granite to the southwest; Cheyenne warriors lying on the ground dead or wounded, their horses wandering around while Tall Bear and Quiet Owl still faced the devastating power of the Whitacre's Spencers.

Then as he thought about the Cheyenne, he stood picked up one of the pieces of firewood he'd collected and drew the symbol that Tall Bear had told him to use for identification. The arrowhead, semicircle then the back end of the arrow.

He tossed the dried branch onto the fire as he sat back down, refilled his coffee cup, then slid the skillet off of the fire grate onto the ground to cool.

Lin then looked at the symbol and smiled. The odds of him running into a band of Cheyenne was dropping these days as the Lakota Sioux were pushing them westward and the white man was pushing both tribes. He doubted if the symbol would deter the Lakota. Maybe that's how he'd meet his end. He surely couldn't hold off more than a half dozen with the Winchester '76.

He ate directly from the skillet and only finished half of his surprisingly tasty supper, leaving the rest for breakfast.

As the sun set over the Black Hills, Lin sat with his back against the saddle drinking his coffee while he watched the deer return to the valley floor from the trees. It was a good-sized herd of about thirty animals and some of the young bucks were looking frisky.

After watching the deer, he reached into his pocket and pulled out the cheap chain that he'd found at the burned-out cabin. The heat had made the cross curl slightly, so he pulled out his knife, set the small cross on the wide blade then pressed it flat again before sheathing his knife.

He then held it into the fading light, letting the cross twirl in the light breeze wondering why the woman had stored it. Was she worried that she might not survive childbirth? He would have expected that she'd want to have it on her when she went into labor. Maybe that was it. Maybe she was keeping it safe until the baby began to arrive.

Lin walked to the stream then rinsed the cross as well as he could before sliding it back into his pocket knowing he'd probably be wondering about the mystery for the rest of his life.

By the time he slid into his bedroll, he was resigned to having another nightmare. He'd spent hours trying to soothe his mind but hadn't come close. He stared up at the Milky Way before the moonrise and as usual, it left him in awe of the cosmos. He continued to gaze into the starry night until his eyelids slowly closed, and he fell into a deep, troubled sleep.

————

Sometime during the night, Lin jolted awake screaming as he bolted upright in his bedroll. His heart was thumping wildly against his ribs as the recalled the horrific scene that his mind had created. *Would they never end?*

He was certain that if they didn't end soon, the madness would arrive because he would be too scared to go to sleep until he was exhausted. Then his nightmares would interrupt that sleep. A solid night's sleep was necessary to keep sane, and he wasn't going to find it if he couldn't calm his troubled soul.

He was already so tired that he lay back down and was soon asleep despite the fear of more nightmares. When he opened his eyes again, the sun was already well up in the sky, so he quickly slid from his bedroll and pulled on his boots.

After taking care of nature's demands, he washed and shaved in the cold water of the stream before restarting his fire to have his leftover breakfast and some coffee.

Once the frypan and coffeepot were in place on the cooking grate, he stood, stretched and began a slow walk along the stream to calm his frantic thoughts. He finally was able to push them away when he thought of Julia and wondered if she was still having nightmares. Julia. How different things would have been if those six bastards hadn't schemed to make themselves rich by ruining the lives of seven innocent women. Their lives were hard enough as it was, but those sons-of-bitches had to make it harder. *Why should he feel so damned guilty about killing animals like that?*

He returned to his fire, slid his warmed-up bean and sausage mix from the fire and added some coffee to the boiling water before sliding it onto the ground as well.

Lin had just poured his coffee when he heard hoofbeats behind him. He didn't have to look to know that he had Indian visitors, the question was which tribe was visiting. He was never good at determining the difference between Cheyenne and Lakota, but he finally stood with the cup of coffee in his hand and turned to face the large group of warriors.

He made no threatening moves as it would have made no difference at all. He had only five shots in his pistol and his Winchester was twelve feet away, so he just watched as the sixteen Cheyenne approached. They must have been leery after losing so many of their men to the Whitacre brothers last month, so they traveled in larger groups.

When they were about fifty feet away, the band stopped and stayed mounted, but one warrior slid from his horse's back and walked toward him with his hands unencumbered by weapons.

He stopped just five feet away then ran his eyes from Lin's toes to his head before he asked, "Do you come here to take gold from our mountains?"

"No, I come to find peace for my soul."

The warrior snorted and said, "You lie. White men come here for gold, but you foolishly came with only one rifle."

Lin replied, "I left all of my other guns at home, including the ones I used to save Tall Bear and Quiet Owl," then pointed to the symbol he'd carved into the dirt.

The warrior looked down at the divided arrow and asked, "You are the man who kills from far."

"I am, but I have killed too many and it is driving me into madness. I cannot do it any longer."

The warrior tilted his head slightly and then said, "What you are saying is woman talk. Warriors do not speak this way. Men know the way of death and the way of life and accept them both."

"I can accept my own death, but I do not have the right to take other men's lives."

The Cheyenne shook his head and said, "What is this nonsense you speak?"

"As you have said, I am the one who kills from far. It is unfair that I can kill them before they even have a chance to kill me. I am nothing but murdering them. That is what tortures my spirit."

"Again, you speak silly words. When I fight, I seek every advantage. Why should I let my enemy be able to kill me? If he has a bow, I will shoot him with my rifle from far away. White men have been doing this to my people for many years now. Sometimes, talk of honor in dying is the talk of fools. There is honor in a warrior's death, but not if it is given away. It is the way of the warrior to take lives. I have taken many Sioux and white lives and find no shame in it."

"That is war, not killing as I do. It is not the same."

"Bah! It is still war. These men you killed. Are they good men? Good warriors?"

"No, they were all bad men, but some were not good warriors. I blew up a mountain a few days ago southwest of here, killing fourteen men who had bought women from men who had taken them from their homes. I then killed the six men who stole them in gunfights. None of them were good warriors. They were no threat to me, and I killed them all."

The Cheyenne's eyes widened as he asked, "That was you that made the mountain fall? We heard the thunder then went and found the rocks and were happy that those thieves had been crushed by the mountain that they had been raping. Killing such men is nothing. It should not bother you."

"Yet it does. I have been trying to make peace with myself and have failed because I am taking their lives from them."

The warrior then stared past Lin and said, "Turn and look at the mountains behind you."

Lin turned and looked at the Black Hills as they appeared almost yellow in the bright morning sun.

The warrior continued, "The mountains have been here before your grandfather was born and will be there long after your grandchildren die. Our lives are nothing but a blink of the mountain's eye. When you killed these men, you did not take their lives from them, but ended it sooner. It was their time for dying."

Lin nodded slowly and said, "What you say is true. One of the women that was taken to the mining camp told me that what would happen between us was inevitable. Maybe that was the key to all of this."

"What is inevitable?" he asked.

"It means that it was going to be, no matter what else happened."

"So, it is. Those men died because it was their time. Those that follow the evil path always die sooner than good men."

Lin looked at the Cheyenne and said, "Not all of the time."

The warrior smiled and replied, "That is true. Most of the time, then."

Lin smiled back and held out his hand.

The warrior shook his then said, "I am Hawk Who Waits. Tall Bear is my brother."

"Thank you for sharing your wisdom, Hawk Who Waits."

Hawk Who Waits nodded, returned to his horse mounted, then waved before he wheeled his horse around and the band of warriors trotted away.

Lin then tossed his cold coffee away and returned to his fire to have his breakfast. As he ate, he thought about what Hawk Who Waits had said and two things struck him. First was that whether those men died at his hand now, or from the hangman's noose a year later, when viewed in the eyes of the mountain, it was insignificant. But more importantly was the concept that Julia had first raised that first night together – inevitability. Men who violated the laws of men and God would die because of the way they lived. It was inevitable. It was their fate the moment they took to the outlaw trail.

But was the answer that simple? He'd been dancing around similar answers before but had focused on what the men had done to deserve their fates more than the inevitability of their demise or the relative insignificance of what they truly lost.

The longer he ruminated on the matter, the more he began to believe that he no longer needed to feel guilt for what he had done. He'd never hurt a man who wasn't wanted for crimes that would get him hanged, including every one of those miners.

He finished eating then cleaned up his campsite and began saddling Homer and loading the packhorse. He'd start back a lot sooner than he had expected to be returning but would still have to spend one more night on the trail. He needed to see if his new way of looking at his problem would give him a good night's sleep. If he had just one night free from his nightmares, he'd swing by the Lampley farm and see if he could help Julia then maybe convince her to join him in Cheyenne.

So, just forty-five minutes after the Cheyenne had disappeared from view, Lin had Homer and the packhorse saddled and headed south.

As Homer climbed the rocky slopes of the Black Hills, he wondered what he would do if he had reversed his slide into madness. If he married Julia, he wouldn't want to return to the isolated life of the bounty hunter, so maybe he would take Sheriff Ward up on his offer to be a deputy sheriff in Albany County. The sheriff was probably right when he said that Lin knew the county better than he did, but he knew Laramie County even better, and his house was there. If he took the job, he'd have to move to Laramie, which wasn't bad, but his house suited him.

But that all was dependent on what happened tonight after he closed his eyes.

———

As Lin was crossing the Black Hills, planning and preparations were underway at the Barber and Lampley farms for tomorrow's excursion to Cheyenne. It was a substantial event because it involved all of the family members, including the babies.

The Lampleys had many more horses available, so their wagon would be driven by Jim, who'd have Anna, Marge and Teddy with him in the driver's seat. The wagon would only have two travel bags with their clothes for the one night's stay in Cheyenne.

Julia, Pete and Bill would ride horses alongside, and they'd loaned two horses to the Barbers so their wagon wouldn't be so full. Julia had selected the buckskin mare as her own and named her Helen.

Once they arrived in Cheyenne, they'd have lunch then the two couples would go to East Construction to arrange for the one half-completed house to be finished and a second one built. They also wanted to have a second barn built. They expected to be a little short of cash, but Julia and Mary had offered to handle any overage. Julia had also given sixty dollars to Pete so he could buy something for himself, not knowing that her mother had already snuck him fifty dollars herself until Pete told her. She still gave him the money.

While the couples were at the builders, the rest of the families would do their shopping including a trip to F.E. Warren & Company so Wilma Barber could buy her sewing machine.

They'd stay at the Inter Ocean Hotel for the night then do some more shopping the next morning including a return to F.E. Warren to order the furniture for the new houses before returning that afternoon. Marge and Bill had expressed a need for some new baby furniture as well.

It was going to be a hectic two days of spending a lot of money that they could never in their wildest dreams have anticipated.

Even as the discussion was progressing, Julia was making her own plans. She knew where Lin's house was and how to get inside. Now that her mother was back to her normal self, she decided that she'd go to his house and wait for him to return. After she'd talked to her mother, she began to believe that it was possible for her to be intimate with Lin, and even the possibility of a pregnancy no longer loomed large.

It was her mother's revelation of Julia's own conception that had changed her perspective. She'd enjoyed a wonderful childhood and loved her family, never knowing that she wasn't her father's daughter. If that was possible for her, she knew that she could do the same for a baby that might be inside her now. She had no doubt that if she told Lin she was pregnant, he'd have the same reaction that her father had when her mother told him, and that made all the difference.

––––––

Lin decided that he'd spent the night camped right at the base of the destroyed mining camp. If he could manage a dreamless sleep there, he'd be sure that his problems were behind him.

So, late in the afternoon, he pulled Homer to a stop at the stream where he'd stayed the night before then unsaddled him and unloaded the packhorse. After letting them wander to drink and graze, he set up his camp in the same spot a few hundred yards from the mining camp. When it was done, he picked up his Winchester and walked to the rubble-filled valley.

After reaching the edge, he intentionally sought out MoMo's remains and studied them for almost two minutes before entering the destroyed mining camp. He spent two hours climbing and traversing sharp-edged rocks as he worked his way deep into the valley finding what was left of nine bodies. He checked the gold seam he'd seen two days ago just out of curiosity, having decided not to tell anyone.

By the time he returned to his campsite to make his supper, the sun was already sinking behind the mountains to the west and he was anxious for the night to arrive.

Lin quickly made his meal and skipped the coffee so he'd be able to fall asleep easier. He washed his skillet in the stream, rubbed some bear fat into the cast iron then set it back in its pannier before picking up his bedroll and his Winchester and walking back to the mining camp.

He stretched out his bedroll just fifty feet from MoMo slipped off his boots and gunbelt then slid inside as the last of the sunset was dying.

He was so anxious to fall asleep, that he found it almost impossible. He closed his eyes then a few minutes later, they'd pop open again and he'd watch the stars. This cycle repeated every few minutes for more than two hours after moonrise, and he began to wonder if he'd ever fall asleep. Lin finally stopped trying to force himself to nod off and just closed his eyes and thought about Julia.

Rather than using the happy memories of Julia to push aside the bad ones, he just let them flow through his mind as they were. From that stunning first night when she'd told him that she wanted him to take her with him, then the 'hanky-panky' and non-proposal marriage. Lin found himself smiling as he saw those dancing blue eyes as she said, 'hanky-panky'.

He was still smiling when he was no longer listening to Julia, nor was he in his bedroll.

He was out in a bright, green field with a bright summer sun overhead. The landscape looked so familiar, yet he couldn't quite place it. Then he looked down to his hands and found them holding a weapon he hadn't fired in more than twelve years and suddenly, he knew where he was and why he was here.

He brought the Burnside carbine level and brought the sights on a gray wolf about sixty yards away as it walked right at him, snarling as saliva dripped from his mouth with his yellow eyes staring at him.

He heard a voice behind him shout, "Now!"

Lin squeezed the trigger and the carbine slammed against his shoulder as the .54 caliber bullet spun out of the muzzle and just a fraction of a second later buried itself into the wolf's skull, throwing the animal almost straight back.

He then turned and asked, "Why did you want me to shoot him, Papa? Why didn't you do it?"

His father smiled at him and replied, "Lin, it was important to realize that sometimes, it's necessary to kill. That wolf was mad and was a danger to our family. Do you understand now?"

Lin looked at his father's face and answered, "Yes, Papa. I understand."

"Now, Mister Chase, you go and marry that young woman and make me a grandpa."

Lin laughed but before he could answer his father was gone, and he felt his heart aching for him to return. His father had died three years earlier and he hadn't been there when he'd passed.

The dream image remained as his eyes opened as the full moon glared down at him and he understood not only what his father had told him, but that he would no longer be plagued by nightmares. It was the final step toward finding peace within himself. A peace that would allow him to continue to do whatever was necessary to stop evil men.

"Thank you, Papa," he said softly before closing his eyes to return to a quiet sleep.

CHAPTER 8

Lin awakened from the first good night's rest he'd had since the killings and walked quickly to his campsite to get Homer and the packhorse ready for the return ride to Cheyenne with the much-anticipated stop at the Lampleys.

He didn't even start a fire for breakfast, but quickly saddled Homer then loaded the packhorse and was moving quickly down the long slope shortly after daybreak.

––––––––

The preparation for departure at the Barber and Lampley households was anything but quick or orderly, but by the time Lin was passing the location where the wagon wheel had broken, the two wagons and five riders were finally on the road to Cheyenne.

––––––––

Lin made good time on the long decline and it wasn't even noon when he reached the black blotch on the ground that used to be the squatters' cabin. He could have cut the corner toward the Barber farm and saved himself a couple of miles but wanted to make this stop.

He pulled Homer to a stop twenty feet from the debris field, dismounted then walked onto the ash-covered ground and made his way to the remains of the fireplace.

When he reached the spot where the woman's burned body lay, he removed his hat then reached into his pocket, extracted the cleaned chain and cross and laid it gingerly on what little was left of her.

"Ma'am, I don't know if this was yours or the other lady's, but it doesn't really matter. I just thought that it was right that you have it now. You never had a chance to wear it when you had your baby, but I think that's why it was hidden away. You wanted it to be there when you welcomed your baby into this world. You may not have been able to give your child much in the way of real things, but you wanted your baby to live a good life and this was all you had to offer."

He didn't linger but satisfied that the necklace was where it belonged, he turned, pulled his hat back on, then stepped around the remaining charred timbers, mounted Homer and turned him east toward the Barber farm.

———

The caravan of Barbers and Lampleys had reached Cheyenne about the same time that Lin left the burned out remains of the cabin and according to their day's plan, they stopped at Ramsey's Restaurant for a bought lunch, which was a real treat for everyone. Pete was even able to get some ice cream for dessert which was the first he'd ever had.

After lunch, they split up, with Mary, Julia, and Pete all heading for F.E. Warren with Henry and Wilma Barber. When Wilma had gushed about buying a sewing machine, Mary had decided that she'd buy one as well. Henry Barber was going to buy a new tiller at R. Rodgers, but it would have to be delivered.

Everyone else went to East Construction to arrange for a multitude of building projects at both farms.

After they'd purchased the two sewing machines, Julia asked her happy mother, "Mama, if it's alright with you, I'll leave you with the Barbers and ride over to Lin's house. I'd like to see it."

Mary smiled and replied, "You go right ahead, dear. If he's there, I wouldn't expect you to be returning with us tomorrow, either."

Julia returned her smile and said, "He's not back yet, Mama, but I'll wait there rather than come back."

Mary looked up into her tall daughter's eyes as she said, "Things will be better, Julia."

Julia nodded then turned and headed for the store's entrance, pulling on her dark gray Stetson as she cleared the doorway.

Before she made the ride to Lin's house, Julia stopped at Harrington's to buy new clothes. She wanted to look special for Lin when he returned and spent more time than she had anticipated before leaving with a large bag of clothing. She had her personal items in the saddlebags but had splurged on a mirror and brush set in addition to some scented soaps.

Ten minutes later, she'd made the turn north and hoped that Lin had returned but was almost certain that he hadn't. She hadn't told her mother about the underlying feeling of dread that Lin would never return to his house. When he'd told her about the nightmare in which she had been the one who had given him his own Colt to kill himself, she had been quietly terrified that he would actually do it. She was planning on staying in his house for as long as it took until he walked through the door.

Twenty minutes later, she spotted the small house and barn and had to smile despite her misgivings as she imagined Lin taking a bath in that contraption of his.

After another twenty minutes, she dismounted, walked Helen into the small, empty barn then spent some time unsaddling and brushing the buckskin mare. She made sure the small trough and feed bin were both full before leaving the barn with the door open to let Lin know she was there.

She crossed the dirt yard, climbed the three steps onto the porch holding her bag of purchases in her left hand and her saddlebags over her shoulder as she turned to look south toward Cheyenne in the small chance that Lin would be riding down the trail. The path was empty, so she turned to the dinner bell and pulled it down heard the latch open then holding onto the steel triangle, she pushed the door open. With the entrance clear, she released the dinner bell and with a smile on her face, walked into Lin's domain, closing the door behind her.

Julia removed her dark Stetson and hung it on a peg near the door before she began to inspect the house, finding it was almost exactly as she'd imagined it would be. The heat stove was in the northwest corner of the room with a coal bin beside it. There were two easy chairs, a couch and a low table on the left side of the room. Kerosene lamps dotted the room on almost every flat surface, including one that hung overhead in the middle of the room.

She strolled out of the main room and saw the locked room on her right, which she knew was the equipment room where he kept all of his guns. To the left was his bedroom, so she turned, opened the door and went inside then set her saddlebags and the bag from Harrington's on the floor near the bed.

Everything was surprisingly neat and tidy, and he'd even made the bed before he'd left. Julia felt a little guilty as she walked to the bed then sat on the edge and slowly laid down on top of the quilts.

When her head rested on his pillow, she could feel his presence and closed her eyes trying not to let that morose dread creep over her. She'd worked hard to get past the horrors of that one night at the mining camp and didn't want to slip back into a dark persona, especially not now that she was in Lin's house and he could be returning any minute. It was that thought that let her mind wander into believing he was nearby, and she'd soon hear the door open.

But after two minutes of just fantasizing, Julia opened her eyes, swung her legs off the bed then stood and walked to his large dresser. She opened one of the drawers and smiled as she saw all of the dark clothing that matched what she now wore. When he'd ridden off to the Black Hills, he'd been wearing a much lighter outfit, so she thought that she looked more like Lin Chase, the bounty hunter, than he did.

She laughed lightly then closed the drawer left the bedroom and headed for the kitchen and that bathing contraption that she'd been so anxious to see.

As soon as she laid eyes on it, Julia giggled and then spent a few minutes examining its workings before investigating the rest of the kitchen. There was more than enough food for her to stay for a while, but she still had over eight hundred dollars of the money that Lin had left for her and that would last her a long time. She just didn't want to spend a penny because it would mean that Lin hadn't returned.

Her inspection completed, Julia decided that she'd try out the bath, so she started a fire in the cookstove then filled the cistern as Lin had explained. She released the valve under the cistern to fill the pipes then returned to the bedroom to disrobe. She'd dress in her new, very feminine clothes with the hope that Lin would soon be there to see her in a dress for the first time.

———

When Lin had passed the Barber farm, he noticed that no one was out working the fields which struck him as odd, but he thought they might be in the house planning on how to spend the money he'd left them, so he'd continued without stopping to the Lampley farm.

As he neared the Lampleys, again, the lack of activity initially aroused his concern, but the likelihood of another attack of both farms by outlaws was so remote as to push that possibility aside.

When he arrived at the farm, he didn't dismount until he reached the barn, left Homer and the packhorse at the trough, then just quickly dismounted, opened the door and noticed the missing wagon and horses.

He grinned, then walked to the tarp, recovered his Sharps-Borshadt and his second Winchester then slid the scoped rifle into it scabbard on Homer and the second Winchester into the packhorse's scabbard. After sliding a box of the .50-110 cartridges into his coat pocket, he loaded the rest of the ammunition into his saddlebags before he finally turned, closed the door and mounted Homer before setting off down the short access road then turned east toward Cheyenne at a medium trot.

————

Julia had almost forgotten the second half of adding the cold water to bring the bathwater's temperature down but had caught her error just before sticking her foot into the almost boiling water.

"That was stupid," she said to herself as she tiptoed to the pumps and filled the cistern again with the cold water.

Five minutes later, Julia slipped into the tub and sighed. It took her a lot more time and work to have a hot bath at home and then there was always the issue of sharing. Baths were almost always shared, so none could linger and just enjoy the soothing, warm water. She washed herself using her new scented soap then shampooed her hair using the same soap. As she washed, she looked at the same calloused, rough hands that she'd shown to Lin that first day and wondered if they'd always be that way. Once she was clean, she simply stayed in the water and let her fingers and toes wrinkle like raisins simply because she could.

————

Four miles away, James Whitacre was mounting his dark brown gelding after talking to Joe Darling at the Bon Ton Livery and gotten the directions to that bastard Chase's house.

Ever since that day he'd seen Willie hanged, he'd plotted his revenge. It was just a question of coming up with the best way to get it done. The problem was he knew that he was no match for the bounty hunter with firearms and even attempting an ambush was risky. It was only after he'd exhausted all of the complex plans that he returned to the simplest option. He'd just walk up to his door, knock and then when the door opened, he'd shoot the bastard. When he discovered that Chase lived four miles out of town, it made it even better. He originally thought of the act of revenge being almost suicidal but now, he knew he'd be able to just walk away, leaving Chase's body in his doorway.

He didn't draw attention to himself as he calmly walked his horse west out of Cheyenne, looking for that trail that went north to Lin Chase's house.

————

Julia had carefully dressed in her new clothes then made some coffee as long as the cookstove was hot. She was sitting at the table drinking her coffee as she tried to imagine where Lin had gone. She was pretty sure that he'd revisit the mining camp site but didn't know where he'd go after that.

Wherever he had gone to find peace, she hoped that he not only found it, but discovered it quickly so he would return to his home and to her.

––––––

Lin had kept a fast pace as he felt drawn to Cheyenne knowing that Julia was there. He was excited to tell her the news that he was free of his mental chains and would be able to help her. His only question now was where to go when he got to Cheyenne. He guessed that the families would spend some time at East Construction arranging for the new houses but didn't think Julia would be with them. He couldn't imagine her spending a lot of time shopping, either. She'd probably be with her mother and Pete, but where would they most likely be?

He was approaching his normal cutoff to his house and was still debating with himself about where he should go when Homer made the decision for him and the gray gelding suddenly veered to the left to head for his barn.

Lin was going to turn him back to the road when he thought he may as well divest himself of the packhorse and supplies, then give Homer a rest before riding to Cheyenne. It was already late in the afternoon, but the sun would be up for another four hours, so he had plenty of time.

––––––

James Whitacre spotted the small house and was pleased when he saw smoke coming from the cookstove pipe because it meant that Chase was in the house. He pulled his Remington pistol and let the horse walk as he made sure that all six cylinders were loaded. He didn't intend on just firing a single shot. He'd empty the pistol into that son of a bitch.

———

Lin had passed the Lewis ranch house and soon spotted his house and observed smoke coming from the cookstove pipe as James Whitacre had just noticed. He was alarmed at first and reached for his Winchester, but then the possibility that it might be Julia inside radically altered his mood, and he slammed the Winchester back home and stepped up the pace. If the cookstove fire was burning then it was highly likely that Julia was trying out the bathtub and the idea brought a smile to his face as he recalled her laughter when he'd told her about the contraption.

He was still a mile out when he saw a rider approaching the house from Cheyenne and stared at the man. He didn't recognize him but at a mile, even with his extraordinary vision, that wasn't possible, so he continued to watch the rider. There were no more ranches or farms north of his land, so the stranger had to be going to his house and that was enough to increase his level of concern and Homer's pace.

Then Lin watched as the rider dismounted outside his house and drew his pistol. It was only then, when he saw the mass of gray hair and beard that he recognized who he was and understood what he was planning to do.

While he knew he wasn't in any danger, if Julia opened that door then Whitacre may pull the trigger before recognizing who she was, or he may not care because if she was in his house, then she was important to him.

Lin instantly understood what he needed to do. He could fire a warning shot to let Whitacre know he was twelve hundred yards away and not in his house, but believed that if he did, the old man would never engage him. His only recourse would be to take Julia as a hostage, and he didn't want to try and make another shot past her.

He let Homer keep fast trotting as he pulled his Sharps-Borshadt from it scabbard yanked off the telescopic sight's lens caps, and had to fish a cartridge from the box of ammunition before he drew his gray gelding to a halt and opened the rifle's breech and slid the long cartridge home. He didn't have time to adjust the scope and recalled the last shot he'd taken with the rifle and estimated the current range at another two hundred yards.

At the house James Whitacre knocked politely on the door as he cocked the Remington's hammer. His fury was building as his moment of revenge neared.

Julia was still sitting at the kitchen table when she heard the knock and jerked slightly at the unexpected sound and then smiled. Lin was home.

She hopped up, then after taking one step, she stopped. *Why would Lin knock on his own door?* This was his house and he would have seen Helen in the barn and would know she was inside. Then she thought that it was probably Pete or someone else of her family and began to walk again.

She soon reached the door and started to pull it open.

Lin had acquired Jim Whitacre in the scope and was convinced of his identity and purpose as he released the first trigger and squeezed the second. The Sharps-Borshadt slammed into his shoulder and the bullet was propelled out of the muzzle at more than fifteen hundred feet per second.

Julia was still smiling as the door started to swing open expecting to see a familiar face looking back at her while Jim Whitacre was just as expectant knowing that he'd soon be pulling his trigger.

The door opened and two startled people stared at each other.

Julia saw the cocked pistol and was preparing to slam the door closed and in that brief moment of decision for Jim Whitacre, he decided to shoot the woman then go inside so he could kill Chase.

His right index finger tensed when Jim Whitacre was slammed to his right as the massive slug of lead with its enormous amount of stored energy rammed into the left side of his chest. His Remington discharged, the .44 ripping past Julia and burying itself into the heavy back wall of the main room.

Immediately after firing, Lin set Homer to a canter, as fast as he dared with the trailing packhorse with the Sharps-Borshadt still in his right hand. He witnessed James Whitacre's sideways lurch and knew he'd hit his target, but he also saw the reflexive firing of the pistol into the open door. He couldn't see Julia, so he was panicking as he rode as hard as he could to his house.

Julia stood frozen in place with her hand still on the door as she stared straight ahead. She knew that what had just happened took place in just a few seconds, but it had been so vivid and so intense that it felt as if it had been much longer.

She blinked, took a deep breath then looked down and to her left at the old man's body. She'd been so shocked by his threatening appearance and sudden destruction that she hadn't even heard the rolling boom of the big round when it had passed. It was only after she'd spend another twenty seconds staring at the body that she understood that he'd been shot at long range and that meant…

Julia quickly stepped out of the house turned to the west and spotted Lin just a couple of hundred yards away, then put both of her hands over her face and began to cry out of immeasurable joy and relief.

Lin's panic vanished when he saw Julia walk out from the doorway, apparently unhurt. He wasn't convinced she hadn't been wounded, so he kept Homer moving quickly, slid the rifle into its scabbard without bothering to reattach the lens caps and waved.

Julia waved back, her face covered in a big smile and still-flowing tears as she laughed giddily.

Lin hopped down from the saddle as he slowed Homer fifty feet from Julia who'd leapt from the porch and was trotting towards him.

They slammed into each other, wrapping themselves together so tightly that Julia wasn't sure she could breathe, but it didn't matter now as breathing was secondary.

Lin kissed her passionately for fifteen seconds before releasing her enough so she could breathe then asked, "Are you all right, Julia?"

"I'm fine. He was going to shoot me, Lin!" she exclaimed then asked, "Who was he?"

"He's the father of the Whitacre brothers. Sheriff Ward told me that he'd said he was going to kill me, but neither of us paid too much attention to it because we hear it all the time."

"He would have shot me just because I was in your house, wouldn't he?"

"I think so. He probably thought I was inside and would have wanted you out of the way."

Julia shuddered then turned her head to look at Whitacre's body.

"What happens now?"

"I'll load up his body on his horse and take it into Cheyenne to see Sheriff Templeton."

"I'll come with you, Lin."

"You'll need to make a statement anyway."

Julia then looked into his eyes and asked, "How are you? Are you better or will this make everything worse?"

"No, I'm fine now. Would you believe I was given the answers to my problem by a Cheyenne warrior? I'll explain later, but I'm okay with my life now. How are you doing, Julia?"

"I wouldn't be waiting for you if I wasn't doing better, and I have you to thank for it."

"Me?"

"You helped my mother and she helped me. When you explain how the Indian helped you, I'll tell you how my mother helped me."

Lin nodded then kissed her again before saying, "I'll just get that old bastard's carcass on his horse then I'll have to unload the packhorse and saddle your horse."

293

"I'll get changed then I'll saddle Helen while you take care of the other things," she said.

Lin then stepped back slightly and looked at Julia. He hadn't noticed that she was wearing a well-fitting dress until she mentioned it.

"You look very attractive, Miss Lampley," Lin said.

Julia smiled then replied, "Thank you, Mister Chase, now I'll get changed and I'll saddle Helen when I'm done."

"Helen?"

"You know. Homer, Helen of Troy. I thought you'd appreciate that."

Lin laughed and said, "I named him Homer because he'd always be able to head back to the house no matter where we were. I'm not as well read as you are."

"I can remedy that, sir."

"Well, you go and put on some riding clothes and I'll take care of this grisly business."

"I'll be out soon," Julia said before she quickly turned and walked into the house, leaving the door open.

Lin couldn't help but admire Julia's form as she left and wondered how much better she was now. She did seem to be much closer to the first Julia he'd met. He'd just shot a man standing just a few feet in front of her who was preparing to shoot her, yet she seemed unfazed by the whole incident.

He didn't even give a second thought about the shooting would have any impact on him anymore. If ever he needed to kill a man, James Whitacre was the one.

He returned to Homer then led him and the packhorse to the barn where he found Helen staring at them.

Lin quickly unloaded the packhorse leaving everything in the barn for now then let Homer join the packhorse and Helen at the feed bin and trough while he walked to James Whitacre's brown gelding, took his reins and led him to the porch where Whitacre's body lay half off the edge.

He slid the body to the ground, glanced at the large pool of blood on his porch, then picked up his pistol, removed Whitacre's gunbelt, wrapped it around his Remington and dropped it into his saddlebag. He then lifted the surprisingly light corpse and flipped it onto the saddle before taking two pigging strings that he always had with him and tied the wrists and ankles together.

He was just finishing when Julia exited the house and Lin smiled when he noticed that she was now dressed as he used to but filled the clothes much better than he ever had.

"I'll go and saddle Helen," Julia said as she approached Lin.

"While you're doing that, I'm going to try and get some of that blood off the porch."

"Okay," she replied as she headed for the barn.

Lin trotted into the house and walked to the kitchen, immediately noticing the light floral aroma left by Julia's use of her scented soap. He then filled a bucket, shaved in some soap chips and grabbed his bristle brush.

He dumped the sudsy water on the porch and scrubbed the thick boards with the brush before returning to the kitchen and refilling the bucket with fresh water.

When he rinsed the porch, he was pleased that the blood hadn't soaked in that deeply. It was one of the odd things he'd requested from the builders. He asked that the floor varnish from inside the house be used on the porch as well. It was just a quirk at the time, but it was useful now.

He left the bucket on the porch then closed the door hopped to the ground then led Whitacre's horse to Homer where he tied him using the packhorse's trail rope to provide some gap between Julia and the body.

Julia led Helen from the barn then they both mounted and set their horses to a slow trot as they took the trail road to Cheyenne.

Lin shouldn't have been surprised when she asked, "How far out were you when you took that shot, Lin?"

"About a thousand yards, but he was a pretty clear target this time."

"Do you know what an absolute shock it was first to find an old man pointing a gun at me one second and then just have him tossed aside as he fired the next moment? You have no idea how utterly strange and confusing that was for a few seconds until I recalled your shots at the target range and then I knew you were there. I never even heard the Sharps' report I was so shocked."

"You seemed to have recovered well. Probably better than the last time I sent a bullet in your direction."

"That's because the first time, I knew what you were going to do but this time, I thought…"

She paused then said, "I thought I was going to die. All I could think about in those few moments was that I would never going to have a chance to be with you."

Lin looked over at Julia and said, "We'll talk for a long time when we get back to our home, Julia."

Julia smiled at him then nodded without saying another word.

Neither spoke again by an almost unwritten contract, understanding that they would spend hours in conversation later when they were alone.

———

It was early evening when Lin and Julia rode into Cheyenne leading James Whitacre's body-draped horse into town, pulled to a stop before the Laramie County Sheriff's office and dismounted.

When they entered the office, Deputy John Draper was still at the desk with the soles of his boots pointed at the front door and his eyes closed. When Lin closed the door, his eyes popped open as he jerked his feet to the floor.

"What do you need, Lin?" he asked.

"John, I have a body for you outside. He's the father of the Whitacre brothers and he showed up at my house planning on killing me and was about to shoot Julia when I got him."

"No kidding?" he said as he stood and crossed the floor.

They left the office, crossed the boardwalk and the deputy examined the body for a few seconds.

"Can you take him down to Shaw's mortuary and then come back to write your statements?"

"I'll do that. Julia, did you want to stay here?"

"No, I'll come along."

The deputy turned to go back into his office as Lin took the horse's reins then began leading him down 19th Street past the Catholic church, the Congregationalist church then two more blocks to Shaw's Mortuary.

Julia was about to comment on the number of times that Lin had made a similar walk leading body-draped horses but decided to hold her tongue because of their delayed deep conversation about their perceived release from their demons. She believed that she no longer had any concerns, even if she was carrying a child, but Lin had just shot a man when he had told her that he was worried that the next one would drive him into madness, and she wasn't convinced that he'd truly achieved peace with himself. She wouldn't be sure until they'd talked and then slept together. The second step in the process would be where she would discover if she was past her own difficulties.

Lin was already past thinking about the gunfight if it could be called that. Julia appeared to be herself again and had even joked about her dress and her buckskin mare just minutes after the shooting. Most women, or men for that matter, would have been much more shocked by those incredibly intense few moments when death was imminent and, suddenly the threat was destroyed just inches before your eyes. Yet Julia had rebounded quickly from the traumatic episode and even now, seemed perfectly content as they led a horse carrying the body of her would-be assassin. It was what he had expected of her after that first day and she'd exhibited such strength of character. He'd only find out tonight when they slept together. He had no intention of giving into the inevitable. Tonight, he needed to make Julia comfortable and already had a plan for doing just that.

———

Forty minutes later, they were back in the sheriff's office, talking to Deputy Draper as they wrote their statements.

"You shot him from a thousand yards on horseback?" exclaimed the deputy.

Lin didn't look up from his writing as he replied, "About that. It wasn't really a difficult shot because I had a large target and that telescopic sight. The toughest part was to avoid rushing the shot because I could see him with that pistol facing the door and knew that as soon as Julia opened it, he'd fire. I fired and had to wait those long two and a half seconds, willing that bullet to travel faster. It got there probably a second or so before he was going to fire. There's a bullet hole in the back wall of my main room for evidence, if you want to see it."

"No, that's alright. Besides, you need to come back in tomorrow and see the boss. He's got a ton of vouchers in his safe for the six bastards you chased down. I think he said the total was twenty-seven hundred dollars."

Lin didn't reply as he finished and signed his statement, then set it aside to let the ink dry before standing beside Julia.

"Julia's family is in town right now, so we'll be back in the morning to talk to them anyway. John, if you want that horse and rig, feel free. I don't have any more room at my place

299

anyway. There's a Winchester in the scabbard and his Remington pistol is in his saddlebags."

"Really? I appreciate that, Lin. You don't care if I sell the horse and tack, do you?"

Lin smiled and answered, "Not at all, John."

Julia finished her statement set the pen down then stood and hooked her arm through Lin's and said, "We'll be going home now, Deputy."

"See you in the morning, Lin, ma'am," John said as he rose.

"See you tomorrow, John," Lin replied as he turned with Julia and left the offices.

After they'd mounted, Lin asked, "Did you want to go to the hotel and talk to your family and let them know where you are, Julia?"

"They know where I am and they don't expect me to come back with them tomorrow either, but we'll talk to them before they leave. They're planning on heading back after lunch."

"Then let's go home, Julia," Lin said as he smiled at her.

"Let's," she replied before nudging Helen into a walk.

They arrived at dusk and by the time they'd unsaddled and brushed both horses, the sun was setting in spectacular style over the distant mountains.

Lin took Julia's hand as they stepped onto the porch then pulled his triangle door opener and they entered the dark main room, removed and hung their hats then spent a few minutes lighting lamps.

"I'll start supper while you clean and put away your rifles," Julia said as if they had just returned from a day's shopping.

"Then we can talk," Lin said as he began unlocking his equipment room.

"Definitely."

———

Julia was still wearing her dark britches, shirt and vest as they sat down to eat and talk. Lin had already filled the cistern, drained it into the pipes and filled it again. It was one of the nice things about the simple system. As the water in the pipes expanded from the heat, the added volume of heated water would flow back into the cistern. If there was already cold water in the cistern, it would begin to heat up as well, but there was never any danger of bursting pipes anywhere because the pressure remained low. Lin had planned on using the tub before going to bed to wash off the two days of trail dust, but it soon became obvious that it wasn't going to happen.

Lin cut a bite-sized piece of the thick slice of smoked pork as he asked, "Where do you want to start, Julia?"

"Can you tell me about how you were able to stop the nightmares? Are you still worried at all about them returning or other things?"

"I'm not worried at all, Julia. I told you briefly about how I'd been helped by a Cheyenne warrior. His name was Hawk Who Waits, and he was about my age. He basically told me I was a woman for thinking the way I did because warriors have to kill to protect their families and their tribe and should take every advantage available to do it. That was pretty much what I'd been telling myself for a long time; that the men I was chasing were evil and didn't deserve to live, but it never worked. But then he pointed to a mountain and said that compared to the life of the mountain, our lives were just like the blink of an eye and killing them just made that blink shorter. That put everything in a whole new perspective, and I thought I was completely cured of my problem."

"But you weren't?"

"I think I was, but it was a dream I had that night that made me realize that I had nothing to be ashamed of or feel guilty for doing. When I was a boy of about twelve, we had a problem with a rabid wolf that was killing our stock. I accompanied my father out into the fields hunting for the animal and watched him shoot the wolf with his Burnside carbine but really hadn't thought about it since then.

"In my dream, I had the carbine in my hands as the wolf stalked me. I heard my father tell me to shoot the wolf, and I did. When I asked him why he hadn't done it, he said that the wolf was mad and would hurt our family and that sometimes it was necessary to kill. Then I knew for certain that I would have no more nightmares or qualms about doing my job.

"I wished the dream about my father would have lasted longer, though. He died three years ago from cancer of the stomach and I wasn't there when he passed away. No one in the family even knew he was sick until the last few weeks, and he asked them not to tell me."

"You didn't tell me about your father before," Julia said softly.

"I know, but I don't know why I didn't tell you. But in my dream, the last thing he said was 'go and marry that young woman and make me a grandpa.'"

Julia poked at the food on her plate and asked, "And are you?"

"You know I want to marry you, Julia. It's almost all I've been thinking about since I left your farm to go to the Black Hills."

Julia continued to stab at her smoked pork as she asked, "I know that, Lin, but what about the other part? Will you try to make your father a grandpa?"

Lin put down his fork and just stared into Julia's deep blue eyes for almost a minute.

Finally, he replied, "Tell me about how your mother helped you, Julia."

Julia nodded, but kept her eyes on his as she began.

"After you'd gone, my mother and I were sitting in the kitchen and she asked if I was going to marry you. I told her that I would but that I still had many worries and concerns about what had happened and didn't know if I could be intimate with you. Then she told me that it would get better, and I pointed out that she'd gone into her shell after what had happened. But when I told her that I understood why she'd had such a reaction because it was the second time it had happened to her, she said it wasn't the second time, it was the third."

Lin didn't comment when she paused, but noticed she wasn't close to tears, despite the topic.

"I was stunned when she told me that because none of us knew about it. She'd been raped when she was seventeen and thought she'd never get over it when she told my father, who then married her anyway because he loved her."

Lin then said, "Just as I will marry you, Julia. It's because I love you and want to make you happy."

Julia smiled at Lin then said, "I know, Lin, and that makes all the difference. You see, when my mother told my father she'd been violated, she also told him that she was pregnant with me. I never knew that I wasn't his daughter through conception because he always loved me and treated me as he did his sons. Honestly, I always thought he loved me a little more than the others which made me feel special. It was probably one of the reasons I never married, too. I always compared other boys and men to my father.

"After my mother told me about my true parentage, I knew that if I was pregnant, I'd still love my child as much as I could. It doesn't matter who the father is. Not to me."

Lin said, "It doesn't matter to me either, Julia. When I went out on that soul-searching ride, I stopped at the burned-out squatters' cabin. I found the remains of one of the pregnant women in the rubble. It wasn't much, but I knew it was one of the women. I then found a loose rock in the fireplace that they must have used to hide whatever they had of value, which wasn't much. Inside was an old tobacco tin that contained a few charred one-dollar notes, thirty-seven cents in loose change, and a small, cheap chain with a tin cross.

"I took the chain with me cleaned it up as best I could, then when I returned, I laid it on the woman's remains because I believed that it was important to her. I think that she might have been keeping it safe so she could wear it when she went into labor, so the start of her baby's life outside her womb would have some meaning beyond the squalor of its birth.

"If you have a child inside of you, Julia, I'd be honored to be his or her father. I'll love our baby as much as I love you. No child deserves less."

Julia reached over, took his hands in hers and said, "Thank you, Lin. I already knew that was how you'd feel about this. My mother told me that when you spoke to her, it was as if my father was talking. That was why she was sure that you'd react just as he did. She said that when she confessed her pregnancy to him, all he said as that they'd have to speed up the courtship."

"So, Miss Lampley," Lin said, "How about if we speed ours up even more? Let's get married tomorrow."

Julia smiled and said, "I thought you'd never ask."

Dinner was then forgotten as Lin stood with his hands still attached to Julia's as she rose then he kissed her softly to consummate the official engagement.

When the kiss ended, Julia said softly, "Our food is getting cold, Mister Chase."

"I suppose we do need to eat, ma'am."

Julia laughed as they each took their seats and ate their chilled dinner without comment.

By the time they finished, the sun was down, and Lin had a lamp burning in the kitchen as they had coffee. The conversation had moved from what would had happened to what would happen tomorrow, not later that night.

"We leave around eight o'clock, and we'll go and find your family and let them know about our wedding. I think we'd better plan for the afternoon because we still have to go see the sheriff."

"Okay," Julia replied as she swished her coffee in the cup.

Then she asked, "Lin, are you going to keep being a bounty hunter now?"

"No, I don't think so. It's not that I'm suddenly ashamed of it or that I'm even worried about getting all bolloxed up again. I just don't want to spend so much time away from you."

Julia smiled and asked, "Then what are you going to do?"

"Sheriff Ward asked me if I'd be a deputy in Albany County because he's down to one deputy, and I've been thinking about that. What do you think?"

"Wouldn't we have to move?"

"Yes, ma'am, and that's my only real problem with taking the job. I like Laramie, but I'm much more comfortable here. The good news is that we don't have to make that decision for a week at least. Money certainly isn't a problem. Even my beloved fiancée is loaded."

Julia laughed and patted her currently empty pockets before saying, "Not at the moment, King Midas. The money you gave to me is in our bedroom."

"Well, just the same, ma'am, money isn't an issue. But before we get married, Miss Lampley, there's something that I have to warn you about that might change your mind."

"I doubt if that's possible, Mister Chase, but what is this terrible secret?"

"I don't do laundry, so the dirty clothes will be your responsibility."

"That's it? That's your big problem? I've been doing laundry for ten years, so I'm not going to worry about it."

"Oh, so you enjoy doing the laundry?"

"No, I hate it, but it has to be done. So, did you just keep buying new dark clothes or just ride around in the rain?"

"Oh, no. Once a week, I'd drop off my dirty clothes at the Chinese laundry then pick them up two days later."

"Then why will I have to do the laundry?"

"I didn't say that you had to do it. I just said it would be your responsibility, ma'am. I figure that the thousand dollars that you have in your possession would last about fourteen years' worth of laundry. By then, we can probably negotiate for continuation of the service."

Julia set her cup down, stood, took two steps to her left and plopped down on Lin's lap, putting her right arm around his shoulder.

"I think we can negotiate a better deal now, Mister Chase," then leaned down and kissed him.

Having Julia on his lap and her lips on his had an enormous impact on Lin as he slipped his arm around her waist and pulled her closer.

She pulled her head back slightly and whispered, "Let's go to bed and do what is now incredibly inevitable."

Lin asked quietly, "Are you sure, Julia? Are you really sure?"

"Almost, but I need this to be completely sure."

She slid from his lap and took his hand as he stood then blew out the lamp before they walked slowly down the short hallway into the open door of the bedroom. the bright moonlight making the room almost a milky white as they entered.

Julia may have wanted this badly for so many reasons, but once she entered the bedroom, the imminence of intimacy brought the worries of her inability to let it happen take hold of her thoughts again. She tried to push them aside, but the more she tried, the more persistent they became.

Lin, despite his almost crushing lust for Julia, knew that more than anything else, she needed tenderness and was determined to let her know that she was loved.

Once in the bedroom, he held her softly and kissed her.

Julia was so focused on keeping those horrible memories at bay that when Lin kissed her, she didn't even have the same reaction she'd had on their earlier kisses, which disappointed her and only confirmed that she really wasn't past her concerns.

Lin could sense the difference and knew Julia was already in doubt, so after the kiss, he kept her in his arms, but instead of progressing down the expected path, he asked quietly, "Julia, what's wrong?"

"Nothing," she replied quickly then kissed him as soon as she finished answering, but even as her lips were pressed against his, tears began to well in her eyes and flow onto Lin's cheeks.

Lin leaned back slightly then used his fingertips to wipe the tears from her cheeks before saying, "Julia, it's alright. You're just worrying too much. Why don't we just get some sleep? Okay?"

Julia nodded, but the tears didn't stop. She'd failed and knew it would never be right. All of her brave talk about putting everything behind her was nothing but talk. She'd never be able to be with Lin and that hurt more than anything else.

"I'll get changed," she said hoarsely.

"Okay. I'll go and put away the coffee cups. Let me know when you're done," he said as they separated.

He turned to leave the bedroom when Julia said quickly, "Lin, I'm so sorry. I wanted to be your wife so badly and I've messed that up, too."

Lin smiled at her and said, "Julia, I'll always love you and you'll be the best wife any man could hope for. You haven't messed up one thing since I've known you. I'll be back in a little while."

"Okay," she replied before he left the room.

Julia was going to close the door but decided to leave it open as she turned to the dresser where she'd stored her new clothes. She had bought three nightdresses in anticipation of this night, and when she pulled the top one from the stack, her tears began to fall again. Lin was just being the thoughtful man he always was when he'd told her she hadn't messed this up. She knew better.

Julia changed quickly into the nightdress almost angrily threw back the quilts and slid on to the bed before pulling the quilts back to her chin. She was going to tell Lin that she was in bed but didn't because she was ashamed of herself and announcing that she was in bed was almost an admission of that disgrace.

Lin had long since cleaned up the coffee cups and had a problem of his own. He normally slept naked and knew that it was out of the question tonight but simply didn't know what he should wear to bed. He knew that most married men in town slept in nightshirts or even pajamas, but he didn't have anything like that.

As he sat at the table in the moonlight, he went through his whole wardrobe thinking of anything that he could wear to bed that wouldn't scare Julia. After five minutes of thought, he finally decided he'd just take off his boots and belt and sleep in his shirt and britches. He slept in them on the trail, so he was used to it, but it would be really odd with Julia sleeping nearby.

He assumed Julia was already in bed, so he stood and walked down the hall turned into the bedroom and saw Julia's face almost framed by the top of the quilts and the pillow as she lay on the right edge of the bed.

Julia watched as he sat in the straight-backed chair and pulled off his boots and socks then slid his belt out from his waist.

He stood then walked to the bed and asked, "Would you rather I sleep above the quilts, Julia? I'm used to it."

"No, that's okay."

Lin nodded, pulled back the corner of the quilts and slid underneath leaving a three-inch gap between him and Julia as if one of them was contagious.

Once his head was on the level as hers, he rolled onto his right side while she remained on her back, staring at the dark ceiling.

"Lin," she asked softly, "when you left to chase those men, you told Pete to keep me company at night and tell me silly stories. Why did you do that?"

"Because I was worried about you. I thought you were going to have a terrible time after what had happened, and night times are always the worst time to be alone because all we have is our thoughts. You had no one with you those nights, Julia. Your sisters-in-law had your brothers and Wilma, Mary and Bess Barber all had their husbands, but you had no one to help you."

"But why did you want him to tell me silly stories?"

"If there's one thing that I've learned in my years doing that gruesome job was that laughter always helped keep me going. If you look hard enough, you can find humor in just about anything. I wanted Pete to tell you silly stories to get you to laugh and feel better."

Julia finally rolled onto her left side facing him and asked, "Can you tell me a silly story, Lin?"

Lin smiled, then touched her face with his fingertips and began his silly tale.

"Now, you may not believe this about your intended, Miss Lampley, but I've never been a drinking man. It's not that I'm a preacher or anything, despite my very parson-like form of dress, but I still remember my first taste of beer and thought it was disgusting, so I never tried one again. Don't even get me started on what whiskey tastes like. Anyway, it was a hot summer day and I was in a saloon in Custer City over in Dakota Territory when I was hunting down a middle of the road outlaw named Pius Sanders. That was his real name, by the way. I guess his parents thought he'd be a pope or something when he grew up.

"Now, Pius was a frequent visitor to saloons as most outlaws tend to be, and I suspected he was in this one. It was called The Gold Rush Saloon and it was seedier than most. You may not be aware of this particular unwritten rule, but one does not go into a saloon and not buy some form of liquid refreshment. So, if

I had to enter one of the drinking establishments, I would always ask for a sarsaparilla, and if they didn't have one, I'd order a beer but just let it sit.

"I walked into this one, moseyed up to the bar and ordered a sarsaparilla, not expecting that they'd have one, but in one of the bigger surprises of my life, the barkeep reaches under his bar and pulls out a bottle of sarsaparilla and sets it in front of me. I gave him his nickel and pulled the cork as I looked around the room.

"I spotted Pius sitting at a table in the corner nursing his whiskey and staring at me. I didn't know if he understood who I was or not, but I was ready if he did, so I walked over to the table near his and sat down. He continued to watch me, but I pretended he wasn't there. I took a big swig of my sarsaparilla and then set it down.

"Just when I put the bottle on the table, I watched a big old wasp settle on the lip and then crawl into the bottle, which immediately killed my desire for the drink. Well, Pius, who was still paying attention to me suddenly stands up and saunters my way, his half-empty whiskey glass in his hand, which kind of surprised me. He sits down, uninvited I may add, and stares at me.

"He doesn't say a word for another thirty seconds before he drawls, 'Are you a sissy or somethin'?'. I noticed that his hammer loop on his Colt was off and both of my hands were on the table, so I wasn't in a very good position to do anything spectacular. If I dropped my right hand to my pistol, he'd have been able to shoot me before my fingers touched metal.

"So, I played for some time and asked, 'Why would you call me a sissy, mister?', and he replied, "Cause you're drinkin' sarsaparilla, that's why'."

I leaned forward slightly and said, 'You ain't from around these parts, are ya?', and he's a bit confused and says he isn't, then asks me why it mattered. I told him that if he was then he'd know that when you ask the bartender for sarsaparilla, you get a bottle of the special stuff. Now, he's interested and asks, 'Special stuff?' and I answered, 'You bet. It has a real bite, too.' He licks his lips and looks at my bottle and asks, 'Can I have me a swig?'.

"Then the fun began when I just nodded and he grabbed that bottle before I changed my mind and upends it, dumping the sarsaparilla into his mouth along with the wasp. I thought I was going to have to flip the bar table on top of him, but I didn't need to do anything so dramatic when Pius jumps into the air, throwing the bottle across the room and begins hopping around like a big, stinky frog that stepped on a hot plate.

"While he's jumping around, he's shouting 'You bathdard! You thun-of-a bitch!' because his tongue had started swelling after a very surprised wasp took defensive measures. I just stood then walked behind him pulled his pistol and tied his wrists behind him while he was still hopping around. I guess the rest of the patrons thought it was too funny to intervene, especially when he began shouting, 'Thtop this bathtard! I'm Piuth Thanderth!'. They were all laughing too hard to care and just enjoyed the show. And that, Miss Lampley, was my wasp-assisted capture of Pius Sanders."

Julia was laughing almost from the start of the story, and had tears sliding down her face by the time he finished.

Lin just watched her happy face and was glad she'd asked him to tell her a story.

As Julia's laughter slowed to just a damp smile, she said softly, "Thank you for that, Lin."

313

"You're welcome, Julia," he said as he looked into those dark blue eyes just eight inches away.

Julia was still smiling as she put her right hand around his neck and kissed him, and felt the same rush she'd felt the first time in the barn then she slid forward pressing herself against Lin.

He didn't ask her if it was okay this time but slid his hand behind her back and slid his lips to her neck making her gasp as she pulled his head closer to her answering the question he hadn't asked.

All of her focus was now on Lin and how he was making her feel. He didn't touch her anywhere but her face or back as they continued to kiss for another few minutes then Lin slid his left hand down her back and caressed her soft curves making her to catch her breath.

Julia then began to unbutton his shirt and slide her hands across his chest as she let herself become a willing partner in their lovemaking. Without realizing it, Julia suddenly understood the difference between giving herself and being taken.

After a few more minutes, both were free of clothing and Lin still tried to restrain himself as he let his hands explore Julia, yet always gently and with soft words of love but was finding it more and more difficult the longer they progressed.

Julia found herself totally immersed now and wanted more but was hesitant to ask until Lin found himself almost at wit's end and said in a normal voice, "Julia, whatever you want me to do, just tell me."

After hearing his request, Julia told him exactly what she needed as all inhibitions disappeared in an instant. Nothing was off limits any longer and Julia found that she reveled in the release from the last of her doubts.

———

Ten minutes later, as Julia slid closer to Lin with their bodies bathed in sweat and their breathing finally returning to normal, she said softly, "Thank you, Lin."

Lin kissed her on her forehead, pulled the quilts over them and said, "Goodnight, Julia."

Julia sighed before whispering, "Goodnight, Lin."

———

Lin's eyes opened just enough to see Julia's tranquil face just inches from his as she slept. His own sleep had been dreamless, and he felt more aware of everything as he lay beside her. He could hear the light sounds of Julia's breath, smell the delicate, flowery scent of her hair and skin, but mostly, he could almost feel her serenity. This was the immense reward for almost two weeks of constant danger and terror. These few seconds that he spent just gazing at her balanced the scales.

He was still studying her face when Julia's eyelids slowly parted revealing her dark blue, smiling eyes.

"Good morning, Lin," she said softly.

"Good morning, Julia."

"I never thought anything could be so wonderful. Not just last night but waking up to see your face."

"My scratches are healed then?" he asked with a smile.

Julia touched his left cheek and replied, "Not yet, but they'll be gone soon. But more importantly, the horrible visions that drove me to make them are now just a distant memory. That is why I said, 'thank you' last night."

"I know. I could see it in your eyes, Julia."

Julia smiled and asked, "We're naked and in bed, Mister Chase. What do you think we should do?"

Lin kissed her quickly and replied, "I, Miss Lampley, need to use the privy and we have a lot to do today. As much as I'd rather spend time here with you, we need to start our day."

Julia laughed before she hopped out of bed and began dressing while Lin did the same. It was an odd experience for both of them, especially for Julia. She had always thought of herself as almost prudish until she met Lin, but after one night, she found no shame or embarrassment in dressing in front of him.

———

After firing up the cookstove, Julia cooked breakfast and the water that was already in the pipes from Lin's aborted attempt to take a bath last night was heated for a shared bath. It wasn't a communal bath as the tub simply wasn't big enough, but Julia went first while Lin shaved in the nearby sink. That meant that Lin would have a residual floral bouquet for a few hours from the water, but he didn't mind that much.

It was just before nine o'clock when the couple mounted their horses and set out for Cheyenne, arriving less than an hour later at the sheriff's office.

When they entered the outer office, Deputy John Draper was at the front desk and Sheriff Luke Templeton was standing in front of the desk with his back to the door. He turned when Lin and Julia entered and broke into a big grin.

"Lin, John told me you had some fireworks when you returned to your house yesterday."

"Yes, sir. It seems that the Whitacre brothers' old man decided to carry out his threat about getting revenge for his sons."

"Come on back to my office. I need to talk to you for a few minutes."

"Sure," Lin said as he took Julia's hand to let her know she was coming with him.

They followed the sheriff into his large office in the back of the jail where Lin held out a chair for Julia. Once she was seated, he sat in the second chair and assumed this was about the vouchers that the sheriff was holding for him. He didn't think that he would face charges for shooting Mister Whitacre.

As he waited, the sheriff opened the small safe in the corner, took out an envelope, closed the door again and sat down before sliding the envelope across the desktop.

"Those are the vouchers for those six bastards, Lin. They total twenty-seven hundred and fifty dollars just in case you didn't know."

"I didn't really care about it in this case, Luke. Is that what you wanted to see me about, or is there a problem with my shooting James Whitacre?" Lin asked as he slid the envelope into his coat pocket.

"No, no. I already talked to the county prosecutor about it this morning and he had no problem with it. What I wanted to talk to you about was totally different. I heard that you were getting out of the bounty hunter business. Is that true?"

Lin was a bit surprised as he didn't believe he'd told anyone other than Julia.

"It is. I didn't think I could ever shoot another man after those last six. It was eating at me, but I've gotten past that. Now the reason is that I don't want to be gone that long from Julia. We're going to be married soon and I'll be taking a deputy's job with Jimmy Ward in Laramie."

"That's what I was going to ask you about. I lost Ralph Scranton two days ago when he found out that Albany County was short two deputies. His family lives in Laramie and had applied to be a deputy there a couple of years ago, but Jimmy didn't have any more slots. Now, I'm short a deputy and was wondering if I could talk you into staying in Cheyenne."

Lin glanced over at Julia then looked back at the sheriff and said, "I'll be honest with you, Luke. The one thing that bothered me about moving to Laramie was leaving my house. I'd be honored to be one of your deputies."

Sheriff Templeton grinned stood and offered Lin his hand as he said, "That's great! You just said you were getting married, so how about if you start on Monday, the 19th?"

"I'll see you then, boss," Lin said as he shook the sheriff's hand, "but right now, Julia and I have a lot of things we need to do."

Sheriff Templeton smiled at Julia as he said, "Congratulations to you, Miss Lampley."

"Thank you, Sheriff," she replied as she stood and took Lin's hand.

"Call me Luke. He has to call me boss or sheriff."

Julia laughed as she and Lin turned and left the sheriff's office and as they passed Deputy Draper, he said, "Glad to be working with you, Lin."

"Same here, John," Lin replied before he and Julia exited the jail and stepped onto the boardwalk.

"Where do we go next?" she asked.

"Before we go and meet your family, wherever they may be, we need to head over to Miller's Jewelry on 17th Street and choose our wedding bands. It's only two blocks, so we can walk and maybe we'll bump into some Lampleys along the way."

"That sounds like a sound plan, sir," Julia replied as he started walking while she glided alongside.

As they headed for the jewelry shop, they were spotted by Pete as her entire family was walking in the opposite direction to go to Craig & Gardner on Eddy Street to add to their furniture purchases.

Pete shouted, "Julia! Mister Chase!" and bounded away from the other family members reaching Julia and Lin in a few seconds.

"When did you get back, Mister Chase?" Pete asked.

"Late yesterday afternoon. Why don't we wait for everyone else to arrive, so we can tell them what happened at the same time. Okay?"

"Okay," he replied as he turned and waited for the others.

Mary was twenty feet away and could see how happy Julia was and already anticipated what their news would be but could not have imagined the whole story. News of the unusual shootout hadn't boarded the gossip train yet.

Julia was smiling as she told her mother the news that she and Lin were going to be married that afternoon and everyone was invited to the ceremony which would be held at the county courthouse.

Because everyone had already expected that part of the news, there was no shock or surprise, but congratulations were offered and accepted. Then Julia told them about the arrival of James Whitacre at the door with his pistol and Lin's shot to eliminate the danger which resulted in an extended, boardwalk-blocking explanation including Lin's decision to remain in Cheyenne as a Laramie County deputy.

Finally, they agreed to meet for lunch at Ramsey's Restaurant on 16th Street at noon to finish the story before going to the courthouse.

Fifteen minutes after Pete's shout, Lin and Julia separated from the crowd of Lampleys and walked to Miller's Jewelry to buy their wedding bands.

The selection didn't take too long but Julia's fingers were larger than most women, so they had to wait while the jeweler resized the ring to fit. As they waited, Lin looked at the different displays and saw something he wanted to buy, but not now.

With the box containing the rings in his pocket, Lin and Julia then went to the bank and Lin deposited the vouchers into his account, which along with Julia's cash, now contained $12,988.65. He then had Julia added to the account using her new name, which did make her giggle slightly. Lin almost laughed as she did, having never heard Julia giggle before.

They left the bank and went to the county land office where he had her added to the deed for the house. Julia didn't giggle when she signed *Julia Chase* this time, but she did smile. While they were in the county offices, they did all the paperwork for their upcoming nuptials and set the time for one-thirty. Judge John Allen would perform the ceremony.

With everything done, they barely had enough time to make the walk to Ramsey's for their lunchtime meeting with the family. When they entered the restaurant, they looked for the family but couldn't see them anywhere.

Lin pulled out his pocket watch and checked the time, finding it was ten minutes past the hour, so he asked a waitress, "Has a large family arrived for lunch?"

"Oh, you must be Mr. & Mrs. Chase. Yes, they're in our reception room because there were so many. Please follow me."

Lin took Julia's arm as they followed the waitress past the diners in the almost full main floor to a short hallway and approached a large door. After she swung it open, she smiled then returned to the main part of the restaurant.

Lin smiled back then when he and Julia entered the door, the room echoed in applause from the combined clapping of both the Lampley and Barber families.

The couple entered the room then Jim Lampley guided them to the seats of honor at the head of the long table where they sat down.

Henry Barber, as the oldest adult males stood and said, "Lin and Julia, we heard about your wedding this afternoon and thought you should have a proper sendoff. The staff at

Ramsey's was very helpful and gave us this room. We couldn't be happier for you both."

Lin expressed his and Julia's gratitude and told them that the ceremony would be at the county courthouse at one-thirty and all were invited.

After they took their seats, waitresses began bringing in trays of food.

As the plates were being set on the table, Julia leaned over to her mother who was seated on her left side and whispered, "Thank you, Mama. You were so very right about everything."

Mary smiled at her daughter and replied, "Love fixes everything; doesn't it, Julia?"

Julia nodded, then kissed her mother on the cheek before sitting straight and taking Lin's hand in hers.

During lunch, Jim and Bill told them about their contracts for the new construction and the new furniture that they were able to afford. Mary gushed about her new sewing machine that was already in a crate in the wagon while Pete just wanted to talk about the long shot that had saved his sister.

The food and conversation pushed the time to the point where everyone left a good portion of their desserts on the table as they poured out of the reception room then left the restaurant and paraded to the county courthouse.

The marriage ceremony itself was almost anti-climactic after the events that had led to it. Vows and rings were exchanged, the newlyweds kissed, and everyone applauded when they were pronounced man and wife. There were no photographs taken of the couple before or after they returned to the judge's offices to sign the papers.

After accepting everyone's congratulations, Lin and Julia mounted their horses, waved to the families and rode west out of Cheyenne.

When they were back in their house after taking care of the horses, there was no race to the bedroom to consummate the marriage. So many things had changed in their lives in such a short period that they just took off their hats and coats then sat on the couch to talk.

"Now that we're an old married couple, Lin, what happens next? What do I do? I can't just sit around the house. There's not a lot to clean and there's no laundry. Cooking doesn't take that long, either."

"I've been thinking about that, ma'am. This house was perfect for a lonely bachelor like me, but it's barely acceptable for two people. I think we should use some of that money in our bank to expand our home and barn and probably the corral. We'll go to East Construction tomorrow and arrange for that, and you can talk to the architect and decide what you want. Then if you'd like, I can show you how to shoot one of those Winchesters. I have a nice '76 that I picked up along the way that you can have. How does that sound?"

Julia smiled and said, "I was wondering about the house and wasn't sure if you wanted to have it modified or not."

"We'll be needing some more bedrooms, Mrs. Chase."

"How many do you want to add?"

"Well, it's cheaper once they start, so it would be silly to add just one. I think we should add three bedrooms and an office with a library. Maybe we should add a back door, too."

Julia then asked, "Could we have a fireplace, Lin?"

"Yes, ma'am. Anything that you want."

Then Julia asked softly, "Anything?" the question being an obvious invitation that was immediately accepted.

––––––

The next day, Lin and Julia entered East Construction and met with the architect, who told them because of the way the house had been built originally, the additions wouldn't be difficult at all. Rather than expand the existing barn, they found it would be cheaper to add a second, larger barn to the east of the small barn and put the large corral in between. When they went to the office of the manager, he told them that because of a sudden increase in their workload west of Cheyenne, they'd be using crews from Calland Lumber but would be supervised by his foremen.

––––––

Two days later, Julia and Lin stepped down from the Chicago, Rock Island and Pacific train onto the platform in Walnut, Iowa so Lin could introduce Julia to his family. It had been a surprise to Julia when he'd made the request, but she'd agreed quickly, wanting very much to meet his mother and the rest of his family.

Over the next couple of days as they went from house to house, Lin was surprised how many new nephews and nieces he had. His mother was tickled pink about his marriage and decision to settle down to a 'respectable' job but thanked him profusely for the sewing machine anyway.

Julia wasn't hesitant to talk to her new family about what had happened to her and the other women and how Lin had single-handedly served an appropriate measure of justice on those men who'd committed the crime. Lin's sisters and mother were all astonished about Julia's candor and proud of Lin for doing what few others could do.

After four days of almost constant talk and visiting, Lin and Julia boarded the westbound train. They spent one day in Omaha so Julia could do some shopping before taking the long train ride across the Great Plains to Cheyenne.

During their visit, Julia found that she wasn't pregnant, and despite her acceptance of the possibility, the absolute assurance that when she did have a child, it would be hers and Lin's lifted her spirit even more.

———

On Monday, the 19th of June, with construction well under way at the house, Lin Chase was sworn in as a Laramie County deputy sheriff by his new boss, Sheriff Luke Templeton, and then spent the next few weeks learning the parts of being a lawman that didn't involve bullets, especially the paperwork.

Lin was still adjusting to the new job when the work was done at their house and all of the furniture and miscellaneous necessities were freighted to the house from Cheyenne and Julia directed their placement before doing the necessary redecoration.

For more than a month, everything was routine, and the only real excitement consisted of a few bar fights and petty thefts, none coming close to serious violence.

That would change soon.

———

On the morning of the 24^{5h} of July, Lin was at the desk when a telegram arrived from the small town of Chugwater, about forty miles north of Cheyenne. He accepted the message, read it and then carried it back to the sheriff's office.

As he handed it to the sheriff, he said, "Boss, there's been a killing up in Chugwater."

Luke took the yellow sheet read the short telegram and growled, "I guess they didn't want to give Western Union more than two bits. All it says is that a man was killed by a stranger."

"Want me to go up there?"

"This is right up your alley, Lin. I'd ask them for more information, but it could take a few hours and by then, you'd already be there."

Lin nodded, turned and left the sheriff's office then as he passed the desk, grabbed his hat pulled it on and exited the county courthouse.

He had to saddle Homer, but twenty minutes later, he was leaving Cheyenne. Because Chugwater was north of the city, Lin decided he'd swing by the house and see Julia and tell her that he wouldn't be home that night.

When he was just a couple of miles out from the house, he heard the sound of Winchester fire and didn't panic. He'd given Julia the Winchester '76 and she'd been practicing with the repeater almost daily now. She wasn't a great shot, but she was above average.

He pulled Homer to the back of the house, which now had a back porch and door, dismounted and walked to the target range where Julia was concentrating on her target and hadn't heard him approach.

Lin was fifty feet behind her and waited until she fired before saying loudly, "Good shot, ma'am."

Julia was startled but turned with a big smile on her face then set her Winchester on the flat rock and walked toward her husband, threw her arms around his neck and kissed him.

"That's high praise coming from my sharpshooter husband."

"I just stopped by to tell you that I'm leaving for Chugwater in a few minutes. It's a town about forty miles north of here and there's been a killing I've got to investigate."

"Will you be back tonight?"

"If I am, it'll be late. Don't wait up for me."

"Of course, I'll wait up for you. I have all of those new books to keep me company until my husband returns and ravishes me again."

Lin kissed her again before he said, "I've got to go," then when she turned to pick up her Winchester, he slapped her behind softly before heading back to the house.

Before he left, he packed some of Julia's biscuits and a half jar of honey along with his usual smoked beef. He and Julia exchanged waves as he rode cross country heading northeast to pick up the northbound road to Chugwater. He had one of his non-scoped Sharps in his right scabbard and one of his .50 caliber Winchester '76s in the left as he set off. It was a warm day, so he didn't have on his heavy, large-pocketed coat but just wore a vest with his badge prominently displayed.

Even in his days as a bounty hunter, he knew that it was always dangerous to be a stranger entering a small town after a shooting. Some of the local citizenry would be trigger-happy and might take a pot shot at an unknown rider entering their town. The badge should act as a safety shield against unwarranted gunfire.

As she watched Lin ride away, Julia felt an uneasiness creep over her. This was the first time she'd watch him ride into danger since they'd been married and somehow it was different. She didn't understand why she would feel the eerie discomfort now and not when he'd ridden off to hunt down the six murderers.

She continued to stare as Lin receded in the distance then finally shivered and returned to her target practice.

Lin picked up the northbound road and set Homer to a medium trot, expecting to arrive in Chugwater in the early afternoon.

———

It was just past two o'clock when he first spotted the collection of buildings that made up Chugwater, and twenty minutes later, he rode into town and headed for the small dry goods store, stepped down then entered the establishment after tying off Homer.

"Thank God, you made it, Deputy!" the owner exclaimed when he spotted Lin.

"What happened? All I know is that someone was shot and killed by some stranger."

"This tall feller, even taller than you and probably forty pounds heavier, just walked into Poor Joe's Livery down the street and said his horse died and he needed another one. Joe offered to sell him one, but the man just pulled his pistol and shot him, right through his gut."

"Alright. What was the victim's full name?"

"His name was Joe Miller, and he was a good ol' boy who never hurt a soul."

"Which direction did his killer go and how long ago did he leave?"

"That murderous bastard left about six hours ago and headed west, cross-country."

"What is the horse's coloring?"

"He's a dappled gray gelding, almost like yours, but lighter."

"Did he arrive carrying his own tack or did he have to steal a rig from the livery?"

The proprietor shrugged and replied, "Beats me, Deputy. Nobody thought to ask Joe before he died and none of us even saw him come into town. We were lucky to get as much from Joe as we did."

"Okay. I need to rest my horse for a little while and get him some oats and water. Is the livery open?"

"Yes, sir. You passed it on the way in."

Lin nodded, then left the store untied Homer, mounted and trotted down to the livery and walked him into the open barn.

He let Homer drink and feed as he examined the livery's interior, saw the blood splattered across some of the wood and the big, dried pool of blood on the floor. There were so many footprints and scuff marks that he was sure there was nothing else worthwhile in the barn, so while Homer grazed and rested, he walked to the small eatery halfway down the main street and had a steak that was pretty good. He knew that many of the citizens were probably displeased with him for not rushing after the murderer, but Lin knew the difference in time wasn't as important as being prepared.

He paid for his lunch, then forty minutes after arriving in Chugwater, he and Homer left town, picking up the departing trail of the lawbreaker easily as he made his way across the open ground.

As he tracked the killer, he tried to match his description with any of the wanted posters he had memorized and came up empty. Men that large would be easily identified, so either he wasn't wanted at all, or he'd come from outside the territory.

Then he realized that there was something else odd about the situation as he followed the trail at a medium trot. He hadn't seen a dead horse anywhere and hadn't noticed any vultures either, which he should be seeing by now. That meant either the man had come from the north or east but even then, he should have spotted the vultures.

The large birds could be seen from a long distance and a dead horse would attract a lot of attention. If this stranger's horse didn't die, *how did the stranger just walk into town?* He arrived early in the morning on foot without a horse, so Lin needed to find the man's footprints when he entered the town.

He'd been concentrating on the departing hoofprints and now that he looked, he didn't see any human footprints. He had assumed he'd walked in from the same direction that he'd ridden away, but he obviously hadn't. So, he expanded his search to see if he could pick up the telling footprints the man must have left as he walked into Chugwater.

Not wishing to lose his original track, he began a series of ever-widening S-curves, scanning the ground and after thirty minutes found the set of footprints about two hundred yards north of the hoofprints he'd been following and brought Homer to a stop. The footprints were large and deep, so it was the killer. He was a big man, but the prints weren't deep enough for a man carrying a heavy saddle, saddlebags and probably a Winchester.

Lin then stood high in the stirrups and studied the terrain, looking for possible ambush sites. The only thing that made any sense to him at all was that at least two men had ridden close to Chugwater then set up in a well-hidden ambush location.

Once they were ready, the big man had walked into town, claimed to have lost his horse and shot the liveryman, knowing that a county deputy would be sent from Cheyenne. The next question was why they would go to such extraordinary lengths to lure a deputy sheriff into an ambush. He'd only find the answer to that question if they tried to drygulch him and failed, and he didn't intend to let them be successful. As Sheriff Templeton had said before he left, this was right up his alley.

Satisfied that he'd arrived at the only possible conclusion, he started Homer forward again with the late afternoon sun in his eyes. The footprints and hoofprint trails weren't that far apart, but were headed in the same general direction.

"Here he comes," Wes Easley said loudly as he readied the Sharps rifle.

"Are you sure you can hit him from far enough out?" asked Saul Pruitt.

"Trust me. I'm better than he is."

"You didn't see him shoot between that woman's legs and kill MoMo," Saul replied.

"From what you told me, that was with a Winchester at fifty yards, and that long-range shot that killed all of your pals was into a dynamite shack. Hell, I could hit that thing at over a mile. There's nobody who's as good as me."

Saul nodded as he watched that bounty hunter, now deputy sheriff approach. He was still two miles out. They were well-hidden behind a long, thick growth of bramble bushes but allowed Saul a decent view of the eastern landscape.

Saul had somehow survived that incredible blast by one of those quirks of fate as he was hiding behind a large boulder already and his only injuries were a temporary loss of hearing. After the women had gone, he'd spent the rest of that day scavenging the mined gold from any of the pouches that he could find. Like Lin, he'd seen the rich vein of gold, and knew that he could return and become a rich man but first, he wanted payback on the man who'd killed his best friend, MoMo.

He'd walked to Laramie then taken the train to Denver where he'd cashed in his gold and searched for someone who could do the job for him, finding Wes Easley by reputation. He hadn't come cheap and he was the one who had come up with the plan when he discovered that Lin Chase was now a deputy sheriff in Laramie County.

It had taken a few days to find the ideal spot for the ambush and then the quick murder to get the locals all worked up and request the law. Their only concern was that the sheriff might send his other deputy, but Wes thought the odds were much better that the sheriff would send his newly hired sharpshooter to investigate.

Now the plan was coming to fruition as they watched Lin Chase riding straight at them.

Saul wasn't going to play any part in the actual shooting, simply because he couldn't hit anything past fifty yards even with a Winchester, but he had confidence in his paid assassin.

———

Lin had seen the massive collection of thick brambles and as it was the only real obstruction in line with the horse tracks, he took the safe approach and assumed it was an ambush site. If he was wrong, it would cost him some time, but he'd rather waste the time than his life.

Lin then began angling gradually toward the northwest away from the thicket without trying to appear too deliberate. It was an obvious ploy as the drygulcher had left such an obvious trail for him to follow that when he began moving away from the tracks, then they might suspect he was aware of their plot. He was also ignorant of how many men or what kind of weapons they might have behind those brambles, so he decided that he'd leave about eight hundred yards of space to give him time to react.

"He's changing direction," Wes snarled as he watched with his loaded Sharps in his right hand.

"Why would he do that?"

"I'm not sure yet. He should be following the tracks I left."

"Do you think he knows we're here?"

"He might figure someone's here to ambush him which would make sense, but maybe he's looking for some signs of other riders. Let's just watch him for a while. It's all we can do anyway."

"Okay."

———

Because Lin was well aware that his shift in direction had spooked any potential ambushers, he decided to give them at least some reason for the drift away from their track. So, after he reached the eight-hundred-yard radius, he dismounted and appeared to be inspecting the ground while he began planning to flush out the men who might be trying to kill him.

After just a minute, he figured that he'd just ride to the west, keeping the same distance and then charge to the south to get around the brambles. He knew that the men would probably run to the other side, but if he did it quickly enough, they wouldn't have time to mount their horses and even if they did, they'd be flushed out of their hiding place and he'd have a better idea of the enemy he was facing. He'd probably separate them from their horses too, if he did it quickly enough.

Lin then mounted Homer and set him off at a medium trot to the west, keeping his head straight ahead but his eyes on the distant bushes.

———

Inside the brambles, Saul saw him ride away and said loudly, "He's getting away! Shoot him! Shoot him!"

Wes growled, "Shut up!" but aimed his sights on Lin as he crossed in front of him at eight hundred yards. It was a difficult shot, but not too bad as he didn't plan on shooting Chase on the first shot. He'd shoot his horse out from under him and then kill him at his leisure.

He released the first trigger of his Sharps then squeezed the second trigger, releasing the hammer which punched the firing pin into the center percussion cap of the .45-90 Sharps cartridge. The heavy round was rammed down the rifled barrel, beginning to spin as the soft lead was cut by the steel grooves before bursting from the leaves of the bramble patch.

———

It was the one thing that Lin hadn't expected because it was almost an unwritten rule in gunfights that nobody targeted a man's horse. He should have realized that even unwritten rules didn't matter to some men.

So, when he spotted the burst of gunsmoke from the thicket of brambles, he immediately slammed his heels to Homer's haunches and dropped to his gelding's neck as he prepared to turn him toward the shooter.

His left hand was tugging on Homer's reins when the bullet arrived and slammed into Homer's gut, right behind Lin's saddle skirt.

Homer screamed and twisted violently throwing Lin into the air. He landed in an awkward roll fourteen feet away as Homer writhed in pain before going to the ground in a giant cloud of dust.

Lin was stunned by the sudden change and the loss of his friend but knew he didn't have any time to waste. For a few more seconds, he had the cover of the dust still hanging in the air, but it wouldn't last long. He scrambled to his feet but stayed low as he raced to Homer who was on his side and still crying in pain as massive amounts of his blood spilled onto the ground making a thick, dark mud puddle.

Lin pulled his Colt, cocked the hammer and didn't care if he was wasting ammunition or not as he aimed it as his long-time companion and pulled the trigger, ending Homer's life and his pain.

He didn't have time to mourn or to let anger take hold of him as he pulled his Winchester free then tried to yank his Sharps from under Homer, but it was stuck hard. He sat near the rifle, and just as he'd done with Orville, he put his boots on his gelding and pulled on the rifle's stock. It didn't move, but as he strained, he spotted a second cloud of gunsmoke explode from the brambles and quickly released the rifle and dropped into his back. As his spine felt the hard ground, Lin heard the round buzz a foot over his chest and then gave up on the Sharps. He'd have to depend on the Winchester.

He didn't waste any time digging through his saddlebags for extra ammunition because he had such a small window of time while the shooter reloaded. So, just a few seconds after the bullet passed, Lin snatched his Winchester and bolted from Homer's body and ran southwest.

———

Wes Easley initially thought he'd hit Chase with that second shot and seen him go down, but still reloaded, stabbing a third long cartridge into the breech. Once it was loaded, he glanced toward the dead horse and what he assumed was a dead Lin Chase, then was shocked to see his target suddenly stand and pick up his Winchester. But when Lin began to run, he brought his sights to bear on the racing lawman and a slight smile crossed his lips as he led his target.

As soon as he began to run, Lin had started his own countdown, assuming that the shooter was good with the Sharps. He gave him three seconds to reload and another three to acquire and lead his target, so as soon as he started his sprint, he began to count down loudly,
"Five…four…three…two…one…turn!"

336

Wes Easley knew he had him this time when he pulled the trigger, but even as the Sharps slammed into his shoulder, Lin had begun his sudden turn directly at the brambles.

Easley couldn't see if he'd hit Lin yet because of the combination of the bramble leaves and the gunsmoke, so he used those critical seconds to reload and cock the hammer.

Lin was within three hundred yards now and flopped to a prone position as he tried to control his rapid breathing. He didn't have a good target, but he had marked the source of the gunsmoke. He cocked his hammer and set his sights on the spot as his breathing slowed knowing he had to wait just another few seconds to steady his sights.

Behind the brambles, the gunsmoke had cleared enough to get a glimpse of the ground outside and for the second time, Wes Easley believed he had killed Lin Chase when he saw the dark shape on the ground.

He turned to Saul Pruitt and shouted, "I got the bastard! I told you I was better than he was!"

Lin heard the shout, but the only thing it meant to him was that there were at least two men behind those damned bushes. He squeezed his Winchester's trigger at the spot he'd marked, then quickly levered in a second round as the first sliced through the air.

A grinning Wes Easley turned to verify that the great Lin Chase was dead on the open ground when the .50 caliber bullet ripped through the leaves and branches as if they didn't exist, then slammed into his chest, just above the notch in his breastbone. There was no chance for the killer to scream or so much as grunt as he dropped to his knees as if to pray then his hand released his Sharps and he fell face forward into the thorny bush.

Saul had turned to thank him for his expertise when he witnessed Easley's chest explode just ten feet away. He was frozen in place for another ten seconds as his eyes bulged in disbelief. This was worse than Momo's death because now, he knew he was going to die. Just seconds later, another shot ripped through the thick bush and then a third, all aimed where Easley's body lay on the ground.

He dropped to his hands and knees and crawled to where his paid assassin lay on the ground, picked up his heavy rifle and crawled back to his spot, stood and cocked the hammer. He then looked through the branches and spotted Lin Chase with his rifle aimed right at him, so he hurriedly aimed the Sharps, then pulled the trigger, waiting for it to fire, but nothing happened! He didn't think it was loaded but had no idea how to load the damned thing. *Why hadn't he been paying attention when Easley had used the gun?*

After his third shot, Lin held his aim, but didn't fire again because he didn't think the shooter was there anymore. He must have moved left or right, and that presented him with a problem. He couldn't stay here anymore, so he jumped up and raced straight at the brambles in a sporadic zigzag, knowing he was getting too close now and if the shooter fired at this range, he wouldn't have time to react.

By the time Lin was within two hundred yards, Saul noticed the second trigger on the Sharps and thought he'd try using the rifle again. He stepped into a small break on his side of the brambles but didn't see Lin yet until he took one more step and spotted him running right at him. Saul lifted the rifle and aimed it at the zigzagging deputy and pulled the second trigger.

If Wes Easley had been alive to shoot the rifle, Lin would have been cut in half at that range, but Saul was a miner with all of those injuries that accompany that job and missed Lin by a good two feet.

Lin slammed his boots into the dirt and quickly brought his Winchester level and began wasting ammunition as he blanketed the site of the gunsmoke with six rounds of fifty caliber bullets.

The second of those bullets slammed into Saul's right shoulder, spinning him around and throwing him to the ground making the others all fly over his head as he screeched in pain on the ground.

Lin quickly raced along the front of the long, thick bush with his Winchester in his left hand and his drawn and cocked Colt in his right. He reached the end of the bush after thirty seconds, turned around the edge and almost ran into their horses that were fidgeting against their reins from nervousness. He noted three horses, but soon spotted one screaming, squirming man bleeding from a mangled shoulder and the silent body of a large man just ten feet further away.

He kept his pistol on the wounded screamer as he approached, but the man didn't even have a pistol, so he uncocked his Colt, slipped it into his holster and pulled the hammer loop in place.

"You murderin' son-of-a-bitch!" screamed Saul as Lin drew near.

"Who the hell are you?" Lin asked.

"You murdered my best friend and then blew up our mountain!"

The news surprised Lin because he didn't see how anyone could have survived that blast.

"I guess you're going to be the last of those miners to die, mister."

"You gotta help me. I didn't do nothin'!"

"You did a lot of thing wrong, mister, including trying to kill me. Now I'm just going to let nature run its course. You try and tell God that you didn't do anything wrong and see what that gets you. I'm thinking it'll be a one-way ticket to Hell."

Saul didn't say another word, but just glared at Lin until his breathing just stopped.

Lin then walked over to the second body that matched the description that the proprietor had given him, All he did was to take his gunbelt from his waist, throw it over his shoulder and then went through his pockets. He found just under five hundred dollars in cash, and a receipt for two boxes of .45-90 Sharps cartridges from Fieldstone's Firearms in Denver. It had been made out to a man named Wes Easley.

That name sent a chill up his spine. Superb sharpshooters all know who the others were that shared that level of skill and Wes Easley was the only one he considered to be his equal. The big difference between him and Easley was that Easley's skills were for hire without any restrictions. He wasn't wanted anywhere because he'd never been linked to any of the disappearances that he'd caused. He was a meticulous planner and always targeted his victims in either remote locations or from a distance far enough away that he'd be able to just walk away from his sniper hole.

After he had taken all he needed from Easley's corpse, he returned to the unknown miner and went through his pockets. He had nothing that identified him at all, and only twenty-two dollars and change in his pockets.

Lin picked up the Sharps and guessed that it was probably only one of a few that Easley possessed, but he'd never know where the others were and didn't really care.

He then walked slowly to the horses and slid the Sharps into the only empty scabbard. The other scabbard contained a Winchester '73, as did the only scabbard on one of the other horses. The third horse, the stolen animal, didn't have a rifle.

He pulled the saddlebags of the miner's horse and after rummaging through the contents, found an astonishing thirty-eight hundred and fifty dollars in currency inside. He left it there, wondering if the miner really believed he'd leave the bushes alive. Easley's shadowy reputation was that whenever his employer went with him, it wasn't unusual for him to return alone.

He then mounted Easley's handsome, tall black gelding, took the reins of the other two horses and rode to where Homer's body lay on the ground where he dismounted.

There was nothing he could do for his dead friend but spent another forty minutes working his Sharps and his saddle free and then hanging his gear over the miner's saddle. Once it was done, he returned to his slain horse, removed his hat, laid his hand on his neck and offered a silent prayer for Homer. After a minute, he stood, pulled his hat back on then mounted the black horse and headed back to Chugwater.

As he rode back to Chugwater, he hoped that that was the last he'd ever see of those miners. He knew that they would no longer populate his dreams, but he didn't want to find any more of them alive, either. Even after he thought they were all dead, one had surfaced and caused the death of another man just to find some measure of revenge. At least the other one could hardly be classified as innocent.

He'd been in the manhunting business for six years and had never had a single case of revenge unleashed in his direction, and now he'd had two in less than sixty days.

Lin walked the horses into Chugwater and pulled up to the nasty-looking saloon which was the only place he could find open.

He dismounted, entered the squeaking batwing doors and walked to the bar.

"Did you catch that murderin' bastard, Deputy?" the bartender asked.

"I left his body out west about fifteen miles out if anyone wants to go and get them, and I have the stolen horse outside. I'll just leave him there and you can handle it. Alright?"

"I'll tell the mayor in the mornin'. Did you want a drink, Deputy? It's on the house."

Lin smiled and replied, "Only if you've got a sarsaparilla."

"Sure thing," the barkeep said as he reached under the bar, pulled out a brown bottle and handed it to a disbelieving Lin.

"Thanks," he said as he popped off the cork and upended the bottle, emptying its contents in just seconds.

Before he put it back on the bar, he took a quick glance at the bottle, didn't see a wasp, smiled, then tipped his hat, turned and left the saloon. He mounted Easley's black gelding and attached the miner's pinto gelding to the saddle and started back for Cheyenne, estimating his return sometime before nine o'clock. There was no real reason for him to return to the office tonight, so he decided to go home to Julia.

The concept of having someone waiting for his return was new to Lin and it made him pick up the pace a bit. The big gelding was fresh, and the trailing horse wasn't carrying much weight, so he wasn't pushing either animal in his rush to see his wife again.

———

One of the additions to the house was to place two rocking chairs on the front porch. It was a warm evening, so even after the sun had set, Julia remained on the porch looking south toward Cheyenne waiting for Lin. She knew he might not be back until the morning, but she found it difficult to concentrate on her reading, so she just moved to the rocker and waited. Despite the peaceful surroundings, she had her Winchester leaning against the wall behind her. Julia Chase was not going to be surprised again.

The last glimmer of sunlight had disappeared in the summer sky, when Julia heard hoofbeats coming from the wrong direction and bolted from the rocker, grabbed her Winchester and stepped down from the porch. She walked deliberately around the eastern edge of the house and spotted a rider coming from the northeast trailing a second horse. In the dim light, she didn't know who was coming or for what reason and cocked the repeater's hammer.

She was about to shout a challenge when she heard Lin shout, "Julia!" and laughed in relief and joy with her husband's return. She released the Winchester's hammer and waited for him to get close.

When he was about thirty yards out, she noticed he wasn't mounted on Homer which created a bit of concern.

Lin dismounted ten seconds later, let the reins drop and threw his arms around Julia and just held her close without saying anything.

Julia asked, "What happened to Homer?"

Lin stepped back slightly and replied, "I'll explain as I unsaddle these two and put them in the barn. I just wanted to know how happy I was to see you. I didn't know if you'd gone to bed already."

"Not if there was a chance my husband would be joining me tonight. Now grab those reins and you can start telling me what happened."

Lin took the gelding's reins in his left hand and Julia's free hand in the other as they walked to the new barn.

"It was an assassination attempt, Julia. One of the miners had survived and I guess he scrounged a lot of the dead miners' gold and hired a sharpshooter. What happened was when I arrived in Chugwater..."

Julia didn't even break stride as she listened to him narrate the story even when he told her about Homer. Julia didn't ask a single question while they just unsaddled and brushed the horses and Lin continued talking.

Once the horses were put away for the night and the saddlebags were hung over his shoulders, Lin and Julia left the barn and entered the house.

Twenty minutes later, they were in bed in the darkened room and Julia began asking her questions. She knew that this was his life and fretting about it wouldn't make any difference. She'd decided almost from that first day when she'd decided that Lin Chase was going to be her husband, that she would do nothing but be there for him when he needed her.

Then after all of her questions were answered she knew that he needed her as much as she needed him.

———

The next morning, Lin rode the black gelding into Cheyenne and trailed the miner's pinto, arriving at the sheriff's office before eight o'clock. After tying off the horse, he removed the cash-filled saddlebags and entered the office, finding John Draper already at the desk.

"How'd it go, Lin?" he asked.

Lin hung up his hat and replied, "That shooting was just to lure me into an ambush. One of those damned miners survived and hired an assassin. Is the boss in?"

"Not yet. Grab a cup of coffee and tell me what happened."

Lin nodded, walked to the heat stove and filled his cup with coffee and was about to drop the saddlebags on the floor when their boss entered the office.

"Boss, I need to talk to you about this one," Lin said before he sipped his coffee.

"That bad?" the sheriff asked as he walked to the desk.

"Not bad as much as different."

"Tell me about it."

Lin told him the story while John Draper listened intently.

"He intentionally shot your horse?" the sheriff asked in surprise.

"I'm sure he did. A man with his reputation wouldn't miss that badly, even at that range at a moving target. But a horse is a lot bigger target and he wanted to be sure."

Both lawmen shook their heads as Lin continued talking and when he finished, the sheriff just shook his head.

"What did you do with the bodies?" the sheriff asked.

"I left them where they were. I only had one spare horse, so I just told them in Chugwater that the bodies were fifteen miles west of town."

"Sounds like a fitting end to a damned horse shooter," the sheriff growled.

Lin asked, "Speaking of horses, if it's okay with you, boss, I'll keep the black gelding to replace Homer."

"You can keep him and all the rest, Lin. The county doesn't have any rules about turning in recovered property yet, which is kind of surprising to tell the truth."

"What about the cash? There's over four thousand dollars in that saddlebag."

The sheriff paused when he heard the amount but then said, "Keep it. They were trying to kill you anyway."

"I'll tell you what. At the risk of sounding like I'm trying to buddy up to you, why don't we split it three ways. You and John have been at this business making a lot less money than I have, and this will even the scales a bit."

"Are you serious, Lin? That's over thirteen hundred dollars!"

"I'm serious, boss. Besides, maybe you'd make Elizabeth happy if you showed up at the house with a new sewing machine."

Sheriff Templeton laughed and said, "That would be an understatement, Lin. But if you're sure, then I thank you for your generosity."

"Same here, Lin," said John Draper, "but I won't be buying my wife a sewing machine, if that's okay."

"Unless you got hitched yesterday afternoon, John, I don't think you have a wife," Lin replied.

"That's why I won't be buying her one," he said as he grinned.

They divvied up the money then walked out to the horses and the sheriff thought the pinto would be appreciated by his ten-year-old son, Matt, which accounted for everything. Lin was going to keep Wes Easley's Sharps. It was the only .45 caliber version he'd own, but probably had more range than the Big Fifty, but not the punch at the end, although it was still considerable.

Lin deposited the money then dropped his Sharps off with Paul Bergerson to have it repaired and refurbished before he stopped at Miller's jewelry to buy the small piece that he hadn't bought when he and Julia had bought their wedding rings. While the sheriff went to buy his wife's sewing machine and make his deposit, John Draper was left in the office until Lin returned.

———

That evening Lin told Julia about all that had happened, including the addition to their bank account as they ate dinner.

"The county doesn't want the money or horses?" she asked somewhat surprised.

"I think it's more of an oversight than anything else. They've spent so much time chopping up Laramie County over the past ten years, they probably haven't had a chance to remedy it yet. You forget that Albany County, Carbon County and Crook County were all cut out of the original Laramie County which made it kind of confusing when Laramie became the county seat of Albany County."

"I didn't forget that, Lin. I never knew it. You forget that, unlike you, I haven't been here that long."

"I apologize, ma'am. I keep forgettin' that you ain't nothin' but a hayseed sodbuster girl."

Julia laughed and kicked him under the table before she drew more serious and said, "Lin, I missed my monthly. I don't want to get too excited yet, but I think I might be pregnant."

Lin leaned over the table, kissed Julia then smiled and said, "It was inevitable, wasn't it, my wife?"

Julia smiled back as she nodded and said, "Inevitable."

––––––––

Julia's inevitable pregnancy went well and while she grew, so did the sheriff's department when they added a new deputy, Abe Lynch, in November. Abe was as green as possible with no law experience at all but was the son of a county commissioner. He wasn't a bad sort, just a bit lazy and uninterested. He wound up doing most of the desk duty, which the other two deputies appreciated.

Just before the new deputy was sworn in, the county passed an ordinance requiring all property that was collected by county employees be turned into the assessor's office. Surprisingly, it was driven not by the rumors of the large amount of cash that Lin had recovered, but by the appointment of Abe Lynch, when two of the other commissioners accused Abe's father of trying to enrich his son at the county's expense. The argument had resulted in the new ordinance, and Abe's father had to vote for it to prove that it wasn't his intention which of course, it was.

INEVITABLE

———

On the afternoon of February 21st, Julia went into labor and Ellie Madsen, the midwife was in the house with Mary Lampley, who'd been living with them for the past two weeks, helping her daughter and waiting for this day.

After six hours of labor, she lay on the bed, bathed in sweat in her exertions, when Lin entered the room to the consternation of Mrs. Madsen. He ignored her protests as he stepped close to Julia and smiled at her.

Julia tried to smile back, but she had another strong contraction, and she grimaced in pain then after it subsided, she exhaled sharply and looked back at her husband.

Lin reached into his pocket and pulled out a thin silver chain with a small silver cross, pulled it wide and placed it over her head.

Julia managed a smile as he stepped back, and without another word, he turned and left the room to return to his equipment room where he'd been since she went into labor.

It wasn't until the wee hours of the morning before Lin heard a baby's first cries from the bedroom and wanted to rush into the room to see Julia but had been warned that it wasn't his place and stayed at the table drinking his bitter, cold coffee. He had his Sharps-Borshadt on the table and had cleaned and oiled it until it was almost new. It was the last of his rifles that he'd worked on to keep his mind busy. He'd even done the same meticulous cleaning and oiling to Julia's '76 and the pistols.

Now he just anxiously waited to be allowed to see Julia.

Julia. The woman he almost didn't meet at all if he hadn't made that fateful left turn into the Lampley farm. He'd thought about that often over the past ten months, and it gave him the willies. If he'd been just a little earlier, he would have continued straight on through to Cheyenne. A little later, and it would have been too dark for him to notice the farm as he had for almost three years. If he hadn't been trailing the Whitacre brothers' horses and weapons, he may not have stopped. There were so many 'ifs' that could have kept him from ever meeting Julia.

But he'd made that turn, seen the dark blue eyes, and been stunned by her request and her manner. He'd always wondered if there hadn't been a guiding hand that pushed him to make that turn.

Julia had told him that first day that when she first met him, she knew that he was the one man that she had been waiting to find. Maybe she had willed him to make the turn. But whether it was fate, Julia's magnetic desire, or maybe it was simply inevitable that they should meet, it didn't matter. He had found the one woman who would share every moment of his life.

Lin was so deep in thought he was startled when he heard Mary said, "Lin, you can come in now."

He didn't rush in but quietly walked behind his mother-in-law into the bedroom where he saw a smiling Ellie Madsen and then looked to see his perfect wife holding a newborn child in her arms. Their child.

Lin walked slowly to her side and sat in the straight-backed chair near her head, smiling at her and their baby.

"Isn't she beautiful, Lin?" she asked quietly.

"She takes after her mother, Julia. If she grows up to be half as beautiful as you, then I'll have to have my shotgun ready."

Julia smiled and asked, "Why did you bring me the cross, Lin?"

"It was just something that I believed was the right way of welcoming our child into this world, Julia. To me, it was just a way of telling our newborn child that even if we have nothing, we can give them what is most important. When Faith is ready to have our first grandchild, you can give it to her."

Julia reached up with her free hand and touched her fingers to Lin's scar-free face.

"I promise to do that, Lin, but it's a long time away."

"I know, my love, but it will happen. Just like you told me that first day we spent together. It's inevitable."

EPILOGUE

By the time Faith Ann Chase was seven, her father was still a deputy sheriff of Laramie County and now had four fellow deputies, none of whom were sons of county commissioners. Abe Lynch only lasted six months when his father was found to be embezzling county funds but was allowed to leave the territory rather than face arrest. His son went with him.

Lin had stopped accepting pay for his deputy duties in 1883, because he had started a shooting school at his house and had students from as far away as Ohio and Canada come to learn the techniques of long-range shooting. He organized shooting contests using repeaters, Sharps and other types of sniper rifles that drew a large following.

By the time that the school was underway, he and Julia had two more children, both boys, named Earl, after her father, and Stan after his. Her mother had moved to Cheyenne to be with her only daughter after Earl was born in 1882, and Lin had a small house built just fifty yards from their home, which she shared with Pete, who decided that he didn't want to be a farmer.

It was Pete's arrival that had triggered the shooting school when he had asked Lin to show him how to shoot and casually mentioned that he thought a lot of men would want to learn.

Lin still helped the sheriff, especially in the winter months when his school was shut down.

The gold vein that Lin had found was rediscovered in June of 1881 and the entire valley was purchased by the Rocky

Mountain Mining Company for the outrageous amount of six hundred thousand dollars. Unfortunately, the vein petered out after recovering less than two hundred pounds of gold, and not much more was found elsewhere in the valley, resulting in the firm's bankruptcy.

Faith was married in October of 1896 to John Templeton, the sheriff's youngest son and went into labor with their first child on July 11th, 1897 wearing a silver cross hanging from a thin chain that her mother had given to her.

Julia had told her that she'd worn it each time she had entered into childbirth that had resulted in her four beautiful children and represented the greatest gift that any parent could give to her child.

Love.

BOOK LIST

1	Rock Creek	12/26/2016
2	North of Denton	01/02/2017
3	Fort Selden	01/07/2017
4	Scotts Bluff	01/14/2017
5	South of Denver	01/22/2017
6	Miles City	01/28/2017
7	Hopewell	02/04/2017
8	Nueva Luz	02/12/2017
9	The Witch of Dakota	02/19/2017
10	Baker City	03/13/2017
11	The Gun Smith	03/21/2017
12	Gus	03/24/2017
13	Wilmore	04/06/2017
14	Mister Thor	04/20/2017
15	Nora	04/26/2017
16	Max	05/09/2017
17	Hunting Pearl	05/14/2017
18	Bessie	05/25/2017
19	The Last Four	05/29/2017
20	Zack	06/12/2017
21	Finding Bucky	06/21/2017
22	The Debt	06/30/2017
23	The Scalawags	07/11/2017
24	The Stampede	08/23/2019
25	The Wake of the Bertrand	07/31/2017
26	Cole	08/09/2017
27	Luke	09/05/2017
28	The Eclipse	09/21/2017
29	A.J. Smith	10/03/2017
30	Slow John	11/05/2017
31	The Second Star	11/15/2017
32	Tate	12/03/2017
33	Virgil's Herd	12/14/2017
34	Marsh's Valley	01/01/2018
35	Alex Paine	01/18/2018

Made in the USA
Las Vegas, NV
19 September 2022